BURNING SHADOWS

JON C. ALBERT

Get It Write Publishing - New York State

First Edition 2024 by Get It Write Publishing

ISBN: 979-8-218-37921-6

For my Father and Creator. I cannot thank You enough for both the blessings and challenges in this life You have given me. Without both, I would not have found who I truly am or discovered the courage to become the 'me' that I continue to redefine through Your loving guidance. May people see the light hidden in these dark words.

Secondly, for my favorite creations—the two halves of my heart—Taylor, my favorite gift; and Jenny, my angel and my muse.
Neither of you will ever fade, die, or grow old for me.
And now, you never will for anyone else, either.

—Jon

"Between Two Lights"

The Sun may be the bravest fool
For chasing hopelessly the Moon
As, star-crossed, these celestials
Defy the stars on which they're strewn.
They endlessly pursue each other,
Kept apart by gravity;
Yet they would tear their stars asunder—
Love, for them, is blasphemy.

Funny how a god of love
Would build them same and sew their seams—
To tear apart their married hearts
To only watch their passion bleed.
Doesn't matter—absent god, intention flawed, or rapid flow—
The River leaves The Broken awed
And takes them in the undertow.

Perfect one, I am the Sun who seeks to infiltrate your night—
To catch the perfect Moon you are and make myself your satellite.
Moths are simply butterflies who learned to love the night
Into which they're blameless born,
Within the dark, between two lights.

Beautiful, you are my dream, as I lay sleepless here tonight.
Space between is darkness—and uncertainty—between two lights.
When we are all that's left, remember we are all that's right.
We are more than just the gravity—or you and me—between two
lights.

GENESIS

ARI

Lacrimosa….

God is a fire. He is a flame eternal, great and sprawling, consuming all who dare to touch Him.

We are made in His image, as we're told—little embers that flicker, dance, shed heat, and make shadows—and as a flame upon a candle, we are watched as we glow, sometimes brightening, oftentimes dimming. Yet though we waiver or blaze; change color or shrink; spread or remain stationary; one truth is clear: whatever we make of ourselves or choose to do with our brief lives is of our own will. But all things aside, we are merely watched, weighed, and ultimately judged by our Father Flame, the Source that gives us brief existence in how we compare to Him in our effects upon the darkness. He, that very same Source that would watch us—whatever our journey—burn in whatever mode we select, the wax of life dwindling and melting at our own selected pace, until there is no more wick of life left to consume; until we are snuffed out, the purpose always eluding us, but within, we know the purpose to be the burning itself—the light expelled or the shadows made.

God is a fire, and we are each, in our own little flickering embers, a part of Him; and through us, He burns on until one of us is but ash and smoldering wax.

The easy rain that fell outside was a brooding, soothing soundtrack to my thoughts as I turned them over and over in my mind. What I had learned of God in my experiences was what I had envisioned that He had learned of me, which, in the grandest scheme of things, had been absolutely nothing. They say He sees all things and that He is the sole witness—He and His Watchers—to all things that are done. In my mind, if He is busy watching, He does not have the capacity to hear. I do not think He does either of the two, and I do not believe He cares, nor should He have to.

We are not His responsibility.

My prayers, either unanswered or ignored, were pointless pleas.

I twirled the wine glass in my hand.

Love is blind, and God is Love; therefore, God must also be blind, and if this is true, then my life would have been radically different from the grey, insufferable diatribe that He had been recording for me—the one that I would lament over during the eternity for which I had sacrificed so willingly and so woefully.

I was never what one would consider a good person—not in my own eyes, at least. Always striving for perfection, be it in achievements or imagined moments, I failed. My failures were always great, never shy of grandiose, and I had become hardened by the shortcomings throughout my life, my mediocrity only ever showing its mediocre face when I truly showed my potential. Perhaps my failures were the only perfect portion of me.

The irony….

You see, my weakness is, was, and always has been one thing—women. I kept them on my private little pedestal, and unfortunately I worshipped them as I believed they deserved. I have always maintained that they are the fountain of life, a beautiful carriage that carries the seeds that hold within them the promise of the future. Maybe that is why God never allowed me to have one of my own—His Divine Jealousy.

But who am I to judge a Judge? The conflict that this produced in me was damned-able, yet the conflict was not the sufferer here. I was. I would suffer, a scapegoat for my own curious misunderstanding. Much akin to my metaphor, I would flicker and I would die, a minuscule fire, a brief reflection of God; only I was burning without much purpose but to provide heat and light for those that were around me, having no illumination or warmth to experience for myself—a joke, a bad one—and in my desperation to experience, appreciate, and bask in the warmth of the others, I decided to host a party.

And with a little 'bonfire' at the center of it all.

What a wonderful notion!

If God truly is a fire, He would be there in spirit—the only way He could be present, I suppose—and He would be amongst us, myself the host in place of Him and the attendees as my angel guests. And in our drunken, free-spirited Pagan circle, He would once again regain His throne at the center of us all, giving us gravity, light, warmth, and love, along with the capacity to do so, ourselves.

Yes, God would be at the party.

Had He the ears or eyes with which to receive my invitation, all the sins I was planning to commit would happen in shadow, away from His sight, beyond the reach of His Light.

I looked at the clock on the mantle of the living room fireplace. I took in the aroma of leather and smoke that surrounded me, ensnaring my senses.

Three o'clock, about a quarter past….

I began to feel drowsy as I contemplated my guest list. The wine was not helping.

Maybe He will show up….

I sat there, eyeing the fire as it glared back at me. The calls I needed to make were to be few but selective, knowing the few would notify many.

I smirked to myself, nodding to the flames, as if some silent agreement had been reached.

Many preparations had to be made if this evening were to be a success. I did not have the luxury of patience. Waiting—the waiting itself—would have to wait. I laughed to myself, a sort of self-mockery amid these thoughts of pseudo-cleverness.

The fire shifted, catching my attention.

I set my wine down, settling back into my recliner. I closed my eyes, feeling the fire's warmth fill the room around me.

"I will see you all very, very soon," I said.

No one heard.

No one but the autumn Tennessee rain.

JORDAN

Somewhere between the lightning and the thunder in her eyes, there was a yet more striking, silent darkness. Whether it was rage, melancholy, indifference, or freedom—whatever it was, it provoked a subtle dread in him. She could hear his frail voice cracking on the other end of the line. She knew he could feel the static of her wrath. Among the shattering of his composure could be heard little echoes of failure and guilt. She thought she could just make out the soundtrack of nail-biting.

"I'm sorry!"

'Sorry' was all that Jordan had been hearing for the last half hour. *These over-scripted, over-practiced apologies….*

She could think of no response. Her capacity to care had withered. She sat in silence—a chaos of nothing—in panicked apathy.

She ended the call before she knew she was ending it. The empty apologies became a whirlwind of numb demeanor around her, and in the dull howling of the blunted word-violence, she calmly hung up and set her phone down next to her crystal ashtray. Pushing her fingers through her rich, shining blonde hair, she picked up the crushed-out joint resting in the center of it, blew off the ashes, and lit the charred end, inhaling with rage.

Asshole! You're all the same, you little boys!

The phone began to ring again. It wailed until it returned to sleep, Jordan ignoring its cries like a bad mother.

She focused on achieving a new level of numbness.

Another hit.

And then another.

The phone began ringing again, and Jordan stared like a statue, dazed, gazing at the ember glowing at the end of her joint. She could feel all those specific shades of green molding to her interior with every inhale, her indifference to her broken life reflected in the grey pallor of the weightless smoke.

The ringing stopped.

What more could you possibly say to me?!

Wait….

Different ringtone….

Jordan answered speedily, relief spreading over her.

"Jordan? Jordan, are you okay?"

Hannah.

"Yeah, I'm fine," Jordan said.

"Are. You. Okay?" Hannah repeated, unconvinced.

Jordan took in the odor that began to fill every corner of her living room.

"Absolutely fine," she exhaled.

She was not fine, but she was strong. She was mildly irritated that Hannah had repeated her question, as if Jordan's first response was not enough.

Hannah broke the abbreviated silence. "Fine enough to go to a bonfire tonight? I mean, it's a party, but there'll be a fire there. Sounds pretty fun to me. We should go!"

Fire….

Jordan thought long and hard about the proposition, perhaps too long. She distanced herself from the situation, herself, and the world in general. She was a bright and fearsome star, yet somehow the world seemed to always have her kept in the shadows of a corner in the world's tiniest, most secret box—locked, and the key long ago rusted away. She would escape this prison of oppression and become Pandora herself, with all her little deceits unleashed in planned irresponsibility upon the old world. She would establish a new world, a mint reality where all things pristine are obtainable, but her hands would become worn and dirty during the quest.

It is the journey.

And so—

Even in our metamorphosis from flaw into the flawless, though we toil and climb and scrape our foolish ways toward the summit, once we reach that shining nirvana where all is without mar, we still cannot bear it to ourselves to suffer the looming mass of terror that grips us as we see our imminent, eternal failure, because the dirty, grimy fingers that have carved the pathway to this point of enlightenment cannot fathom the pain of reaching out, lingering in pause, and soiling with a proud, reserved touch that perfect surface—the surface of that same shining trophy of perfection that we sought and fought for during the miserable entirety of our dimly-lit lives….

Jordan took her final drag. "Sure," she said.

"Awesome! Pick you up at ten?"

"Sure, yes, but can you make it ten thirty?"

'Sure' was the key to possibility. 'Yes' was the portal to oblivion.

Jordan waited for Hannah to hang up before she set her phone on the table by the ashtray. Her thumb and index finger had begun to burn with the heat of the smolder she pinched so delicately—as delicate and warm as she, herself. Dropping the dead remnant in the ashtray, she took a sip of coffee, and, bringing her knees to her chest in a gathering motion, Jordan secured that lock with a childlike double-handed hold upon her mug—a comfortable statue upon her living room couch.

She was a fierce and quiet bundle as she modestly indulged in the occasional gulp of caffeinated bliss. She was a tidy heap of form-fitting grey leggings and ankle socks of red—the same violent hue that was her oversized shirt—and the scene melded like melting wax into a daze that sometimes comes with coffee. A blur of crimson and grey was the last unfocusing sight her tired eyes would see for a while.

Red and grey.

Flame and ash.

Exhaustion set in.

Darkness. Peace.

She nodded off, both excited and spent, the slightest aroma of Colombia clinging delicately to her motionless lips.

Passion.

Indifference.

Jordan Subra fell asleep as the rain outside dissipated beyond the opaque window.

HANNAH

Hannah Knox set her phone down on her queen-sized bed and rolled onto her side, resting her head on her elbow. Her dark, silken hair fell gently about her face.

I'm lonely.

I need this party.

She shrugged as she picked up the remote to begin what would be another evening of Bram Stoker's dark genius on screen. As the film began, she poured herself a glass of sauvignon blanc. Taking a large gulp of it, *Dracula*'s symphonic background supplied the soundtrack for her private pre-party. She had only time to pass before picking up Jordan in a few hours and she had plenty of wine.

She never felt the need to spend much time getting ready for evenings out. The hair on her legs grew slowly and thinly, so shaving was not as common an inconvenience for her as for other 'average' women. Her creamy complexion was light brown, the result of a mix of her mother's Cherokee blood with the Italian olive shade that she inherited from her father. She was a stunning beauty, perfectly proportional in every manner conceivable; her rounded, distinct curves a storm of feminine power, and with that power, she defeated many a masculine foe.

She always got what she wanted, but she was not spoiled or wont in confidence. She was simply physically overwhelming and had grown to know a perpetual air of self-comfort and awareness in recent years. She was an intellectual as well, well-versed in all her passions of art, history, music, and, of course, fashion. Even in her denim skirt and fitted orange shirt—which only further accentuated her perfect frame—she was a grand vision of simple successes, all combined with her skin and spirit. It had not always been this way, and she had, since her womanly transformation, always appreciated her great physical fortune. She earned everything she ever obtained or achieved—looks aside—so naturally, anything that ever came easily to her was easily turned away.

What she saw of life through her almond-earthen eyes was a miracle to her. Hannah was a lover of moments and of life in general. Yet here she was, watching her favorite film of the undead and his ventures with mortals through the unrelenting throes of passion and pain. She thought of her best friend, Jordan Subra—that vibrant blonde that never thought much of herself—yet was not unconfident; the same young woman that was equal to her in intellect and passion, but lacked Hannah's outward appeal that cannot be learned and can only be discovered by the bold. Of the two she-cats, one was a nurturer, the other a huntress.

One comforted.

One devoured.

Tossing her hair from her face, she sat up, lifting her glass to her inviting lips, savoring the acidic aroma, granting passage to another glorious sip. As it trickled, drop by drop, into her quickening blood, Hannah contemplated upon her beautiful life and how the glitter that clung to its surface was a collection of a thousand tiny mirrors that reflected the light that the rest of the world had ascribed to her. The result was a display of light dancing upon her smooth flesh, a movement subtle yet outspoken and unheard. The world never seemed to understand the troubles and struggles she silently suffered.

Because how could they? Beautiful people don't have any problems, after all, do they? Psh! Mediocre morons….

A bit of light shone through the lifting rain outside, softly illuminating her infallible skin.

Hannah had always wanted love—to love and be loved—but despite her flawless appearance, unlimited mind, and open invitations, the void she kept secretly within was never filled. In the realm of permanence, she was overlooked and underappreciated. Her reputation was that she was a lady of the night, the unconditional warmth of the day always eluding her, yet she craved for the one man—that hidden man she had never met and only read about—to sweep her off her feet and carry her, eternally, into the sweet, bask-worthy heat of perpetual sunlight.

But love is a mutual choice. We fall into it, but we must choose to keep falling. The fear of the fall is the first step toward climbing out—escaping. But why would we want to escape something like love… something, or someone? Especially when we want it so badly, yet when we have it, either we're suddenly 'too good' for it, or it's 'not enough' for us. We chase it with all we have, yet when it becomes a reality, we flee... I flee.... Like, we suffocate on the lack of air on the mountaintop but want more air, and yet seek the next highest summit. Love is something to beautifully drown in, and those that struggle for air fail to give in to the gorgeous lostness of it all. We love how we drown until we realize we are dying for it, and most people panic in the desperation to survive... but shouldn't we be willing to die for love if it is real? Shouldn't we be willing to die for that which makes us feel most alive? THAT is what separates the two ideas. If we are not willing to die in it, it is not really love. And even though I know the truth, I cannot accept anything but perfection. I drown as I breathe, and I clamber for the surface, though I want to drown. I want to suffocate on air I've never breathed before....

Will I ever figure it out?

Love was lasting, and without another that so desperately wanted love, she would simply give in to her episodes of lust to bide the empty nights, bestow a brief flash of light unto the void, and carry the burden of the brevity of both into a future that she hoped would promise a more hopeful tomorrow. Poised to strike, she wished to be stricken. Hungering for an equal, she craved to be savored, yet every time, her standards of a perfect man intervened. Lust and love—she needed the combination, but in such a small town, men were either grown boys or self-proclaimed kings. She despised both options on their own, but she did desire the culmination of the two.

But men like that simply do not exist. Might as well cry while I dance to the music of the single life.

Hannah wanted confidence and sensuality; intellect and creativity; a mind and a heart; and these nearly unattainable standards kept her single. Men wanted her and women wanted to be her, and in her confidence born of lessons learned from past failures, she understood one undying truth—biding her time was all that she could do.

Independent yet craving company, these stones of men that she hobbled over to keep her from the churning waters of commitment kept her safe in her own eyes—the little nourishment she needed to keep her alive as she lay in wait for the opportunity of the 'big kill' to present itself.

She was not lonely—simply alone—and she would not be deterred from her tireless quest of finding 'the one'.

The movie was halfway finished, and her glass of wine completely empty save for a few drops that had collected at the bottom. Draining the dregs, she refilled her glass, watching as the flickering television light played within the newly poured contents of her glass. In darkness, with the window blinds sealed closed, she sat pondering the cinematic themes and how the wine was the purest thing in the room around her.

Maybe I am condemned, too, if only for my undying passion and strength….

In her sobering realization, one that reminded her of her unwarranted aloneness, she met the conclusion that tonight she would give someone—someone unexpected—a genuine chance to know her—an opportunity that her nearly impossible standards would never have allowed before.

She needed this party.

Many—acquaintances and strangers alike—would be there, and there was nothing more perfect for her than the mixture of familiarity and adventure that this would present. She concluded her deepening thoughts, wishing only to numb her made-up mind, forcing herself to allow the woman within to simply go with the unabated flow of life and enjoy in quiet darkness her favorite film.

In what seemed like moments, the credits began to scroll onscreen, her heart full and her mind empty. Her comfortable and cozy apartment had become too quiet for her liking.

She finished her second glass of wine. Setting the glass on the nightstand beside her comfortable bed, she sprang, with an intoxicated stumble, to her eager, pretty feet. With a stretch and a soft moan, Hannah proceeded toward the upstairs bathroom to prepare for the evening.

She stripped off her shirt and slid her skirt down to her ankles, playfully kicking it from her toes into the laundry bin by the bathtub. There, in her undergarments, she shed those last coverings and examined her naked, natural beauty in the mirror above the marble counter of the bathroom sink, exposing her flawless body to herself.

Hannah turned on the shower, the water warming to a steam, and once the mirror had fogged, she stepped into the cascading warmth, proceeding to clean herself in a delicate manner. The suds from her luffa were a million tiny fingers caressing her, and she watched as each soapy wave slid beautifully down her fit frame to her feet, disappearing into the drain, taking away all the invisible dirt and grime that had collected upon her.

Dripping wet and smelling of her apple-scented body wash, she stepped out, drawing a towel from the rack mounted to the wall. She dried her face and body, taking time to appreciate with her hands her own curves, and wrapped her sopping hair in the embrace of the towel. She poured a third glass of wine and went about her clothing selections.

Setting her glass on the nightstand, Hannah went to her closet and picked out her favorite pink panties with white lace, along with a bra that matched. Laying these on her bed, she went through her clothes, hoping to find what matched her mood.

Hmmm….

She settled on dark, stone-washed jeans—

It's going to be chilly later.

—and complemented them with a simple black V-neck shirt, along with her favorite black Converse low-top shoes. She drew out a pair of pink socks—as even the unseen wardrobe had to be uniform—and tossed her selections on the bed beside her undergarments. After more thoroughly drying her hair, she sat on the towel, which she had folded and lain on her askew comforter.

She was naked and vulnerable to none but herself and the watching darkness.

My mood….

Leaning back, with wine freshly poured just a few feet from her, she followed the lines of her body down to her thighs and, caressing herself from her knees to her nether regions in a back-and-forth motion, Hannah began to moan with soft pleasure as she maneuvered to her secret place, massaging and making play with her passion's source.

With her eyes closed, she took notice of the coming exquisite feminine odor as it filled the surrounding air, her sense of smell confirming her mounting lust. As she drew her nimble fingers deeper inside herself, she writhed with ecstasy, accidentally knocking her clothes onto the floor, paying them no mind. And then, once she had reached the point of her gripping climax, her fingers wet with the result that only that form of intense desire can create, she felt that tiny, pleasurable explosion ignite within her. She buried her face into a nearby decorative pillow, arching her back, lifting her waist into the air above her. She exhaled a gasping moan into the muffling thickness of the pillow. She rolled over onto her side as she vibrated, a faint, glistening trickle carving a soft path down the smooth topography of her clenching thighs.

The darkness watched with all of the darkness's dark intent.

She lay there for a few moments before collecting herself.

Yeah, definitely my mood. Let's get to this party!

She arose, washed her hands, freshened herself, and put on the outfit she had so carefully selected—and had so carelessly knocked into the floor—for the party. She brushed her teeth, tied her shoes, gathered a few things she might need, and walked calmly and confidently out the front door, which she locked behind her.

She started out of her apartment parking lot and, turning onto the street, called Jordan to warn her of her coming arrival.

No answer.

She tried again.

Still, no answer.

Probably stoned….

She turned up the radio and drove into the night, speedily approaching her friend and a night of promise and possibility. She lit a cigarette, exhaling the smoke through the cracked window, and drove on, smiling, toward Jordan's apartment.

A lonely glass of sauvignon blanc remained on her nightstand, awaiting her return.

ARI

Success.

I had prepared my home for comfort: a fire in the fireplace, a bonfire outside prepared for burning, and a wide selection of liquors and wines on the kitchen bar. I had spent almost every moment I had getting myself and the house ready for such an occasion. I looked from the slow blaze in the fireplace to the clock from my favorite spot to relax—my living room recliner.

Half past eight. A half hour to spare before—

Headlights had begun disturbing the peaceful shadows of the yard as they carved slowly into my realm of nocturnal paradise. I watched a small group of them through the large living room window as they made their way down the driveway.

Friends…. Friends always show up early.

Strangers never show up at the beginning. They always feel obligated to make such an impression.

No excitement for the coming guests stirred in me. I neither got up nor made any effort to do so.

With a glass of cabernet in my hand, I waited in my bright crimson cotton button-down, accentuated with a black tie, along with black slacks and patent black leather shoes to match. The drinks were out, the food was displayed, and the bathrooms were stocked with all sorts of amenities for my guests: extra toilet tissue, hand soap and sanitizer, moist towelettes, mints, eye drops, single cigarettes, and individually wrapped toothbrushes for the overnighters that I placed behind the mirror of the medicine cabinet between the floss picks and ibuprofen. Even an unopened box of tampons sat awkwardly on the sink countertop of the upstairs bathroom. I had not had to buy anything of that sort in years, and as uncomfortably strange as it was to have such a feminine thing in my house, I gained a sense of pride from it. I had indeed taken great precautions. I and the house, one and the same, were prepared to receive our guests.

"Let it begin."

I stood up from the recliner with reticence, making sure to keep my wine from spilling, and made my way to the kitchen to top off my half-empty glass. After setting the bottle back in its place, I leaned against the countertop, cabernet in hand. I heard the first of the car doors shut through the void of my backyard. I swirled the glass around and took a sip.

The house was set, the guest room beds made, and the doors unlocked. Beautiful music played from the living room, setting the classy tone I planned for the evening. It was time to light the bonfire. It was time to send Him *His* invitation.

I and the house were—

—*Ready*.

Now, what only mattered was—

—*Is everyone else?*

Success, indeed.

The doorbell rang. Looking down into my wine, I smiled with an evil seductiveness.

JORDAN / HANNAH

Jordan awakened to a knock and a ringing.

Hannah….

Bleak awareness, blurry consciousness, and Hannah's phone call were her only waking thoughts.

"Hello?"

Hannah replied. "Hey, let me in!"

"Ugh, okay. One second."

Jordan stirred, rubbed her eyes, and, setting her phone down, stumbled in her sleepy stupor toward the door. When she opened it, perfection stood before her, dressed to the casual nines in clean black Converse shoes. Her friend—her best friend and favorite foe—once again was indirectly challenging her to be her feminine best.

"On the hunt tonight, I see. How do you expect me to keep up?" Jordan smiled.

"By being you," replied Hannah softly.

Jordan laughed. "You always know the words, don't you?"

"Hardly. I simply comment on obvious truths. Um, speaking of… you aren't going in *that,* are you?"

"Hardly," mimicked Jordan. "Not with you looking like *that!*" She smiled again.

"I guess I'm going for comfort. It's going to be chilly later. Need a hand getting ready? You have sex hair," Hannah teased.

"I'm just exhausted. Well, I *was* exhausted. I guess I've slept away the night since I talked to you. Want to come in? I'll need only a minute."

"You always say that, and it always takes an hour," Hannah teased again.

"Well," said Jordan, gesturing toward her home's interior, "if you didn't always look so damn incredible, I wouldn't have to try so hard!"

Hannah walked through the doorway, the smell of cannabis

lingering lightly throughout the living room. Jordan, seeing the surprise on Hannah's face, offered it to her.

"I'm going to burn one down first. Might make time pass more quickly in the meantime—"

"Absolutely," Hannah interrupted. "The wine is wearing off, and I refuse to go into a party sober. Roll it up."

Hannah rarely ever partook in such activities but Jordan always enjoyed those giddy moments that they shared over their private smoking sessions. Taking a seat, she opened the little drawer of her coffee table, drew out the necessary contents, and began to crush a choice nugget in her kaleidoscope grinder, cigarette papers only an inch or two to her right. As she ground up the bud, she asked, "So how much have you had tonight?"

"Not much. Well, not *that* much," Hannah laughed.

"And you drove here?" said Jordan, concerned.

"Of course. Takes more than a glass or two, or three," she smiled, "to get the better of me." She thought back to the abandoned glass on her nightstand.

"Always so confident," Jordan teased back. "Hell, if you got pulled over, you'd only get a dinner invite anyway."

Jordan said this jokingly, but she and Hannah both knew there was a glimmer of hidden truth to her words. A slight discomfort had begun to descend upon them, but before it could take hold, Jordan interrupted the awkwardness as Hannah took a seat next to her. "So, what should I wear? We can't look the same. I don't want to overdress, and I can't undersell myself…."

Rolling the paper with focus, Jordan licked the adhesive with a slow, careful motion and twisted one end. She blew lightly on the moist gum to dry it, then she asked Hannah, "Will you help me out?"

Hannah, eyeing the freshly spun joint in Jordan's pinching grasp, nodded saying, "It isn't like you need much help. You *are beautiful*, you know. It makes me so uncomfortable when you compare us. We're friends. Besides, I've never been good where it counts—I've never had much of a real relationship—and you've always…."

Hannah broke off as Jordan's body language shifted. Jordan noticed her reaction's effect on her friend. The word 'relationship' had moved Jordan, which in turn moved Hannah. Hannah shifted her posture inwardly, focusing with increasing concern.

"So that's why you seemed so… off… over the phone," said Hannah. "What's wrong?"

"I'm single now. 'Last straw' type shit," sighed Jordan, trailing.

The way Hannah had been attempting to comfort her friend's insecurity had finally extinguished itself; her trump card burned and withered before her eyes. True, Jordan *was* extremely pretty, but she always envied Hannah in the innocent way that friends sometimes envy one other. The solution came to Hannah and spewed from her lips before the thought had registered.

"You're wearing a dress. You have to be sexy tonight. Drunk boys never can appreciate beauty…. You have to entice them, and quietly so. Sexy first. Beautiful after."

As Jordan contemplated, she delicately placed the joint between her pouty lips and ignited the end. The ember glowed, residual ash falling away, and inhaling, she passed it to Hannah. "You're right," she said, struggling to hold the smoke within herself. "I have only one or two, though. And you said you think it'll get cold later?"

"That doesn't matter. Beauty is pain. And, come to think of it, heels, too," Hannah said.

Jordan could hardly argue and caught between her siren-of-a-friend's logic and her own quiet, brooding sense of revenge, she could not disagree. Hannah, with mild difficulty, took a hearty drag of smoke, and holding it, she passed the joint to Jordan, who gladly received it. Jordan responded with a simple nod, took another glorious drag, and handed it back to her friend.

"I haven't shaved my legs in days," exhaled Jordan, feeling the stubble on her shins.

"You go and take care of that," Hannah said. "I'll find your dress and shoes and all that."

"Okay," Jordan whispered, smiling. She took the joint from Hannah, dragged it haphazardly, and passed it back. Bolting upstairs, a trail of nearly indiscernible smoke issued from her lips leaving a faint cloud behind her.

Hannah turned on the television and, having consumed what she deemed her limit of cannabis, she placed the half-finished marijuana cigarette in Jordan's crystal ashtray. "Partly cloudy with a chance of rain tonight," came the voice of the weatherman. "And a chance of thunderstorms around midnight."

She sat in silence for a time.

Hannah became restless, stood up, and climbed the stairs. As she ascended the steps, she could hear the sound of running water. Steam lightly billowed through a beam of light that emanated from the crack in the bathroom door, left slightly ajar. For a brief time, she was dazed at the top of the stairs, trapped in a moment, left speechless in witnessing Jordan's naked body, one that she had never laid eyes upon in the years they had known one another. She paused, looking on at the statuesque beauty in the nude, and as Jordan disappeared behind the shower curtain, Hannah broke from her trance and continued toward Jordan's bedroom closet. She now, in this brief moment of friendly service, had witnessed the 'goods' that she had promised to accentuate and make more enticing.

Perfect.

Now, Jordan Marie, what would you like to silently say tonight?

She quickly browsed through the closet until she found Jordan's small collection of dresses. One in particular stood out immediately—a slinky black one that would accentuate Jordan's powerful body.

Perfect.

As Hannah exited the closet, her eyes were captured by a stunning pair of red high heels that hung with several other pairs of shoes on the rack on the back of the closet door.

Cliché, but sexy.

She grabbed them from the door and made her way downstairs to the living room couch.

Eventually, Jordan emerged from the bathroom. She, in nothing but a towel, descended downstairs, with Hannah on her couch, and Jordan's black, figure-fitting dress on a hanger on the living room door. Hannah had finished the joint, something over which Jordan became thrilled. Hannah's honesty was always most forthright whenever she had partaken, so she knew this choice of wardrobe to be the correct one.

"Hope I wasn't too long—"

"Are you kidding me?" Hannah interjected. "Record time, especially for a stoner like you," she giggled. Jordan could not fight the innocent, playful smile that stretched across her face. "Well, don't ruin it now! Get ready!"

"Right," Jordan said, nodding.

Jordan grabbed the dress and hurried back upstairs to her bedroom. She stepped into it and slid it up her body, taking a moment to appreciate the newly acquired smoothness of her legs. Satisfied with the result, she shimmied the dress over her breasts, smiling at the choice Hannah had made for her.

Hot.

When she descended the stairs once more, Hannah watched as this dream of a girl made her way into her presence. She had never seen Jordan so outwardly sensual, the dress she had chosen doing wonders for Jordan's petite, curvy figure.

"What do you think?" asked Jordan.

"I think you'll need this," said Hannah, handing Jordan a lipstick of powerful red. "And… these," Hannah added, picking up a pair of intimidating high heels that matched the hue of the lipstick, which she set back down by the couch.

"Heels? You sure?" Jordan asked, confused. "But it's—"

"—A bonfire?"

Jordan nodded. Hannah repeated, "Beauty is pain, even if that pain is simply inconvenience. Or impracticality."

Jordan, once again speechless, nodded again, though she silently agreed with a slight apprehension.

"Come on! We have to be there by eleven," said Hannah. "Fashionably late means nothing if everyone's hammered when we show up!"

Jordan acknowledged Hannah and quickly sat down next to her. She put on her high heels and then walked across the living room with a confident feminine stride to the downstairs half-bathroom, where she applied her lipstick of passionate red. She kissed a bit of toilet paper, discarding it along with the excess crimson, and walked into the living room to be revealed.

"How do I look?"

Hannah was stunned. For years, she had been Jordan's friend, yet here in this moment she could barely comprehend this transformed woman before her. "Oh my!" was all she could say.

"So, I look okay?"

"Great. Wonderful. Absolutely stunning. You totally look the part," praised Hannah.

Jordan lit up. A compliment like this was nothing like anything her ex-boyfriend had ever told her.

"But I'm nervous. I haven't dressed up like this since New Year's," Jordan admitted.

"I remember, and I also remember—correct me if I'm mistaken— that you had to tell many a nervous boy that you were seeing someone. Tonight is a different story, is it not? Own it. You look hot."

Jordan revealed a grin too genuine to describe. She sat down next to Hannah, crossing her legs at her ankles, and opened the little drawer in her living room coffee table.

"Hurry up," said Hannah. "Fashionably late, you know."

"I know. Nervous, still, you know."

Hannah exhaled playfully and heartily. She could not tease Jordan and her innocent nature, especially in Jordan's current state of insecurity. "I want one for the road, two for the party, and one for the hangover," Jordan added.

"Not a bad plan, but please hurry," urged Hannah. "I'm ready to drink!"

Jordan set to work. Hannah watched on as Jordan, in her speed and precision, rolled four cannabis cigarettes of professional quality in no time. Then, putting them into her cigarette case that normally remained empty, she slid the compartment into her green purse—the only one she owned—and slung it onto her bare shoulder.

"Ready?" asked Hannah.

"Ready."

Getting into Hannah's sedan, Jordan had a thought. "What if I meet someone—"

"Look, if you need protection, I've got you covered," Hannah said, her clever double entendre going entirely unnoticed.

"Alright."

Jordan still, despite her sensual appearance and her friend's preparedness, felt a bit of nervousness steal over her.

What if? What if....

She closed off her mind, ignited the first of four, and relaxed as Hannah turned on the radio. Pink Floyd, her favorite band to fade into, was halfway through a paralyzing guitar solo. This relaxed her, and exhaling, she reclined in her seat, Hannah pressing harder on the gas, the two of them driving into a collective unknown—a new comfortable uncertainty gripping them both.

ARI

Stranger things have happened.

I took another drink. Then another. Then another. The previous day's hangover had dissolved, and so had I, into the din and humdrum heyday that my typically quiet house had become.

People in the kitchen talking; old friends and those becoming friends, maybe enemies; couples and singles alike, dancing in the living room; and I had not yet stepped outside for a single moment since I first opened the door. I was drunk, yes, but not in a loose fashion. I was, simply put, at heights that must be experienced and cannot be described. I was floating, but just above the floor.

I was standing in my living room, surrounded but alone, drawn in by the allure of the un-imprisonable motion of the fireplace pyre, and as I stared into the face of the flames, they stared back, a glaring, roaring, tangible abyss.

God.

But then again, He could be outside, waiting....

I kept a glass of wine, red and fierce, in my hand and tarried about, making sure my guests were comfortable. Every care had been taken to ensure a carefree time was attainable by all. Nothing but laughter and conversation filled my home. All were hysterical with happiness. All had something to contribute, I thought, save for me—except the house itself. And in a way, I offered myself—as I and the house were one—as a center for the activities of the night. I had floated from guest to guest, my count of them becoming slurred and diminished by the time I had reached about the seventieth one, and I realized in that very floating that I knew very few who were present, if I 'knew' anyone at all.

Conversation had happened here and there in dissipated episodes, yet I felt disconnected, the party growing more and more 'American nineteen-twenties' by the minute. My host status was becoming lost in a tumultuous void of unknowing. Anonymity was becoming the theme for me, my identity askew amongst the crowd that was, in large part, ignorant of who I was or what purposes I served in this little social game. I was the host not playing host, becoming a guest myself, I suppose, and had, in that transformation, become a guest anonymous, unnamed, unmentioned, and unannounced.

Exactly why I'm here alone, again. Comfort in the chaos.

"Perfect," I uttered quietly to myself. I tasted my wine with care, paying special attention to the distinct aroma and flavor notes as it tantalized and numbed my senses.

The party was only to reanimate and redefine my dull, understated world, anyway. In my living room to which I had retreated, I was happy—irretrievably happy. I wore a smile like armor ever since my guests had first arrived, but they had hit up the bar in the kitchen almost immediately, never leaving the ample liquor selection, save for the small crowd in the living room of which I was now a part.

I had chimed in on conversations at random and broken intervals, but I had not become fully engaged by a single one. It would take a miracle, a burning miracle—a *God* miracle—to attain and retain my attention, and I had seen nothing of the like in the hours during which the party had commenced.

I stood there in front of the hearth, watching the fire dance to the whimsical genius of Mozart. I casually sipped my wine, listening to the current concerto that illuminated the otherwise empty talk of nothing that filled the room around me, and I stood in lonely peace, enjoying the steady, unintelligible roar that emanated from the mouths of the people in my lonely presence.

All that enraptured me was the fire in the fireplace.

The fire....

It burned and so did I.

It was flickering as I was burning out, like little flames of life desperately reaching out to be fed.

It filled the house with comfort and warmth and had given the dwelling the tonality of invitation, an attitude of attraction, and a mood of fleeting wonder. It was alone, burning, and completely unnoticed, much like myself, save by one.

I, the witness.

I watched it crackle and dance in its brick cage, and somehow it thrived in that little world in its bright loneliness. It was much like me. It *was* me! Yet the fire was still God.

It's a wonder no one else is watching. My time....

I simply could do no more but stand and watch, wait and listen.

I in my abode, my Sheöl, and He right there in front of me, dancing.

Passion.

Forgiveness.

Illimitable.

He was in His little Heaven and I was in my great Hell, and still, He was the One burning, not me. All the screams that supposedly thrive in the darkness of damnation—*this mortal Hell*—were but shrills of joy and murmurs of happiness. Echoing waves of ecstasy and stupefied bliss permeated me, filling me, pulling every outer energy deep within my core, rattling toward me in continuous waves from the people that filled my home.

I stared at Him.

He stared at me.

The duplicity was almost numbingly overpowering, yet the quiet emotion that was building was undeniable. In our silent conversation, we were learning of each other. We were one and the same, and in that realization, I decided He had in fact accepted my invitation, sarcastic as it may have initially been; but He had, in the end, obliged.

I fed Him another log from the small wood pile I kept next to the fireplace. I had to keep Him alive.

God must never die.

If God dies—the Source snuffed out—there is nothing from which to feed.

We are all fires.

The conversation I had earlier within myself played out like a recording from what seemed like eons ago.

Waiver or blaze?

Wax of life….

Shadows made.

During the entire exchange, I may have never once blinked. The heat felt good upon my face; the light was subtle, yet fulfilling; and the shadows dancing on the ceiling were but creatures of myth, moving to the silent song of God's voice—a song that they alone could hear—but I could hear music as well, feeling it deeper than emotion.

Wolfgang. Wolfgang Amadeus Mozart.

I swooned. I was lost. I was slightly drunk.

If He were truly there in the flames, as I knew Him to be, I was also burning—a little piece of Him burning right along with Him.

Beside and within.

Clever.

If I were burning, I would burn up, reduce to ashes, and

recombine with the Inferno at the end of it all. I would return to Him, my Source. And as I pitched yet another log into the fireplace, sipping my wine, I realized that we must feed Him to give Him life in the world—this Hell.

Our prayers and thoughts and loving gestures are offerings to Him. Sometimes He gives back. We are the tinder and He the purpose, the font of all flame.

He and I were One. The house and I were One. He and the house, therefore, were also One, and in our little trinity, we contained, harbored, and ruled over the entirety of the sin that was taking place around, between, and within our triumvirate collective. The fire in the house was comfort. The fire in my face was desire. The fire in God was Love.

Comfort, desire, and love.… Is there anything else we ever feel aside from these or their lack thereof?

We were complete in our combination, all an equal part of the other portions, all relying on the fastidiousness of the rest. I stoked the fire with the metal poker I kept by the hearth. I swept the ash that had drifted upon the floor back to the flames. I closed the chainmail grate and guzzled what remained of my deep red wine in a mighty gulp.

Mozart relinquished his symphonic rule over the transparent multitude.

After a brief silence, Beethoven intervened with his mighty "Moonlight Sonata".

The moon.…

Looking to the clock above the mantelpiece, I saw that it read half past ten.

And I need a refill.

"And I want to see the moon, too, Ludwig."

I looked God straight in the face and nodded. He simply carried on with doing what fires and gods always do—dancing and whispering.

But will God go with me?

"Do *You* fear the darkness?" I asked aloud.

The logs shifted, sparks flying up through the chimney, fresh ashes landing in a peppering fashion upon my patent leather shoes, soiling them. I laughed at the coincidence.

But there are no coincidences.

I reopened the fireplace grate, adding yet another log to the fire, acknowledging the pyre in the hearth one last time before making my way to the kitchen for more wine. I carefully closed the grate—the gate of Heaven.

And then outside into the darkness.

"And you will come with me."

I checked my pockets for my matches and cigarettes and, floating mostly unnoticed through the raucous din of the kitchen, I grabbed a half-full bottle of wine from the counter and made my way out of the back door with empty wine glass in hand, the bottle tucked under my arm.

Ludwig van Beethoven was the distant soundtrack to my departure. I left the fire burning in the hearth.

God must never die.

God must never die.

JORDAN

The cool, autumn air rushing past the cracked windows of the sedan whispered warnings.

I feel good.

Something made her uneasy, anxious as she was in her overly excitable state of mind, and the mixture made for much confusion—a confusion that dripped slowly into the bloodstream of her confidence.

I must look a total mess.

The hair she had brushed straight had become lightly tossed about her brow by the wind passing through the window. As the pair of girls turned onto a country road, she looked from the passenger seat out of her window, watching stars and treetops pass overhead.

She shifted, uncrossing and re-crossing her legs, enjoying one smooth leg caressing the other, dragging her palms up her shins. She shivered. She lightly squeezed her calves, experiencing their supple elasticity and silky texture. The light of the moon shone through the windshield—a brilliant, defined shine glowing upon her knee, fading as it crept up her exposed thigh, equally as plush as the rest of the ensemble.

Jordan turned to Hannah in the driver's seat just in time to see her drop her cigarette into the floor of the sedan. Hannah moved in a controlled panic, keeping the car moving forward with one hand on the steering wheel and one hand on the floor, all while peeking just enough for minimal sight over the dashboard. Her eyes drifted up and down, road-to-floor-to-road, as she fought time in her attempt to not burn the carpet.

Hannah fumbled around, finally eyeing the glowing ember on the floor, a quiet "Shit" escaping her lips as she picked up the burning cigarette.

"That could have been a disaster," she said coolly.

"You really should quit that habit, you know. You're so

beautiful, and eventually those are going to ruin that," advised Jordan.

"I'm trying to quit," Hannah replied. "Well, I've *tried* to quit, but I've been drinking, too. Besides, have you ever tried a cigarette after sex? It's so incredible, lying there next to whomever, both so relaxed and tame; the wildness sweated freshly right out of you. Memories like that attach themselves to things, and then they become habits."

Jordan blushed at Hannah's response, her color change entirely unnoticed.

She thought of Hannah, dressed in nothing but her perfect flesh and a veil of smoke, drifting like her current thought around Hannah's toasted olive skin, lingering like a ghost around and within her. Jordan considered herself a woman made for men, yet she lost herself in the momentary imaginings, having to pull herself back to reality, back to Hannah fully clothed—her best friend and nothing more.

Jordan shifted once more, again uncrossing and re-crossing her silken legs, amazed at the self she exhibited—the self that Hannah had summoned out of her.

"You know I haven't," whispered Jordan. "'Douchebag' and I haven't slept together in so long. Our last time was on our anniversary.... I guess a year was enough for him. Almost to the day he started cheating on me. The bastard...."

"And you stayed so loyal to him the whole time, even when you were suspicious. You were *such* a great girlfriend, dealing with his shit the whole time. Why did you not end it then? I couldn't go half a year without getting any."

Jordan interrupted this time, quickly coming to her own defense. "I guess I, well...." She paused. "I guess I thought he'd come around, that it was simply a phase. I suppose I forgive too easily, to put it simp—"

Hannah's retort was abrupt yet compassionate.

"You didn't recognize your worth," she said. "You still don't, obviously. You were almost too timid to put on that dress! Hell, you almost didn't come with me tonight. I could hear your hesitance over the phone earlier. Forgive, forgive, forgive, and forgive, Saint Jordan!" she joked. Jordan thought Hannah had become erratic and overreaching. "I think it's high time for our little saint—"

Their eyes met.

"—to sin a bit tonight," Hannah continued.

Hannah's voice caused Jordan to blush once again, but this time it was out of shame—the shame of her allowing Hannah to turn her on with her sultry tone. Jordan turned away as Hannah did, both looking ahead into the glow of the headlights, the road passing in a grey, continuous stream as they drove on toward their destination.

Jordan felt a distant heat touch and rise in her, the warmth of a thousand stars gravitating around her, trapped in the magnetism of her gravity; yet they were currently too distant to make her truly burn. "Let's do it," Jordan uttered. She paused a moment, and in that pause, those far-off stars seemed to gather closer and burn brighter. "Teach me."

"We're almost there," was Hannah's smoky reply.

As they crested a hilltop, the trees cleared, and the moon, whose light shone strongly from behind a gathering of clouds, lit up the night air. Even from the mile-and-a-half distance from their destination, Hannah and Jordan could see the magnificent lights of the house nestled between two moonlit hills, and the spectacle battled for attention with the looming moon.

There can be no victor.

Almost thoughtlessly, she procured one of her joints from her purse and lit it, inhaling slowly.

"*One* for the road, eh?" teased Hannah

"I'm just feeling it. The whole vibe of the scene is a bit overwhelming, isn't it? I mean, look at that house, and *look* at that *moon!* Seems more like a night I should feel instead of see to experience it, don't you think, Hannah?"

Hannah's only response was a smile.

Jordan took down almost half of the number to herself, watching with childlike astonishment as each ghost exhaled lingered in front of her before being pulled against its will, out of the window and into the night. Jordan passed the remainder of the joint to Hannah, who took it gladly, yet Jordan never broke her gaze from the window or the vivid nocturnal canvas that was painted and living beyond.

She felt something of a connection, once again, with the smoke. She felt gray, weightless, and disconnected. She floated, lingered, and drifted seamlessly out of and beyond the transparency of the windows of life, defragmenting as she escaped. She had become smoke, a product of something burning or something that once burned, and all she could deduce was that she, here and now, was the smoke to Hannah's fire tonight. Hannah, who was so obviously defragmented herself, burned also, but in tinier, quieter bursts. Jordan was the smoke of the fire of all those distant stars—those little pieces of Hannah.

After all, Hannah had invited her, Hannah was driving her to the party, and Hannah was rescuing Jordan from her loneliness. Hannah had broken Jordan from within the shell of herself and brought her into this little world of hers. The longer Hannah burned, the longer Jordan existed.

"Thank you," Jordan said. "Thank you for tonight."

Hannah simply shrugged her rounded shoulders, passed Jordan the joint that was nearing its end, and activated her turn signal before making a left turn into the driveway. The headlights of other cars were following down the road behind them and several pairs of brake lights were ahead of them—the parking of countless cars along the driveway ahead.

Jordan took no offense to Hannah's indifferent gesture, shrugging, herself in the process, and looked down the driveway as she took a long draw from the short roach and tossed it out the window into the yard. "Yes. Feel. Instead of see…." mused Hannah.

Out there in the darkness, Hannah joined Jordan in the air, her heat reaching up and out to her, commingling with the smoke that was Jordan, high in the shallow atmosphere. She thought this to be very appropriate because, after all, they both were indeed *high*. Jordan, much akin to her smoky metaphor, drifted. Hannah led the way. Jordan, willing yet helpless to fight it, simply followed.

The car slowly traversed the driveway into the subtle valley where a little universe waited to be born.

Jordan turned to Hannah as she motioned to light a cigarette. Her lighter had ceased working. In frustration, she shook it several times, each time grinding the flint and steel, trying to make the spark into flame. Jordan looked on with comical pity, a playful smile stretching lazily across her face, and she reached into her bag to hand Hannah her lighter as Hannah tossed hers in a miniature rage into the back seat of the sedan. Both laughed at the extreme reaction. Hannah took Jordan's lighter with a smirk and a wink.

Hannah succeeded in producing a tiny flame. She lit her cigarette, Jordan carefully watching herself drift, once again, from Hannah's lungs, past her lips, and finally up and out the window into the mystique and darkness of the autumn night. Jordan unbuckled her seatbelt, watching as approaching trees began to crowd the view of the sky again.

Hannah smoked.

Jordan *was* smoke.

HANNAH

Hannah was mesmerized.

The light reflecting on Jordan's legs was a crippling embodiment of a soft, unspoken power, like dew upon a flower or the glistening of a fang in the mouth of a hungry lioness. The wind was screaming past the gap in Jordan's window, the calling-out of a million invisible voices that cheered aloud the haunting memory of a distant regret.

Between the whispering wind and the sound of the radio, there was nothing—nothing but Hannah and Jordan and that reflection on Jordan's legs, too strong and proud to release Hannah from its hypnotizing gaze. Jordan squeezed her calves.

Damn!

Jordan turned to Hannah, Hannah quickly shifting her gaze from Jordan's legs, her cigarette lost to gravity in the clumsy chaos of the shuffle. Hannah felt the heat rising in her face in embarrassment.

"Shit," she mumbled as she bent down, still driving, expertly finding and removing the cigarette burning the fibers of her sedan's carpet.

This is so embarrassing….

The conversation continued in a blur that Hannah would not absorb, so lost was she in Jordan's pretty display of feminine might. She recalled something along the lines of sex and cigarette philosophies, but these were lost to the blankness of the brief present, turning almost instantly into forgotten words, seconds, moments, and breaths. She drifted back to reality as Jordan's voice brought her back.

"I suppose I forgive too easily, to put it simp—" Jordan said.

"You didn't recognize your worth," Hannah interrupted, the frustration building until it exploded from her mouth. "You still don't, obviously. You were almost too timid to put on that dress! Hell, you almost didn't come with me tonight. I could hear your hesitance over the phone earlier."

The sadness in your voice….

"Forgive, forgive, forgive, and forgive. Saint Jordan!"

Hannah watched as these words weighed upon Jordan, her newfound confidence softly shunned, though Hannah could not define why or how. A darkness gripped her—a desire of an evil kind, branching out within—beneath her skin. Hannah panicked, and in her panic, she vomited words that to her were threadbare and thin, a nervous attempt to repair what she perceived as damage to Jordan's fragile inner light.

"I think it's high time for our little saint to sin a bit tonight."

Hannah realized that she had leaned in toward her best friend as she finished her sentence. Jordan shifted her body in a sinuous manner, making it obvious to Hannah that she had indeed somehow darkened the otherwise bright aspect of Jordan's view of herself. Jordan looked up, meeting Hannah's gaze with hers. Shocked innocence veiled her face. Their eyes remained locked only for a moment, Hannah looking away with an awkward quickness, to focus on driving the sedan—a responsibility that she had been carelessly abandoning. The cannabis and spirits from earlier were still lingering like weak yet ardent ghosts within her flesh. As she stared through the windshield, the dim light beyond the dashboard faded, along with the road and the darkness. A scene began to play itself out in Hannah's imagination.

Jordan's place. The crack of the bathroom door. That playful, inviting, thought-provoking beam of light….

In her conscious dream, Hannah was once again outside Jordan's bathroom. She was also prepared this time—more daring and braver. As Jordan's second foot passed beyond the shower curtain with nymph-like grace, Hannah nudged the door open inches at a time. An occasional creak forced her to be stealthier, but this was a daydream. She was in no real danger. Regardless, Hannah shut the door quietly behind her.

Hannah was nude herself all-of-a-sudden, looking blankly into the gradually fogging mirror that Jordan's reflection was also previously within, though she now remained hidden beyond the curtain. Jordan began humming a song, and the combination of Jordan's soulful, sultry voice gave Hannah goose bumps all over, no crevice or hidden place unaffected. She looked down at her arms and breasts, all seemingly tingling in the rising steam of the lavatory.

The song stopped.

Jordan's voice had ceased its melody.

Only the steady cascade of the falling water made any effort to make its presence audible.

Moments passed, then the shower curtain burst open, the fabric loudly rustling, the plastic curtain rings clanging together with agitated abruptness. The shock of the commotion caused Hannah to quickly look up, her eyes scorched by the power of Jordan's dripping body, no sign of her innocence anywhere nearby.

Hannah looked into the reflection of Jordan's eyes in the mirror, the power of Jordan's naked body dominating her peripheral vision. Hannah turned slowly, shifting her gaze to Jordan's feet. Starting with her pedicured toenails, Hannah gradually lifted her witnessing eyes upward, directing with expert skill, this movie that played in her head.

Those petite ankles…. Those thighs…. A freckle here, a scar there…. So beautiful.

"Hannah," said Jordan's dream twin, "I can only tempt you so long as you resist..."

Hannah could think no more. She rushed into the shower, taking Jordan by the shoulder and pressing her into the shower wall. There, with her right knee bent between Jordan's legs, she raised it, massaging Jordan's secret with her curiosity. Taking Jordan gently by the throat, she grasped her wrist with her other hand and pinned it against the wall near the steaming shower head. As the water encased them both, Hannah pressed on, massaging and tempting.

She watched as her victim's eyes rolled gently upward, her head turning downward, her legs shaking with pleasure and anticipation. Looking up at Hannah with a stern gaze—one that paralyzed her—Jordan pushed Hannah's knee away from her. Hannah looked away, ashamed.

Just as her chin began to fall toward her chest, Jordan caught Hannah's face and lifted it. Hannah slowly closed and opened her eyes, Jordan's eyes reflecting Hannah's right back at her, and as those mirrors reflected back into each other, the depths of forever were opened to be seen. Hannah could only register the meaning of this moment for a short while before it was finished. She could only avariciously respond as her counterpart's face softly collided with hers, their lips melding, the steam of the shower making the moment wholly romantic.

As Hannah closed her eyes, she fell in love with the thumb pressed to her face in front of her ear and Jordan's fingers cradling the back of her head, all becoming helplessly entangled in the wetness of Hannah's hair. Jordan kissed Hannah. Hannah returned the favor. In the shower's heat, lost and in a fog, their joined hands, once locked to each other, began to part. Hannah released Jordan, and with that merciful hand, she carved a soft path down Jordan's arm to her chest, over her breasts, and finally plunged, with a reserved sensitivity, toward Jordan's inviting center.

She stopped short of her goal.

Jordan had begun massaging her lower back, the indentations of her dimples becoming Jordan's fingers' haven of comfort. Hannah opened her eyes, ceased kissing, took a breath, and stepped back. Opening her eyes, Jordan said, "Huh, I imagined you were braver than that."

Jordan shrugged. Hannah blushed, her hand still gently lingering on Jordan's secret place. Jordan looked down, smiling.

In a flash, Hannah and Jordan lay on the shower floor, Hannah caressing Jordan into an explosive frenzy, the water glistening as it clung and dripped from their unified skin. As Jordan's cries peaked, Hannah quickened her stroke, ultimately releasing Jordan from her prison of dissatisfaction. Jordan looked up, spent, and beaming. She then spoke in what sounded like a distant echo.

"Let's do it…"

"What?" asked Hannah, exhausted. "But we just did. Want to go again?"

"Let's do it…."

The last echo snapped Hannah back into the real world, away from her perverse imaginings. "Let's do it," Jordan had said. "Teach me."

In the aftershock of what she had witnessed in her imagination, Hannah could sense a sort of steam from the shower still lingering in the atmosphere around her. Her heart was beating rapidly in nervousness and excitement.

I need to calm down….

Hannah cleared her throat and spoke to Jordan.

"We're almost there."

Transcending the hill before their destination, Hannah watched as Jordan drew another rolled joint from her jade handbag. As she lit it, Hannah jokingly remarked, "*One* for the road, eh?"

"I'm just feeling it," responded Jordan, and Hannah understood her meaning perfectly. "The whole vibe of the scene is a bit overwhelming, isn't it? I mean, look at that house, and *look at that moon!* Seems more like a night I should feel instead of seeing, don't you think, Hannah?" Hannah smiled in her appreciation for Jordan in this moment. Hannah loved Jordan for the poetic scope of her own little world.

I need to relax….

Jordan had exhausted nearly half of the joint before offering Hannah what remained. Though she craved the release, Hannah waited patiently, readily taking it—

—Perfect!—

—when Jordan offered it. Still, Hannah could not shake the feeling that something was different about Jordan. It was neither good nor bad, whatever it was. It was simply something different, something alien to Jordan's usually placid demeanor.

Jordan parted her beautiful ruby lips, exhaling a cripplingly soft "Thank you. Thank you for tonight."

Hannah, hoping to avoid another inappropriate daydream, merely shrugged, returning the joint to Jordan. Hannah activated her left turn signal as she prepared to guide the car into the driveway of the massive house. The collective red glow of brake lights—guests parking—could be seen at the end of the path. A few pairs of headlights were winding down the hill with the arrival of even more guests. Jordan then shrugged, dragging the joint once more before discarding it out the window. Watching the cherry of Jordan's joint fade into the darkness beyond the window, Hannah repeated what Jordan had said previously: "Yes, feel instead of see."

Hannah thought over these words, examining Jordan's frame. Jordan's crossed legs and the textures they bore were driving Hannah to the brink of silent madness—

Feel…. instead of seeing…. Feel….

—but the changing scenery interrupted. The trees had become denser, and the driveway had become steadily darker. Hannah drew out a cigarette, placed it between her lips, and attempted to light it. Her lighter produced no flame. Hannah shook it vigorously—

Piece of shit!

—and attempted to spark it multiple times, all to no avail. She threw the lighter over her right shoulder into the backseat, and just as she parted her lips to ask Jordan for her lighter, Jordan held one out for her.

Jordan was smiling, and the reassuring look she gave Hannah caused Hannah to laugh and smile as well. Winking playfully, Hannah took her up on the offer and lit her cigarette. With a satisfied sigh, Hannah exhaled the smoke out of her window. She thought back to the shower of her dream and how the smoke was very much like the steam that had surrounded them in the warming depths of the deep desires of her imagination.

Jordan unbuckled with obvious anticipation for the party to come. Hannah laughed silently to herself.

Why unbuckle? The ride has only just begun....

EXODUS

ARI

I couldn't handle the real world, so I created my own, and now that utopia has fallen as well. When a deity is your only company, you tend to look crazy to everyone else. You talk to yourself, have fights with yourself…. But it's like arguing with an echo. You get tired of the repetition of things you've already said and said and said….

All these people, and nothing more than an introduction and a welcome exchanged with any of them.

Host, indeed.

And they are my parasites.

Being in the house had become too much. I had organized this whole affair to escape my dismally lonely world, yet I had remained inside, hardly social, and somewhat anxious. My friends brought dates if I even dared to call them friends. They had no need for my attention—only the house, a place, and a party. I was not entirely sure I wanted a conversation yet anyway. After all, I wanted only the crowd and the noise. I craved invisible company.

I suppose I got that from all the talk with God to which I had been wholeheartedly committed.

I suppose I was invisible, myself. After all, was it not I who had been keeping my sole company this whole time?

As the host, I knew I was a tool to be used.

The emotional trickery of alcohol can be quite the foe, and I was losing the battle.

The back door closed with a soft click. The back porch had been flooded with people—a debaucherous horde. I recognized no one. It was perfect. To this degree, I seemed to fit right in.

On the other hand….

A voice, friendly and familiar, interrupted.

"You look a bit distracted. I won't have a self-pitying bastard host any party I plan on attending for very long."

The smile I heard in the voice kept my frustration with its

rudeness at bay. I turned slowly, instantly relaxing at the sight of the smiling man half a foot taller than myself.

"Michael. Off work early tonight?"

Michael Law, ladies and gentlemen….

His reply, a well-planned dialogue, felt like something he had been composing for some time. Immediately, I got the idea that he had been preparing what he was going to say long before his arrival. He might have even missed me a little bit, which would explain such a well-versed, overstated introduction.

"Ari, I'm telling you, if those old folks don't care for themselves once in a good while, then what the hell's the point?"

I knew he had skipped out of work without notifying anyone. He was no longer in his scrubs, dressed in a deep grey V-neck shirt and dark jeans. He continued speaking before I could look to his shoes.

"I refuse to take their autonomy away. They are no better than machines without it at that point, simply waiting for someone to boot them up and give them direction. Mrs. Avery won't let me wipe her ass anyway. Stubborn. Stubborn, but very strong."

He spoke as if I knew this woman. He continued. "Very self-reliant. She's got no one—no one but me, really. Oh, don't look so worried, Ari. I told her I was coming here, tonight. She even asked if I needed a date."

He chuckled to himself in his recollection of this woman.

The typical hubris of a self-proclaimed alpha male.

Give me a damn break.

"She isn't here—don't worry," he continued. "Too much inconvenience to carry all that machinery around. Besides, I told her she was too far out of my league. That seemed to make her whole night. She even offered to introduce me to her granddaughter, and Mrs. Avery swears she's a nice girl. Apparently, she comes in from time to time to check in on the old lady, but I've never met her. I gave Mrs. Avery my number in case anything happened, and, hell, maybe she'll even slip it her granddaughter's way!" he said, nudging me.

You never change, do you?

"Sweet lady. Said she would be reading and didn't want to be disturbed—her little way of telling me she would be fine and to have a good time." He nudged me again as if attempting to quell my obvious concern.

Okay, let's move the topic forward, Michael, for my sanity's sake.

I took advantage of his pause to interject.

"So, are you?"

"Am I what, Ari?"

"Having a good time?" I asked.

"The best! Only been here about thirty minutes and I've already been scoping out the prospects," he said.

I knew you'd come for the girls. Only a half hour to find me, huh?

He swept his straight blond hair from his face, his blue eyes glistening with the play of the light. He looked especially stern yet not unfriendly.

"But that is exactly why I've stopped you," he said. "You look glum, sad as hell. The biggest party I've seen since I can recall, and you, *oh host*, are skulking like a sad kid. Cheer up. Saw you talking to yourself by the fireplace…. Can't be a good sign, Ari. So, what's the matter? Where *is* your accomplice?"

"Accomplice?"

"The one you invited out with you in the living room… 'And you will come with me.' Sound familiar?" he asked. We both smiled. Mine faded as I gazed down at my shoes, still peppered with the ashen remnants of God.

"No one," I said. "No one at all."

A distant rumble of thunder echoed in the far-off night.

"Thunder?" Michael asked, looking into the trees in the backyard. "Damn, at least it's far away. So much for the fire."

"Shit, the fire! I should have lit it by now!" I cried in panic.

"What? You haven't started it yet? But this was advertised as a bonfire, *Ari*. That's like going to a bar without girls or drinks!"

"I know," I said. "I was just on my way to—"

Michael nudged me again. "Good thing you've got a friend that's already got it going." He turned to examine a beautifully dressed wonder of a girl as she passed us by.

Red head….

I exhaled with complete relief at Michael's favor. He was still watching the auburn-haired beauty make her way away from us.

Pick up your jaw, but….

"Thank you, Michael."

So, that's what took you so long to get to me…. Maybe I shouldn't assume who you are, now. It's been so long….

Turning his sights back to me, he said, "There you go getting soft again, Ari. Shall we go down to the fire and dry you out?"

Always the alpha….

"Sure. It couldn't have been built to last very long."

He shrugged off my funny jab, ignoring it, as if he had heard me speaking at all for the presence of the girl that kept him gawking.

"Well, let's go, then," he retorted. "I'm gonna need a drinking partner!"

I looked up into his face and nodded in acknowledgement. I pulled the cork from the bottle under my arm, poured a glass for myself, and handed him the rest.

"You'll want to let that breathe for a moment. Let the tannins go to work," I said.

This bottle's been open quite a while. Just a test, Michael. We are more equal than you are willing to admit.

"Ari," he said, "I love you, brother, but damn it, I'm here to get drunk." And with that, he turned the bottle up, taking several large gulps in rapid succession.

"Such a waste of a great wine…" I sighed.

"I'm drinking it. It'll get me drunk. Where's the waste? You handed me the bottle, man. If you wanted me to be classy, you should have brought another glass." He then winked at me in comically rude fashion.

"I didn't expect to bump into anyone familiar. I've been enjoying the solitude. Still, that's an expensive wine, Michael."

"Well, I may be 'wasting this vintage,' but that's better than wasting the evening. Mrs. Avery expects stories—epic stories tomorrow—and I have no intentions to disappoint."

Thunder rumbled once again from far away.

"She loves stories, that woman," he continued. "I read to her all the time. So, let's get to it, shall we? To the bonfire?"

"Yes, let's go. I've been getting this together all day. I could go for a little social interaction."

Partly a lie, but now you've dragged me into the gauntlet. I appreciate it.

Aside from a little cleaning here and there, I truly put almost no effort into the planning of this whole thing. Why did I say that? That's not you, Ari. Kings do not compete. They have no competition. Stand your ground. After all, you've got an actual friend here now, no matter your friendly 'competition'.

"And I could go for some girls," he said. "Sharpen that silver tongue, man. If your words can't melt them, maybe the fire will."

Another distant echo of thunder crept through the darkness, passing through me.

"Come on," he said. "No fire can stand up to a crying sky. We have got to beat the rain!"

I gave no response.

We started down the back porch stairs, dodging guests in a slow, wavering motion, with Michael following closely behind.

"So, your accomplice? Is it God or Beethoven with us tonight?"

"Neither, or both," I said.

"So much for clarity," he joked.

"Well, Michael, who would *you* invite?"

"Of the two?" Michael asked. "Well, Beethoven would be shit for company, honestly."

"How so? He's brilliant!"

"He's fucking dead, Ari. Can't be all that smart. Not like the deaf bastard could hear a word I said, even if he were still living," Michael said, laughing to himself.

I stopped abruptly at the bottom step as wine exploded from my mouth in laughter, some splashing back into my face from the glass. I did not mind. Michael was cheering me right up.

Good friend. I shouldn't be so hard on you. I'm just stressed. I'm sorry.

I lifted the glass for another drink when an aftershock of laughter halted me from doing so. Through the residual smile from that much-needed fit, I asked Michael, "And of the other?" I began wiping my face with my hand.

"Who? God?" Michael asked. "Now, I don't know much on the subject. Neither of us are really fans of the church, and I, myself, have never seen any miracles, but as hard as it is to prove a god does exist, well, try proving that one doesn't, Ari. I don't think 'He' exists, or maybe 'He' does, but either way, I just don't fucking care. But it's very difficult to tell, for sure, if I'm being honest. He's here, He's there, He's everywhere, and look around—nowhere to be found."

Thunder.

And I see his point entirely. Probably why I'm so badly wanting my invitation to be accepted…. Hell, maybe I don't believe it at all, either. Half taunting, half pleading for Him to show Himself, so either my plea will be honored, or my taunt will just piss Him off, completely. Either way, by rage or by grace, there are two ways this can work.

"Of course, we can't trust our eyes with everything," Michael said.

The alcohol was affecting Michael already.

The wine was not affecting me at all, and that is how I knew, indeed, that it was.

He always hated the idea of anything being greater than himself. Here he was, being a fair-minded philosopher. I felt strangely proud of this progress.

I guess it has been quite some time since we've caught up and all that….

"In fact," he continued, "of the senses, sight is the bastard child. Sight is a traitor." He took another sip of wine.

If sight betrays, then why lend it so much credit? You didn't mind the sight of that hot redhead 'lying' to you, did you?

I decided to challenge him further. My words were meaningless as I spoke, but I knew he could not tell the difference from the elevated position of his inflated audacity.

"But see, Michael, what about hearing? We can't believe everything we hear, surely. Sight may betray, but the ears.... Sight is too heavily relied upon. People panic in the dark, and for no good damned reason. The ears can be tricked, too, but the eyes are much easier to believe. Sight can inspire or scar far worse than hearing can. I mean, what traumatizes more, typically? Visual memories or audible ones? Sight, *right*? So with sight, we trick even ourselves sometimes, seeing what we *want* to see. In sight, we *per*-ceive...."

"But in sound, we *re*-ceive," he said.

Wow, that was actually insightful. Has it been so long since we've spoken? Not bad, Michael. Not bad at all.

"Exactly," I said, feeling briefly that I was now the one who had become the serpent in my garden. "What we see is either false or real. It's black or white. Perception and possible mistakes in recollection only surface once the message is relayed. It gets skewed in the handoff. Perhaps a deaf genius like Beethoven wouldn't be such awful company after all. He could *really* give us some sense of insight. Does that sound right? Do you see?"

I can be clever at times.

He laughed at my play on words with a mannerly, dry laugh and nodded in understanding. "I see just fine. And I feel great! That wine of yours is really getting to work! How do you feel, Ari?"

His question crept upon me like a stalking shadow. How I had felt all day had been the only thing on my mind, yet I had no response. "Ready" was the only thought I could translate into spoken words.

"Alright, let's keep moving, then," he said. "Probably time to throw some more wood on that fire that you didn't start."

"I know," I said, laughing. "Maybe we'll find some more firewood underneath that gratitude you're digging for." I began to walk toward the fire, with Michael instinctually following at my side. He chuckled to himself.

"You and your words, Ari. You're too emotional for a man. You're so sensitive. But you're in tune. I'll give you that," he said.

"Sensitivity is the source of sensation. If you aren't open to feeling, then you won't feel. It's simple," I retorted. "The more sensitive I am, the more I feel. And isn't that what truly makes us not simply live, but feel alive? It's my desperate attempt to keep myself wholly human, I guess. Make sense?"

"You are killing me with this cheesy wordplay, you clever bastard. See. Sense. Just shut up," he laughed.

"It's all accidental, I promise," I said.

Ari, you liar.

"Just part of my programming, I suppose," I continued. "But before we trail too far, we still have to discuss smell and taste."

Michael thought for a moment. "Well, brother, smell… well, it isn't important, honestly. To be born without the ability? A blessing. I for one wouldn't be as disgusted by the odor of this world's bullshit," he said in a serious manner, though his brash phrasing was hilarious to me.

Okay, who is this man? You're still so much yourself, but you have changed…

"Smell is nice, it's convenient, and it plays its part," Michael pressed, "but I could do without. Changing old people's diapers at work sure would be a lot easier if I didn't have to hold my breath sometimes. Smell is good, but not a heartbreaking loss. Except perfume. Women's perfume…. Some women smell good enough to break a man. But that's it, I suppose. Well, food, freshly cut grass, the salt of beach air… but definitely women! Some smell so lovely…. This conversation is losing its potency," Michael laughed.

And you almost sound insightful, if not for the baseness you keep returning to. I swear….

As he broke off, I could smell the fire. I could smell that holy realm where we kept the ark of our covenant, where God waited for us in all His fervent glory. We had reached the tree line, where the foot-worn path led down to the hollow. I stopped suddenly, Michael bumping into me and almost toppling me.

"What, Ari?! Almost spilled your precious grape water!" Michael laughed.

"Taste," I said.

"I'm not tasting a damned thing. You've made me spill it all!" he said. "You're not letting this conversation go, are you?"

"How can we afford to?" I asked.

"Well, if we wrap this up, can we please, please go down to the fire? We *should* be talking about this *there*," he said as he pointed down the wooded hill, into the shadows of the forest, toward the flickering flames. "Women would eat this subject up!"

"Eat it up… and *taste* it in the process?" I said. "Taste is certainly worth discussing."

"Yeah, for sure, but with *them!*" he said.

You're right, Michael. I'm drunker than I think, maybe. Why do I keep this stupid conversation going, as if I need to prove anything. The battle of wits was fun, while it lasted. Let's have fun. It's been too long, brother.

The silhouette of a crowd began descending the hill from the house, slowly coming toward us and the fire, Michael gesturing in its direction. I studied the approaching shadows, drawing on all the possibilities that were approaching.

God and His Gravity.

I looked at Michael with what must have been a solemn, curious look.

I turned to the shadowy mob as laughter and loud outbursts issued from its amorphous collective. Michael took a drink from the bottle in his hand.

"You're hosting tonight," he said. "Be the host. You've got quite the attendance here. Your plate is full tonight, and you're going to need help finishing the meal. I'll help you however you need, so long as we wrap this up soon. I plan to party my ass off until the sun rises, but that doesn't mean it will get here any slower. Taste, Ari?"

"Taste…. I'm out of wine. I don't really feel up to going back to the house, though, and with all those people on the porch—"

"You don't need to," he said.

I can't just pray for wine. I don't want to go all that way, but I must.

"But I want more wine," I said. "I've been drinking moderately all day. If I lose my momentum now…."

He smiled a smile that relaxed me and my anxiety assuaged.

"I took a bottle down there with me when I built the fire earlier," Michael said, chugging what remained in the bottle he held, tossing the cork into the surrounding darkness. "It's not the nicest wine— sorry, Ari—but I thought it would be a nice party gift for our host."

I smiled. "Thank you, Michael."

I don't care what it costs. It means a lot to me and thank you. Thank you.

"I wouldn't thank me, Ari. Like I said, it's cheap, but it's red, and I know how you're always like, 'the redder, the better,' whatever the fuck that means. World-class guy, and relatively normal. You can be a pussy sometimes, but you know who you are, which is rare. Sorry if that's a bit off topic."

"World-class should be the standard for *normal*, I believe," I said.

"No doubt, my man. No doubt," he chuckled. "So," he said, gesturing down the hill. "Shall we?"

Yes. Absolutely.

The approaching umbral mass began to merge with, envelop, and surpass us as it passed us by and through until it melded into the shadows of the trees. The fire blazed in the distance of the dark, wooded background, and Michael and I suspended our conversation in momentary silence.

In that silence, I heard the vaguest whisper, unformed yet looming. Something called for my attention, and as I peered around the void, the only thing magnetic enough to draw my nocturnal focus was the moon. A cloud passed over it as I studied its face, and somehow, I saw a bit of myself within it. I felt like howling.

Bright, cratered, and more aged than dates and times can fully represent, I felt the meaning of the moment pass through me like oil through a sieve, and as we exchanged glances—the moon and I—we were juxtaposed. That celestial beauty had descended to be amongst the mortals like us. I was rising, onward unto power, as the king of the night. But where was the Earth around which I revolved? Where was my queen? My satellite? An elbow in my side brought me back to reality.

"Ari! Ari, did you *see* that?!"

"Huh? No, what?" I responded to Michael's crazed voice.

"That crowd, man! Two dozen people—*all girls!* Give it a minute, then we've got to go!" he loudly whispered.

"Absolutely. Don't want them getting those hands on that bottle. Not a wine like that," I said with a devious smile. "But it's red and I need it."

"Let's finish up this conversation first," he added, being respectful of our friendship in the face of such obvious temptation. "We have another moment or two. We still have to get back to God."

There was no way he could have fully known what he had said to me just then. Michael was speaking of the beginning of our philosophical talk, but I had been talking to God all day.

"Yes, Michael. Yes, we do," I said, letting our recent tense history go.

"Can it wait? Can God wait just a few more minutes? Those girls, dude," he said.

A reprise of thunder, far more distant yet stronger than those prior, met our ears.

"And red wine," I said. "After you, sir."

"Much obliged, sir," he responded. He was off.

I lit a cigarette and dropped the match by my shoe after fanning it out in the autumn air. Chemicals coursed through my body. I followed Michael down the path toward the fire in the hollow. I kept my quiet eyes on the fire as it grew with the constantly changing perceptions of my steady approach. Voices beckoned us into their presence. The sirens were calling, and the sailors, Ari and Michael, were willingly pursuing doom disguised as pleasure.

"Lotus-eaters…" I mumbled to myself.

Michael called back over his right shoulder. "What's that? Inviting Odysseus to dinner with Beethoven and God? Quite the guest list you've compiled," he laughed. "I could go for a siren or two, actually. I may never set sail from *that* island again, ha-ha!" he bellowed, motioning toward the delicious appeal that emanated from the fire and its guests.

Michael, I don't think you need me to sharpen this 'silver tongue' of mine, at all. You're clever tonight and in good spirits, on top of your looks. I could leave right now and he would be fine, but I wouldn't. What's wrong with a little recklessness from time to time? I can't live inside my head forever, can I?

The echo of his *ha-ha* reverberated off the surrounding trees and doubled back to us as it commingled with yet another far-off peal of thunder. The small crowd's din was tempting our interaction. In fact, it begged for it.

The sirens continued calling.

Beautiful….

The captain has set his course.

Michael turned and stopped me at the edge of the hollow where the trees dispersed, and the fire roared like a lion at the center of the rigid circle.

"So, Ari, is God joining us?" he asked.

"Yes, I think it would be safe to assume so," I said, looking over his shoulder, peering into the blazing monument that he had ignited. The flames climbed much higher than the five-feet-tall stack of logs that fueled them. The entire grove was illuminated in all shades of red, orange, and black, the colors dancing and swaying around and through one another.

"Assume?" he asked, looking around suspiciously. "Funny, I don't see Him *anywhere.*"

As Michael turned away from me to continue to the crowd of girls talking and giggling by the fire, it was *me* who stopped *him* this time, turning him roughly. I felt like an animal spirit of sorts had formed and tossed in sudden passion in my center. Grabbing the back of his neck in a stern yet comfortable embrace, I tugged at him to pull his face down to the level of mine. I drew him in close.

"You said it yourself," I said somewhat mockingly. "Sight is the bastard, remember?"

We both smiled.

"No, Ari. *You. You* are the bastard, showing some actual balls for once! Now let me go before you gain my interest over *them*," he said with a joking smile and a wink.

I don't always like you, but I'll always love you, Michael Law.

JORDAN

Jordan lurched with the parking motion of the car. Stars peeked through the silhouettes of branches and leaves. Hannah cast her finished cigarette through the window, leaving it open and the car running. Jordan heard the thundering echo of a quiet, approaching storm. Hannah opened the visor mirror to check her face, Jordan following suit.

"As if you need to do anymore," said Hannah.

Jordan smiled at herself in the mirror. She saw herself as truly beautiful in that brief eternity, perhaps for the first time. Deep in the nebulae of her eyes, she was beautiful, valuable, and worthy of existence. The sound of Hannah's rustling and the muffled voices of those walking the driveway were the soundtrack to her new discovery. Unblinkingly, she became comfortable with being lost in herself, as if her eyes were windows to her own soul, and in the rearview mirror of her best friend's sedan—an infinite loop of reflecting glass mirroring reflecting glass—they looked perpetually into themselves and each other. Jordan was becoming lost in the labyrinth that was Jordan, and she did not understand why anyone would take her for granted in these timid, yet grandiose reflections.

Jordan fought to keep her eyes open to hide from Hannah the tears she could feel building. As those juxtaposing images of herself flashed in her mind, she became exhausted, her emotions confused and blended: anger, optimism, love, and indifference. Neither felt entirely correct. Her eyelids slowly closed, their meeting applying the final pressure that forced the first droplets to course down her cheeks. Hannah called from beyond the cold, confused, peaceful darkness.

"Ready? Hey, are you all right?" Hannah delicately laid her hand on Jordan's hand, which she had helplessly positioned on her lap. "Are you all right?"

Jordan took Hannah's hand willingly and softly. "I mean, he… we…." broke into an arrhythmic song from her quivering lips.

How could anything so beautiful be so easy to discard? But this is all makeup and paint. I'm not even that beautiful….

"I'm not even that beautiful," she whispered, broken, through coursing tears.

What? What are you….

"Jordan…."

"What am I doing here? I should be home watching movies or something. I can't do this," Jordan said, choking on her own voice.

"Of course, you can!" Hannah leaned in, squeezing Jordan's shaking hand a little more firmly. "Be brave." Jordan felt the soft sting of the caress of Hannah's full lips as they broke through the small river running down her cheek.

The asteroid that ended the reign of the dinosaurs—crashing through the unprepared atmosphere, obliterating the bedrock—an exhibition of complete death in the finest sense, with a preparation for a new birth following closely behind.

The life, the panic, the death, the peace…. Then, again, the life.

Hannah scowled, pulling her hand free from Jordan's loose grip. "*He* lost *you*, Jordan. And you *are* beautiful." Her expression softened with empathy. "Don't ever speak about yourself like that. You are a knockout, especially tonight." Hannah's sincerity was evident in her smile.

Jordan, lost in a jumbled abyss, began to dip her head downward, tempting yet another brash encounter with the echoes of the falling pieces of a pearlescent, broken heart. As gravity was bringing her eyes down and the tears along with them, a force, calming and gentle, intercepted. With her thumb and forefinger, Hannah cradled Jordan's chin and turned her face toward her own. Jordan, with closed eyes, flushed a new wave of sadness from them, that soft reminder of compassionate human company bringing a warming glow to her. She opened her eyes to Hannah, whose own were now glistening.

"Jordan… you're a gem. No one cares like *you* do. He was never good for you. You *had* to know that. He's not good enough for you!"

Thunder.

"He… he… it's just…."

Hannah took her hand from Jordan's face to wipe the emotion from her own eyes. "It's just what? I told you. Everyone told you so. Regardless of tonight, the distance beforehand. No one makes someone they love suffer with distance like he did to you. It was bound to end, no matter how much you loved him."

"It's just…. I don't know," Jordan said sadly.

She then laughed, the mixture becoming beautiful, comical, but overall maniacal, as the dormant star that her insides had become began to warm with a polar shift, a new reaction taking place within her core. She was preparing herself for the reception of a new beginning—a new life.

Hannah's hands, the hands of that new Gaia, wiped away the tears that coolly clung to Jordan's cheeks, and somehow, the veil also that had covered her innocent, searching eyes for so long. In that stark, abrupt revelation, Jordan became her own world again. Only now she was becoming a solitary celestial body seeking a new star—a hopeful stone, cast by some divine hand, tossing and tumbling through nothing, in patient wait for a sign from the universe to reassign her to a new orbit. Yet she was unaware, as she might be, of the air she was breathing. She watched Hannah laugh quietly to herself as she witnessed Jordan's evolution from sadness to insanity to revelation. The pair of them were a hysterical sight, half-laughing, half-crying, and both fully embracing the moment they shared.

"We look like completely crazy bitches," Hannah laughed, wiping the last tear from her eye.

"Yeah," said Jordan, uncrossing her legs and leaving them uncrossed. "Thank God no one is watching."

"Well, let's not say *that*," said Hannah, her voice gently muffled by the cigarette that she had just placed between her pouty lips. "Someone *might* be looking. It's dark, and in the darkness, I feel like someone is *always* watching."

A rumble of thunder rolled outside the car.

Jordan laughed, remnants of her sadness banished from her face with finality. "Maybe you are the crazy bitch, then, Hannah. You're paranoid…. The weed…. It's making us… weird!" she laughed.

Hannah's response was a flick and a flame, a lighter being sparked, and the soft, pleasurable exhale of smoke that escaped her lips. She merely smiled at Jordan's comment. Jordan loved that smile.

Wicked.

Beautiful.

Thunder.

"Maybe. Just maybe," Hannah said quietly, a little vesper of smoke escaping her exquisitely shaped mouth with each breathy syllable.

Jordan could still feel the creeping hands of her high holding her, massaging her, and relaxing her. She crossed her smooth legs once more, their silkiness exciting her and their newness inspiring a quiet desire for more. This intimate sensation seemed to blend somehow with her muted frustrations, her opaque confusion, and her suddenly newfound anticipation that was just beyond her reach, calling from the shadows of the night. She stretched for it—yearned for it—yet once again, these realities lingered in another realm, beyond her sight, either too small or too large for her to comprehend in her present scope of life. Baffled by herself and these invisible thoughts she almost did not have, she lost herself in Hannah's smoky breath as it crept, billowing, through the cracked window like an amorphous ghost.

You set me free, Hannah. With every exhale, you show me to myself. It's like I am the smoke—the byproduct of your carelessness. That's the magic. I am so damn careful, and you have no cares in the entire world. I don't mind the 'me' that I am. I'm pretty, with or without this makeup or these heels. They are sexy…. ha-ha! Some are sexy and imply danger. Smoke means fire, and fire is dangerous. The mystery…. But it also makes life possible…. Fire is life. Yes, Hannah, that must be it! You are so in control, yet you have no cares. I am not in control at all, yet I worry about everything…. You inspire me, you do.

Hannah dropped her half-finished cigarette out the window. Jordan watched in slow motion as it slid down the exterior of the pane, the cherry exploding like a tiny supernova on the window's ledge before its residual sparks spiraled into the shadows. Jordan closed her eyes in reflection.

Fire moves. I need motion. No fire can remain stationary for long. Fire consumes. It consumes, or it dies.

"I don't want to warn anymore," Jordan mumbled.

I don't want to come with a warning. I want to come out of nowhere. I want to be selfish. I want to destroy, either for good or bad. To be a force to be reckoned with, that's what I want to be. And I know that I can!

"I want…. I want…."

With her eyes closed, Jordan was stunned in her private darkness as full, luscious lips gently collided with hers, the passion and abruptness of their arrival catching her completely off guard.

Thunder again.

She swooned, trapped in a vortex of passion. She missed being touched this way.

But it's Hannah! This is too much! Wow, what a good kisser! You taste like smoke. You taste… familiar….

Where is this coming from?!

No, this isn't right! But it feels right. It feels good, and I'm kissing her back? What the hell is going on? I'm lonely. I'm so lonely. I need someone….

No.

I need 'me'.

No. I need time.

"I need time!" Jordan blurted as she pushed Hannah away from her, and she immediately regretted her tone and force. She sat in disbelief, looking at Hannah and watching the slight tinge of embarrassment and shock play out across her face.

"I… I don't know what came over me. I'm sorry, Jordan," Hannah said coolly. "I'll give you your time." Hannah rolled up her window as she spoke. "Lock the car. Come find me when you're ready to talk." Collecting her lighter from the back seat, she quickly stepped out of the car. Hannah was either embarrassed or insulted. Either way, she fled.

"Wait. Han—"

The closing door cut Jordan's sentence short, leaving her in an unfamiliar mood with only herself and her thoughts.

She didn't seem too upset. She's just horny. Or caring. Hannah, you're insane! I'll forgive you. It's fine, really, but I need to think. Or drink. You are my friend.

"You showed me the smoke that brought me to the fire. Hell, you literally brought me to the fire with this little bonfire. Doesn't really seem so little…. Great, I'm talking to myself."

Jordan sat alone in darkness. She sat in confusion, though she felt so comfortably confused.

"Fire," she laughed.

Thunder called out once more into the silence of the night.

HANNAH

Fortune favors the bold.

Hannah took one last decadent glance at her passenger's gorgeous figure as she shifted the car into park. Her only thought was of her own chemical urgency as she casually dropped her cigarette butt out the window.

You look so beautiful—amazing. I need to catch up.

Hannah lowered the visor to inspect herself in the mirror, a sense of competition, friendly and fierce, rising inside her. Jordan seemed to acknowledge the challenge as she mimicked Hannah by checking her face in her own mirror.

"As if you need to do anymore," Hannah said with the intention of flattery. Hannah checked her eyebrows, her eyelashes, and her teeth—all the essentials.

Not bad.

She smiled at her own self-approval. She turned to Jordan, who had an expression of melancholy on her face.

You haven't spoken for some time. Thinking about him, no doubt, the worthless piece of…. Ugh, I hope she's ready for this. Jordan, are you…?

"Ready?" Hannah asked, facing her ghost of a passenger. Jordan's response was silent sadness.

"Hey," Hannah said, her voice lowering. "Are you all right?"

Hannah already knew the answer. The response was muted and booming, like a whispering bomb—Jordan's silent, distant contemplation.

In the ineffectiveness of her words, Hannah rested her hand on Jordan's, her own desperate attempt to calm her companion. She felt a warm jolt creep through her chest as Jordan's hand opened to receive hers, closing in a loving, appreciative grasp.

Jordan….

"I mean, he, we…" Jordan said, her emotions causing the words to sound broken and incomplete. "I'm not even that beautiful."

You are so beautiful, even in your frailty.

Especially because of your perfect frailty....

"Jordan...."

"What am I doing here?" Jordan asked in a rhetorical fashion. "I should be home watching movies or something. I can't do this."

Please don't be this way. Be strong.

"Of course, you can!" Hannah said, unable to resist her urge to lean in close to her friend, squeezing more tightly that complementary hand that kept electric warmth running through her veins. Jordan was shaking.

You shouldn't be scared.

"Be brave," said Hannah, as she gave into her empathy. Impulse urged her, as if against her will, and Hannah leaned out into the darkness, pressing her lips to Jordan's tear-stained cheek.

What a beautiful monster I have made!

Hannah's hand withdrew from Jordan's grasp.

"*He* lost *you*, Jordan. And you *are* beautiful. Don't ever speak about yourself like that. You are a knockout, especially tonight."

Especially tonight.

"Jordan... you're a gem. No one cares like *you* do. He was never good for you. You *had* to know that. He's not good enough for you!"

A roll of thunder rose and steadily diminished.

Well, maybe not entirely true. They really were so beautiful and hopeful together in the beginning. I guess we all drift away at some point.

"He... he... it's just...."

Hannah felt her heart quiver seeing Jordan this way. Hannah's heart broke for Jordan's as it broke for itself.

"It's just what? I told you. Everyone told you so. Regardless of tonight, the distance beforehand. No one makes someone they love suffer with distance like he did to you. It was bound to end, no matter how much you loved him."

"It's just...."

What is it, sweetie?

"I don't know," Jordan continued. Then she let out a laugh, surprising Hannah, bringing with it an air of relief.

Oh, thank goodness... This could have been rough...

Hannah let out a laugh of her own, mirroring Jordan, relief spreading over her.

"We look like completely crazy bitches," Hannah laughed, wiping her eyes once more.

"Yeah." Jordan moved to uncross her legs, which is how they remained.

So unladylike of you, miss.

Hannah's heart smiled an almost wickedly enticing smile.

"Thank God no one is watching," Jordan said.

"Well, let's not say *that*. Someone *might* be looking. It's dark, and in the darkness, I feel like someone is *always* watching."

The fucking creeps out there….

A second wave of thunder echoed outside. Then came a giggle that fell from Jordan's lips as Hannah placed a cigarette between her own.

"Maybe you are the crazy bitch, then, Hannah," Jordan said, confirming what had caused Jordan to laugh. "You're paranoid…. The weed…. It's making us… weird!"

Yet another relieving laugh followed. Hannah lit her cigarette, inhaled that first delicious drag, and exhaled it, smiling directly into Jordan's eyes. There, Hannah was trapped, and she froze for a moment.

Wicked.

Beautiful.

Thunder.

"Maybe. Just maybe," Hannah said, her words carrying off in another noxious cloud of smoke.

Jordan crossed her legs again, and Hannah was watching.

The contact there, thigh on thigh. The press of their touch on one another…. So erotic…. Supple…. Classy….

Hannah took a hit of her smoke and exhaled slower this time, as though wounded by the sight of Jordan. She was only halfway through her cigarette, but she had had enough. She dropped it out the window, the lit end bursting as it collided with the door's exterior at the window's base.

"I don't want to warn anymore," Jordan mumbled.

Oh, honey, you were just coming back…. But let it out, please.

Let me have it.

"I want…." said Jordan.

I think I want you right now.

"I want…." Jordan repeated.

So do I, sweetie. So do I….

Jordan's voice crackled, and Hannah had finally broken.

So many emotions—all at once.

Okay, Jordan….

Keep your eyes closed….

Hannah took a deep breath. Her eyes glittered with hope, honesty, and feeling. She vibrated inside, and the next wave of thunder that rumbled outside the car felt to Hannah as though it had come from within herself. She leaned in, placing her willing, wanting lips upon Jordan's.

Hannah became irretrievably lost in the moment, feeling as if she were flying. Jordan, to Hannah's great surprise and satisfaction, kissed Hannah back.

My   god….

Jordan…. Honey….

You're my best friend…. This can't be happening…. It's too simple to be real….

Hannah became a wildfire and was absolutely glowing with euphoria.

My favorite drug….

Hannah was forced to awaken from her brief dream as Jordan withdrew, and Hannah was crushed and embarrassed by the obvious shame and confusion that resonated from Jordan's complex expression.

Jordan gave Hannah a gentle, quick shove, furthering the distance between them. "I need time!" said Jordan.

Hannah looked into Jordan's eyes.

I…. I've ruined everything.

"I… I don't know what came over me…."

I always fucking ruin everything.

Hannah spoke, her voice weak, yet nurturing. "I'm sorry, Jordan. I'll give you your time."

Hannah began rolling up her window, quickly grabbing the lighter she had thrown into the back seat.

Withdraw. Let her think.

"Lock the car. Come find me when you're ready to talk."

Hannah was outside the door and shutting it before she realized she was leaving.

"Wait. Han—" said Jordan as the door snapped shut, muting Jordan's plea that Hannah knew would only destroy this moment further.

Wordless, she stalked up the driveway, chasing the nothing she felt was before her.

Damn it, Hannah! Damn you! WHY?!

Yet another thunderous clamor permeated the air.

Hannah, shaken by its call, increased her walking space, tearing for the house in an elegant stride of false pride and confidence. Anonymity and new beginnings summoned her from the lights of the approaching abode.

ARI

Amid the darkness of the towering trees, we were two sides of the same incubus, ready to invade these dreams in the form of girls. I ignored their gossipy chatter, opting to utilize my eyes rather than my ears. My perception was self-willed to be flawed to, better myself, be deceived.

Pretty. All of them. None stir a spark in me. Not a glance. Not a cosmic pull.

I looked into the fire. I closed my eyes, taking in the moisture in the air and its clash with the warmth of the flames. My emotion was transparent. My mind was clear.

Michael, however, was coming into a frenzy.

"Hey," I whispered. "Control yourself. You're shaking like a mad man, you fiend!"

"Fiend, my friend? You must be joking, you ass!" he snapped back. With a strong finger, he pointed out the same red-headed beauty from earlier. "You know I'm crazy for a redhead," he said, keeping his low tone.

"You'll go crazy for anything with breasts and a beer, Michael."

"And would you look at that?" he smiled. "She's got both."

"Well, maybe you should say hello."

"Ari, when it's time, *she* will say hello."

I was not exactly stunned by his abruptness. I was secretly hoping he would stay and talk with me.

Great friend.

His bottle met my glass with a crystalline *clink*.

"You've got nothing to drink," he said. "Where is that... Ah! Here it is!" He lifted the bottle from the ground and handed it to me along with the cheap corkscrew he had procured.

"Michael, where did you...?"

"I got it at the liquor store. I wanted to pop this for you," he said.

I was grateful for his thoughtfulness. He noticed and smiled. He took the bottle and glass from me, and with expert quickness, he opened both, filling the glass and handing it back to me, then he set the bottle on the ground between us.

"Again, cheers?" he asked, and with a nod and another *clink*, we commenced the ritual.

"Not bad," I said. It was not vintage, but for all my wealth....
I am not pretentious.

"Don't mention it, man. By the way, we've got company."

That exquisite redhead was heading directly toward us. A siren had strayed from the rest of the pack. She had a look about her as though she could be either the predator or prey. It didn't matter much to me. This girl was damnedable. Her beauty was captivating and intense.

"Told you so," he said, as my face must have said all that was on my mind, which didn't feel like much at all, considering the moment. She was awkward in her approach. This made me feel instantly powerful.

"Hey," she said, her unwarranted excitement making me a bit suspicious. "Um, do you guys party?"

"Do we!" Michael jumped. "I mean, uh, yes. Yes, we party, sweetheart. This man here," he said, nudging me, "is our gracious host, as it happens."

"Oh, so you *do* party!" she laughed.

I could only respond with a glance, a smile, and a sip of wine. She was looking right at me, into me, even, and I was entirely confused by her presence. Michael mimicked her laugh, his little way of stalling for a perfect response. She took a drink of the beer she held in her hand. The exhale that followed was an aphrodisiac, and I noticed the glare of the moisture on her lips.

Beautiful. Sexy, even.

She licked those lips, collecting the portion she had failed to swallow, causing Michael to stamp his feet in uncontrollable excitement.

There's no point in checking his body language....

This girl was seducing us heavily. I was less expressive, but she was also affecting me, and she could see it.

"Well, host, do you have a name?" she asked.

"My name is…." I stammered.

"Host, it is!" she interrupted. Her rudeness had offended me, but because of her appearance, I forgave her, lustfully letting the matter go.

"Fine," I said. "Host, it is. But please, *Mister Host.*"

In saying this, I winked at her, and her response was a wordless shuffle. She took another drink of her beer, shuddering. I was getting to her. Michael hated it, and it was obvious to me.

"Okay, so, *Mister Host,* and…." Michael said.

"Katie," she said, smiling, smiling at me. Michael was visibly growing more upset. He had pointed her out to me, and unintentionally, I had stolen her attention from him.

Smart girl.

"Katie, I'm Michael," he said.

"Michael and Mister Host…. Good to meet you both."

"So, Katie, what kind of party *are* you suggesting?" Michael asked.

"Now, now, Mister Michael, please be calm," she laughed, a laugh that was a bit more hysterical than was necessary. "I have mushrooms. That's the kind of party I'm suggesting. I thought you boys were cute. I was wondering if you wanted to join me."

I was floored. How many more drugs had she brought to my party? There was no telling how many people were about to go crazy, all within my house. She was instantly a problem, but is this not what I wanted from my party? Chaos?

"How much do you have?" asked Michael.

"About two… two and a half grams?" she said, unsure.

"We don't—" I said, but Michael had other plans.

"We'll take 'em!" Michael interrupted, his desperation to win her attention becoming obvious.

"Excellent," she said, pulling a sandwich bag with the remainder of her hallucinogen from her purse. "Now, normally I'd charge you, but for our gracious host," she said, eyeing me carefully, "it's free." With a wink, she held them out for me.

"But I—"

"Oh, don't be a puss, Ari. It'll be fun!"

"I just don't know…."

"We'll take 'em!" Michael repeated, losing none of his previous enthusiasm, snatching the bag from her open hand. "Are you taking some with us?"

"I already have," she said. "We were starting to feel them, so we came down here to be closer to nature."

"To be closer to God," I mumbled.

"What was that?" she asked.

"Oh, don't mind, Ari," Michael said. "He's been talking to *God* all day."

I could have punched him. So brash and bold was he with his statement that the inner animal that I felt within was gnashing its teeth, though it had yet to achieve a bodily form. I forced my anger down, knowing that the alcohol had caused this mood swing. The truth of it all was a lie, but I bought into it anyway.

"God? But He's everywhere. My, my…. You're as crazy as I am, Mister Host! Ari, huh?" she said.

"Yes, Ari. And yes, God, though surely He isn't listening."

Thunder filled the air in and around the grove.

"Sounds like He is," she said, surveying the sky. "Listen, I'm really starting to feel these 'shrooms. You boys figure out who's taking what and come find me, okay?"

"Okay," I said.

Michael simply nodded.

"And bring 'God' with you, should He be any sort of interesting company," Katie said.

With that, she turned and walked back to her friends. I exhaled with relief. Michael was somewhat frustrated with me. We both watched her walk away, her form-fitting jeans leaving very little, yet very much, to the imagination.

"God? God, Ari? God damn it, Ari, you scared her away with all your 'God talk'. Ugh…. I guess it isn't a total loss, eh? I love these things," he said, placing a few caps and stems into his mouth as he chewed them into mush.

"Look, Michael," I said. "I'm simply speaking my mind. I believe what I believe, if I believe it, at all. You believe what you believe. Now, eat your damned fungus and shut the fuck up. Your eyes might finally reveal something to you. In all these people, I'm seeking some reflection of the Source—something actually real. Something out there—something distant—has been clawing at my mind all damned day; and be it something divine or nothing at all, I will seek it out."

Michael was stunned. I had put him only further into second place, our interaction with Katie only making it worse, and he surely hated it—maybe even me. Michael always considered himself the alpha male, and I was putting the frustrating possibility of his submission deeper and deeper into his subconscious, all as he stupidly chewed the dryness in his mouth.

"I'm going with nothing at all," he said. "Listen, friend," he continued, hoping to pacify the beast he saw forming within me, "let's not let a girl—the first one we talk to, even—come between us." He was retreating. "Red-heads aren't even my favorite—crazy bitches—and besides... we have these now," he said as he held out the mushrooms for me to see.

Red-heads have always been your favorite. Don't play a step ahead if you're gonna be an asshole to me about it when you fall two steps behind. Lessons are learned in loss. Lose, my friend—you bastard—and learn. I am not your springboard. Don't patronize me. Damn it, the wine....

"I have absolutely no desire to do those tonight, Michael," I said. "I have a house to watch over."

"Suit yourself," he said, and with that, he forced more into his mouth, relishing to his best ability their dirty flavor. "So fucking stale...." He chased the fungus with my wine. My stomach turned in disgust.

Buffoon.

"Hey, Michael, give those about a half hour and be somewhere safe," called a voice. It was Katie.

"I'll come find you when they do," he said. He turned to me. "Ari, I swear to God, these are already kicking in."

"God?" I asked. "What *god* might you be swearing to?"

"Oh, shut up, Ari. It's an expression," he said. "But seriously, it's been forever. I'm getting... tingly...."

"Then be tingly," I said as I took a sip of wine. "Feel good."

He raised the bottle in acknowledgement. I tapped the bottle with my glass, both of us taking a drink in reconciliation.

"I do, sir," he followed.

"You're welcome, sir," I said.

For what may have been many minutes in length, we sat in silence, listening.

Hearts are beating strongly tonight.

Only the whispers and cracks of embers and shadows filled the empty spaces around us.

A long silence passed before I spoke up. "Give me a bit of that," I said. Michael only looked up and through the treetops, staring blankly at the sky. I sipped my wine. I watched him with agitated patience.

"Michael, I—"

He slowly raised the bag he had clenched in his hand, offering the mushrooms to me, never breaking his focus on the sky. I took them, quickly chewing and devouring a small portion of the bag.

"Ari, I'm definitely starting to feel these," Michael said. "Katie, where is she? Katie? Katie?!"

"Michael, I don't think—" I said.

"Katie!"

"What, Michael?" she called. He kept his sights toward the empty sky above.

"How long did you say it would take these to get going?" he asked.

I swallowed the dusty, earthen texture, the taste leaving much to be desired.

"I don't know." Katie walked toward us. "I already feel them. Took me about a half hour. Of course, I haven't done them in a while, but—"

"It's taken me about two minutes, I think. This can't be… typical… can it?"

"I think you're being ridiculous, Michael. A last name like Law, and you've lost your reason," I said.

"With a last name like Cayne, and you may just be your brother's keeper, tonight," he said. I was stunned by his lack of crass sarcasm. The depth of his words floored me, because his shallow nature was always the forefront of his persona.

Maybe he is beginning to hallucinate….

Katie laughed. She laughed again, then she spoke. "Amazing, isn't it? The feeling of connection with—"

"—Everything?" asked Michael.

"Everything." she responded abruptly. "They must be working for you."

His gaze snapped from the sky as he looked down at me, his eyes locking into mine. "Yes, yes they are," he said, and he quickly resumed his stargazing.

"They are grown by someone I know. Very potent," she said.

"So, I've noticed," said Michael and I, simultaneously.

"They're fertilized a certain way to make them break down in the body easier, so I wouldn't be surprised if you're well on your way, guys," she added. "I sprinkled a bit of something else on them, too." She rubbed her finger along her nose.

Cocaine?! Aw, come on! You have got to be kidding me! This whole place will go to hell before the night's over!

"Awesome," Michael said as he looked down at Katie, then back to the sky, a smile creeping across his face. The shadows cast there spoke of evil thoughts in Michael's essentially pure, but brutish mind.

A look of realization spread across his face. "Ah, shit," he continued. "That might not be good for my job."

I had already walked to the tree line, trying to force myself to vomit. Katie, as only Katie knew to do, began to laugh again.

"Relax, boys. It wasn't much. Just a little something to make the mind dance before the soul offers it a drink."

This girl is clever. Ish....

"How much?" I asked.

"Not much at all," she said.

"Well, alright then," I said, standing and attempting to gain grips on myself again.

"Yeah, come on, Ari," Michael said. "It'd be a terrible shame to miss your shot and ruin that tie or waste that vintage."

I could do nothing but laugh. Be it the drugs or the pure timing of his comment, I was glad to genuinely do so.

My mouth began to tingle with numbness.

Damn it, she wasn't kidding.

"There you go," Katie said. "Simply feel good."

"Oh, I do, Katie," Michael said, taking a great drink of wine.

Katie threw her beer can into the fire, a *hiss* emanating from the flames as the foam of the beer licked them back. Katie licked her gorgeous lips. Michael and I were licking our chops, prepared to devour this auburn lamb that had strayed from the flock. Michael lunged for the kill. The beginnings of a vague intoxication began to work within me, crippling my intentions and making me an eager bystander.

"Say, Kate," he said, his eyes focused within and upon hers, "how about we go in and get you another drink? I could show you around—if that's alright with our host, of course—and we could talk of higher things, or whatever." He shrugged.

I could not restrain myself. "Higher things?" I asked. "You mean talk about you two, right?"

Michael reached out like a corpse that had just awakened. Pushing a bit of hair away from Katie's face behind her ear and caressing her jaw line, he said, "That is precisely what I aim to do."

Katie and Michael both smiled, and in my witnessing, I saw that they had attached themselves, invisibly, to each other in the matter of a moment. Party animals, both of them—one predator, the other prey—and it had suddenly become difficult to define which animal assumed which role anymore.

"Well, what are you waiting for? Go!" I said, my excitability showing my support for whatever Michael had secretly planned.

"Shall we?" he asked Katie, offering his arm to her.

Katie kept her smile and turned to the group of girls behind her, her body still facing us. Nodding, she turned back and took Michael's arm. "We shall."

"Bring me more cigarettes?" I asked.

Keeping his gaze upon her, he said, "Sure, Ari. I won't keep you waiting too long."

"Okay. You know where to find them." I broke off and looked at Katie. "Enjoy the house," I said to her. My entire front row of teeth had lost all feeling.

She giggled.

I watched them as they disappeared into shadows up the path, and I was suddenly lonely again, yet content with my loneliness. I took another drink of wine and placed a cigarette in my mouth. After lighting it, I exhaled into the darkness above. I looked through the smoke and into the air for that which Michael had been staring into so keenly. I saw no trace of God or anything, save space and smoke.

Sight is the bastard…. Sight is the bastard….

Thunder echoed through my thoughts and the crisp autumn air. The storm was getting closer, a storm that was both within and without, and both fronts—soldiers of the human and the natural— snarled at each other from across the imaginary battlefield, preparing to strike at any moment.

I thought of Michael. I thought of Katie. I looked at the crowd that she had abandoned, just as Michael had abandoned me. I was a lone wolf again. I churned with yearning as I smiled at my dark and lonely world, taking another sip of wine.

JORDAN

Jordan watched her reflection.

The shadows that were strewn beautifully across her face clashed in gorgeous contrast with the flecks of the liberated light of the moon. The shadows seemed to darken. The highlights seemed to further illuminate; yet as these foes of dark and light clashed upon the textures of her face, the borders remained equally blurred. This growing sense of stalemate summoned in Jordan the idea of indecision—incompleteness—and upon these uncomfortable notions, she acted.

Jordan leaned across the driver's seat, manually locking the driver's side door. She moved to open her door to make her exit, but suddenly—

—To be touched like that…. To be wanted…. To be craved….

Jordan let out a soft sob of pleasure as she thought of the intimacy she shared with Hannah.

Those gorgeous lips, their caring touch…. She's the only reason I look so amazing tonight—amazing enough to make her do that…! What is it, though? Am I really so desirable?

She inspected herself in the visor mirror, her cleavage and how its perfect symmetries became more obvious; her shimmering legs and how they gleamed even in darkness; and her eyes—how sad and distant and deeply earthen brown they looked. Her blonde hair was super-luminous in the moonlight.

This body is beautiful. This body…. My body….

Jordan inspected the soft contours of her legs. She closed her eyes and began to daydream, drifting, aloft and wavering, into the recent past. She envisioned herself as a witness to Hannah's memories of the night and saw momentarily through what she imagined Hannah's eyes to have seen—the opening door to Jordan's home with Jordan's weakened face behind it. It was the rarity of her decision to smoke Jordan's marijuana, something she rarely, if ever, did. It was the feeling of her care for Jordan as she delicately thumbed through Jordan's closet. Even more so, it was Hannah's patience, waiting downstairs, as she anticipated Jordan's escape from the steamy fortress of the shower.

Why, if you felt the need to kiss me, why didn't you do it earlier? You are not the patient type, but what if…? But so impatient. It makes no sense! If she saw me as anything more than a friend, she would have acted upon it then, right? Might have even tried to shower with me!

Jordan laughed at the thought.

Her imagination, however, was not so lighthearted.

In the back of her mind, far behind her still-closed eyes, a thought began to form.

With me….

A dull roll of thunder, barely audible, softly roared through the silence. The lightning source from which it emanated seemed to lash out from Jordan's heart, her interior becoming kinetic with the charge.

The spark began to smolder.

Hannah, if you had, what would I have done? So naked and frail—the conditions alone would have prompted me to give in. I need to be touched. Maybe you simply recognized my need? Then, why not in the shower? Maybe with all this time to think on it, you just couldn't hold back anymore.

Jordan drifted further.

In flashes of broken, concentrated images, Jordan saw herself through Hannah's eyes—the same Hannah that kissed her so passionately earlier, but one whose role that Jordan could guide and direct in these lonelier, imagined moments of her daydream. In the sedan, Jordan's restless hands increased in their restless state as they— her hands as Hannah's hands—began to touch her, ever-so-cautiously, within the safe confines of the steamy shower of her mind. Her hands as Hannah's hands crept silkily across her knees. Her hands, like her own, did the same. Hannah began to manually pleasure the blonde vessel before her. As herself, she began to do the same. Her fingers, delicate yet determined, began to lift her dress.

Hannah reached out like a nymph, eager to caress her favorite flower in the forest. In the car, Jordan's hands gave attention, tangible and soft, to the same flower. Her mouth quietly opened, her fingers tiptoeing around and teasing the petals, caressing their dew. Her legs began to separate as she inhaled slowly, only to interrupt her circular rhythm with occasional gasps. Her fingers began to moisten along with the soft surface of the flower they grazed upon, and they began to find their way to the center, not entirely against Jordan's wishes.

But deeper than wishes exist needs.

Deeper than need was *her* need, and furthermore, deeper than any need was a burning desire, hot and small, that glowed within. Jordan's fingers, as eager as they were, plunged into unknown waters, only to resurface and re-plunge with the slowness of slow passion. Seeking that tiny ember, she continued her campaign, her face occasionally wincing with a gorgeous pain, her lips quivering.

In the steamy and comfortable shower, she watched Hannah's hands continue their work. Jordan and Hannah paused.

Jordan was Jordan again, and the exchange of perspective was seamless. With Hannah's hand still juxtaposed with her own, Hannah withdrew, a look of curious recklessness playing upon her face. Jordan looked into Hannah's eyes, and Hannah's eyes reflected Jordan's. With an understated smirk, Hannah kissed Jordan's lips. Before Jordan could fully absorb and appreciate the electric contact, Hannah began to descend to her knees, her lips stopping along the way and kissing Jordan's neck with a delicate firmness. Then Hannah's lips moved to Jordan's chest. Jordan looked down at Hannah. Hannah simply stared at the target between Jordan's curvy hips.

"*Hmm….*" moaned Hannah. "Hmm…."

"Hmm… what?" Jordan asked aloud, dreamily.

In the sedan, Jordan was her only audience. In the imaginary shower, Jordan was both an innocent bystander and a victim, willingly taken.

With eyes still closed, Jordan spoke to Hannah. "Do it," she said to the darkness.

Hannah grabbed Jordan's naked hips, and drawing them closer, she indulged herself in the decadent morsel that Jordan offered her.

Hannah pressed a sealing kiss to her cherished flower of the mythical forest, and the weight of each press was nearly enough to send Jordan into frenzy. The heat of Hannah's mouth caused that very same flower to begin a rapid photosynthesis, opening quickly for that morning sun that was giving it new life in a perpetually dark world. The evasive ember within Jordan began to grow. As her nimble fingers delved, they were reaching out, shaking, in hopes of claiming that infantile fire that resided within, but even still, just beyond her grasp.

Jordan moaned.

"But wait…."

Wait, Hannah.

She lifted Hannah's head to better look at her. Jordan looked into

Hannah's deep brown eyes, stroking her blonde hair.

Wait, what?! Blonde?!

Jordan let out a restricted gasp. She was suddenly looking at her kneeling self who had been pleasuring her standing self, Hannah's form replaced with a secondary, exterior Jordan—an avaricious doppelganger. A roll of thunder met her ears in the car's passenger seat as a flash of lightning crossed quickly across her liquid eyes in the shower—those same eyes that were hers and not hers. Jordan's eyes in the real world flashed open at this moment, immediately releasing herself from herself. She was no longer in the shower, and she felt unclean, the parallels and ironies of this discovery sinking into her consciousness. She was in the car, somewhat ashamed, and completely alone.

On the brink of climax, she had horrified herself. That star—that ember that she so desperately sought—had evaded her yet again.

But isn't it the journey that counts...?

Jordan once again was Pandora, yet she felt she had avoided chaos, quickly gathering herself and all the ailments released upon the world, returning them to their innocent keeping place.

"Disaster averted," she laughed.

Jordan collected her belongings, her mind included, and she stepped graciously out of the car. She fixed her dress and looked deeply into the eyes of the sky. They were glistening, like before, but for whatever reason, they seemed clearer and more defined, and they were looking right back at her. The intensity of their gaze focused on Jordan like a beam, concentrated and resolute. She locked the door and shut it, but as she closed the door, her phone slipped out of her hand, landing on its face in the passenger seat.

Damn. And Hannah has the keys…. Well, no turning back, now!

"Maybe someone *is* watching," she whispered into the air. She was flirting with fate.

Soon, silence was all that surrounded Jordan.

All the guests must have already arrived.

No more cars were coming down the driveway and she heard no echoes of footsteps as they trod toward the house. A low din, light yet full, was expelled from the party beyond. She was truly the last to arrive.

"Damn it."

Now, to find Hannah.

Jordan tore her eyes away from the dark expanse forcefully, yet peacefully. The giddy feeling the stars gave her lingered, as did her determination to find her friend and mend the damage done between them.

She had no idea who she was anymore, if she was still herself, at all.

"So many changes—such heavy things—all in one day. Well, at least we have the cooling night to slow this rapid heat."

And yet it is autumn....

Jordan began her lonely march to the house. A whisper of thunder was her sole companion in the stillness and cooling of the resonating Tennessee darkness.

HANNAH

The chilling feeling of the autumn night on the backs of her arms made Hannah walk with a feverish pace. Her hands were clasped to the backs of her arms, her arms across her chest, shielding them from the air.

Hell, maybe it's me….

Her steps were quick and unmeasured and she could not discern whether she was anxious or excited.

The friend she had abandoned was 'Anxiety'. The party and the social roulette it promised brought excitement. She was torn.

Tonight is tearing me to pieces ….

She stopped to light a cigarette, thankful her lighter had begun working again. The low roar of the party sounded like an impaired Gregorian chant to her, and she let out a small sigh of contentment with her first smoky exhale. Hannah quickly regained her stride, a new determination gripping her.

No matter her interpretation, she still looked like a haggard husk of her formal triumphant self—a beautiful ghost trapped by the desire of the former flesh. And the separation she felt showed fully in her blank yet determined expression. Her energy had been depleted by the horrors she had witnessed so far tonight.

I need a drink. A stout one. None of that sugary trash!

Dragging her cigarette in time with her stride, the rhythm of her addiction helped her to keep a sense of control over the brisk nature of her walk. With the achievement of a new level of intoxication on her mind, she doubled her pace.

I have got to calm down….

She stopped. "Calm. Down." Hannah took two quick drags from her cigarette, trying to regain her confident composure. "It was just a kiss. Hell, we've been drinking like thirsting cats all night. At least I have. She'll come to understand."

"She will come to understand," Hannah repeated, the last syllable inspiring her pursuit of the party to recommence.

She rounded the corner of the house—her view of the mansion opening into a beautifully lit display—and the din of the party met her with full, unexpected force. Her arms went limp, her mouth dropped open, and she suddenly forgot about the slight chill around her as she surveyed the social mass before her. She dropped her cigarette, smoke escaping her lips, pleasantly shocked at the number in attendance.

"Hell yes," was mingled with the smoke, both pulled against her will from her awe-stricken mouth. And lighting a fresh cigarette, she began her walk into possibility—the ever-approaching future.

The present had other plans. She was in desperate need of a bathroom.

She scowled. "I'll bet the line is huge. Oh, well."

Already, she could feel the eyes of lust on her as she traversed the frantic scene. In all their desire, what they could not see or comprehend was that this unknown creature, Hannah, nameless and possible, was suffering quietly for that very same sin.

She made her way to the steps of the back porch. As beautifully ornamented as it was, Hannah could only watch her feet as they expertly conquered the steps, one by one. She reached the top, but her scurry to the toilet was rudely halted by a boy.

"Hey, gorgeous. Where have you been all night?"

"Move," Hannah responded immediately, her impatience obvious. She never looked at his face. "What, sweetheart? Move?"

She pushed him out of her way, moving for the back door.

"Hey, I just wanted to—"

The door closed behind her, silencing him. She could not believe the speed at which she had escaped.

He could have been really nice…. Whatever.

She shrugged off her thoughts and set out in search of a bathroom. She passed through the kitchen, cutting through the crowd with slight difficulty, taking care not to bump into anyone or be noticed.

Nice or not—'gorgeous'? 'Sweetheart?' I don't buy it.
My goodness, I have got to piss!
Where the hell—?

In her rushed panic, passing what she thought to be the living room, she heard classical music resonating from within. The brooding melodies were applying their dark soundtrack to her desperate quest. She rounded the hall and began climbing the staircase at the end. As she raced for the top, the silence that began to grow became increasingly more apparent.

Nobody's here. Perfect.

About halfway down the hall, a single beam of light shone through the darkness and it cut the darkness with its bright blade, practically calling out to Hannah. She ran for it, bolting inside and locking the door behind her.

She quickly seated herself, the biting cold of the porcelain seat shocking her warm caramel skin. She immediately began conducting her intended business, a wave of relief sweeping over her in the process. She could hear a pair of footsteps ascending the stairs outside the bathroom door. Just as she motioned to flush the toilet, however, a duo of voices grabbed her attention. They were hushed but clear in the silence of the empty hall outside.

"...and this is the main guest bedroom."

"Michael, it's beautiful in here."

"*You're* beautiful in here."

"Michael, stop it...."

"I can't help it, Katie. You're beautiful."

The sound of a closing door ended what Hannah could hear of the conversation. Her cat-like curiosity piqued, she washed her hands and soon left the bathroom with a certain investigative desire to eavesdrop on the goings-on down the hall from her. She slowly opened the bathroom door, avoiding making any sound, leaving it ajar as she crept down the hall. A single beam of light emanated through the door frame, gently lighting the corridor. Hannah crept closer and closer, her heart racing faster with each step toward the spectacle of her intent.

JORDAN

Jordan walked alone along the driveway, following the swelling din of the party that increased with each step.

She approached the house, the sheer size of it intimidating her. She had seen larger, but something about this one was more attractive to her; more inviting.

But this was to be a bonfire? Such an elegant ritual for something so modest....

The size of the crowd shocked her completely.

Maybe a hundred people, at least....

Too much for right now. Way too damn much.

"I hope Hannah's not in there somewhere," she whispered to herself. "I can't deal with this many people right now."

She stood there, regardless, hoping to catch the eye of anyone who seemed to be having a comfortable conversation. Anxious, she craved to be calmed, yet no one even lifted an eye to this gorgeous new arrival.

"No telling how many people, and not one damned look!" she vented to herself.

Bored, she began to mosey her way along the outside of the great mob that made up the outdoor scene. Scanning faces with focused quickness, she searched for her friend in the unintelligible crowd.

After a few long minutes of searching, she began to lose hope.

I'll check the house in a moment. I need a moment....

Jordan made her way to the rear of the party, noticing the intense gloom brought on by the presence of the dark woods that loomed nearby. She took a glance at the immense house, the rear of which faced her and the trees, and she began to daze.

Her blurred focus was somehow broken by the crunching of approaching footsteps from the dark forest beyond. As she turned, she saw a couple—a boy and a girl—modestly lit by the outdoor lights of the house.

What a handsome couple....

The figure of a giggling red-headed girl emerged into the light of the backyard from what looked like an entrance into the forest, walking alongside a tall, smiling man.

A handsome man.

I am in no position to flirt. Besides, they're all over each other. I want that.... Not that one, though.... I want mine.

Jordan thought about her predicament—her urge to pursue a taken man.

The couple walked past her, the girl stupidly giggling at every word the boy said, though Jordan could not understand what he was saying to illicit such an absurd response. Passing Jordan, the boy's sight strayed from his cackling muse for a moment, looking at Jordan and catching her gaze. He smiled—a lazy, friendly smile—and Jordan caught every nuance of his silent flirtatiousness. He looked at her with kindness but appeared, himself, devious and cruel. She felt a rush, full and cooling, wash over her. Jordan shuddered as he turned back to his hysterical companion, the sound of her laughter beginning to irritate Jordan. Jordan's ears had become the chalkboard upon which this other girl's voice scratched like sharp nails. Jordan felt a sudden disdain for this girl she did not even know, and the pair of them seemed in that moment much less attractive to her.

Whoa   I've got to chill out.

Jordan remembered the joint she had stashed away in her bag. She had been saving it for the hangover, but she was on the verge of a panic attack, caught between both her thoughts and her urges and the battle they waged with one another beneath her skin. She needed to decompress and collect herself, but she could not imagine smoking it here.

But where?

Jordan looked around for a place to be alone to smoke and to collect herself.

With nothing but a crowd between her and the house, she turned back to the trees, pursuing the path from which that hideously beautiful couple had emerged earlier.

It seems dark down there.... It might be quiet, too. It's worth a shot.

Jordan took a deep breath, making her way to the opening in the tree line. As she arrived at the gap in the trees, she looked back at the house, pulling out her joint. She lit it and inhaled the first drag of decadent cannabis, closing her eyes slowly. She took in the sounds— the party, the forest, the night—but as she opened her eyes, a faint glimmer of fire caught her eye, nestled in a grove in the heart of the dark woods.

She took another hit, held it for a moment, and exhaled. She watched as it trailed away into the darkness above. Breaking her gaze from the sky, she looked down to the path, making her way to the burning heart of the party—the fire, itself.

The path was not a difficult one to navigate, but in heels, the steady decline into the grove was a tedious chore. Still, she kept moving, determined as she was to abandon civilization for a few private moments.

Jordan had smoked her joint about halfway down by the time she reached the fire. There were not many people there.

Perfect.

There was only a group of girls, a few miscellaneous people fervently talking with apparently new acquaintances, and a man who stood alone, staring into his wine glass as he swirled it.

At least I'm not the only one here alone tonight.

Intrigued by him, Jordan kept her distance.

She flicked the cherry of the joint onto the ground and put the remainder of it into her handbag. She approached the group of girls standing near the fire.

Social camouflage.

She could not think of how to introduce herself, however, so she awkwardly tapped the girl closest to her on the shoulder. As she turned, Jordan asked her, "Hey, do you have an extra cigarette?"

I know I shouldn't smoke, but this stress is killing me worse than cancer ever could.

"Sorry, girl," was her response. "We're about to leave to go get some more. We've been here for a couple hours now, I think. You can ride with us, or you can have one when we get back. I'm Alicia, by the way. And you are—?"

"Jordan. I'm sorry to bother you," Jordan said. "Do you know anyone here? Who is hosting this thing anyway? I got invited by a friend of mine, and she might be the only one here I know. You haven't seen her, have you? Gorgeous brunette? Name's Hannah?"

"No, honey, I haven't seen your friend. I don't think I know a single Hannah, to be honest," Alicia responded. "But as far as the host… why, he's standing right over there. Some of us were debating how best to introduce ourselves, but he's a quiet, keep-to-yourself type. Get my drift?"

I understand that 'drift' perfectly.

"Besides," Alicia continued, "I'm sure he's taken, not to mention rich and boring. Men this wealthy don't stay single for very long at all, but God bless the women who put up with all their nonsense. I can't see a wealthy man like that making much time for any woman at all, or ever putting her needs above his love for money."

"Surely he can't be all that bad," Jordan remarked. She looked up at that moment, realizing that her host was looking right at her. He quickly retracted his eyes from her, and she mimicked the same action, blushing.

"Don't waste your time, honey," Alicia said. "You seem like a nice girl, and I hate to see a nice girl get tangled up in all that pretense. He seems nice enough, but a wolf always shows its true nature eventually."

But don't we all? The lies eventually run out.

"Does anyone know him?" asked Jordan.

"He had a friend down here earlier," Alicia said. "They were drinking quite a bit together, from what I could tell. He probably went to the bathroom or something."

"So, he isn't alone," Jordan said.

Just lonely…. Human….

"No, I think the wealthy are more alone than anyone. Maybe you *should* go talk to him. But be careful. Remember what I said if you do. Loneliness can make for some pretty bad decisions, especially if two lonely people latch onto each other for the wrong reasons."

"No, I just… well, I don't know. I'm just not sure—" Jordan's words were cut off as her eyes met the host she had been hearing about.

Shit! He can probably hear us! Damn it, Alicia!

His eyes interrupted her sentence with their intense glare. He was studying her. He seemed to realize her observation as he averted his eyes to the ground, stooping to refill his glass with a bottle that rested on the ground by his feet. By the light of the fire, she noticed his shoes were very shiny, and they were black to match the pants and the tie that draped over a gorgeous red shirt. Jordan smiled at his adorable awkwardness.

"Look, you've clearly gotten his attention. Go. Talk. To. Him," Alicia said. "Just tread with caution. And don't be hurt if he doesn't give you what you want or need. A man can buy a girl the whole world over, but if he doesn't make you happy without buying your happiness, he's not worth a bit of your time. That's not true, entirel— look at that. He's got a cigarette for you, I'll bet." As she said this, the host was drawing a cigarette from his pocket. He had lit a match, and Jordan thought deeply about the classic appeal of this action. The thought began to simmer in the back of her mind.

"Let me know how it goes, honey," Alicia said. I'll be right here to party with you if you get shut down. Here, take this drink with you. It's vodka. You don't want to show up empty-handed." Alicia handed her cup to Jordan and turned to her friends.

"Okay," Jordan said, taking the cup from Alicia's hand as she kept her eyes upon this mysterious man. She stood there, watching him as he looked up into the heavens, smoking his cigarette. After a few drags, he dropped it to the earth, crushing it with his foot.

"I'm going in," Jordan said to a distracted Alicia.

"Good luck, Jordan. Enjoy your night," Alicia said, keeping her back to Jordan as she spoke.

Jordan took a drink from her cup, which she found to be delicious and fruity, and began to make her way to her host. As she got closer, his features began to capture her attention: his strong jaw, the well-groomed beard to match, his powerful eyebrows, and his crooked yet genuine smile. She stopped at a comfortable distance from him, Jordan loving how he ignored her as he stared into his wine glass. He had a look of obvious shock on his face as he looked up at her, swallowing his mouthful of wine with a look of modest discomfort. She had surprised him, and he had choked on the reality of it.

He tried to hide the path of his eyes, but Jordan noticed that he was examining her entire body, a dangerous and sexy appreciation sweeping over her. He looked at her shoes. He laughed to himself. This made Jordan very unsure of his intention. She became curious.

They stood in silence, sizing up one another, lost quietly in a darkness that warmed them from within, the fire and all its surroundings momentarily disappearing.

He motioned to speak, but he sipped from his glass instead, the words seemingly catching in his dry mouth.

Jordan stirred with impatience as she waited for him to speak. The suspense was driving her curiosity to madness. She took another drink, folding her arms, her cup dangling beneath her elbow.

He drew another cigarette from his pack. Jordan noticed he was down to his final matchstick as he took it from the matchbox then slid the match across the coarse strip on the side of the container, watching as it ignited and burned, allowing the tip to burn away before lifting it to his cigarette.

He was enthralled by the fire as he pulled the tiny flame in his hands toward his cigarette. Jordan leaned in, with an innocent, playful air, and extinguished his match with a sharp breath.

Laugh at my shoes again, you rich bastard….

Jordan watched with him as the smoke from the match drifted into the night, dead in his hand. Jordan stood there, arms folded, awaiting his response, which never came.

So calm….

Here, allow me to ingite you.

Jordan nodded toward the unlit cigarette that dangled from his stunned lips. His eyes rose to meet hers. She pulled a lighter from her handbag, lighting his sad cigarette for him.

"I'm Jordan," she said, finishing her drink in one go, tossing the empty cup into the fire. "You got one for me?" she asked. Her voice was weak with slight nervousness. Her intent, however, was strong. She watched as his deep, strong eyes softened before her.

ARI

The night was as dark and mysterious as the centers of my focused yet distracted eyes. The moon full-faced and halfway hidden—hidden like my swelling intention—watched warily over the scene, as though made timid by my unclear motive, from behind a band of dismal, seemingly motionless clouds.

Though it was covered, it revealed with its cunning light the mythical wolf in me, poised and ready to permeate my surface. The carelessness of the absent sun had allowed my inner vampire to run rampant, and with my adjusted eyes, dark yet illuminated by the light of the great fire that burned in the middle of the assemblage, I caught her up in the dark magic of my spell in a brief glance she threw in my direction, only to quietly and quickly retract it.

I did not know her name. I did not really need to know. It was not a need, but a desire.

I watched, as I sipped my wine with casual awareness, her every movement. It seemed every move she made—from the slow blink of her open careless eyes to the shift in her exquisite posture—every action, though subtle to those less aware than I, dripped from her like euphoric, liquid sexuality. I could faintly taste it from that brief, barbaric distance as though she was flowing across the wavering light of the fire, right into my glass.

I took a reprieve to gain further consciousness of my surroundings, if only to relieve the mounting pressure that she had planted within me.

I breathed inward steadily, heavily, only then taking notice of the moisture in the air from the day's rainfall that had transpired only hours before.

The earth is sweating just as I am.

I had only then taken account of the bewildering fact that I was mildly perspiring, the salty coating clinging to my receptive skin, and I tasted it on my upper lip, slowly sliding my tongue, savoring the electric sensation.

For the second time, I briefly held her attention, our eyes holding each other's eyes, before the intensity of our married vision forced our impulses to retreat back within ourselves. A chill, too cool for even the autumn air, passed through me and seemingly stretched out, reaching out and into her, as she gave a comfortable shudder at that moment, only a few feet from the flames that crackled and writhed.

That shudder alone laid bare all her mystery that she had kept hidden to herself. It was completely out in the open, yet all that was visible was even more mystery, a puzzle to which I seemingly had all the pieces, but not quite the strategy or skill with which to bring them all together.

I was lost. I was determined. I was becoming irreverently impatient, but I had to wait.

The moon exhibited its full face as it pushed the weakening clouds from its brow, beckoning the wild canine within. The collected predatory instincts of the vampire fought him back.

Patience....

I had to be patient, for a war was about to break loose upon the scene—a war both within myself and right here in this dark grove—between her eyes and mine. Countless casualties had already been accrued with many more little deaths to be died in my transpirations of agony, except, possibly these vague confirmations that were not entirely confirming anything, whatsoever.

I sipped the wine once more and as the alcohol began to do its work, so flooded more thought and more precognitions; but my capacity to engage myself was growing thinner and thinner.

The branches of the nearby tree line, leafless in lieu of the sinister season, swayed in time to a simple, rhythmic autumn breeze, and I distracted my coursing mind with these simple gestures of nature. I gathered the image of the silver light of the pale face of the moon dancing playfully upon the bare branches, and as this searing light touched upon the hibernating limbs, I began to hope to do the same to her limbs.

Her limbs....

I was trapped in the rapture of her astounding beauty—a beauty vicious, hungry and cruel. I wanted to be that light—the light that so enshrouded her in all her quiet glory—and the glow that dwelled upon her skin as well as within it. She did not need the moonlight to be seen because she contained a light—a vulgar glimmer of a spark that resided deeply within—and it was fierce and swift; yet to a less perceptive witness, it might have gone remarkably unnoticed. She may have even had the audacity to be light, itself.

What a perfect role for her: my counterpart, my competition, and my companion.

With every passing moment I was more becoming—and surrendering to—the darkness. In the glorifying imagination of an infatuated man, she was liquid light while I was solidifying into shadow. She was the image of a gorgeous vixen—a she-fox—and she had, unbeknownst to herself, waltzed haphazardly into the presence of a wolf.

The wolf was poising itself to strike.

The wolf was gnashing its terrible jaws.

She so innocently reveled in modest terror.

I knew her to be relaxed, as I matched her modesty in my gaze, peering timorously over the rim of my wine glass; and as I studied her rhythmic, downy composure surrounding itself with all the mystery and melancholy of the dark, she seemed brave to me—no fear of the shadows around us and no fault in her awareness—and she was either completely ignorant, or indifferent to, the grand vision that I had bestowed upon her in these brief images of time.

I shook these thoughts away, downed the remnants of my refreshment, and refilled it quickly with the bottle whose loyalty had held it steadfast in the grass by my feet.

I must be dreaming you….

Taking down half the cup's contents in a hearty gulp, I topped it off with what had remained of the bottle, sluggishly discarding the container with a slight hesitancy that mimicked an intoxicated apprehension. I drew my cigarettes from my front pocket along with the necessary matchstick box. Setting my wine upon the ground, a bit drunk now and slightly careless-feeling, I experienced a mild fleck of difficulty in returning to an upright state.

I, cautious and nurturing, drew a cigarette from the box, closing it with a satisfyingly cardboard-like snap, putting the remaining unchosen away in their keeping place.

Taking a match from its box, I pressed firmly the cigarette with my wine-bittered lips, licking at the soft, bristly cotton of the filter with my wine-bittered tongue. I softly pressed the head of the fire-bearing end of the match to the rough, friction-breeding surface of the matchbox, and with what could have been interpreted as either expressive and revelatory or minute and inconsequential, I pulled the match with an aggravated eloquence that must have rivaled the commotion of the first spoken words of God. With that matchstick of Creation, small and perishable and useful, I ignited my cigarette, bringing death and relaxation to my exhilarated, energetic, intoxicated paradise.

I inhaled and embraced that little death, yet another casualty of the ongoing battle. Drawing the smoke with my mouth, the ember glowed with such a passion as though in competition with the central bonfire, the sun of our little social solar system.

Hope. This is hope.

The pride and effort in that cosmic initial drag symbolized hope for me, suddenly, and closing my eyes in a subtle swoon of personal exploration and discovery, I inhaled the hopes and dreams that were generated by that tiny, insurmountable star that I had enkindled with my own hands only a fraction of a moment prior.

Exhaling the smoke and all its allure out into the crisp, autumn air, I watched as it drifted into oblivion among the stars. It floated away, up and towards the moon, catching little rays of light as it rose soundlessly into soundlessness.

It disappeared as I motioned to lift the cigarette for a second drag and I exhaled that one in the same fashion as before.

I was looking down again, lost partway between thought and thoughtlessness, eyes fixated upon the awkward space between my feet. Bringing the glass to my mouth, I took another large gulp of the wine, ingesting the fluid with quickness, hoping it would alleviate my dazed state. Taking a third drag of gorgeous nicotine, I released the smoke from its prison of my lungs, closing my eyes once more. Tossing what remained of the lightly used cigarette into that awkward space between my feet, I crushed and twisted it with my right foot. I was becoming anxious, and the way that I was wasting my cigarettes proved that to me. Mid-motion, I delved slightly deeper into the vortex of wine, gazing into my glass with haunting suspicion, examining the play of the light upon its unpredictable surface. I noticed I had been crushing my discarded source of addiction and pleasure for an unnecessary amount of time. Ceasing the action to spare myself my self-embarrassment, I went for yet another grand draft of the wine that by now was making me positively glow from within. I swilled it down after savoring its distinct earthy flavor and presence, and let it pass warmly and casually into my body.

Lowering my glass from my face, I realized that I was fully and undeniably becoming the recipient of her attention. She was now standing no more than two feet away from, and in front of, me.

Those eyes, the perfect mixture of saint and seductress, burned hungrily at me. They were like two dark suns, rising simultaneously on the same horizon that was the rim of my glass, and where their light commingled and lingered was where she had enraptured me—my own personal paradise of euphoric damnation—both scorched by a sinful desire and quenched by the salvation of clarity.

Around those eyes dwelled a pretty face. Her eyebrows, well-groomed and ever-so-slightly asymmetrical, gave her a clean, curious look: inquisitive, frail, and precise. Her eyes, vaguely reflecting fire, projected hope of some generic sense, and were focused and calculated as they took my measure. Her nose, perfectly proportional, flared its nostrils, simply and quietly, as she subconsciously breathed in my pheromones. They silently penetrated her psyche, caressing her emotions, and as the chemical reactions became physical within her, her mouth—beautifully drawn with full lips, lending much to the exquisite dimples that accentuated her flawless smile—twitched with anticipation.

Her hair, a luminous blonde, only further and more completely rendered by the light of the looming moon, flowed in gorgeous strands down to her small, rounded shoulders; all while keeping her sweeping, full bangs from the magnetic heat of her eyes. Her lips were pouty and inviting. Though the slightness of the light may have been fooling me, I could tell that she had exceptional skin, perfectly soft, and not so much as more than kissed delicately by the destructive light of the sun.

What began in her beautiful face roared like a sensual waterfall, cascading down her frame. Her arms, thin yet supple, begged for a squeeze from overeager hands. Her hips were full for her small size, the bottom of a curvaceous hourglass that completed its sinuous shape as it wrapped delicately in perfect symmetry her full, well-shaped breasts that hid smartly behind the top of a stunning form-fitting dress of black. From the delicately hemmed bottom of her dress extended two legs, shapely and fit; her thighs of a strong proportion, which granted only more of the supple frailty that inhabited her strong calves and simple ankles. Those calves, though I could not examine them fully from my current frontal view, were well-defined and smooth. I just knew.

What I had not noticed until that moment was the source of her legs' commanding stature—the incredible effect of high heeled shoes.

Her feet were small, as were the shoes, but they accelerated so aggressively an already bold woman in physical terms. Crimson, lifting, and stern, those red heels were catching and keeping my attention. Open-toed, exposing perfectly pretty French pedicured toenails, the shoes made her a vision, a vision that would have stood several inches shorter if not for their use; and as we stood eye to eye, I owed much to the donation of the shoes to her height, as we were more evenly matched because of them.

My eyes were at the level of her eyes.

My mind was at the level of her mind.

I rendered her anew with each and every bat of my lashes, a new revelation spiraling into my thoughts each time she batted hers.

I laughed slyly to myself as I studied this girl. Shoes, so damnedable and a reason to be damned, were lightly caked in places with earth and dirt and grass, the red luster shining through in most parts with confident diligence.

In the few moments in which I digested her stunning presence, she scarcely moved. Her lips quivered, her eyes shook with light, and her heart pounded, in a rhythm made obvious by her quickening, supple chest; but externally, she stood quite still, psychically begging me to speak.

I sipped my glass again, nervously, letting the liquid courage commence its sobering work. She shifted in a pretty, uncomfortable awkwardness, folding her arms with impatience, her drink dangling haphazardly from beneath the hand that was suspended beneath her right elbow. She drifted for days, it seemed, in her own mind, searching for some thought that might kindle a conversation.

I drew my cigarette pack from that same familiar pocket, placing one chosen at random between my lips, as taking my attention from her would have been helplessly impossible. I pulled the final matchstick from its box, struck it, and as the flame danced only an inch or two from the tip of the tobacco, she extinguished it with a playful sweetening gasp of a breath that nearly took my smoky breath from me. The whisper of smoke drifted from the burnt match, rising slowly above and away from us. We watched it ascend as its journey played out.

Coolly and confidently, she procured a lighter—from where, I could not discern. She struck it, held it out for my use, and lit my cigarette. As the aroma of the tobacco infiltrated my nostrils, she cocked her head to one side, flashing a quick, innocent smile to the group of friends she had abandoned to introduce herself to me. In the motion of her turning—her eyes becoming more curious, more inquisitive, more interestingly dark, and infinitely more focused—she carelessly or carefully revealed a neckline too perfect and too casual to attempt any expression with human language.

That very neckline that so stirred the Child of Darkness deep within—he and his wolf pet were communicating in the deepest, darkest depths of desire, and I basked in the sensation of their mutual empathy developing inside me.

The eyes of the blood drinker glared into the eyes of his companion in eternity and the canine glared directly back, an intimate understanding going unspoken between them. With a nod, the specter relinquished control of his hound. He was quickly following in pursuit, both clawing and tearing away at the same goal—starving, wild and giving in.

Passing me, he gripped my wrist, dragging me in tow at a preternatural pace, inhibitions lost to the wind passing over and by us.

Her gaze never broke from mine. She was studying me.

Delicately furrowing her soft, manicured brow, she delved into what seemed to be a fragile courage, shifting slightly and flashing me a brief, beautiful smile. Gesturing with a subtle nod toward my cigarette, she, over the course of what seemed a miniature lifetime, parted her lust-worthy lips, raised delicately her hand in a motion suggesting request, and spoke—

"I'm Jordan," she said, taking down the rest of her drink before discarding her cup into the fire burning next to us. "You got one for me?"

In the sound of her voice, I heard a faint echo of sadness and separation. She, however, was not distant herself.

Jordan…. Her name is Jordan….

MICHAEL

He was a devil in the dark.

HANNAH

She was a curious creature, listening intently to the sounds beyond the door as she approached with a sneaking apprehension. She could not betray her curiosity. Her hormones would not permit such betrayal. She got close to the door, her ear tuned in to the noises beyond.

All she heard was whispering and subtle laughter. Smiles were practically audible in the optimism of their voices. It made Hannah jealous.

The whispering and laughing turned to the sounds of kissing and gasping. Soft moans echoed from within the room.

Whatever he's doing, he's doing it right. That girl is going crazy!

Hannah heard another sharp gasp, louder than the one before. A laugh, something almost sinister, soon followed. "My turn," Hannah heard her say. Hannah heard a belt buckle and a zipper. Her stifled moans were only interrupted by his hard exhales of satisfied disbelief. He laughed gently.

The smug bastard.

Soon, the sound of bedsprings caught Hannah's curious ears.

Tossing her onto the bed….

Hannah then heard a feminine giggle before a long, satisfied moan of pleasure.

At least someone is getting some action.

The noises of shared pleasure beyond the door were driving Hannah insane.

The sounds….

The friction.

God, this is hot.

Hannah felt a heat rise in her. A fire was beginning to burn, one that only passion could quench.

His pace quickened. Her breath was strictly exhales, and Hannah began to breathe more heavily, herself.

"Oh my god, oh my god, Michael ..."

Faster. Louder. Michael.

Hannah felt a very concentrated excitement rise in her. She was torturing herself with her naughty, hidden curiosity, but Hannah could not tear herself away from the door and its dangerous romance.

"Michael... Oh!"

"Yeah?"

"Yesss!"

"You got it, babe."

"Oh my god, just shut up and—! Give it to me!"

Hannah could hear the animal this 'Michael' had become. The sound of him doing as he wished with this unfortunately fortunate girl had aroused Hannah. She listened on as more breathing and more sharp exhales echoed through the door. The sound of the bed's headboard began aggressively knocking on the wall behind it.

"Yes! Oh my god...."

"Baby, I'm close."

"Michael, keep going. Don't stop yet. Don't you dare stop, Michael. Don't you st—"

A brief silence seemed to conquer the scene before a sharp female inhale broke the stillness of the air. The screams that followed were loud, even for being stifled by the heavy door, and the vibrations of the voice struck a very sensitive nerve in Hannah's core. His rhythm did not falter.

"Katie—"

"Go ahead, baby. I already got there—twice," Katie sighed.

The selflessness between these two....

Her response pushed Hannah over the edge. The sound of bedsprings left very little to her overly excited imagination. Hannah allowed her mind to wander in search of intimate scenarios that were unrealistically both rough and romantic. The powerful sound of his release caused Hannah to bite her knuckle as she fought to keep silent in the dangerous, sensual darkness.

"Mmmm.... Perfect," said the exhausted female voice.

Hannah moistened in the tense quiet she struggled to uphold in the presence of such passion.

Perfection, indeed.

Hannah's fingers danced around her neck, tantalizing her before they made their way past her waist. She began massaging herself through the soft fabric of her stone-washed jeans. A gentle roll of thunder moaned from beyond the window at the end of the hall. A gentle roll of thunder moaned from beyond the doorframe. All around Hannah, a storm was forming—the storm of the century.

She was a ship tossed to and fro in a frothy, relentless sea, and lightning seemed to strike all around her.

"Let me get you some water, honey."

Hannah heard movement and the click of a light being turned on, a bit of it showing from underneath the closed door.

Hannah then became very still.

"No, I really want a cigarette, though…."

"Shit, I gotta remember Ari's cigarettes…. I'll be right back—!"

The sound of the doorknob turning brought a shocked and surprised Hannah to her feet. She stood there, unsure of what to do, draped in a tapestry of confusion and embarrassment. She was clothed, yet fully exposed, and a messy-haired, well-built, shirtless man, apparently named Michael, was the sudden audience to this awkward state with which she and her confident demeanor were not at all familiar. Silent thunder, once again, rolled on within her shaken soul. Hannah forgot herself in this moment of powerful, brief discovery.

ARI

My cigarette had fallen from my lips. The wolf of my spirit and the vampire of my lust were halted in their tracks.

Supernatural as these metaphors made me feel, the realness and genuine quality of this mesmerizing person before me had stopped them in their imaginary places. Even they could appreciate this exquisite creature, their various forms of lust aside, one of which was unlike anything either of them had ever before encountered in their collective centuries of life. Taken up completely in confused bewilderment, they sat stock still, eons of experience eluding them in the euphoric uncertainty of this light that stood before our trinity in the form of a girl.

And she had a name—Jordan.

"Hello? Are you drunk?" she asked.

How confident. Those red shoes. And my cigarette, lying helplessly there, down there in the—

"Mud," I said.

"Mud?" she asked.

Shit, Ari?! You idiot! Say something! Anything else!

"On your shoes. It's okay. I think a little dirt adds character, don't you?" I said as I winked at her. I was not off to a good start with this conversation as I had craved her more than anything I had ever seen. Even in the dark, I watched as she turned a brighter shade of red, eclipsing the movement of the firelight already present on her face. Whether it was the fire or my embarrassment at my lame words, my face burned.

So far so good for a stupid person, you moron!

She shrugged, her body going limp in the action.

"Yeah, I guess I really didn't dress for the occasion," she said flatly.

I'm an asshole, all of a sudden. Thanks for rubbing off on me, Michael!

I had deflated her, and it was obvious to me.

Time to recover, Ari.

"Are you kidding me?" I said. "You.... You look... damned fantastic tonight. Sorry to be so honest. I don't socialize much. I apologize."

She lit up again. Her body reacted to my words, and the motion that was taking place all over her body was provoking my ego.

"Honest? Talk shit about my shoes, *then* call me beautiful? You're a very confused man, aren't you?"

I am not egotistical.

She was testing every limit of my self-control, and I was looking less like my true self with each passing moment.

How can I be this nervous right now? Get it together, Ari!

I tried playing it coolly, but I panicked.

I opened my mouth to speak, but a playful wink from her luxurious brown eyes silenced my unspoken words.

"Relax, I'm only messing with you," she said.

Oh, thank God! I'm so embarrassed, still.

"But seriously, do you have a cigarette?" she asked again.

I had completely forgotten about her need that had even brought her into my world. I scurried to the task, reaching into my pocket, my recent panic evident in the shaking of my hands. Eventually I located a cigarette for her.

"Here you go, Jordan," I said. "I'm afraid you'll have to find a light, though. Some rude bitch of a girl came over and blew my last match out," I flirted. "She was pretty, at least"—I smiled—"except for those awful, dirty shoes." I threw a playful wink at her, again, and she smiled, knowing fully well how hard I was trying to flirt.

Ari, you're pathetic and hopeless. She'll be gone before she even gets that thing lit. For the love of God, stop fucking winking at her!

"It's okay. I'm sure she didn't hang around for too long. She probably wasn't into the whole fake money, douchebag thing." She winked right back at me. I was speechless. Fortunately, she broke the awkward tension by reaching into her bag, once again pulling out her lighter, and using it to light her cigarette.

The smoke that flowed from her mouth was a fountain of desire, and as it rose, it took me with it.

Fake-money thing? So you know me....

"Ah, so you know who I am." My gaze remained transfixed upon her fleeting exhale.

"I know you are the host, but I do not know your name," she

said. "Even if I did, I would not know *who* you are. That could take a lifetime."

She was philosophical as well, and I was intrigued. I turned my attention back to her, forgetting the smoke that I had watched climb to heaven.

A lifetime…. Ari, can you just imagine….

"Ari," I said, putting a cigarette into my mouth. "Welcome to my home."

"It's beautiful," she said. She reached out with her lighter to light my cigarette. Keeping my manly pride intact, I took it from her, taking the liberty of letting my hand linger upon hers in the process. A movement of her fingers told me that she did not want me to let go, so naturally, I let go. I lit my cigarette, dropped the lighter back into her purse, and took another sip of wine, a drag of nicotine following.

"Thank you. Would you like some wine?" I said. "It's cabernet. The best, in my opinion."

Like hell, it is. Cheap trash. But I am thankful Michael brought at least something, I suppose….

"I'd love some. My friend and I came here to drink some over a girls' night," she said, "but I've lost her. Have you seen her? Her name is Hannah."

"Here, have some," I said, handing her my glass. "Sorry, I've been a loner all night. I've got just my one friend here, and he's off… entertaining guests. You're the first new person I've truly met tonight. Should we look for her?"

A look of deep thought passed over her face. "No, it'll be alright. We'll find each other, somehow."

Yes, we will, Jordan. Yes, we will.

"Have you been looking long?" I said.

"Feels like forever, but I arrived only a bit ag—" she said.

"Would you like a tour?" I asked, taking a page from Michael's book, interrupting her with my unbridled juvenile excitement. "We can look for your friend in the meantime."

"I appreciate the incentive, Ari, but it's probably for the best. You wouldn't understand," she said.

"Why wouldn't I understand, Jordan? I may be wealthy, but I'm still human. We can talk if you nee—"

"I know, but it's personal stuff. You're a real nosey bastard, you know that?" she said. She was teasing me.

"It's my house, Jordan. I like to stay informed on who is who and who is here. Of course, tonight, I haven't a clue who any of these people are, to be honest. I kind of like it this way. More mystery and all...."

We both sipped from the wine in turns.

We turned in unison to the fire that blazed near us. The outline of her body with her back toward me sent a jolt from my feet through my legs, and I shivered as I studied this statuesque human that had changed my whole outlook on the night in only a fraction of time. I liked her. I already knew that.

"Beautiful," escaped my lips before I could stop it.

"What's that?" she asked over her shoulder.

"What a beautiful fire," was my attempt to recover, but I realized after I spoke that I was still talking about Jordan, in a way. She was indeed a beautiful fire, smothering with her heat even the literal fire that gave us light in the grove. Even so, I was the one burning. This connection to my constantly running thoughts of the day embedded her deeply within my consciousness.

She was now the fire.

God would have to wait.

I had an angel, visible and tangible, right before me. She was His messenger, wingless and real. He was an absent parent, silent and stern.

Both Jordan and God burned in contrast with one another before my irretrievable gaze. I was wholly astonished, questioning fate and what cruel karma would come to bring balance for this meeting for which I felt I had been preparing all my life. I was happy.

What cruelty would take it away?

Yet another woman in my life to invoke the wrathful punishment of a jealous god....

What a beautiful fire.... And to think, this whole meeting started with a match, extinguished.

The bonfire shifted.

Maybe You're listening, after all.

JORDAN

Ari's unlit cigarette fell from his gaping mouth.

"Hello? Are you drunk?" Jordan asked.

Jordan immediately regretted those words. She felt rude to her host. He was attracted to her—that much was clear—but she had not gained anything from her comment except a creeping lament that perhaps she was not as confident as she saw herself to currently be.

I'm here to find Hannah, not flirt around, anyway.

"Mud," was his response.

Mud? Of course he's completely fucking weird..!

"Mud?" she said.

"On your shoes…" he said. He had continued to speak, but she had tuned out the words, lost in dizzying thought.

I look amazing tonight, I thought, and all he sees is the dirt on my feet?

She blushed, frustrated with herself and embarrassed.

"Yeah, I guess I didn't really dress for the occasion..." she uttered, withdrawing.

"You…" he said. "You look damned fantastic tonight."

Jordan's mood immediately lifted. He had brought her back as quickly as he had pushed her away. "Sorry to be so honest," he continued. "I don't socialize much. I apologize."

She hardly knew how to react, her insides confused and interested and empty. She had nothing to lose. Her emotions lashed out through her mouth, her mind unable to hold back the wrathful syllables. "Honest?" she said.

You want to be honest, buddy? Honestly?

"Talk shit about my shoes, *then* call me beautiful? You're a very confused man, aren't you?" she asked.

Damn, Jordan. He's only flirting. Maybe a little bad at it, but you don't really want a smooth talker, do you? You want something real. But he's rich? He's probably a total fake.

But you could have things. Your life could be so easy. Just spend his money and return his love, that's all.

No, that's not you. Those things don't matter. He's handsome, that's for sure… And he's 'here.'

And 'here' is all I need now.

"Relax. I'm only messing with you," she said, attempting to make amends for her rudeness without making it a subject of conversation. She remembered that she had asked him for a cigarette. Now, however, she actually needed it for its use as opposed to the excuse for rough introductions. "But seriously, do you have a cigarette?"

He so awkwardly went about searching his person for his cigarettes. She had him.

Be cool, Jordan. Keep your emotions close. Keep them imprisoned. They are dangerous right now. To you…. To him…. To Hannah…. Keep your feelings hidden.

"Here you go, Jordan," he said. "I'm afraid you'll have to find a light, though. Some rude bitch of a girl came over and blew my last match out."

Asshole.

"She was pretty at least—" he continued.

Better.

"—except for those awful dirty shoes."

Artist. And a bastard.

He winked at her.

Again, Jordan vomited words with no control over them or herself.

"It's okay. I'm sure she didn't hang around too long. She probably wasn't into the whole fake-money douchebag thing," Jordan said.

Nice one, Jordan. Let him know who's boss!

She returned his wink with a sarcastic wink of her own. Watching his lip begin to quiver, she awaited his response. She had no desire for his wealth, nor did it matter to her.

"Ah, so you know who I am," he said.

She had revealed herself.

"I know you are the host, but I do not know your name," Jordan said, digging for a way to be more personal with this awkward interaction.

Show him the real you, Jordan. Stop caring and just go for it!

"Even if I did," she continued, becoming more fully herself, "I would not know *who* you are. That could take a lifetime."

Great, now I'm sure he thinks you're trying to be deep-minded and trying to

He was interested. He was engaged.

"Ari," he said as he placed a cigarette into his mouth. "Welcome to my home."

Restart.

"It's beautiful," she said, reaching out her lighter to light Ari's cigarette. Though she had intended to light it for him, he took it from her hand, the touch of his fingers upon hers sending an electric flow throughout her body. She looked at her hand and the lighter loosely gripped within it. Ari let his hand remain on hers for a moment.

She did not want him to let go.

As he lit his cigarette, Jordan watched as a look of childhood innocence played out on Ari's face. He took a sip of his wine, then exhaled his smoke as he dropped her lighter back into Jordan's handbag. The smile accompanying his exhale shook Jordan.

"Thank you," he said. "Would you like some wine?"

Hannah….

Jordan glided out of her mind, her attention caught by the fog of past lamentations.

Ari was speaking, but she had not heard the words. The mental image of her drinking wine with Hannah had momentarily distracted her.

Wine….

"I'd love some," she said, hoping to keep the conversation moving, even though she felt a bit dull, herself, now. She could not keep herself from asking about Hannah, worried still, as she was. "My friend and I came here to drink some over a girls' night, but I've lost her."

Maybe for good….

"Have you seen her?" Jordan pressed. "Her name's Hannah."

Was I wrong to be so blunt with her? Is it mistrust? I already miss her, but out of nowhere…! What came over her, I wonder?

Ari seemed to be inside her head, reading well into her thoughts as he spoke.

"Here, have some," he said, handing her his wine glass.

Maybe I will. I think I'm the loneliest person here tonight.

"Sorry, I've been a loner all night," he continued.

So, you're all alone and I'm alone….

"I've got just my one friend here, and he's off… entertaining guests," Ari said.

So, we've both lost a friend, finding each other? Interesting….

"You're the first new person I've truly met tonight. Should we look for her?" Ari asked.

No, Ari. I'll find her. We're still searching for each other, now, anyway. I still need more time before I can face her, honestly. I must find myself, first.

"No, it'll be alright. We'll find each other somehow," Jordan said.

"Have you been looking long?" Ari asked.

My whole life, Ari. My whole life, I have been looking, searching. Even in the presence of others, I've always felt alone.

"Feels like forever, but I arrived only a bit ag—" Jordan said, as Ari cut her off.

"Would you like a tour?" he asked. "We can look for your friend in the meantime."

"I appreciate the incentive, Ari," Jordan said, "but it's probably for the best. You wouldn't understand."

But maybe you would…. I guess only time will tell.

"Why wouldn't I understand, Jordan?" Ari asked. "I may be wealthy, but I am still human. We can talk if you nee—"

"I know," Jordan intervened. "But it's personal stuff. You're a real nosey bastard, you know that!" Jordan teased. She smiled to herself, reflecting his own.

"It's my house, Jordan," he said. "I like to stay informed on who is who and who is here. Of course, tonight, I haven't a clue who any of these people are, to be honest. I kind of like it this way. More mystery and all…."

The word 'mystery' made Jordan shudder as it escaped his lips. That was all the night was to her anymore. She felt once again the chill of the cooling night, though the fire behind her kept her warm. She sipped from their shared wine, handing it back to him. She studied his lips as they savored the flavor.

What a gorgeous man! These silly, meaningful gestures…. How they grab my attention.

Lost in thought, Jordan turned away from Ari to the fire. She was too eager to give herself away, and realizing that, she decided to separate herself from him, though Ari would not let her leave him that easily.

"Beautiful," he said as Jordan peered into the fire.

It is beautiful, Ari. But I know you mean 'me'. I'd like to hear you say that again.

Jordan turned her head, keeping her body still.

"What's that?" she asked, pretending she did not hear him. She was distant, yet playful in her inquisition. She wanted to keep him interested but needed her personal space. It was the only way to keep herself safe from his innocent charm.

She was smoke before she met this man, simply a warning, to the world that a fire was close by. She could not discern from which exact point his own heat emanated, but this man—this Ari—had built more than one fire—the fire before her—tonight, and she began to feel the embers of something alive and new as his undeniable warmth embraced her.

She felt like the smoke to Hannah's fire all night, yet now that she was here, she—with the help of Ari's relentless compliments—had grown into something sprawling and formidable. She stood there, facing the small inferno, and as she pondered these thoughts, her feet seemed to stand stronger, the earth beneath them giving way to this newfound strength.

Ari, do you really think I'm beautiful?

"What a beautiful fire," he said.

The quiet emphasis of his smooth voice crept over her flesh, leaving a static chill in its wake.

'Beautiful' was the steel, 'fire' the flint, and together, as if wielded by invisible hands, they collided, forging the newborn star that she, in these unlimited yet fleeting moments, had become.

She was a nebula.

The gravity of Ari's words had condensed her, and she—once a scattered and formless cloud—began to take form. She had become a proto-star, hot and young and born again.

Then let me be fire.

As Jordan gazed into the heart of the bonfire, she felt the strong impulse that it seemed to look back into her—deeply into her heart—she and the fire becoming one and the same.

The fire itself responded with a stir.

Jordan kept her smile as she watched the ashes from the embers' quiet commotion drift through the carrying air and land gently, like a comforting hand on a troubled knee, upon Jordan's dirty red high heels.

HANNAH

Hannah stood in the hall in the shadow of a doorway. The light that came from within was soft and yellow, and the air was comfortable yet thick with the scent of pleasure. Hannah licked her lips.

"Can I… help you?" the boy asked.

"I'm sorry," Hannah panicked. "I was using the bathroom, and I…"

"Yes?"

"…I heard a noise…."

He laughed an evil laugh at her comment. "I'll say you did."

The girl's voice, tired and satisfied, called from the disheveled contents of the bed. "Michael, who's there?"

"I don't know, honey. She says you're loud as hell, though. Redheads," he laughed. "Redheads…. What's your name, sweetheart?"

"H-Hannah. I'm Hannah. And you must be…."

"Michael. Michael Law."

"I've never heard—"

"I'm a friend of the host, you see. This might as well be my house—by association, of course."

Hannah was unimpressed with his blatant flirtations. Still, she was interested in this ape of a man, who, while terrible with his rough words, had a sense of eloquence and charm about him. She was intrigued.

"Sorry to intrude. I've never been here before. This place is so big. I just wanted to take a look around."

"Michael, who the hell are you talking to? Go get those cigarettes and come back to bed! I'm not finished with you yet, mister!"

"Hang on one minute, Katie. I'd like to catch my breath if you don't mind. Now, as I was saying, Hannah, I know the host. Anything you need," he said, gently grabbing her arm, "you let me know."

He has to be incredibly intoxicated. No one is this damned confident! She's literally right there, and he's hitting on me! You bastard. You confident bastard.

He continued. "I was about to have a cigarette. You may have one with us if you wish."

"Michael, I still have some powder left. Go get those cigarettes and we'll do some more," Katie said as she sat up in bed, her naked torso fully visible in the quiet light of the dimly lit room. "Oh. Who's your friend? She seems very… nice," she said, taking no liberties in covering herself.

"This is Hannah. She was checking out the house and she heard you."

Hannah, embarrassed, stepped into the room, slipping underneath and past Michael, the ability to avoid staring at Katie's body eluding her completely. She thought of Jordan.

"Hi. Sorry to intrude. I'm Hannah."

"Very nice to meet you, Hannah. Care to have a chat with me while I wait on this slug to bring me a smoke?"

"Slug? More like a snake," he said, turning and leaning on the doorframe in a relaxed, cocky pose. Katie merely rolled her eyes. "Cigarettes!" she said, dismissing Michael with a flick of her wrist. He made an exhale of impatience but made his way into the hall, nonetheless. "That's more like it. Now, Hannah," Katie said, leaning in. "I could use a conversation while I break this powder down. Do you party?"

"I've done that only a few times, in college, before I dropped out. It doesn't bother me, though. Do whatever you want."

"Would you like to do some? You seem frazzled. Care to shake that all away?" Katie said.

Hannah obliged timidly, but eventually she took a seat by Katie at the foot of the bed. For all her giggling, she seemed sweet enough to Hannah.

That's her evil. She's an innocent little devil.

"Now, Hannah, when he gets back with those smokes, you're more than welcome to have one. If he isn't comfortable with that, well… I have my methods of persuasion." Katie smiled, her teeth flashing in the dim light. "What are you doing here all alone? Don't you have any friends that can eavesdrop with you?"

"No, I brought my friend, Jordan, but well… Hey! I wasn't eave—"

"You were eavesdropping," Katie laughed, but Hannah took her tone as playful. "It's fine, I promise. I understand. If I were you, I would have done the same—no lie. That man, Hannah, he knows how to use it. I couldn't help myself."

Hannah was suddenly comfortable in her presence, and all the awkward things about this Katie began to form a picture, one that was coming slowly—very slowly— into focus.

"Yeah, I'm sorry about that. But… it's nice to meet you!"

Both girls laughed. Katie stuck out her hand to shake Hannah's. Hannah took it with reticence, shaking Katie's hand slowly. The two laughed at the strange relationship that began to form under these strange circumstances.

"Very nice to meet you, Hannah. Now… this 'Jordan'. Where is she?"

Hannah thought for a long moment before she responded. She wanted to speak, but the words fell apart in her mouth. Either that or her heart simply had not yet the strength to carry the weight of the reality. "I don't know," was the only response Hannah could conjure. After a pause, Hannah asked Katie, "So how about that coke?"

Hannah felt she had nothing to lose, and she had not done any hard drugs in a long time, but the need to escape the real world was weighing on her quickly. Her inhibitions were falling apart faster than a crumbling star. She was a nebula, desperate to condense. Beginnings and ends were flashing through her mind at a rapid pace. She knew the drug would speed up her mind, but the thought of a vice sounded appealing.

"How 'bout that coke, indeed," came Michael's voice from the door. "Is it ready, yet? I found his cigarette stash. Ari's got a new cigarette machine in the game room. Pretty sweet. They're just out in the open by the boxful. Guess he's planning on throwing more of these parties. It must be that. He doesn't smoke that damned much!"

Katie had been preparing the powder on a thick book that Hannah deduced did not belong to her. Katie let out a forced laugh, that same giggle that drove Hannah mad earlier. Like a ghastly blade, it cut her to the core, yet now it seemed to garner her attention— another mystery unsolved in the unknown that this girl had come to be. She seemed to only laugh like that with Michael, Hannah noticed.

Carrying what seemed to be a liquor bottle and cigarettes, he sat down on the bed next to Hannah, his back to Katie. Katie paid no attention to either of them as she began to roll a fifty-dollar bill into a tube.

"So, are we all friends, now?" Michael asked. "I didn't miss anything *scandalous* while I was gone, did I?" he joked.

Katie took a line through her nose, giving her nasal passage a good, hard tug to take in any loose particles that came anywhere near her face. She grimaced for a moment before commencing a series of sniffles. Michael took the book and read the cover. "Bram Stoker.... You just did blow on *Dracula*...."

"That's my favorite movie!" Hannah said. "What a beautiful story. Horrifying, sure, but what romance."

And, what the fuck. I just watched that movie....

"Yes, Michael, we know a bit about romance, don't we?" Katie giggled and began to rub Michael's chest from behind him, pressing her breasts to his back.

He was reading the first page to himself as she did this, pretending to not notice her.

"Hannah, I think you should go next."

"No, no, it's fine. You go ahead. I'll wait."

"No, but I insist!" Katie said. She snatched the book from over Michael's shoulder. Quickly, she brought out more chunky powder, instantly beginning the task of breaking it down, cutting it into lines. "Hannah, you need to lighten up. You look a little... tense?"

"I am, I guess. Rough start to what should have been a fun night," Hannah admitted.

"Why... is it not fun?" Michael asked. "I thought we were getting along here."

"Jordan," Katie said.

Hannah simply blushed with embarrassment. She was not, however, offended.

"Jordan? That your boyfriend, Hannah?" Michael asked, nudging her.

"No, *she* is a friend"—*friend*—"of mine. She came with me tonight. We had a... 'fight,' if you will. We might not be on such great terms right now. I don't want to talk about it, really."

"I understand," Michael and Katie said in unison. They laughed at the coincidence.

"Then don't talk," Michael continued.

"Yeah," Katie agreed. "Just do. Too much time thinking is degrading to a good life, as life is lived by *doing*. Thinking doesn't accomplish anything without action. Get those bad vibes out of here! You're up," she said to Hannah, handing her the freshly-adorned book—that exquisitely decorated book—that had a nicely-formed line of white cocaine resting on the leather cover. Katie handed Hannah the bill she had used for a straw.

"Yeah, superstar. Action," said Michael. As his words echoed in Hannah's head, she lowered it, shrugging all the weight of her shoulders as she took an inch or two of numbing bliss into her skull. Immediately, that old sensation that was not unfamiliar took her body over, starting in her sinus cavity, and spreading to her skin, her fingertips, and other places that—until this moment—had gone untouched for a long time. Instantly, she was changed. All her problems left her mind as she tried to cope with this changing perspective. She became hot all over, energetic, and driven with no real purpose.

Michael was next to do a line, and Katie followed suit. Hannah let it pass to Michael as she was still getting used to the change. "Give me a cigarette," she said.

"Well, well. Sounds like it's going to work on *somebody*," Katie laughed as she honored Hannah's abrupt request, handing her a cigarette from her pack.

"Sorry. I just feel…. I just feel…."

"Like doing something?" Katie asked.

"Yes! That!" Hannah laughed.

"Here, do this line first, then light your cigarette. We'll plan once you've accomplished that much," Katie joked.

Hannah needed no support. She finished her second line in half the time of the first, a chalky drip beginning to work its way down the back of her throat. "Drainage," she said.

"Ah, you're so close, Hannah. It really kicks in once you get to that point…."

"Wait. This isn't even as far as it goes? I guess I don't remember very well. It's been so long. Oh. Oh, shit…."

"It's okay, baby," Katie said. "We're here. Here, have some water." As Katie spoke, she handed Hannah a bottle of unopened water. Apparently, this room was stocked for such late-night, exhausting endeavors. Regardless, Hannah was thankful. She chugged most of the bottle, using some to pour into her palm, using it to chase the chalky substance through her nose, down the back of her throat.

"Like a pro," Michael said. "So, you *have* done this before."

"Yes, very well done," said Katie.

Michael and Katie began to snort water as well from the bottle they had been sharing already. The both sniffled and swallowed hard.

I am starting to feel really fucked up right now….

Hannah began to shuffle in her growing anxiety. She lit her

cigarette, determined.

"What's wrong, girl?" asked Katie. "You were fine a minute ago." She set the book and bag of white aside. "It's okay. You can tell me."

Hannah thought long and hard about what to say. Her walls had fallen. Her inhibitions had fled with her increasing inebriation.

"Well, I kind of… kissed her earlier. She was just so… timid! So scared. I care about her—I really do—and she looks so hot tonight." Hannah ashed her cigarette on the carpet. Katie set an ashtray before her as Hannah continued. "I was so proud of her. And I saw her body when she was changing earlier."

And I must admit, it changed me, too….

"Look, I'm straight. Not a gay bone in my body. I do like men… but something about the way I saw her, though! It came from an honest place—it really did! More from my heart—and my imagination, definitely—but just… it's driving me craz—"

A soft finger pressed itself to Hannah's lips, silencing her.

"You talk too much," Katie laughed. "Hush. So, you maybe wanted to experiment. Big deal. I'm bisexual. I've had only two girlfriends, but they were absolutely beautiful people, inside and out. I've dated mostly boys, even almost married one, but there's something restricted about that whole institution. Marriage is like sex to me. It can ruin or it can strengthen. It really depends on how it's used, if you ask me. I like it to last about fifteen minutes—sex, that is, not marriage of course," Katie laughed. "Any more is just pointless without recharging, to me. But if they get off sooner, who's to say that passion didn't drive them there faster? It's flattering to me. I can tell when they're surprised." Katie smiled at Michael, and so did Hannah. "I can tell when it's me, or if it's them. Let's see, what was my… oh, yeah! Don't worry about it, is what I'm saying. She was your friend first, right?"

"Righ—"

"Then be friends. Friends kiss sometimes. It happens. Men and women. It doesn't have to mean anything. It can, of course, but it doesn't have to."

"But it did—for me, at least," Hannah said quietly. "I'm not sure she understands why I did it. She's probably so confused. Hell, I'm the one that did it, and *I'm confused*!"

"Don't be," Katie said.

Something clicked in Hannah's heart. Be it drugs or a paradigm shift, it caused her body to quiver.

With that, Michael stood slowly from the bed. Katie eyed him with an excited apprehension, watching his every move. "We need to get this off your mind, Hannah," Michael said, his gaze taking in every bit of detail that her physical form offered his hungry eyes. The drugs were causing him to sweat profusely, Hannah noticing that she was beginning to sweat, herself.

"Drink water, you two," said Katie. "No need to dehydrate to death."

"I don't know," Hannah said. "I kind of feel like dying would be okay on a night like this."

Dracula.... Not living, but not dead, either....

"Well, then," said Katie, "why don't we kill you just a little bit at a time?"

"You read my mind, honey," Michael said.

Vampires....

Katie's lips and Michael's hands began to cover Hannah with kisses and squeezes. Her hands, almost against her will, found their way into their hair, massaging their scalps as they caressed her with lips and hands. She was a criminal in the shadows, and Hannah was slowly becoming her own victim as she, lying down, chased the dream of herself through her mind.

Soft.... Just what I imagined it to be....

Jordan. I wish it were you.

Numb in mind and body, Hannah's spirit sank into the depths of a tingling, dark, numbingly comfortable abyss.

Now 'this' is a party....

ARI

There she was, and there I was, and we shared in the night and its sinister light.

We, there together, were all that was beautiful in an ugly, unfamiliar world—a world full of strangers, all of whom, looking in on us, could in no way understand the foundations and structures by which this focus of the world that this 'we' had come to be.

We knew nothing.

We knew everything.

We were ignorant and knowledgeable.

We were hopeless and saved.

She glowed like an explosion frozen in time. She but stood there; and the universe, in all its jealousy, had its greedy eyes upon her, envious of the light that she expelled. She was a goddess, and at the core of her heart, a star burned—and it burned for me. Every beat of her heart was a pulse of photons, each individual particle flowing from an inner hidden pain; and each photon alone held the power to destroy utterly the insistent darkness that surrounded us in this grove. Billions of stars enveloped us, showering us in gazes of awe. Countless shadows crept too close for my comfort.

Where there is light, darkness is never very far away. But if she is light....

My thoughts grew dark with my newfound revelations and I knew that this path of darkness would not ever bring me closer to her. She was keeping me warm, warmer even than the deity that was merely feet away.

The changing of the guard....

The fire shifted in an ominous way, the topmost wooden tier collapsing into the center. I watched as the inferno caved in. The wind, like a bellows, stoked the blaze as it settled into a fresher bed of churning coals.

It had been several moments since either of us had said a word.

This was a miracle to me. We simply stood in the presence of one another, smoking our cigarettes.

No girl had ever let me simply *be*. Those before either wanted toys—cars, clothes, or credit cards, ignoring the 'me' beneath it all, using me as a means to some tangible end—yet here this girl stood, silent for what seemed like blissful forevers; and even with her back to me, she had intrigued me. She was art before. She was real now. She was the uninformed, unaware guardian angel who, given her stance of bold indifference, was somehow saving me—saving my delusions of romance, at least—delusions true and full of comforting and contact and reconciliation.

Why do I deserve any less?

I had wealth, sure, and the looks to go along with it, but what haunted me for many of these past years was a strong desire to no longer be alone. Flames of the past burned either too quickly or too slowly, either living fast to die young or remaining so stagnant that they never truly lived. Both outcomes always proved tragic for me, and I must admit that none of them ever did fully satisfy me in any aspect.

Then, there was Jordan.

She was there but distant. She was both the object after which I chased and the hunting companion running adamantly at my side. I was starving for her heart—the very one that pounded only feet away in exciting pursuit of the chase.

Life had always been a meal for me, my plate full, yet I kept piling on more, at least in my younger years; but it had been empty for some time, as I had been. All I had done for these past lonely seasons was stare at the vacant plate and the reflective void of its surface, the reflection of myself within the frame of its perfect circle, reveling and analyzing. All the while, I never savored a single morsel.

I suppose it was because I had always felt lonely, as if no one was ever there with which to partake in life and all its various flavors.

Now, at least, I had a dinner guest—one whose conversation would slow the eating, one whose presence could inspire the desire to taste again, and one who should give a purpose for the eating—the instinct of survival, itself—in the first place.

I was starving for her heart, but I did not wish to dine alone.

Everything and nothing.

Victory or defeat.

Life.

Death.

I had thought in terms of black and white all my life. In the fires of my soul, wrong and right were the errors of the lifelong trial. Desire was the pyre, misdirection the matchstick. The fire that resulted scorched the color from my world, leaving it to be a desolate hell of colorlessness. Black and white were all that remained of an immature, overeager youth. That youth was now a man, however, but my world had remained much of the same.

Where the black and white separated, there was grey. Wherever black and white blended, there was grey. And here, among the neutrality of the pallor of my world, a most beautiful shade of grey stood before me, indifferently and unknowingly coloring my world. She was becoming the candlelight by which I saw in darkness—both within and without—allowing my tired eyes to finally see what the world had kept from me for so long.

Perhaps there had always been color.

Maybe I just needed someone to pry my eyes open for me—to teach me the existence of color and its immeasurable value.

My once neutral view of my once neutral world began to display brighter hues, mobbing quickly in whatever direction it was in which I was heading. I had no bearings on my destination. I knew only to keep moving.

Yet here I stood, nearly motionless, sipping my wine. I looked on as the colors flowed from her, bleeding into the darkness, saturating the dismal dark and its impartiality.

Was it lust or was it love? Nothing was any mixture of black and white anymore, from what I could tell. I continued to drink my wine, as a purveyor in an art gallery, and as I analyzed and pondered the sole display, I found myself lost in her perfectly imperfect colors and shapes of this canvas living in three dimensions.

Art—the only thing in this world with a voice that can speak to us without a word….

"What time is it?" she asked, interrupting my monologue of thought.

Time and its urgency….

"A little past midnight. It's already tomorrow," I said.

The latter sentence sounded ridiculous to my ears as it escaped my mouth. I suppose I still had jitters, not that that was a bad thing. Regardless, the statement left a bitter, awkward taste on my tongue, but just when I felt I was failing, she reassured me.

"No, Ari," she said to me. "It's only another chance for today."

Thunder, stronger than the prior rumbles, echoed through the trees.

I shuddered in the moment—in Jordan—and the combination of the two enveloped me within an atmosphere of ecstatic magnetism.

JORDAN

Stay silent. Make him think. Make him sweat it.

Let him watch. Let him speak first.

Let it drive him mad. Make him go crazy for you.

Feel the heat on your skin and his eyes on you.

This silence is killing me, but words can do so much more damage. Damn it, Ari! Be a man! Say something!

…But I'd almost rather you didn't at all.

You're sweet. A little clumsy in almost every way, but you're sweet. Genuine, I think. I could be wrong, but I guess I'll find out. I do love how nervous you are around me.

Even if it's only for tonight….

Everything begins with a moment, and this could be that moment. This could be that beginning.

Ari, you make me burn! As hot as this fire is, and yet I feel your eyes on me even more intensely…. You are uncertainty. You are the safety and the danger from which I am protected. So, now that we are here, how do we proceed?

Am I so pathetic that I throw myself at the first man that pays me even a little attention? He seems different, though, for sure, but how can I know? I could simply be tonight's prey, but then again, so could he….

But I didn't feel so appetizing earlier. I only fear being wanted because I'm wanted… because he wants me. Without his eyes of desire all over me and through me, I wouldn't even be having these thoughts. I'd still be looking for Hannah, lost, and searching. And yet, here with you, Ari, I feel so… so… found… so seen….

You give me the capacity to fear you because you do want me. If you didn't care, why, there would be no emotion to question. Why the emotions are even there, I've no idea. I don't even know you!

He isn't talking, still…. Well, I like that, I suppose. Men always think words are the way to win a woman. I suppose they oftentimes do—words do hold power. But tonight, I am no mere woman. Not simply just a woman, no.

No.

Not tonight. Tonight, I am blazing and soaring and burning and flying—a phoenix soaring on the winds of change.

The space that you give me gives me the air I need to burn and to breathe and to fly… to survive.

Yes, keep silent so I may continue to burn for you—for both of us. Untouchable yet inviting. Warm and bright. Keep silent so that I may know you better without your clumsy words to make us both stumble over them. Anyone can appear to be anyone else by saying the right things, but that doesn't feel like your style. You seem to have no goal—no endgame—in mind. Your confidence in your quiet nature is fascinating and refreshing. Let the silence speak for you.

Let it speak for us.

To hell with it! I can speak for myself!

"What time is it?" Jordan asked, breaking from her thoughts.

Time… what even does that word mean?

"A little past midnight," Ari said, reminding Jordan he was still there with her. "It's already tomorrow."

It can never be tomorrow, Ari. Tomorrow doesn't exist. How can it, when it is forever in the future, just beyond our grasp? By the time we arrive at tomorrow, it's become today. These fleeting moments—by the time you reach out your hand to touch them… they are already gone.

"No, Ari, it's only another chance for today," Jordan said. She felt her eyes flash with reflections of two fires—one within and one without.

Both flames—the one inside Jordan and the one outside—were binary. They orbited each other with a wild yet governed fervor, both the counterpart that allowed the other to perpetually appreciate the gravity of its cosmic twin.

And it's the same with me and you, Ari. Tonight, at least. And maybe for more 'todays' to come. Perhaps you burn yourself, sir. And maybe I am the reason for it.

Which burns hotter? You, me, or the fire? Do we all owe our heat and gravity to the other? Which star glows with more passion tonight?

The darkness—even as it watched from a distance infinite and up close—could not decide which.

HANNAH

Katie sat back on the bed with a look of disappointment on her face. Hannah sat upright at the foot of the bed, her legs crossed in front of her, the memory of the last few minutes replaying within the fog of her mind. A blank stare mirrored Katie's emotionless face, and Michael sat on the bed's edge, his head hung in shame.

He turned in Katie's direction in a sloth-like manner. His embarrassment was well-disguised, and for anyone uninitiated, was basically non-existent.

"I'm so sorry, honey," he said to Katie.

"That happens sometimes, Michael. I know you don't do these things very often, Mister Doctor," she replied.

Michael laughed an appreciative laugh. Hannah took his lighthearted dismissal as illegitimate and was not convinced that he had recovered completely from his all-too-recent lack of potency.

"Yeah, I don't know if that makes me feel any better," Michael said with his eyes focused on the floor in front of him. Katie embraced him from behind once more, her breasts pressing firmly into Michael's strong back.

"Listen, Michael, you gave me hell last time, didn't you?" she said as she gave him a nurturing hug, clasping her hands just above his navel. She laid her head gently between his shoulders, her face turning to Hannah, who could only look down at her half-dressed body in blank confusion. "So, why don't we just say that you and your 'friend,'" she said, placing her hand on his lap, "take a little break—let the powder wear off for a while? Besides, I'm sure Ari could use a cig—"

Michael snapped out of his thoughts of self-pity, lifting himself and Katie slightly with a physical shock. "Shit! I completely forgot! There's no telling how lonely he feels by now. We've been up here for at least a half hour!" Michael said.

"Michael, sweetie. Breathe," she said, kissing the spot between his shoulders where her head once lay. "You're getting yourself worked up. This is his house, after all. If he doesn't like the way things are, I am sure he is most capable of changing the circumstances. He knows where to find those cigarettes. If nothing else, he knows we came up together. Men this loaded aren't stupid, Michael. He knew what you— I mean, *we*—were up to. Still, you did promise."

Remaining silent, Hannah listened in more closely, her distant eyes coming back into a more concentrated focus.

Clumsy manners tend to trip over themselves....

She watched as Michael stood, finally, removing Katie's hands from his body as he rose. He turned around to her, bending to meet her eyes with his, mere inches from her glistening, gorgeous face.

"But I'm his friend, Katie. Maybe the only one here tonight who really knows him. He's only the *host* to everyone else." Michael then looked to Hannah, a devious smirk slowly spreading over his features. She was looking back in perplexity. His grin intact, he transferred his focus back to Katie, who had not broken eye contact. Hannah was certain she had not even blinked.

Michael kissed Katie's hands with closing eyes as she closed hers in time with his. Hannah watched as these two carnivores, who earlier were devouring each other, including Hannah, set their primal natures aside. Hannah looked on in detached amazement. Their earlier demeanor was, to Hannah, an aggressive display of sexual warfare, she being the innocent casualty caught amidst the back-and-forth of their fierce chemistry. Now it seemed the proverbial dust had settled, and preparations were being made to survey the damages.

Hannah shuffled in discomfort and curiosity. "So, you know who's throwing this thing?" she asked. "This house is magnificent. What does he do? Why does he have so few friends here?"

Michael kept his focus on Katie's eyes as he responded. "Yeah, Ari. He has expensive taste, and that isn't limited to his possessions. He's not an asshole or anything—not really the elitist type—but he does like to keep his circle small. He's just very, very careful about who he lets into his life. He's not the kind of guy to brandish his wealth, either."

Hannah's intrigue deepened. This Ari sounded like a prince with a strong modesty or a pauper with a crippling ambition.

"But surely someone lives here with him!" Katie said.

"No, Katie, he likes solitude," he said, kissing her forehead.

She stammered as she responded, clearly affected by Michael's affection, despite his earlier embarrassment. "Who cleans? Who cooks?"

"Ari. And Ari. He's quite the talented man," Michael said. "Never had much luck with the ladies, though. I have no idea why."

"That makes no damned sense," said Hannah, "unless he's ugly as sin or just completely awkward."

"Awkward would be closer to the truth," he said, turning to Hannah, resting his head upon Katie's as he embraced her. "But he isn't awkward. Not completely. Just… just quiet, I guess. He likes to read and study history. He loves philosophy and different religions. But I've never seen him talk to 'God' like that," continued Michael, trailing to himself. "He's not crazy, but then again, I haven't seen him in some time. I suppose his sanity could be starting to waiver a bit, lonely as he is. But talking to God!" Michael laughed. "It's just bullshit."

"Now don't be mean," Katie said, pulling away from him.

"If you're the only friend he's got here, it's probably best to not make fun. He's lonely. He wears the mask. But underneath—."

"You're probably right," Michael said, retaking control of the conversation. "I'm sorry. I know you were talking about 'God' earlier, too."

"Did I say God?" Katie asked. "I love the universe, the earth and the stars. It is a miracle that we're even here right now, given the incredible odds, but I can't imagine a god making this place. Seems to me that a god that intelligent could make something so much more, beautiful as it is. If there is a god Anyway, long story short, I'm not offended, and thank you for the cigarettes, Michael." An innocent, playful grin formed on her face.

He looked from Katie to Hannah, releasing an impatient exhale.

Michael put on his shirt and shoes, and without a word, made for the door. Hannah and Katie both watched him with longing eyes as he crossed the floor.

"Can I get you ladies anything?" he asked, which made Hannah laugh as she acknowledged his casually playful banter. Simultaneously, it had elicited a modest scowl from Katie that was pointed in Hannah's direction.

"No, I'm fine," Katie said.

"I'll take some water if you don't mind," said Hannah.

"Me too, actually," said the redhead. "If you don't mind, that is." She kept her eyes on Hannah, and, to the recipient of their attention, they seemed to radiate some hot, glowing emotion that Hannah could not identify. The sound in Michael's voice that followed made Hannah think that he had seen it as well.

"Alright," he said, and with a pause and a wink, he shut the door behind him.

Katie giggled her famous giggle as she put her shirt back on, leaving her satin bra askew on the bed.

"My god, was that awkward," Katie said to herself. "How in the hell…. He was ready, and then he wasn't. I know coke can do that to someone, but damn, what timing…. You ever see anything like that?" she said to Hannah.

"No, I—"

"No, that's right. A girl like you doesn't have to use these… *vices*… to have a good time. You strike me as one that always has it together."

Jealousy.

"What makes you think—?" Hannah began.

"I think that because of how *quiet* you've become," said Katie coldly.

"Well, I told you I tried it in school," Hannah said. "But no, I've never seen that happen before. But don't think that's because I'm some *prude* or I think I'm *too good* for it. I know how to have a good time, *Kate*. Don't you *ever* forget that."

Calling Katie 'Kate' seemed to change the atmosphere of the room around them. "God, I hate being called that. It's too short. Biting. No eloquence to 'Kate'. 'Katie' rolls off the tongue and flows. Hannah, such a *pretty* name. But I won't call you 'Hann' if you don't call me 'Kate' ever again. That cool?"

"It's cool," Hannah said. "I didn't mean to offend you, but I hate it when people look at me and think I've got it all together. I know I'm beautiful, not to be pretentious, but I didn't earn this body. I do appreciate what I look like—I do—but it doesn't make me who I am. And it damn sure doesn't give anyone the right to judge me, even if it is sort of a positive judgment. Beautiful people aren't always successful. Those that can make people smile the most aren't always happy themselves. You can't judge people, just like books. The cover doesn't tell all. People aren't like books, yet they are. You can't judge either by their covers, sure, but you also can't read into people as deeply as you can books. Books don't analyze the reader. But people… people are always judging, especially if they are silent… or 'listening'," Hannah went on, the drugs she had done making her mind a hurricane of thought. "Maybe they are just as judgmental as people.

And perhaps, in their silence, they have even more to say. What am I blabbing about? My mind is absolutely racing right now."

"Well, Hannah, you've been silent for some time," said Katie, reaching for the lightly powdered book by the bed. "What judgments have you been thinking on?"

Hannah let out laugh of discomfort at Katie's appropriate yet stern question. "I suppose I haven't been judging anyone but myself," she said. "I thought there was something wrong with me, like he didn't want me in the room. Still, I can't help being glad that it didn't happen. I have never had an experience like that. After the 'Jordan incident' earlier, I think I've had my fill of 'first times' tonight. I'm glad it didn't happen. I can't help wondering what that would be like, though... *not that I'm ready for it.*"

As Hannah spoke, Katie prepared another two lines of cocaine. When the brunette finished speaking, Katie handed the book to her—two perfectly symmetrical lines of powder lying on its leather cover, parallel to one another.

"Here, this will help you think."

"No," said Hannah. "My mind is racing enough as it is."

"Suit yourself," said Katie. And with that, she took both lines through her nostrils, one immediately following the other. She choked slightly, and her eyes watered for a moment. "Oh, that's good!"

"Are you sure that's not too much?" asked Hannah. She became worried. She did not know much about the substance except that Katie seemed to have no concern for the negative effects such a habit might have on her.

Carpe Diem.... Carpe Noctem....

Katie, who had already taken to snorting water from a water bottle, cleared her sinuses with aggressive inhales. Anticipating the drip that she so loved, she let Hannah's question linger.

After a brief silence, Katie responded. "Too much? You sweet girl, you. No amount of this stuff is too much. In my experience, there never really seems to be enough. No matter how much you do, you always want more."

"I know the feeling," Hannah said.

Friendship... it can be that way. I guess friendship—even love itself—can be a drug, and it can be just as harmful as any actual physical drug when overdone or done incorrectly.

Katie gagged then smiled in contentment. "You know the feeling, do you? I thought you didn't do this stuff very often."

"I don't," Hannah said. "I guess I was speaking of other things. I feel incredibly symbolic right now!" She laughed at her own words, comparing people and books to friendship and narcotics.

These pointlessly circular thoughts, and how they never end. Coke sucks.

"I'm sorry if I offended you, too, Hannah," Katie said, interrupting Hannah's rapid dialogue. "My mind is racing, as well. I just hide it better. I'm kind of ashamed to say that I'm used to this stuff. I'm not a junkie—don't get me wrong—but if there's a party, I like to *party.*"

"Typically, I do, too, Katie, but my mind is heavy, and now it won't slow down—no matter how I try."

Katie lowered her eyes, peering through Hannah's flesh to the very soul inside. The glare in them spoke of danger, yet there was a soft comfort in her expression—a place where Hannah could see the cocaine going about its mischievous work.

"You know what I think?" Katie said, lifting her head.

"What's that?" asked Hannah.

"I think you need a distraction." Katie lowered her voice.

"Should we join the party, you think?" Hannah asked. "Michael should be back soon, shouldn't he? I can wait here with you until he gets back."

"No, we don't have to go anywhere," said Katie. She had gotten to her knees and was inching toward Hannah in a slow, lustful crawl. "The party is... *all here.*"

"What do you *mea*—?"

A kiss, soft and full, met Hannah's lips, interrupting her innocent question. It wasn't like the rough, impersonal kisses Katie had administered to her before Michael's departure. These lips, ripened with the confidence of mind-altering drugs, were fully dedicated to their quest of both finding and bequeathing affection.

How soft. How delicate.

Hannah began kissing back. The reciprocation took control of Katie, and pulling herself away from Hannah's face, she studied her closed eyes. Kissing the sealed lids that covered the windows to Hannah's hopeful soul, Hannah opened them, revealing to Katie a soft submission. Acknowledging this, Katie could not contain herself, and, grabbing Hannah by her gently shaking thighs, she pulled Hannah's body toward her, her strength surprising Hannah completely.

Hannah felt the same tingling feeling that she got from her daydreams of Jordan earlier.

But this is real. This can happen.

As Katie pulled Hannah close, Hannah voluntarily wrapped her legs around Katie's waist, using them to hold her in a vice grip between them.

Katie leaned down to Hannah, kissing her. Fighting her inner thoughts of shame, Hannah wrapped the frame of Katie's face with her shaking, uncertain hands. Katie turned and kissed the insides of Hannah's hands, making sure to give each finger its own special attention as she stimulated Hannah. The drugs were forcing Hannah to act against her nature, but by those same effects, she did not care and just went with the flow.

Hannah could practically feel steam filling the air around them.

So hot….

So 'Jordan', all over again…. Fuck it. Here's to new experiences. Fucking drugs. What a stupid yet amazing….

Hannah threw her head back, moaning in soft ecstasy as Katie kissed her body. She was a comfortable stranger to Hannah, and if she lost Katie, she truly lost nothing. The same was not true of her blonde friend.

Might help to get the 'poison' out of my system so I can better talk to Jordan later. Less chemical emotion might mean more practicality.

She banished these thoughts, fearing another drug-induced, sad silence.

Taking control, she let her red-headed counterpart's hands continue their pleasurable work. As her intentions changed with her increasing desire, Hannah reached for Katie's pants, which were still not fully secured from their earlier failed exploits. Katie began to kiss Hannah's exposed neck. As Katie's exhales became steadily heavier on Hannah's neck, she became steadily more aroused, the two of them driving each other to the brink of nearly incurable insanity.

Katie's flower moistened, as did Hannah's, and the two of them were losing themselves completely within the moment and each other. A garden had begun to blossom between them.

This is what I've been craving. No strings. No man to break my focus. No friends to lose. This is now. This is incredible. This… is perfect.

Katie moved to Hannah's feet, tearing off her pants, somehow leaving Hannah's shoes on her feet. Katie looked at the pink socks and the pink panties that matched them.

"My, my, Hannah. You are a stunner. Look at these perfect legs…. Such pretty knees…."

Hannah motioned to speak, but her words were replaced instead with a gasp as Katie began to kiss Hannah's immaculate thighs. The excitement this caused forced Hannah to moan in an increasing crescendo of rhythm. This in turn caused Katie's mouth to speed up its lust-filled work.

Hannah could take no more. Pushing Katie from her, she tore off her own shirt and bra. Katie helped her to remove her pink panties. Whipping her head and her hair in the same motion, Katie tossed Hannah's underwear on the bed near them. Hannah then pushed Katie to her back, and as she crawled upon Katie, Hannah pulled her counterpart's pants off completely. The thong that Katie wore struck a nerve within Hannah that lay somewhere between adoration and lust. She quickly administered intimate kisses of her own, applying their gentle, loving texture to the most sensitive part of Katie's body.

"You're quite the natural, you beautiful bitch," Katie moaned.

The gall in Katie's tone was the final straw for Hannah.

That's enough foreplay… bitch.

Hannah grabbed Katie by her hands and lifted her up, resulting ultimately in the two of them seated, their naked bodies facing each other in the honesty of the veiling shadows. As Katie's hand crept between Hannah's thighs, Hannah explored Katie's secret place as well, and as they shared their secrets with one another, something unknown and forbidden began to form. Hannah felt connected for once. She felt completely free, imprisoned as she was by passion.

With their hot, unified breathing, they took one another to new, ever-increasing heights. Their hips began to gyrate with the coming climaxes, and the rhythm of their movement only made the air around them more humid. A heavy mixture of feminine pleasure filled Hannah's nostrils. Hannah quickened her pace and sharpened her accuracy.

Katie leaned in, the pulse of Hannah's hand making the smooth connection of a kiss difficult. Eventually their lips met, Katie's tongue reaching Hannah's, her thighs clenching as Katie's hand simultaneously found the center of Hannah's flower, prodding it with sensitive fervor. Hannah returned the favor, and after seconds of concentrated, selfless pleasure-giving, both girls were rewarded as they reached their synchronized peak.

Hannah exploded inside, letting out a scream of satisfaction.

"That's a good girl," Katie said, exhausted.

How long has Michael been gone?

Both of their bodies clenched and shook amid the ebbing shockwave of their shared climax. They released each other from their passionate grips, opting to embrace one another's shaking, perspiring bodies as the waves of pleasure steadily faded. They lay beside each other in silence, placing little romantic pecks all over each other's faces, their hands clasped in mutual compassion and companionship.

"That was…." Hannah drifted.

"Perfect," Katie said. "Damn, that felt great."

I can't believe that just happened!

"Now, I *really* need a cigarette!" Katie said, laughing, her voice shaking slightly still.

"I could go for one, too," Hannah said. She looked around, finding a pack lying on the floor.

Michael must've left these behind. Silly man.

"Here," Hannah said.

"Where did you—?"

"No questions."

"Thank you," said Katie. "This should help me get back down to earth."

Why would an angel ever want to be a part of this hell?

Hannah lit two cigarettes, handing Katie one as she kept the other. Katie took the cigarette, a grateful expression spreading over her face.

"So, when were you gonna tell me that you had some?" Katie asked, blowing a cloud of smoke into the air.

"To be honest, I'd completely forgotten about them," she said.

Lies.

"I got lost in the moment," she continued, "but I'm glad it happened this way."

Truth.

Hannah's private world was being shared with this girl, and the honesty was becoming nearly too much for Hannah to accept. Katie giggled again—that same giggle that only Michael could once bring out of her. It spoke of connection. It spoke of something real. It was no longer a nuisance but a comfort to Hannah.

"You're pretty great, Hannah," said Katie. "That was the best I've ever had with a girl. I'm sure the disappointment with Michael didn't hurt, but I can't blame him, and besides, you just… I don't know how to say it!"

"I had no idea I had that in me," Hannah blushed. "Maybe this stuff isn't so bad after all." She was looking at the drug-dusted book near them. "Though I'm sure I'll regret that decision later."

"You won't regret it," Katie said. "Now, cuddle me 'til Michael gets back. You've got me good to go for another round with him."

So, am I just some pastime until what you want really comes along?

"I don't know," Hannah said, exhaling a large cloud of smoke.

Katie's eyes followed the cloud as it billowed into the air. She studied it as it lingered, floating above them, as did Hannah.

Up, up, and away….

"If you don't know, then let me teach you," Katie whispered, drawing Hannah's willing face back to her own.

There they sat in naked silence, smoking. The quiet din of the party outside was a world growing increasingly distant—the reality in which Hannah was trapped—a distant, private daydream from the harshness of the real world beyond the walls of the bedroom.

Their secret embraces in the dark meant the entirety of the world to Hannah. She had upset herself and Jordan earlier with her overzealous pursuits, and in the comfort of a stranger, Hannah was finding what she had wanted all along—the thing that had driven her to compromise a beautiful, untainted friendship with the one she loved most.

Perhaps now, with a clear head, she could address the wedge that she had driven between herself and Jordan, her fantasy realized, and she was coming to understand that this was something to not truly be shared, in honesty, with one so close to her heart as Jordan.

Fantasy should stay fantasy.

Now that her reckless lust had been satisfied, there was nothing to prevent her from mending the gap and making whole again what had been broken through the impact of her unchecked, untamed emotions.

Katie laid her head upon Hannah's chest, both enjoying the quiet of each ˏother's comfortable company. Both girls finished their cigarettes, putting them out in an ashtray next to the powder-peppered book.

They continued their embrace, and as they lay there in the still heat of each other's arms, the darkness moved all around them, carrying upon its currents the lingering odors and magnetism of the room within its invisible mass.

Katie giggled. Hannah smiled.

Hannah caressed Katie's soft, red hair with a slow rhythm. Katie rolled over, her body turning toward Hannah, and she curled up inside Hannah's safe embrace.

There in the dark, Hannah had become herself again, carefree, and confident, her companion giving her, in silence, all the attention that she needed. She almost forgot about Jordan. The distance from her recent problems was a healing one, and the all-too-brief sensation that she had shared with this mysteriously open-hearted girl had heralded its coming.

Hannah felt an unfamiliar appreciation for Katie in this moment.

Hands clasped intimately in loving shadows. Hearts beat irregularly, both exhausted by the past and rejuvenated by the present.

All I need—all I really need—is now.

PSALMS

MICHAEL

"All right," Michael said, closing the door. His weak, optimistic half-smile faded with the heavy truth of his thoughts.

"My god, that was awkward," came through the door in a muffled whisper, clearly from Katie's mouth.

"I'll say it was," whispered Michael into the darkness of the hallway. His thoughts became overcast.

Gotta stay positive. With drugs like this, atmosphere is everything. I need a cig… shit! I left them in there! Can't go back now. Not during girl talk. Not after something like that!

"You worthless little boy! Can't get it up?! What's wrong with you? What the hell?" I'm sure that's what they're saying right now….

I can just hear them. I need Ari. This is awful.

Michael made for the game room that he had visited earlier, taking a pack of cigarettes for himself and one for his host friend. Pocketing them, he made his way to the bathroom.

After finishing his business, he washed his hands, splashing his face when he finished. He used a nearby towel to dry his hands and face, and looking into his own face in the mirror, he began to feel a change come over him. His body began to tingle, and though he could not decide why, his face appeared different—foreign—to himself.

The mushrooms! I forgot all about those! Gotta move before I get weird!

Michael did not move.

He stood for several moments, eyeing his reflection with a stern, curious expression. His facial contours began to move, though in which direction, he could not decide. In the mirror, he became separated from the background, and the colors in the room began to intensify in hue. In an optimistic panic, he decided to escape this scene of self-exploration. Tearing his eyes away from himself, Michael turned to leave the room, bursting quietly into the hallway.

Can't take those waters back to them, after all. I'm sure they can find them. I've got to get the hell out here!

"Shit, it's dark out here!" he whispered to himself. He could see the stairs lit by a subtle light coming from the first floor. As he took his first step toward his way of escape, however, he was distracted by a sound that he was not entirely sure he had heard.

Moaning… a girl's moan. No, two girls! Katie and Hannah? Without me? That is so hot. Go back? No. Don't. Oh well, I got what I needed. Why shouldn't they? Damn, if I'd only not been so weak!

Positive thoughts, man! Think positive! You're a badass. Don't let this one thing get you down. It's the drugs, Michael. Hell, man, you're talking to yourself.

Michael laughed in a hollow tone.

Oh, well. Plenty out there. I'm coming, Ari.

He shrugged his shoulders, regret lingering on his skin, and made his way for the stairs.

As he looked from the landing down to the floor below, the steps began to stretch away from him, making them seem infinite.

Damn… that's not very good, is it?

He took up the challenge, stepping carefully onto the first step as if he had no trust in its stability.

So far, so good….

He continued his descent from the ever-distancing summit. Halfway down the stairs, a duo of people passed him, and his eyes followed them suspiciously.

"Hello," he said, trying his best to keep calm. They responded, but Michael could not hear them, and as his eyes followed them, he found himself looking up at the stairs behind him, becoming enthralled as they stretched up and onward, ever reaching into the worsening darkness above.

Holy shit, that's scary. Scary and… awesome!

Michael took a few more cautious steps toward the floor below, his courage increasing with each downward stride. With three steps left, which seemed like many more to Michael, he leaped with awkward composure, landing on his feet loudly and clumsily at the bottom.

"Made it," he said. He thought he could hear the echo of his own voice.

Smoothing his shirt and slapping his face, he made for the back door, bumping into guests here and there, apologies following as he continued his escape. Once outside the back door, Michael took a breath, drew out his pack of cigarettes, and, packing them with his palm, selected one of them, placing it quickly within his lips. He paused to look around.

So many people… empty…. I wonder what's in there, the collective interior? Look at them all—all these sheep, the pitiful, mindless things. What is their purpose? Do I even have one myself? Am I a sheep?

Michael looked into the sky. The distant clouds from earlier were no longer distant as they loomed, billowing nearly unnoticeably over the darkness of the social collective.

No god there. Only clouds.

Things must be imagined before they are created. Even the artist, with his uncertain instinctual brush, going with nothing but a mental flow, must somehow see his creation in his mind before it is born, even if for but a fraction of a second. God may not be real, and therefore, this world would be no creation but simply just a 'thing'. But then again, if Ari is the artist, and God is his unrealized painting, does that make him any less real? War, friendship…? Even the idea of God forges these things, so is God real in that sense? He or she even seems to have quite a grip on the world. Some ideas can be just ideas—and can be dangerous all the same.

But what of peace? Peace is no danger at all. But what if the idea of peace…. No—those thoughts are for evil people. Good and evil, even morality itself, can exist without a god. This world is a self-devouring cannibal. Look at these people—laughing, flirting, kissing, drinking…. All in hopes of devouring each other. Whether God is real or not, we are made of dust, be it of dirt or of stars, and when we die, we return. Is that all we are? Bits of earth that can reflect upon themselves? Maybe this is where the idea of belonging comes from—bits of separated earth searching to recombine with themselves.

"But we can fathom so much more!" Michael spoke aloud, garnering the attention of a few standing nearby. "Sorry," he said, returning his sights to the sky overhead. They resumed their conversation.

Sorry for what? For thinking? 'They' should apologize to 'you'. At least you understand what they are. Not a single deep thought among them, I'll wager.

We all may be dirt, but some dirt is better than other dirt. Some are barren soil, unable to reconnect. Some dirt grows things and becomes things like mud, and the imagination of a hopeful child makes a mud pie with its hands. Even the useless dirt has purpose, then. Like a cemetery, the soil separating the living from the dead…. But people—people are dirt, Michael? Then we all, alive and deceased, are simply separated by other people—those either existing or unrealized—the dirt in between. Even the dead still exist, regardless of whether in the past or not. The only thing that makes the past, present, and future different from one another is….

The only thing that makes the past, present, and future different from one another is—timing. They exist on different temporal planes. If we can fathom 'future'—future—currently fathom it—then, like an idea, an idea alone, it does exist, which means that it 'is' existing, making it the present! The purpose of the past is to teach us this sole lesson—the lesson of the dead and dying. But then, aren't we all dead? Past, present, and future.... What has happened, the happening and the soon-to-occur.... Aren't we all dead, then? Aren't we all just… just dirt and dust?

Ideas, soil, present, possibility, separation; reality, dust, future, potential, togetherness—Life and Death.

Michael then noticed how moist the filter of his cigarette had become as it lingered in his silent mouth.

If I can imagine these things, then they, whether dangerous or beneficial, are real. They are? Yes, yes they are. All the inventions of the world exist, if only as a thought in someone's mind at first. Then, if God is a thought, great! Back to this again.... If God is a thought alone, surely he exists to some degree, if only in the ideas bred by imagination. That's it! But if it—God—is an idea, even solely a thought in Ari's mind, then he hasn't been created yet, which could mean—damn, my mind is going crazy! Michael, what are you getting at?!

Reset. Okay.

If we are ideas, and God is an idea, either neither of us exists or we both do, one reliant on the other. We exist, so God must, in some form. But who created whom? Which came first? Michael, why are you thinking these things?

At any rate....

Michael drew his lighter out of his pocket, lighting his cigarette, which had become very wet with its time spent between his lips.

If we are dirt and God is dirt, then we are God—dirt creating dirt, a self-manifestation of the other. But if that is true, then God is fragile. God is stardust. God is stardust as we are earth dust, and so delicately do we both thrive within that balance.

But couldn't a god do better than mere sand? Couldn't he do better than to put us by the billions on the beach, only to wash us away? And why so wrathful an ocean? What storm could churn such fury, such rage? Perhaps he hasn't yet realized his full power. Perhaps we were created from a reckless idea.

In the face of the slightest tide, we drift. Yes, we drift. Out into a Great Nothing.

But alas—damn it all!—we drift back into God. Once again, it's all conjoined. Either water or dirt, we are one and God the other, co-dependent. If we consider the idea of God itself, in our consideration, he does exist. Yet if we are an idea in 'his' head, 'we' thrive. And since one or the other must outlast the other into eternity, the idea of the other—despite space or time—lives on. We are both immortal.

And yet, either way, one or the other, humans or God, dirt or water, we are conjoined perpetually. And where the water and the dirt meet—mud. Yet all we do is devour ourselves, churning in a meaningless abyss, whether we're sand by the ocean or dust floating alongside other imagined dust in the empty cosmos....

We are all dead, then.

We are all dirt. We are the dead dirt of the past, the soil bearing seeds in the present, and the dust yet to settle as it lingers into the future.

We are all dead. We are all dust.

Yes, we are dirt, and in the cemetery of eternity, there sits God—a great child—making mud pies on his own grave....

Thunder rumbled through the air, stronger than before, and it caused Michael to recover consciousness of the world around him beyond his deepening thoughts that twisted and unfolded within.

Coming to, he found himself at the edge of the tree line.

"What the hell? When did I get here?"

A wave of emotion washed over him, and as he stood there alone, tears began to accompany his lonely eyes.

What is happening to me? You're on drugs, man. Calm down. This isn't you. This isn't you! Where is this coming from? Is it insecurity? Come now, Michael Law, you've had plenty of ladies, you stud, you. It's only the drugs. These little stupid things can't get you down. Ari will cheer you up. Find Ari. Suck it up, champ.

Michael lit yet another cigarette, staring into the sky and wondering when he had discarded his last cigarette as he exhaled a small cloud.

"Thanks for putting this *God* garbage into my head, Ari. You're making these mushrooms suck for me," he said to himself.

Well, let's get a move on....

Michael stepped out onto the path with unsure yet determined feet. His heightened senses were making him sensitive to the dropping temperature and the increasing feeling of moisture in the air. He shivered with a chill as thunder once again rumbled overhead.

ARI

I was becoming lost in Jordan and her glorious glow as she defied the darkness. She defied me. As God is fire, I was also fire, a miniature representation of His massive fervor. She came at me in echoing silence, like a fiery ocean, wave after wave after wave.

If I even were this idea of fire I so adamantly held to—that I held *her* to—then the meeting of us and these metaphors would cause great calamity, an explosion of the original kind. We were both combined and condemned to that burning abyss, we both becoming gods destroyed by our own creation.

Destruction.

Rebirth.

But after fire comes water. The fire cools. The moisture builds. The air condenses. And then life happens. Sometimes, it happens all at once.

The heat between us was palpable and in the little universe that had formed around us, a tiny world was being born. In our silence, the heat had settled, the bonfire had begun to dim, and as it cooled, a little Earth—a *tiny* world—began to form, gathering in the nothing, drawn to itself and its own desire to exist—a world Jordan and I could share in my mind and in my heart. I homed in on that very Earth where I made settlement, and I sat in waiting, watching—watching like I was God.

The wine began to take hold on my senses at last, and I became even more lost, drifting.

Drifting in the newly formed ocean, a refreshing result of the quieting chaos.

In my pursuit of human beauty, I had lost sight of things supernatural, and all I saw was Jordan, the 'new world' becoming the space between us and where we now dwelled. More imagined time passed, and we were suddenly islands far out in the vastness of unexplored waters. The ocean that separated was an ocean known as God. I decided to brave that ocean's unpredictable wrath—my intoxicated mind slurring the judgment of my good heart—forcing my hand to set my fear of the supernatural aside so that I could be closer to her.

Jordan…. His Jordan….

And I would take her from Him!

I would crash into her. I would detach myself from the bedrock of the Earth itself. I would defy the matter that made me, the forces that moved me, and the Hands that molded us to urge myself across those invisible waters. Crashing into her, we would make a continent, one landform of two, knowing that we had moved mountains across existence to be together—this settlement of the violent clash that, retrospectively, would come to be our meeting.

Ari, you are full of words tonight. Maybe if you spoke them to her she would—

No. I'm watching. I am waiting.

The static from her stone-hard, distant gaze met with the gathering storm overhead. Thunder rumbled as my eyes met the eyes of the sky. They peered right through me. I could feel an increase in moisture in the air and a drop in temperature. The storm was almost here.

What I would do to kiss you in the rain, Jordan. It's like our Eden, in pieces, falling all around us, bringing life to what calamity has turned to ash. I, your Adam, kissing his Eve, camouflaged in verdant innocence.

But rain has destroyed the earth before, too.

And how I stand here, like a predator in agonizing patience. How we stand here like we're waiting for an ark. She is so much more enticing than these metaphors you've made her into. But I…. No, don't put her on a pedestal. At least don't let her see you do it, Ari.

I looked at my watch, my vision full of color yet blurry.

Wait, that can't be right…. Fifteen minutes of silence?! A quarter of an hour of just standing here?! Maybe she's lost interest. Maybe I should say more. But what? What do I say? But she hasn't left. You haven't scared her, Ari. Maybe this is what she needs. Women—they treat every man like their father. They come running to you and sit on your lap, asking with that girlish charm for whatever they desire or need from you. Once they get it, they run off again, only to return when the need arises once more. But that's just how you have to do it. You have to give them what they need, when they need it. When they run away, you have to let them, for only by giving them freedom are you truly giving them your heart, because no matter what, if your heart is with her and you set her free, then your heart is free—and if it's truly hers to have, then she, along with that heart of yours, will return, loving you more for the faith you've shown to both of them.

I was standing on the shore of that peace, peering out into the brooding darkness that hovered there, where the ocean depths met the night horizon. The mystery of their meeting was my downfall. Curious as it was beautiful, this moment, like its metaphor, was all that stood between us. It was magic. It was mystery. She was both. I was becoming neither.

I looked out into that ocean that, once an idea, had become real to me. I began to swim. For all my fear, I dove in. I wanted to beat the tide at its own game, the fear of the tide washing me away against my will, losing my 'self' within her crests and troughs.

After all, how can I offer her anything if I give it all away? But I can't know her value by simply looking. No, I have to jump in headfirst. Only by testing the waters can we judge their resolve. A calm surface may hide a violent undertow. A collection of crashing waves may be the playfulness of kindred dolphins. Sometimes, depths do not reveal their true selves to the eyes alone.

I needed to think on these things, but as I was swimming in my imagination, my thoughts were keeping pace, arrhythmic, and panicked like my staggered breath. In the depths of my soul, I began clawing and scraping and needed to be on dry land once again—secure, standing, and back to the world that contained the glow and heat of the bonfire.

Thunder rumbled through the trees. A breeze moved the spirit of the forest and the branches shivered in respectful fear.

It woke me up from my daydream.

I've been trapped in these symbols and ideas for hours! You aren't getting to know her by thinking about how wonderful she might be, tired philosopher. Talk to her. Even if she is comfortable, don't become boring.

The wine had made me euphoric and clumsy, and my thoughts of everything—Jordan included—may have only been a way to give meaning to myself. I thought for a moment that God's voice—that adamant electricity in the atmosphere—was chasing me. Maybe it was, or maybe it was not, but to feel spoken to in such a way….

Ari….

"Ari!"

I tried ignoring Him.

"What, *God?*" I said.

Embarrassed by my outburst, I looked immediately to Jordan, who turned in a curiosity that was eager but nonjudgmental. A glimmer in her eyes cured my anxiety.

"*God*, man? Ari, it's me, Michael!"

My intoxication was more severe than I thought. In the darkness and a veil of foolishness over my eyes, I had not even noticed that Michael had returned, yet even as I looked Michael dead in his shadowy face, Jordan's was all I saw. I somewhat regained my composure giving my friend the attention he so desperately sought.

In his eyes was a look of great, uncertain terror, a paranoia that I had never seen in him before. The drugs seemed to be doing their best work on him, and reflecting on my deep-thinking silence from before, I had to admit that I was caught up in something similar.

"Ari, so what's up? I'm fucking tripping my face off, man!" he said. "We gotta go!"

"Go?" I turned to Jordan in anticipation of her reaction and watched as she watched us, her concern obvious. The shock of Michael's rude entry seemed to distract Jordan from whatever thoughts were tormenting her.

"Go?" Jordan said. "Go where?"

Her voice sounded so fragile. Perhaps, in my silence, I had wounded her. Maybe she was waiting for me to take charge.

Waiting for me to be a damned man!

"We aren't going anywhere, sweetheart," I said, turning back to Michael.

"The hell we aren't, Ari," he said. "It isn't safe here! Everything's twisted and… and—!"

"But I live here, Michael!" The simplicity of my words seemed to shake him, bringing him back to the real world.

"Oh…. Right…."

"You need to calm down, Michael! You're scaring her. And you're embarrassing *me*!"

"Girl? Oh, that girl over there?" he said, pointing directly at Jordan.

"Michael! Please!"

"Oh, oh right. Sorry. I'm a bit skewed," he said. "Those 'shrooms are doing a number on me—"

"Please, *shut up, will you*!" I hissed.

He exhaled heavily, his shoulders hunching. I knew he was either having a great or terrible time. I could see those dilated pupils, even in the shadows that kept hidden much of his face. I turned back to Jordan.

"Jordan, I am so sorry about all this. I don't—"

"Jordan. Hello, I'm Michael," Michael said, intercepting my conversation completely. He stood there with his hand out, but Jordan did not seem to notice. Her misty eyes—in all their cruel beauty—were focused unapologetically on me. In that moment, I decided in all her imperfect complexity, that I truly did love her.

She was the first girl I had ever met who didn't write me off for my benevolent adversary's fake-tall-handsome charm. I just stared at her—*into* her—and I only did this per the invitation of her warm, clear eyes. I felt a chill, and then a rush of heat, and suddenly, time stopped. Jordan, stock-still, was staring into me. I became frozen by her warm gaze, somehow, Michael becoming shocked at her cold demeanor toward him—a rejection he did not often experience. For once, I forgot all about our friendly rivalry. I was to ignore all those negative ghosts that haunted my life in this realm, and it was all because of Jordan. She knew it, too, and I knew that she knew it, because I saw in her face the reflections of my own expression—hope, reticence, and awe.

Her eyes became teary once again, but a smile, broad and bright, accompanied them this time—that sole image immediately becoming my favorite memory of my entire life, like a wound instantly cauterized. In one fleeting second, she became my favorite scar, and the pain and the healing were simultaneous. It was ecstasy.

Jordan looked down at Michael's outstretched hand, then back into the fire.

"Well, okay…." Michael said, turning to me, shrugging.

"No, I'm sorry. Michael, is it?" Jordan said, keeping her eyes on the fire. "I don't mean to be rude. It's nice to meet you."

"It's okay," he said. "I'm Ari's friend, not some stranger."

Michael embraced me quickly, his arm that was nearer me resting in a protective fashion on my shoulders. I welcomed the big-brother companionship, despite the doubts I had toward its genuineness. I had to keep Michael calm or he would ruin everything.

Still, Jordan's presence quelled my anxiety. Everything felt so good—the heat of the fire versus the heat in Jordan's eyes, her deep resistance versus Michael's comforting touch of loyalty—and I was adamant toward protecting that very feeling. He was being nice, simply for the sake of kindness, for once. He seemed to have no hidden agenda. Very little was mysterious about Michael in this moment, and what a refreshing change it was. I felt honesty radiating from him, but then I came to the realization that his drug-induced fear was real. Michael never let his guard down, ever.

Jordan turned back to me, her smile mimicking the grin that stretched stupidly across my face. Michael saw her smile and then looked at me, confused, as he realized she had made me her focus. He laughed a comical laugh, releasing me from his comforting grip.

"Oh! I see!" he said. "Ari's found himself a girlfriend!"

A look of shock spread across her face as she turned back to the flames. This inebriated wretch of a confidant was beginning to use other tactics to push her away from me.

Schoolyard bullshit….

If you can't have her, no one can, right, Michael?

Michael was becoming obvious, and I began to feel insecure in thinking he was trying to make me act foolishly, as if to lose her, so that he could look better to her, in lieu of making me out to be insecure.

This fucking game of mental chess. Yet I'm the only one with something—someone—to lose. Fuck this. Damn you, Michael.

I could see her embarrassment, which brought me both comfort and anger. I hated how his statement had affected her. I loved that I knew what that meant. I tried forcing a laugh to dilute the discomfort of the air.

"Michael, come now," said my inner host. "We were just talking."

"Talking?!" Michael exclaimed. "Neither of you have said a damn word since I got here!" He lit a cigarette, exhaling through his cheeky smile.

Now I found myself blushing. I could feel the heat in my cheeks and forehead. I was out of polite excuses for Michael.

Jordan spoke.

"Yes, we were just talking, or not. It doesn't mat—"

Jordan's last word hung half-spoken in her throat. Some thought, some recollection, stopped her mid-speech, and I dreaded what her bravery may have cost her—what her bravery may have cost *us.* Sympathy exploded from me in my affection for her.

"Jordan, don't—"

"Ari, it's fine," she interrupted. "I have a lot to think about." With that, she turned and made a quick exit onto the path toward the house.

"But, Jordan, wait!" I called, the echo of my voice pushing her further with every wave of sound. I motioned to go after her, but Michael held me.

"Let her go," he said. "If you care like I know you do, let her go. The night's not over yet."

His philosophy was gold. My ears of silver knew its value. My iron heart softened to the sound of his truth.

"But damn it, Michael! What a gem she is!"

Without missing a beat, Michael handed me the pack of cigarettes he brought me, saying, "I'm sure she is, but whatever is weighing on her mind, she needs to face it alone. She knows what it's like to be around you. You were awkward at best, but she stuck around. That's got to mean something, eh?" Michael laughed to himself. "She's felt the heat," he said, pointing to the fire. "Let her remind herself of what it's like without you again. Let her remember the cold."

Brilliant, Michael…. Just brilliant…. I'm not a fan of your actions, but you are right. Maybe you weren't playing games, after all. I need to calm down. I am not the insecure type. What's worse, you not being mindful of how what you've done has affected me, or me letting you affect my life, in the first place? I need to be stronger. You're right.

His last words calmed me in a most salubrious manner. As Michael released his grip from me, I slid the cigarette pack into my pocket as I became wholly catatonic. I watched in hopeful misery as Jordan disappeared into the darkness of the path toward my house, becoming increasingly further and farther away from me.

A silent tear coursed down my cheek.

I missed her already.

I felt weak for so intensely missing someone that I knew so very little about.

JORDAN

Jordan was miles away, her feet firmly planted in the earth, her mind aloft in the graceful palms of a resolute, elegant breeze. She felt quite comfortable with being torn between earth and sky. She counted herself as one of the stars, those distant glimmers caught in the absolute embrace of nothing, and it had been this Ari—this well-spoken mystery—whose modest, silent, emotional honesty had elevated her.

She could not speak.

She only waited.

Ari…. Oh, Ari….

"Ari. Ari!"

A man appeared from out of nowhere. Jordan continued staring into the fire. She had no interest in giving this man any attention. She wanted Ari. She was not Hannah. She did not distort or bend to achieve her desires. She stayed true to her honest intentions.

She ignored what he had said next. She could hear only the distant echoes of panic in his tone, the words muffled in a panicked din. She lost herself in the opera that was, this time, that man, playing the chaotic score that reflected, in words unheard, the dull quintessence of her thoughts—whatever those thoughts were. As she pulled herself from her swoon, Ari's voice became clear to her as she looked intently upon him.

"Go?" said Ari, his eyes locked upon her.

Jordan shivered.

She had to know that her attraction to Ari was not grossly in spite of her loneliness. She had to know that, in his great wealth, this comical honesty she had come to know was not a routine—a mask—that her handsome host wore to woo his prey.

"Go? Go where?" asked Jordan, unblinkingly.

He could be a wolf. But I don't see it….

"We aren't going anywhere, sweetheart," Ari said.

No one ever sees the wolf coming. Sheepskin, teeth, and death. That's it.

Ari turned to his friend. Jordan turned back to the fire, its crackling voice whispering to her as, once again, the rusty opera that was this friendly stranger's voice took over the private grove.

But even wolves fear fire.

Wolves. Fear. Fire.

Time passed as she pondered this thought, accentuated by a distant voice. She returned to the real world, summoned by the sound of her name. It sounded like a dying reverberation, crawling to her ear from miles away.

Jordan....

It was Ari. She heard no hunger in his bark. She feared no teeth ready to bite.

"Jordan, I am so sorry about all this. I don't—"

Jordan returned to reality, confused and curious. She was clueless, given her recently drifting mind, as to why he would even have a reason to apologize. She did not care, for her own sake at least, for someone else owed her an apology—someone whose carelessness had driven her to tears and insecurity and self-doubt.

This party, where she had met someone real, who did not have to speak to inform her of who he was, was somehow revealing to her a purpose for her struggles, healing her as time went on.

Your ex-douchebag was a smooth talker, wasn't he? Pah! Disgusting. But this Ari.... It's so simple with him. I suppose I should be thankful. Well, okay, then. But still... his apology....

She became curious, her curiosity interrupted as Ari's friend crudely introduced himself.

"Jordan, hello, I'm Michael."

She detected his wool disguise. She heard his famished jaws.

Jordan looked past the carnivore, right into the hopeful eyes of the man behind him. She ignored the desperate maw that she felt so lasciviously craved to devour her.

Tears welled up behind her eyes in her fear of Michael's intent. His tone felt devious to her, though she tried to ignore it. Tears gathered in her desperation for Ari to rescue her; and it was all too much for one moment—one night. Ari's face was stern but soft. She could hear the heart that, despite the strength of its rhythm, was still so eager to listen. She looked at the hand that lingered—held out for her to shake—though she wished for the touch from another. She peered back into the fire for answers.

"Well, okay…." said Michael. His voice sounded deflated. Jordan felt rude, though it was only her strength that made her behave this way.

"I'm sorry. Michael, is it?" She kept her eyes on the fire while speaking. "I don't mean to be rude. It's nice to meet you."

"It's okay," Michael said. "I'm Ari's friend, not some stranger."

The wolf, luring me in, even with its tail between its legs….

Jordan broke from her thoughts. She looked away from the penetrating, reflective face of the fire and looked once more at Ari, a smile resisting her resistance, an obvious happiness claiming her visage. The smile he returned made only more concrete the smile she had worn. They reflected each other, mirrors to each other's sense of wonder and happiness.

"Oh! I see! Ari's found himself a girlfriend!" Michael said.

Typical 'wolf' bullshit…. Whimpering when defeated. You passive-aggressive bastard…. I could never give myself to anyone like you, ever, ever again!

Jordan could feel her face turning red as she shot her eyes to the ground. She stared at her dirty, crimson heels as her face grew to feel just as red, her anger at Michael's move to ruin this moment feeling just as filthy.

Her attention was claimed by the fire once more.

A chuckle, barely audible, escaped Ari's lips.

The confidence…. The quiet confidence….

"Michael, come now," Ari said. "We were just talking."

We aren't 'just talking,' Ari. We are communicating. Even if it is just talking, at least you are talking with me, not at me.

"Talking?" Michael said.

Yes. And no.

"Neither of you have said a damn word since I got here!" Michael said. He lit a cigarette that dangled in the loose embrace of his smug smile.

Yes. And no. Or… is it… yes or no? Oh, I don't know! But, if I don't choose, I can still choose. If I decide to not decide, I have only possibilities. And possibility does not yield to consequence!

Jordan knew that Ari was beginning to feel at least a tinge of embarrassment from the uncouth behavior of his guest—his supposed friend. She could hear the embarrassment in Ari's voice, though he covered it well as he spoke to the wolf, calming the beast before he had to kill him.

Jordan decided to spare Ari the choice of murder or mercy. She spoke up.

"Yes, we were just talking," she said.

But it isn't simply talking! Michael's right on that account. We've barely said a thing, yet I feel I know him so well. I feel him, and that's all I care about.

"Or not," she added in lieu of her recent realization.

But it is! It is so much more! Ari, you have no idea! Michael! You are even more clueless. Even though I am a bit vulnerable tonight, it doesn't matter. It doesn't matter!

"It doesn't mat—" Jordan said, her thoughts making themselves physical and heard despite her intention to keep them buried inside. She caught herself before she could finish her sentence, the lie of *'it doesn't matter'* self-destructing as it passed her lips, dying and fading before it could poison Ari's soft heart.

Because it does *matter! This night and the fire that illuminates it. Ari, you are the night—dark and calm and beautiful. And I will be your star, bringing a new day. Without your vastness in which I thrive, I am merely burning fuel, burning in, and for, nothing. But you give me a stage, make me your actress, and watch in silent awe. I see how you look at me. Why, I haven't seen such longing since—*

—Damn it! Damn it all! I need time to think! Or time to not think at all…. How the fire draws me in…. I have to escape this fire. It makes me linger and ensnares my attention.

Ari pulled her mind from her thoughts as she spoke.

"Jordan, don't—" he started, but Jordan's mind was caught between two men like a planet trapped between the orbit of binary stars. She was pulled in two directions, her lack of control stirring in her that old panic that she had not felt since kissing Hannah earlier. Michael's presence was not helping matters.

Hannah! I'd almost forgotten you! We have so much to discuss. I'm so sorry, Hannah. That was all so much. But you're still my best friend. It was bound to happen eventually. These times, they aren't easy…. I shouldn't have taken it so personally. Maybe it's my own damned guilt…. I shouldn't penalize you for the way the world is—the human condition.

"Ari, its fine," Jordan said, cutting off Ari's expression of anxiety, an anxiety Michael had implanted. She had much to consider and would continue her time with Ari later. She had bridges to mend. How else would she get him safely to his destination that was her heart? The many chasms that scarred the path to her soul—her innermost self—were better left repaired than their destruction explained. Besides, she was trapped again in a hurricane of logic and emotion, 'Mind' and 'Heart' being the two stars that quarreled in cosmic combat to win her. She once more felt a desire to—if only for a while—

escape.

Only one could listen in such a way that she so desperately needed, and that one was Hannah.

"I have a lot to think about," she said.

Jordan looked back to the fire. Fighting its attempts to captivate her once again, Jordan fled, Ari calling after her.

"But Jordan, wait!" he said.

It was painful for her to leave him in this fashion, but it was better to have the pain of the needle now for the cure of the future. If she did not resolve the complex equation that expanded by the moment in her heart, she would hurt him, and that alone would mean hurting herself.

Jordan cared for Ari. She knew it the moment she stepped away. *But why?*

The questions that boiled beneath her skin would be answered in time. For now, she had wounds to heal, and the scars they were to yield would speak of resilience—Jordan's newfound will to fight, and fight on—even if she was wrong.

She made for the path, her steps surer and more confident than when she had arrived. She was a different person altogether. Rather, she was the same person, only a more certain, refined version of who she was before, shedding bits that once clung to her that hid the true 'Jordan' that lay dormant beneath.

MICHAEL

Michael's head was an ashen heap of viscous epiphanies as he walked like a shadow into the fire's grove. At first, the fire summoned Michael's attention, but as his dreading of its power welled up inside him, he was reminded of the substances that induced this fear; and the fingers of that fear gripped him, dragging him further into paranoia. It was not until the fire appeared to begin melting into the earth that Michael was able to pull his eyes away, his obsessed state multiplying exponentially with each passing second amid the surrounding shadows.

As he separated his sight from the dissolving flames, his eyes were drawn to Ari, almost magnetically. Michael was at Ari's side faster than he could even realize, the world passing by as a dark, colorful blur.

"Ari," Michael said. He got no response and was immediately troubled.

Is he even real right now? Am I just seeing him? Why can't you hear me?!

"Ari!" Michael said, just shy of yelling at his host's face.

"What, God?" Ari said.

Thank god, you're real. But 'God,' Ari? Are you serious? You aren't still on about….

"God, man? Ari, it's me! Michael!"

Ari's only response was a nod of his head.

Why does he feel so empty? It's like talking to a damned mannequin!

"Ari, so what's up?" Michael said, trying to remain calm and not be overcome by his psychedelic anxiety. His own hands felt clammy to him, and he felt as though his soul would jump out of his flesh at any second. He knew that a surreal climax had yet to occur in his mind. "I'm fucking tripping my face off, man! We gotta go!"

"Go?" Ari said. The word seemed to repeat itself in space, each repetitious echo stumbling over the one before it, eternally expanding as it dimmed in intensity—falling and folding into and around itself. It was beautiful to Michael.

"Go?"

Again, that word overtook his every sense, but it was a sweeter voice.

"Go—"

Audible ecstasy….

"—where?"

The symphony stopped.

Michael looked at the pretty blonde girl that had settled his heart and infiltrated his mind.

Holy shit, what a… My god, girl. You look good enough to eat. Where I failed earlier, I will succeed with you. I swear, I would….

"We aren't going anywhere, sweetheart," said Ari.

"The hell we aren't, Ari! It isn't safe here! Everything's twisted, and—and…."

Neither is she. Oh, baby….

"But I live here, Michael," Ari said.

I mean, I know, I'm just really trying to not freak the hell out right now! Don't be a bitch, Michael. You've got this! Play along.

"Oh, right," Michael said.

Really, Michael? Really?! That's your best improv?

"You need to calm down, Michael!" Ari said.

I am calm.

"You're scaring her!" he continued.

I hope so….

"And you're embarrassing *me*!"

"Girl?" Michael said. "Oh, *that* girl over there?"

Michael, in a rude attempt at humor, pointed directly at her in a grandiose manner. Michael's crass playfulness had done its job in embarrassing Ari.

"Michael, please!"

He only ever gets embarrassed when he's being defensive. So, what is he defending? I know. classic Ari. Finds two things in common with someone he just met and the guy's ready to marry. What a damned shame. All the girls you could get with wealth and looks like that—*wasted.*

"Oh, oh right," Michael said, trying his best to hide his building, dark intent. "Sorry, I'm a bit skewed. Those 'shrooms are doing a number on me—"

I'd like to do a number or two on you, my dear. So…. So voluptuous.

"Please, shut up, will you!" Ari cried, turning to Jordan. "Jordan, I am so sorry about this. I don't—"

No need to apologize, Ari. I've got this.

"Jordan," Michael said, cutting Ari's apology short. "Hello. I'm Michael." He extended his hand in greeting to Jordan.

She seemed to not hear him or see his gesture, something he could not accept. Never had a girl so blatantly ignored him in his most distant memory. Women loved Michael, and he, lost in his own legend, could not swallow this awkward pill of defeat that Jordan had so deftly handed him.

Michael could only stand frozen in disbelief at her coldness, a chill that contrasted wildly with the heat of the adjacent fire.

He was interested. Her ignorance of him only made his interest more powerful. Between his quiet chase of pleasure and the centrifuge of his thoughts, he felt dull. All at once, he accepted his defeat in spite of his confidence, his desire, and his crumbling mind.

He looked down at the pathetic hand that lingered in suspended animation. He hated its coldness. His hand's loneliness was *his* loneliness, and as it floated in nothingness, so did he.

But you're better than this! Get it together, man!

He shrugged. "Well, okay…" Michael said, turning back to Ari.

Michael had changed form. He had gone from embarrassed to insightful; to unsure; to scared; to comfortable; to interested; to aroused—all leading to embarrassment once again. He felt deflated. He recalled the memory of his recent bedroom shame—his impotence and failure.

Jordan spoke. She did not turn to look at him, but she spoke, and it warmed him.

"No, I'm sorry. Michael, is it?" she said. "I don't mean to be rude."

But I prefer that you are rude….

"It's nice to meet you," Jordan said.

Damage control.

"It's okay," Michael said. "I'm Ari's friend, not some stranger." Saying this, Michael put his arm around Ari, the only thing that anchored him. The lustful betrayals that ebbed within were of no consequence. It was only desire. Friendship—companionship—meant so much more.

Perhaps that is what I am always chasing. Waking up next to someone is always the best part. Well, most of the time….

He laughed quietly to himself in his nervous heart.

Michael could see the way that Ari and Jordan were looking at each other. He noticed how she looked right through and past

Michael—and it gave him hope for something real—something real that would never exist for him in his fantastic world. The duality of loyalty versus jealousy confused and diluted his already chaotic wits, so he broke from his thoughts, deciding to be lighthearted and not worsen things.

"Oh! I see! Ari's found himself a girlfriend!" Michael said.

Surely this'll light old Ari up! He looks like he could use a laugh. Always so serious.

Michael's comment had embarrassed both Ari and Jordan.

Perfect. Now maybe we'll have some laughs….

"Michael, come now," Ari said. "We were just talking."

Hearts don't speak, Ari. The beat and the rhythm of their music give a canvas for the words to be painted on. And I've seen hardly a stroke stricken between the two of you.

"Talking?!" Michael said. "Neither of you have said a damn word since I got here!"

Michael internally laughed at his own joke, drawing out a cigarette and lighting it with immaculate efficiency. As he exhaled his first cloud, a smile spread across his face. Despite how he wanted Jordan—her vessel alone—he loved Ari.

Two wolves—Lust and Love—were battling for the final scrap of Michael's sanity. One would thrive and one would perish. He had no idea which one he preferred to feed.

Fuck drugs. This over-thinking is exhausting. I am Michael Law. It's not that I don't like to think.

It's just that I prefer to feel *instead.*

"Yes, we were just talking. Or not. It doesn't mat—" Jordan said, stopping abruptly.

"Jordan, don't—" Ari said.

Michael burned inside as he desired to ignite to her as well, in the vain hope that his lustful wildfire would spread.

His body was frozen.

"Ari, it's fine," she said.

The way they understand each other. Just flawless back-and-forth. Damn, Michael…. Just…. Damn…. I have a lot to think about.

"I have a lot to think about," Jordan said, her voice harmonizing with Michael's thought.

As she made her way quickly to the path in the trees, Michael stood in utter disbelief. The wolf of love was inching closer and Ari began to chase after Jordan.

"But… Jordan, wait!" he said.

Michael grabbed Ari with an athletic quickness, as though unhampered entirely by the substances that coursed through him. He held Ari for a moment, protecting Ari from himself. As the world caught up with Michael's finely tuned senses, he spoke words of heartfelt wisdom to his companion—his most-loved rival.

"Let her go," Michael said. He felt strong and devoted in saying this.

Or is jealousy rearing its ugly head?

I'm doing the best I can, whatever that means…

"If you care like I know you do, let her go," Michael said.

It's so cheesy, but it's like a butterfly—a butterfly wreathed in flame and glamour. She will be back to burn us both. And we will love her for it.

"The night's not over yet," Michael said.

Not.

Even.

Close.

"But damn it, Michael! What a gem she is…" Ari said.

A diamond. Something rarer. Something… more savory….

Michael handed me the cigarette pack he had promised me earlier.

"I'm sure she is, but whatever is weighing on her mind—" Michael said.

—hopefully me—

"—she needs to face it alone. She knows what it's like to be around you. She's felt the heat. Let her remind herself of what it's like without you again."

Ari….

"Let her remember the cold," Michael said.

Michael watched Ari's face shift from shock to contemplation and from that contemplation to a cold, harsh blankness of understanding. With that, Michael released Ari. Ari slid the cigarettes into his pocket.

The lifelessness in him now…. This is a new Ari. Whether for good or bad, what has she done to you?

Michael did not have to turn around to know that Jordan was gone. The tear that formed and forged its way down Ari's cheek told a thousand truths, and they all revolved around Jordan.

You've always been so strong, even for a sensitive one. What has she done to you?

She must be some kind of something….

HANNAH

Hannah drifted in and out of comfortable sleep.

She was at peace, opening her eyes to the dark room, the moon outside adding a subtle glow to the empty room around her.

She turned to study the resting body of the gorgeous gift of red hair that lay beside her. The low voice of thunder outside calmed her into unconscious comfort in between episodes of conscious solace.

Embracing Katie in a nurturing hold, Hannah snuggled close to her, giving and receiving warmth, yet Jordan was her last thought as she gave in to the swoon of the blissful darkness once more, falling once more into a peaceful slumber.

Jordan….

ARI

"Damn it, Michael."

MICHAEL

"I know, Ari. I know."

JORDAN

A million thoughts were rushing through Jordan's head as she traversed the shadowy path to the house. She had become jaded with her metaphorical mind. She had become jaded by the pedestal she had been placed upon—placed there by herself—along with Ari's hushed confidence in her. Her present company was herself, alone, which was precisely what she needed. As numb as she was to herself and the world, for once, loneliness felt comfortable.

Her growing contempt for her ex-lover's betrayal simmered like a potion within her, the cauldron of her heart shaking with the reactive, unstable contents within. She knew the damage he had done to her were the scars that kept her from fully giving in to her interest in Ari, and the rage of her frustrations began to boil. Her thoughts were ingredients adding themselves to the chaotic blend, resulting in a worsening amalgamation of hatred, jealousy, confusion and pain. Jordan's heart physically hurt, a knot forming in her chest as she reminisced on the man who was once hers only hours before. Now Ari had so effortlessly replaced him. Her heart and mind fought a confusing battle between each other, and she was torn between what was logical and what she felt.

She stopped halfway up the path to collect herself. Nothing seemed to comfort her—nothing except the lowering temperature and increasingly present moisture in the air. She could smell the water in the atmosphere. She knew a storm was crawling closer.

Jordan leaned against a tree, emotionally exhausted. Tears found their way to her eyes. She had such momentum around Ari, yet she had left him. Though her growing need to find and confide in Hannah was urgent, she was clueless as to why she had fled.

But this is why. That was kind of too much.... But he did next to nothing! Yeah, nothing but make you feel wanted—but Michael wanted you, clearly. But is that the kind of way I want to be wanted? The animal.... Michael, if you weren't so… so crass, maybe… just maybe…. No. To hell with that. I need someone more refined. To give in to Michael's fake charms… well, I'd be nothing but a whore! Jordan, you've got to stop this back and forth! Ari wants you. He likes you. Don't just be repelled because of your similar magnetism, you idiot!

Jordan's mind was irrational as it teetered on a dangerous ledge. To fall in love was to fall into a pit. To find balance was to prolong the struggle.

Maybe I've just never seen what love really is…. What a shame….

Ari. Damn! What do I do? My god, what do I do?!

She closed her eyes as she spoke her silent latter thought, a desperate prayer of sorts escaping her oppressed soul.

At that moment, a rain drop, single and obstinate, fell upon her nose. It ran down between her nostrils, settling in the crevice of her lips. Jordan allowed the droplet to linger for a while, letting it kiss her in the tender way that only rain can accomplish. She licked her lips, reveling in the flavor. Savoring its texture and what it may have meant, she parted her eyelids in the same slow fashion with which she closed them, her head lifting to the sky.

Jordan laughed to herself. She knew not which deity had responded, but as she saw it, her prayer had been answered, the voice of her heart finally confirmed to have been heard.

The universe, or some part of it, had given back, its voice hushed yet absolute.

So much mystery to it all. Even an answer can be without substance, I suppose. Or maybe I just don't understand. It's not like I can be outside looking in, after all. They can. They watch from beyond their cosmic window, neither time nor space being any obstacle to them. Cruel, unfeeling….

Jordan's second question—the follow-up to her initial plea—went ignored. Neither fateful drops of rain nor disembodied voices acknowledged her call. Again, she was alone. She experienced another wave of salt—a subtle one—that grazed the outer reaches of her sense of taste, her other senses forsaken by her tongue and its resurrection.

The taste had been moments gone, and only when she realized this did Jordan awaken to the fact that she was crying. Much unlike her other outbursts of the night, this one was stealthy—quiet as the drop—that divine particle—that had invoked the coming of this surreptitious emotional release in darkness. Through tear-blurred vision, Jordan turned to look at the fire that she could see in the distance behind her, her back remaining fixed to the tree.

The fire appeared much farther away than it was, be it for the fire's self-exhaustion or—as seemed more symbolic and beautiful to

Jordan—the fire—*just maybe*—was farther away, and gaining more ground in its retreat, if only to spite her.

Or—

Or perhaps I'm drifting away from the comfort, me on my raft of loneliness, lost in a sea of uncertainty. The fire, the island that I, the castaway, have left behind.

To be safe or explore? Oh… but I've 'explored' enough tonight alone! And I've discovered so much. My boyf—ex-boyfriend—is a scumbag. My best friend tried to kiss me. I'm dressed in this impossibly uncomfortable dress… and yet, I've found someone I can just be *with.*

Jordan turned up the path, looking to the house.

And I've left *him! You left him, Jordan. This is why you've got to find Hannah. You need to talk this out. But what if she tries kissing me again?! No, I don't think I could take that. No, that will not do. Especially… especially with Ari! His house! His clothes! That quiet, almost deceptive smile. Those clear, understanding eyes…. Why, I think I'll go mad if I don't see him again. But. Then again. I've got to get myself in order before I can consider him, if even at all! I've got to know that he is what I'm after tonight. The way Michael was looking at me—well, I'd be lying if I said I didn't enjoy the desire I saw in him…. But that would not outlast the night. He would have me, and then he wouldn't. He would use me as a tool—a tool to build a monument for himself—a monument saying, "I have conquered this. For eternity, a piece of this belongs to me. And so weak was my captive, that she surrendered willingly; a victory without struggle." That's what it would say!*

And then, you would simply be another MISTAKE, MICHAEL! You fucking NOTHING! And the world…!

Jordan's tears quickened pace.

…AND THE WORLD NEEDS NO MORE OF YOU! Those cowards that call themselves men, but how they lie to the world as they lie to themselves! They think they're good. They think they're confident. But when the words run out and the party's over—!

"What the fuck do they truly have?!" said Jordan, her words grating past her gritted teeth.

Much like the response she was given by the invisible mouth of the sky, the conclusion to which Jordan came was: "Nothing," she said. "Not a damned thing. And certainly not *me!*" Her passion added vigor to the coming tears.

"Nothing," she repeated, her voice cracking slightly, the pressure inside her head releasing in the form of copious tears—her personal paradise of melancholy. "Why, this whole world is empty. All this emptiness, and it can't produce a single man anymore. Nothing can create nothing and nothing can come of it. But if the world yields nothing, am I the same?"

Am I *meaningless?*

The floodgates had broken, giving way to the weight of Jordan's feelings. Through them rushed a great flow that ran a corrosive course from the infinite capacity of her tear ducts. She could hold it back no longer, the dam giving way to the reckless might of a once contained river of defeat.

Resting her face in her hands, she began to sob. All her frustrations and blessings overwhelmed her spirit; but, as strong as that spirit may have been, it could no longer carry the growing weight of the world that she had placed upon herself.

"And—and… all in…. All in one day!"

Memories flashed by her as though she was waking from a dream, remembering everything—everything all at once. To Jordan, it seemed like what one might experience upon entering the afterlife—all knowledge attained, borrowed from some ultimate mind that had constructed it all, compiling the ultimate encyclopedia. The shock of these thoughts distracted her from her sadness, an interruption that shot her panic dead.

"And what would that 'encyclopedia' say of me now?"

Jordan stopped crying.

Her heart became still as a stone.

It would say….

She wiped her eyes with her wrists, her deep breaths the opera to her emotional skidding, coming abruptly to a violent halt. She composed herself, looking to the sky and sniffling.

It would say….

Jordan smiled. She shrugged.

"Hell, I don't know!" she said, and for the first time in a long time, she smiled on her own terms. *Her* smile, the only one that she could not see herself, lifted her a bit, and she began to feel normal again in this short-lived and fragile forever.

"So, what to do now?" she said. "What to do? Party? Or Ari?"

Her skin tingled with goosebumps.

Take me where you wi—

The peaceful whisper of the evening's modest music was abruptly shattered as a lightning bolt screamed across the sky above, singular and mighty. The light from it blinded her as it slashed a gash through the darkness, like the cut of a neon blade, tearing and howling through the foe that was the night. Dimness fled from its voice and presence. The light faded, followed by the rumble of its wake, and that very wake was a confirmation of violence—of war. The bolt was the blade that inflicted colorful agony upon the neutrality of the hovering abyss. The thunder was the cry of the afflicted. The blood that issued forth was rain.

Jordan listened as the growing hiss of rain colliding with leaves began to fill the forest around her.

Closer…

Closer…

Closer…!

The sound of the thunder took a few prolonged moments to dissipate, and once its voice became silent, the rain had arrived, the thunder being the introductory applause that commenced the rain ballet.

At first, a few scouting droplets touched Jordan here and there, dappling so subtly her warm skin with their tiny, cold kisses.

More completely… this isn't enough…. What should I do?

An infantile gasp passed Jordan's lips. The rain had paused.

Silence.

And darkness.

What should I do?!

"Tell me! Tell me, please!"

Time stood still for a moment. Then, it caught up to itself.

As though a sea had been summoned overhead, rain—heavy and large—came crashing into the earth and all upon it. Every drop to Jordan was as refreshing as it was a reprimand; the pain of each droplet a piece of her washed clean, baptized by the very sky itself. She could hear the muffling of discontent coming from those that were caught in the rain by the fire—the furthest from the dry safety of the house.

She could make out the sound of the embers crackling and sizzling under the kamikaze assault from the pummeling rain. Realizing how soaked she was, she decided to brave the worsening dirt path to Ari's home.

Surely Hannah has a change of clothes I can borrow. Maybe a cigarette….

"I just hope it's more comfortable than this tool-magnet getup!" Jordan said, looking over herself as rain fell all around her. She leaned back against her tree, taking off her heels, taking time to appreciate the softness of the moisturized dirt beneath her feet. She whispered a 'thank you' to the sky in appreciation for its conversation, and she made for the house.

Barefoot, she ran, red shoes under her arm, green handbag over her shoulder. She tore through the torrent toward the house in an elegant half-run. Athletic as she was, her legs were stiff from the discomfort of her heels, her feet feeling just as red and hot as her shoes. The coolness of the rain brought relief with every step, every splash of her stride a temporary escape.

As the rain increased in tempo, so did Jordan's pace.

As the rain grew colder, Jordan burned hotter.

Eventually, she made her way to the patio, up the steps to the back door of the house. The last of the guests who sought refuge from the rain fought their way inside against the stagnant crowd of onlookers. Jordan noted the stupid, blank expressions that they all wore as she tore for the protection of the inside.

It's just rain, people! Well, it is kind of heavy. But still, it's so, so beautiful… if you look at it in the right way. But, come on!

Now, move! Unless you feel it as I do, you've no reason—no reason at all—to stand there—

"—Blocking the damned doorway!" yelled Jordan. She felt incredible, and her rude playfulness showed through her tone of voice. However, she became slightly embarrassed as her introverted conversation became public. The small sea of faces turned from emptiness to offense, though no one uttered a single syllable toward her. Jordan pushed through the crowd, fighting her way to the back door, her eyes on constant watch for the familiar face of Hannah.

No face, either familiar or interesting, was found.

Like it was going to be that easy…. Ugh, am I really going to have to search this house? And soaking wet, too? I should have waited for Ari. At least he would know how to help me get cleaned up. This dress…. It's just… It's just… miserable.

She laughed to herself, but her laugh carried over the murmurs of the crowd. Her outburst caught the attention of a male duo nearby, her dripping, haphazard appearance kept them intrigued. She watched their eyes look her over, drinking in every visual drop of her. She liked the attention, but she wanted Ari's attention, and his alone. She blushed, flattered as she was, but something about it infuriated her.

If not for this dress, would they still see me that way? If I weren't soaking wet—you perverts!—would you look at me the same? Fucking assholes.

"Alright boys, that's enough for now," said Jordan. "Pick up your jaws and move along." She laughed, a burst of pure joy escaping her lips, so impressed was she at the quickness of her own comment. Even a nearby female eavesdropper laughed.

Strong but modest. To the point, but not mean. Calm and concise. Confident and fierce. Playful and polite. Why, if I could just have spoken as well around Ari…. Oh, well….

They wore expressions of shock—shocked as they were by the allure of her attire, the dripping of her dress, and the boldness of her statement—by her presence, altogether. Still, they lingered—*Those boys and their eyes*—blushing.

"Don't get too close, now. I *will* burn you."

The eavesdropper laughed again. Jordan was garnering more attention than she desired. However, she was quickly forgotten as another great stroke of lightning tore across the sky.

Still no Hannah…. And come to think of it, why isn't Ari inside yet?

To Jordan, it all felt connected as the storm building outside countered and balanced the storm growing within. It was because of this that Jordan did not feel the fear that she saw in those around her. As far as she was concerned, the storm outside was of her own sorcery; that she had summoned the wrath of the sky in her reckless cries—the lightning, her tool to ensnare and terrify, its thunder the voice of the god who had heard her pleas—a god who had empathized with the shattering of her full, defiant, worthy heart.

A promise of a storm. A promise… of mercy….

She looked to the door. She hoped that Ari would have come through to her by now.

Well, I can't just wait around. He's probably cleaning up at the fire pit. And I don't want to look needy or pathetic. Hannah….

"Uh, hey," Jordan said, trying for the attention of the eavesdropping girl. "Hey, can I ask you something?"

"I mean, technically you already did," she said with a laugh. "But go ahead, sweetie."

"Do you know where the—"

"Bathroom is?" the girl interrupted. "Yeah, you look like you could use some drying off. There's one upstairs that I used earlier. Down this hall, past the living room or study or whatever—the room with the fireplace? Yeah, just go that way past the room with the fireplace 'til you come to the stairs. Then take those stairs. Take 'em all the way up. Then it's… then it's… uh—well, hell, I don't remember what door. I'm pretty drunk. I'll find a plant if I can't find a toilet, ya know?" She smiled at Jordan with a pleasant smile.

"Uh, okay, thank you," Jordan said, doing her polite best. Her urgency left no time to socialize further.

"Upstairs," the stranger said again, lifting a beer in ovation to

Jordan.

"Thank you again!" Jordan called back, hoping the conversation would die.

My goodness, this house is so nice! I hate leaving this trail of water through everything….

A swell of classical music caught her ear as she traversed the corridor toward the living room. She gave a quick pause in passing, the smell of rich leather and comfortable smoke emanating from the room.

And what a fireplace! It's magnificent! I could dry off here! That sounds so cozy!

Determined to find a towel to dry herself and her attire, Jordan made for the stairs. As she got to the second floor, a doorway some distance down the dim hallway hung slightly ajar from which a proud beam of light cut the dense darkness—much like the lightning outside.

Even inside both the house and myself, I can't escape the tempest, I guess.

I hope this bathroom isn't taken already!

Jordan rapt hurriedly upon the door. She waited maybe half a second before pushing it open, bolting inside, and twisting the lock on the knob.

Then she turned around.

ARI

This frustrating feeling… such a motherfucker!

I turned from Michael, watching as the silhouette that was Jordan blended with the shadows of the trees as she crept up the path into the darkness.

Do I stay or go? Do I chase or wait? Michael says 'wait,' but he could be out for himself. I can't tell…. This wine…. This night…. Where do I end and the emaciated, uncertain monster begins? I cannot tell.

I turned from the shadows to the fire in hopes to be enlightened by its glow.

You crazy bastard, Ari…. Maybe you are insane. Solitude doesn't look so good on you right now.

I clenched my fists. My head began to spin.

Damned wine….

Fucking drugs…. I didn't even want those. I guess we all get dealt a shitty hand once in a while. Comes down to how you play the hand you're dealt, I guess. Don't fold, whatever you do!

I had become the victim of consequence and of choices I had made against my own knowledge, but not against my will. Circumstance took reign over me at my own party—at my own damned house!—so all I could do was accept these circumstances and pray that God had arrived so that He could watch over me. I was feeling less hopeful by the second.

"Michael, I… I'm so…" I began, but 'sorry' was not the word. No, I had revealed my heart, whether I had intended to or not, and it had been wounded in what I felt to be an inadequacy in my attempt to capture this girl that had captured me so easily.

"Don't be sorry," Michael said. "You're better than that, man."

"It isn't 'sorry' that I'm trying to say…. Hell, I can't even say what I need to say. It's impossible!" I said.

"Like defining love with words. It can't be done, Ari. Someone as deep-thinking and loving as you? You know this already," Michael said.

"But why can't I fucking say it?!" I said, getting louder as I spoke. "I'm so good with words… until… until they matter… Until it matters to me…."

I collapsed in a slowly melting pile into the dirt beneath me, becoming one with the ground to which I felt comparison.

Cold. Dirty. Unnoticed.

Stepped on. Walked over.

I was becoming one with my solitude and the quiet, allowing it to embrace me. Silence crept along the tops of the trees, a slight wind billowing, then building with the turbulence that I gripped like a masochist of self-hatred inside.

Then Michael spoke.

"Ari, brother, don't let it matter. Even if it does matter so fucking much to you, let it go. Just let it go, man. She'll be back," Michael said. "She sees something in you. She sees something, and no matter what it is, *something* is a damned good start!"

I empathized with Michael's sympathy, but it did not seem to be enough. I knew in my mind what he was attempting to tell me, but my heart did not reciprocate.

After all, that's why we have both feeling and rationale, isn't it? Because one cannot interpret the other? One knows, understands, and fathoms. One feels, cares, and dwells.

Just like you and myself, Michael. One is action. The other is potential.

You move. I wait. And we're both perpetual in our nature.

I began to feel a glimmer of hope around me somewhere, somewhere close by but just far enough to be out of my reach. My realization improved me somehow, if only briefly, before dissipating into the nothing, and the glimmer turned to heat—fury's heat. I came back to reality, leaving my hopeful daydream.

"But why?! Why can't I figure this out? She's pretty, but that's no mystery—" I said, choking on the words. I caught myself and hung upon the finesse of the word that had just escaped my mouth.

"Mystery. That's got to be it. It's all mystery. She's a mystery. I'm a mystery to myself. I can't figure *me* out!"

"Ari…."

"So how in all this hell am I supposed to figure *her* out?!" I said, my voice increasing in crazed volume. "If I don't know *me*, how can I offer her any-damned-thing?!"

Nothing to give; nothing to add.

"And if I have nothing to give her," I said, rather loudly, "then what the fuck is the point?! God, if only I could reach through. If only I could break through myself, only once…. But, God, please help me." I turned to the fire. I was becoming hysterical. "God, if you would just *give me a sign! Or someone! ANYONE! Give! Give me…. Give me—damn it!*"

DAMN IT! DAMN IT ALL!!!

I stiffened as my guts turned to hot steel and I struck the ground with both fists, hammering the topsoil with the merciful cushion of my unrelenting clenching hands. The fire shifted once more as thunder echoed across the sky, bringing with it a white-hot bolt of lightning that seared the clouds above, cutting my thoughts, as well. Michael shivered beneath the shockwave, and I could feel every vibration in the air, which shook the trees around us. The earth buckled in respectful fear. I sat stock still, my fists reveling in their indentions in the dirt, and the electricity was melding and emanating from the uncertainty and reckless rage within me. I could not ignore the thought, if only for a vain moment, that I had literally summoned this striking spectacle. And in that moment, I felt powerful, though I knew quite well that this was not my doing.

No, I had called upon the power of the Almighty, and the Almighty had answered, using me as a medium by which His voice had come.

Tears began to well up in my eyes as Michael stammered in his inebriated surprise. Sounds, not words, were my reality, and like the heart-versus-mind battle from before, I could not shake the feeling of connectivity I felt with that fierce, hot act of the heavens. I felt tied, finally, to my fate—a fate I had not the previous luxury of knowing. I felt trapped in my circumstance, but now I could see the once-invisible bonds that had tied me and had not yet set me free. I was feeling. Simply put, I felt, and that was something that I had not experienced in a dreadfully long time.

"Finally," I said.

"Finally, what?" Michael asked.

"Michael," I said. "He's here. He's finally, finally here."

"He? Here? Cut the *shit*, Ari."

"No shit, Michael. God is here now."

I had no way of knowing if I was absolutely correct, but I had to believe it.

Thunder rumbled on—the invisible aftermath of the extravagant electric light.

I shook.

Michael began to speak, but I could pay no attention as his focus had become completely overtaken by the sky—its emptiness and splendor. He stared into the black, and the black stared back; but as it stared, nearly unblinkingly, I felt that it also listened. And God did indeed seem to listen after all, as well.

A smile spread across my face as I turned my head back to the dirt upon which I kneeled.

And all in one day. One day!

"We should go inside, don't you think?" I said.

"Ari, you're scaring me. Hot to cold. What's going on?" Michael said. "I thought you were going to do something drastic, maybe hurt yourself. You sure you're okay?"

"Never better. Now the night can really get started." I rubbed my hands together in a devious manner. I then looked up, my eyes lingering upon the distant lights of my splendid mansion. "I have a party to host. Shouldn't I be going?"

"But didn't God just get here? You sure you want to abandon your guest of honor?" Michael laughed.

I paused for a moment before saying, "Michael, just shut the fuck up for once."

Michael seemed surprised but not as taken aback as I had become in my blatant rudeness. I blushed a little, yet somehow I could not ignore the swelling pride that grew in me. I nearly apologized.

I did not.

Michael just shifted, staring, clearly uncomfortable. Then he smirked. The smirk became a smile. The smile became laughter.

"Ari, what the hell? Where did *that* come from? Actually getting some balls about ya!"

I've always had balls. Big, heavy balls. I just don't show mine off to every batting eye on the field.

"You should speak up more often, kid," he continued. "You'd be a lot happier that way."

Before I could contemplate what he had just said, the sound of a heavy rain whispered in the distance, the low hiss of its approach warning us of its arrival.

A voice came from deeper in the woods, a scream made of the mix of surprise and horror. Someone had just been annihilated by the heavy sheets that were descending.

Poor bastard.

"Let's get inside!" Michael said, calling out over the rain's echo throughout the trees.

It was too late.

By the time his last syllable hit my ears, the sky was upon us, pouring all its ammunition in one fell swoop.

The fire hissed and screamed as it was pummeled by the rain. The fire was no god. The rain was, though, and the mortal blaze fell before the unrelenting divine.

I looked to Michael, who was staring into the fire as though the rain did not exist. I was already half-soaked, as was he, yet he seemed unconcerned. A haunting, blank, focused stare ruled over his face. I grabbed him by the arm, and he mumbled something incoherent into the sound of the storm. I ignored it, dragging him in tow, scrambling for the path to the house. I could still hear him mumbling beneath the raucous of the din.

"What's that?" I called back to him as we ran.

"I said," Michael yelled back, "that I like this Ari! Keep it up, and you'll have Jordan wetter than this weather! There's a Jordan River joke in there somewhe…"

I laughed out of courtesy, not enjoyment. I did not catch the remainder of what he said, nor did I attempt to do so.

Tasteless…

Watch your fucking mouth, Michael Law.

I hated him.

I loved him.

I needed no light of any fire to get myself and my companion up the dark, wet path leading to my house. The wooded grove was often my escape at night when my home became a prison for me. My feet knew the path well, and they kept their memory of it intact as they led Michael and myself away from the dark, lonely cold of the rain to the dry, inviting warmth of the illuminated house.

I looked back over Michael's shoulder in the direction from where the scream from earlier had come, if only to assist the guest of mine who found themselves caught up in the wrath of the nighttime rain. In the darkness, I could see nothing but darkness; but even so, I thought I could just make out two tiny lights far behind us.

As quickly as they had been noticed, they were gone.

I turned my head back toward the mansion, and Michael Law and Ari Cayne made for the house—our shelter from the relentless sky.

MICHAEL

Michael watched in regret and sadness as Ari—his best and only friend—fell apart in front of him. This man, who had been through every sad scenario in life, was being defeated once again, and Michael was partly to blame, and he knew it. Ari was losing a battle with himself that Michael could not see, and Michael felt guilty for antagonizing the situation by flirting with Jordan. The psychedelics in Michael's body were beginning to reach the brink of their reservations, threatening to break through and capture him like a passionate prisoner any moment now. His stomach began to tense with discomfort. He could not tell if it were the mushrooms, the wine, Ari's struggle, the drugs, or a combination of either or all.

God damn cocaine.... Why am I so weak sometimes, most of the time...?

I didn't know she meant so much to you. She only just met you. I know your heart moves faster than most, but not even I thought you would take this to heart. We've got to toughen you up. First, we need to fix you.

"Michael, I…" Ari began.

No, Ari. Don't you say it. Don't you dare apologize!

"I'm so…" Ari continued.

Don't let him!

"Don't be sorry," Michael interrupted. "You're better than that, man."

"It isn't sorry that I'm trying to say," Ari said.

Then say it. Things that are harder to say are likely more necessary to be said.

"Hell, I can't even say what I need to say," he continued. "It's impossible!"

Well, of course it's impossible! We aren't meant to find the answer. But the journey is the purpose, Ari.

"Like defining love with words. It can't be done, Ari," Michael said.

Even when we love someone, saying it isn't enough. You've got to show them. Love is a verb. It requires action. Promises only go as far as their results. Otherwise, it's all just lies from the past. That's like something Ari would say….

"Someone as deep-thinking and loving as you?" Michael said. "You know this already."

"But why can't I fucking say it?!" Ari said. "I'm so good with words… until… until they matter. Until it matters to me…."

Then learn. Learn to speak. We cannot read your mind. And you overcomplicate things by bottling these thoughts. I'm your best friend, yet sometimes, I feel I barely know you.

Ari collapsed to the ground in front of Michael.

"Ari, brother, don't let it matter," Michael said, stepping forward. "Even if it does matter so fucking much to you, let it go."

I need to let go, too. I'm fighting the drugs. You already took them, so, take your own advice with it, Michael, and just….

"Just let it go, man. She'll be back. She sees something in you," Michael said.

Hell, haven't we all? Beyond those sad, contemplating eyes lies a good man. But you wear your weakness, though you try to hide it like mismatched socks. Own the peculiar. Embrace the asymmetrical.

"She sees something, and no matter what it is, *something* is a damned good start!" Michael said.

Now, go on and resist. I know you, Ari, you stubborn bastard.

"But why?! Why can't I figure this out? She's pretty, but that's no mystery."

Pretty. Right. You mean hot as hellfire. That dress. That voice. Red. High. Fucking. Heels. Ari.

"Mystery. That's got to be it. It's all mystery," Ari said.

The only mystery to me is, what's beneath that dress…?

Michael's wandering mind was rather quickly pushing him toward the edge of his sanity. His skin tingled. Light was becoming more intense to behold. What colors he could make out in the fire-lit darkness emboldened, stretching themselves, blending into other colors that he had never seen before.

And the fire, to Michael, seemed almost—

Alive.

Breathing.

"She's a mystery. I'm a mystery to myself. I can't figure *me* out!"

I can't figure me out either, but the difference between us is that I know what I want. I always have. And here you are, reaching out to an invisible god for a wingless angel. You aren't being rational….

"Ari…."

But neither am I. I need your help, too, you know. I'm fucked up. Shit, shit, shit. Here it comes….

"So how in all this hell am I supposed to figure *her* out?! If I don't know *me*, how can I offer her any-damned-thing?!"

Or anyone, for that matter….

Nothing to give. Nothing to add.

Michael's mind was bending as was his grip on reality. The trees were coming to life, and they began to dance in the wind as it picked up, raining leaves around them. Michael kept his eyes on the sky and his ears on Ari's voice.

"And if I have nothing to give her, then what the fuck is the point?!" Ari said, his voice shaking like a tremor underground. "God, if only I could reach through. If only I could break through myself, only once…."

Ari's talk of 'reaching through' had flipped the final switch in Michael's psyche. Everything was illuminated, despite the darkness. His body felt like particles of light, all chasing each other like playful children. He might have felt brighter than the bonfire, but seeing it through these new eyes, he knew that he could not be correct. The fire was moving more quickly as the wind slightly increased in might, the dance of flames an aggressive, yet flowing, beautiful performance. Michael was enraptured by it—seduced.

"But, God, please help me," Ari said.

And me, too, if you don't mind….

"God, if you would just *give me a sign!*" Ari continued. "Or *someone!*"

I'm right here, Ari.

"*ANYONE!*"

I'm right here, Ari!

"GIVE! Give me… Give me…" Ari said.

I've nothing to give. Nothing to add.

Michael hung his head. His mind was racing, the world was slowing, and Ari and the drugs were making for a very emotional experience. He hated that he could not snap his friend out of his emotional confusion. Michael had always believed that men fought their own battles, but Ari rarely felt like just one man to Michael.

No matter how nailed down you think you've got the bastard, he always surprises….

Damn it.

Michael's thought echoed out of Ari's mouth, only adding more significance to the small moments made grandiose in lieu of his psychoactive-induced thoughts.

"Damn it!" Ari screamed as he struck the ground, pounding the earth like a child made suddenly aware of its strength.

But it was not this act that stole Michael's attention. At the exact moment that Ari's hands slammed into the dirt, a lightning bolt—hot, fast, and fierce—raced through the darkness of the sky, illuminating for a moment the world that, once mysterious, gained clarity through the flash of bright light. Michael's jaw dropped wide open. The lightning strike had induced the peak of his trip, and his mind melted in the significance and rarity of the moment. Unblinkingly, Michael stared at the sky, waiting for a rebuttal.

Ari spoke and Michael listened as he stared at the great abyss above.

"Finally," Ari said.

"Finally, what?" Michael asked.

"Michael," Ari said. "He's here."

Who's here? Hell, I'm standing here and I'm barely here….

"He's finally, finally here," Ari said.

Please, Ari, don't fuck with me right now.

"He? Here? Cut the *shit*, Ari," Michael said.

Michael was attempting to assuage his panic.

"No shit, Michael. God is here now."

I don't see a god any-damned-where, Ari. And I see quite a lot right now.

"We should go inside, don't you think?" Ari said.

Right. Now that 'God' is here, let's abandon him, just like you did all the others at the party. They show and you disappear. Don't be selfish. Stay with me a little while. I am no god, but I am here. And which is more important? Your present, real best friend, or some absentee father deity who lets the world he made crumble to ashes? Your god is like this fire, Ari. You build it, you give it existence, and your faith in it will only burn you if you get too close. It's time we put out this fire and got back to our lives. If only you had this sort of blind faith in yourself….

"Ari, you're scaring me," Michael said. "Hot to cold. What's going on? I thought you were going to do something drastic, maybe hurt yourself. You sure you're okay?" The words fumbled, barely together, out of Michael's mouth. He was losing his grip on himself.

"Never better," Ari said. "Now the night can really get started."

I wish it would rain already. I'm sick to death of this god talk!

"I have a party to host," Ari said. "Shouldn't I be going?" Michael's impatience with this moment grew in lieu of Ari's changing emotions. Michael had invested in those feelings Ari was sharing, and the sudden change to happiness made Michael feel as though his empathy had gone to waste.

After all, what's the point in helping people if they refuse to face their problems? When they change that face, how do we know that we know them anymore? If I could just get inside your head and see…. But then again, I'd have to eliminate this god bullshit to even tolerate that space.

Michael's impatience turned to sarcasm as he responded to Ari's question.

"But didn't God just get here? You sure you want to abandon your guest of honor?" Michael laughed as he said this, but his joy was cut short by the sword of Ari's voice.

"Michael…" Ari said.

Yes, what, Ari? Go on and tell me what the hell—

"…Just shut the fuck up for once."

Michael's mind went silent for the first time in a long time. Ari had cut him deeply, but somehow, Michael found joy in the opening of the wound.

Fuck you, Ari. Brilliant.

Michael slowly smiled himself into friendly laughter.

I really am going insane. Seems this lightning gave our host a little spark.

"Ari, what the hell? Where did *that* come from? Actually getting some balls about ya!"

I'm proud of you, Ari. I'd fuck you up in a fight, but good on you for standing up for yourself.

"You should speak up more often, kid," Michael said. "You'd be a lot happier that way."

Nothing would make me happier than to see this fire go out, to be honest. The girls inside, waiting….

The sky had answered Michael's thought. The hiss of rain began swelling in the dark distance, growing louder and louder as it quickly made its way toward the grove in which they stood.

I want to be inside that rain. I want to feel it on my skin, in my hair. But Ari, we've got to change our surroundings.

"Let's get inside!" Michael said. His eyes neither blinked nor abandoned his focus on the dark above.

In mere moments, the monsoon was upon them.

In the arrival of the rain, Michael could hear a scream coming from the forest beyond. It sounded strangely familiar to him but was unlike any other voice he had ever heard. It sounded layered, like multiple voices in one accord—a symphony of one. The sound waves multiplied as they bounced off raindrop after raindrop on their way to his hyperactive ears.

Now, who the hell made it past us? Who the hell would stay out here? Spying on us? Watching? If it weren't raining, you shady bastard….

Michael heard the same voice again as Ari grabbed his shirt and dragged him away from the dying fire. The words were in a language he had never heard before, but he somehow understood. It felt cautionary to him, like a warning—like a crying child that could communicate its needfulness without words.

Michael turned to Ari, then back to the dying fire as they traversed the trees toward the house and Michael was stricken with horror. A silhouette of a figure was staring at him through the rain and the smoke of the fire going out. He could only see it in the dark because the silhouette itself was even darker than the surrounding night. Amid what appeared to be the head, two lights glared in Michael's direction. It raised what seemed like an arm in the air, its supposed finger pointing right at Michael. The voice called out again.

"*Law!*"

"Yeah right. Damned mushrooms!"

"What's that?" Ari called back to him as they ran.

He might believe in God, but he'll never believe this shit. He can never know. Then I'd really be hearing about this God mess forever….

"I said that I like this Ari!" Michael called, never taking his eyes away from the living shadow. "Keep it up and you'll have Jordan wetter than this weather! There's a Jordan River joke in there somewhe…."

Michael tried forcing a laugh, but nothing truly funny existed within this situation.

What was that shadow?

Whether real or not, the image haunted Michael, and despite his desire to blame the drugs and alcohol, he had heard that voice calling out to him.

"*Law, Law, Law!*"

It echoed in his mind. Michael could still hear the voice, even as Ari dragged him through the torrential grove, both of them scrambling for the safety and dryness of the house.

Michael blinked, and the figure was gone.

Its voice, however, lingered on the drowning air.

"*Law. Law. LAW!*"

JORDAN

The blissful silence of the room allowed Jordan to breathe freely for the first time in what seemed like days. The sound of the rain was far away. No one was present to engage her in conversation. No one was looking at her and no one was touching her. It was heaven.

With her eyes down, Jordan kicked off her heels, exhaling relief. She lifted her head and looked around, scanning the bathroom around her.

Spotless.

Even the shower curtain appeared to be unused.

Nice.

She was elated to see the various items laid out upon the counter for the party guests. A mansion that belonged to a bachelor, and still, he thought to provide—

Tampons?

Who is this guy?

A twinge in her midsection reminded her of another need for this room. In a flash, she set down her green handbag, she pulled her dress up, sat down and commenced her dire ritual. The rain's lingering moisture almost sent her off the seat, but she caught herself and continued. Relief spread like a needed sickness all over her.

After she finished, she rose, cleaned up, and made her way to the marble sink. The golden faucet that she had not noticed before gleamed with its own light in the bathroom's luminescence. She turned on the water and lathered her hands, watching as the dense suds rolled off her fingertips, dripping softly into the basin. She skipped over the task of drying her hands because—

What would the point be? I'm soaking still.

She looked around the contents of the countertop once more, laughing as her eyes passed over the feminine products. Even a hairdryer lay on the counter, unplugged, its cord gathered perfectly. She chuckled to herself, the echoes of Ari's voice stirring within her, impressed as she was by his foresight and kindness.

And not just for me…. He did this for all of us.

Jordan rummaged around the room for a towel with which to dry herself. She found several in the small closet opposite the stand-in shower. Selecting a silky, royal blue one, she threw it onto her head, patting the moisture away from her hair, squeezing instead of rubbing, and ran her hair in locks through her towel-bearing hands. She took off her dress, draping it over the hook that hung by the sink. Barefoot, nearly naked, and standing there, Jordan examined herself in the mirror for a moment. She was seeing herself from the outside, yet it felt like the first time. She had never been so overwhelmed by affection in her life.

Hannah.

Michael.

Ari….

She laughed again at the plethora of little romantic moments she had shared over the last few hours. Her broken heart had changed her, and this chaotic evening had been the result. Alone, friendless, lost, and in a bathroom, she began to complain within herself, yet changed the course of her mind.

You wanted adventure, didn't you? Well, you sure got it.

The 'me' from only hours ago would have melted down. Not me.

I'm not that Jordan. Not anymore.

Despite her care, her hair remained slightly tousled, a bit too much for her liking, but she shrugged off the stresses of the importance of image, as she was more focused on her interior rather than her shell. She looked down, examining her body up close without the use of the mirror.

Still, I'm a lady. Can't walk around a house like this with this company— this host—and not look amazing. You can do it, Jordan. You know that now.

"Is it pathetic that it took three people's opinions to make me see myself as beautiful?"

Maybe, but you see it now. And that is all that matters from here on. The past is gone. The future isn't here yet and never will be. All you have, if anything at all, is now.

"And that is all I want," said Jordan, lifting her eyes to meet their reflection in the mirror. Her gaze seemed different. She did not recognize the girl in the reflection, and it was a great relief to her.

We don't age in seconds or hours or years. We age in experience.

"Then let's age. Let's experience."

A soft knock on the door surprised Jordan.

Ah! Shit! Oh, no. I hope they haven't been hearing me talking to myself!

"He- Hello?" Jordan said, her cheek against the door.

A voice—strange, sweet, and feminine—answered.

"Hey, are you almost done in there? I've gotta piss like a cow!"

Jordan blushed, realizing her time in the bathroom had become excessive. Given her needs, however, she assuaged the guilt that would have dominated her old self.

"I'm sorry, I had to pee, too!" she laughed. "I was outside when it started raining."

Jordan cracked the door to better converse with the voice that she had already come to trust. She kept her nearly naked body behind the door in case there were others beyond. She sighed in relief once more as she was alone. She had a friendly face and an amazing smile. The girl seemed innocent enough, so Jordan let her in.

"Come in," Jordan said. "But I'll have to stay in here." She opened the door, guiding the girl in quickly, and shut it behind them.

"I don't have the appropriate attire to be seen outside quite yet," Jordan laughed.

The girl sat down on the toilet, going about her business instantly. Jordan could not see her face as she was hunched over, clearly coming to terms with the pleasurable pain of copious urination. Her hair—a rare shade of bright red—was tangled about her face. The pale skin of her legs stood out to Jordan.

Pale and fair. And not a freckle on her.

She finished, the splashing sound of water coming to a halt.

"There! That is so much better," she said. "I've been holding it for a bit, now. Thanks so much…" she said, pausing as she looked up at Jordan, her eyes taking their time examining her. Jordan's skin grew hot as silent flattery poured over her. "…for letting me in," the girl continued, dabbing herself with toilet paper and discarding it into the toilet.

"I'm Katie," the girl said, flushing the toilet, lifting her undergarments back into position.

"Jordan," Jordan said, avoiding a handshake for the sake of Katie's unwashed hands, which Katie immediately went about remedying, speaking as she cleansed.

"So, thanks again for letting a stranger in. Seems like you're trying to get back to the party," Katie said.

"I am," said Jordan, "but the rain really got me good." Jordan pointed to the dress that hung on the wall. It looked smaller to her, despite the water it held, and it made her uncomfortable.

I've been wearing that all night…. No wonder I'm getting so much attention.

Katie gazed upon the lightly dripping dress to which Jordan was referring. "Aw, did you get all wet?"

The wicked, seductive smile that took control of Katie's face could not be ignored. It was fierce. It was personal.

It was powerful.

Katie was the vampire that Jordan had invited inside.

Well, no going back now. You can't run from a vampire. Pointless.

Jordan laughed to herself despite her company.

"What's so funny, Jordan?" Katie said.

"Oh, nothing. Just thinking about the night. It's been crazy, that's for sure!"

"Well, I know crazy," Katie said. "Red hair and all. We have that reputation." Katie laughed. "So, are you enjoying the party?"

Am I enjoying the party? Yes. No. Both. It's all over the place, just like me. So maybe I do belong here. Chaos marrying the chaos….

"Yes, I am," Jordan said, abbreviating her honest thoughts for the sake of expediting explanation. "Now, if I could only get myself ready and get back to it… I have a friend to find and a host to speak with."

"Oh, Ari? I've heard good things. Seems like a nice guy."

Jordan felt suddenly anxious. For some reason, Katie meeting Ari made her uncomfortable

So, you've met him….

Katie looked around the room. She saw the hair dryer then went about rubbing the fabric of Jordan's wet dress.

"Hmm… doesn't feel like it'll shrink from the heat. Might even dry rather quickly with this," Katie said, lifting the hair dryer and plugging it into the wall.

"Good plan," Jordan said. "But I should dry my hair first. Will you dry the dress while I fix my hair?"

"Sure, gorgeous," Katie said, rather playfully.

Oh, no. Here we go, again.

A vampire's seduction. Real-life bride of Dracula….

I'm sure Ari got much of the same. This bitch…. But she seems nice enough.

"Thank you," Jordan said, despite the mild discomfort that came with Katie's comment. Still, Jordan shrugged away the awkward feeling this brought her.

Katie went to the linen closet, procuring a clothes hanger, draping the dress over it. Plugging in the dryer, she turned it on and commenced drying the dress that hung upon the closet doorknob, keeping mind to not let the heat of it linger in one place for too long. Jordan noticed the care and attention that Katie was paying to her task, though her eyes rarely left Jordan.

So, you've done this before. And not just drying dresses. You're Michael in lady form. A she-wolf out on the prowl.

Jordan shook these thoughts from her mind, realizing that, just as Katie was looking at her, she was looking right back. She blushed again, quickly moving to begin dabbing her hair with the silky towel once more.

Jordan moved to the toilet to have a seat as she continued removing the moisture from her blonde locks.

Minutes passed in silence as the two quietly basked in each other's beautiful company.

"So, what brings you to this party?" Katie asked.

"My friend brought me," Jordan said. "I had a rough day. She thought I could use some time away from myself, so here I am."

"And do you know anyone else?" Katie asked. "I came alone."

Jordan held back the laughter in spite of her humor. "Nope. Just me and my friend. I wanted to stay home, but she made me come."

Their eyes met, Jordan seated on the toilet, Katie standing, drying Jordan's dress. They kept eye contact for several moments before Jordan looked to the floor, shaking out her hair.

"May I use that dryer for a few moments?" Jordan asked.

"Good timing," Katie said. "Surprisingly, your dress is dry. It isn't perfect, but I don't think you'll complain."

"Thank you so much, Kate," Jordan said.

"No, its—" Katie stopped suddenly, as though restraining herself from a quiet rage. "It's all good," she continued, relaxing as she spoke.

Jordan took the dryer from Katie, laid it on the sink, and began to apply some frizz-reducing serum she found on the countertop. She stood before the mirror, running the product through her blonde hair then turned on the dryer, blowing out the potential tangled mess. She ran her hands through her hair as she dried, giving her hair a nice, healthy, frizz-free shine and a wild flow to her locks. Katie looked on at the spectacle before her, her arms crossed as she leaned herself against the wall behind Jordan. Jordan could feel Katie's hungry eyes all over her. It gave Jordan another dose of false confidence.

I don't need it. Not anymore.

Jordan continued working on her hair.

"So, you came here with a friend," Katie said. "Is it, like, a boyfriend? Or just a friend?"

I see what you're getting at. All right, girl. If you want to play this game, let's play.

"Just a friend," Jordan said. "My best friend. We got… separated… earlier. It's kind of a ridiculously long story for such a short time period."

Jordan had become content with her hair. It was not perfect to her, but it was excellent, and Jordan had decided that excellence was a far more satisfying goal than the impossible pursuit of perfection.

She turned off the dryer, shook out her hair with her hands, and threw it over her head, allowing it to lie more naturally. Katie walked over to the closet door, took the dress off the hanger, and slowly walked it over to Jordan.

"Thank you."

Jordan took the dress from Katie with slow hands. She slipped the dress up her legs, which still felt incredibly smooth to her touch, and fitted it over her torso into place. Sitting on the toilet for what seemed the hundredth time, Jordan put her heels back on, yet they felt more comfortable this time—less alien.

"Girl, you are so hot. And you are so welcome," said Katie.

Jordan blushed again, and was thankful for Katie and her presence, but she had had enough of this girl-crush game. She wanted Ari, and nothing else would do; not only because of how she felt around him but for what he was. His timidity and hers together would give them both strength, and because of what they could share, they could both make each other better, helping each other grow.

And together.

Or not. I just know that I've gotta get the hell out of here!

"I don't know how I can repay your kindness. I really appreciate your company and help," Jordan said, overcompensating with words to hide her inner discomfort. She looked into the mirror one last time.

Not bad, Jordan. Not bad at all.

She made for the door, grabbing the doorknob quickly, but not quickly enough.

Katie's hand moved in a fast blur, stopping on Jordan's hand that did not have the time to even twist the knob.

She's been waiting. She-wolf, indeed.

"You don't have to go yet," Katie said. "You can stay here."

Jordan stared at the ten fingers on the knob, her gaze trailing from the chaotic spectacle up Katie's fair arms, across her neck, eventually stopping at her face. The soft look in her eyes reminded Jordan of her younger self, yet Katie seemed a few years her senior.

Definitely more experienced. More confident.

"With me," Katie continued. The longing Jordan saw in her eyes was a trap—a vicious one.

Dangerous, yes, but very beautiful.

No! Absolutely not! Not again!

"Well," Jordan said, "I do appreciate the compliment, but—"

Jordan once again was stopped mid-sentence by a flood of unwanted passion. Katie's lips felt amazing, and Jordan felt the impulse to kiss back, but her experience before had caused her grief of confusing proportions, and she simply did not desire to relearn Hannah's lessons from merely an hour or two before.

"I'm sorry," Jordan said. "Thank you, but I've got to go."

Jordan pushed Katie away, turning the doorknob with a fierce quickness. Realizing the door was locked still, she unlocked it, grabbing her bag and shoes in a frenzy; and embarrassed and anxious, she moved to open the door.

Damn it! Fumbling fucking mess!

As the door opened, the light from the bathroom once again filled the hallway. Only this time, the darkness of the hall was not alone. It was not empty. There stood Hannah, staring intently at the blonde and the redhead.

Jordan's mind went blank as her heart filled with the weight of a great nothing. The anxiety took over her entire being, and vision failed her as it blurred in the face of the fear that gripped her in this moment of being caught in the act that she had not performed.

Oh, shit….

Eons passed in moments, and her confidence from minutes before was growing brittle and falling apart and dissolving like ashes in her mouth. She felt a twinge in her stomach, like static from a heat storm, crawling and stabbing her insides. She felt like a child that was about to receive punishment for the actions of another. She was caught and not the culprit. She was about to be judged for a crime uncommitted.

No, no, NO! Why?!

"Hannah, it's—" Jordan said, quickly.

How cliché of you, Jordan….

"Not what I think?" Hannah interrupted.

Don't think. Feel. Remember?

Jordan could find no words. They were jumbled in a heap behind her eyes, recycling themselves at the speed of panic. Her unwarranted shame clung to her like a static balloon, hanging closely, threatening to pop.

To Jordan's brief relief, Katie was the next to speak. "Yeah, we were just having a girl's bathroom visit. No big deal."

No big deal? So aloof. There's no way she even knows what's going on. Wait—did something happen between these two?

Why does she feel the need to explain herself to Hannah? Perhaps I'm not the guilty one, here. Those bearing the guilt are so often the first to point their finger. The accuser is so often the guilty one. It's like a gun that uses judgment for ammo. You can shoot whoever you want to with it, but the finger pulling the trigger belongs to the true offender.

So here I am, the innocent victim, the true offender standing in this bathroom with me. Or was it Hannah? No matter. The weapon has been fired. And here I am, blameless, bleeding out in silence….

"Katie, don't say another damned word," Hannah said, her face gritted and pursed like an angry statue.

I didn't introduce the two of you…. So, you DO know each other. What's the story here?!

"Not yet," Hannah continued. "You'll get your chance to talk."

She doesn't seem like much of a 'talker'. She's more about the 'action'. Gah, she's going to ruin everything! Don't let her speak. Let her words die. Make her go away! I just don't understand….

"You don't seem to understand," Hannah said, reflecting Jordan's thought.

Jordan knew Hannah was speaking to Katie, but the mirroring of her thoughts grabbed her attention, sending a prickly, nervous sensation all over her skin. She could not ignore the power of that unspoken moment, and it ignited her once more, drying the metaphorical sweat that gathered upon her anxious, heavy heart. Panicked yet resolute, Jordan spoke to dilute the building tension that claimed the crackling quiet around her.

But, Jordan, you don't know what happened, if anything at all. Don't go looking like the crazy one, here. The gun is pointed at you. Doesn't mean you have to pull one, yourself. No retaliation. Bring peace, not war. Otherwise, you yourself become a murderer. And you are not a murderer. You are not a criminal. You are a star, burning brightly, and stars make way for life. Don't implode. Don't be a supernova. Don't become a black hole, swallowing all the light around you. Make light. Take this darkness, and make it light, and make light of it. You've done no wrong, except for not being totally honest here. That is your discomfort. Call the spider for what it is and don't let its web entangle you. Don't let your tongue trip over the scattered words that are beneath it.

Jordan longed to pacify the electricity in the air. She could see rage fall over Hannah's pretty face.

Beautiful. Terrifying.

"This is the friend I've been looking for, Katie," Jordan said, her eyes fixed on the cold eyes of Hannah filled to the brim with anger, their luster, in this moment, temporarily lost.

"Oh, your *friend*, huh?" Katie said, the seductive tone not at all lost to Jordan's apprehension. "Well, well," she continued. "What a situation I've caught myself up—"

"Katie. Seriously," Hannah interrupted.

This girl doesn't know what 'serious' is. Seriously inconvenient if anything at all…. Just shut up, Katie!

"Shut up," Hannah said, tersely.

Thank you, Hannah.

"Yes, please," Jordan said.

Tonight, Jordan, you truly are just a reflection of her. She brought you here, she picked out your dress and shoes…. And now she's defending you with your own words you cannot say.

"She and I have a lot to discuss," continued Jordan, calmly.

Don't be a black hole. You are a star. Give light. Don't take.

"Would you please excuse us?" Jordan asked.

Jordan looked at Katie with forgiving honesty. Katie felt, as Jordan could tell, comforted and persuaded by Jordan's kind tone.

"Well, I suppose I'll just be making my exit, then," said Katie.

See? Give light.

Katie motioned to leave the other two girls in peace, seemingly getting the hint that Jordan had expressed and Hannah demanded.

However, Hannah had stopped Katie, blocking the doorway with her arm, forcing Katie's attention on her powerful, demanding presence. Jordan focused on Hannah, watching her unbridled strength pour from her. She looked to Jordan like a waterfall of supremacy, crashing down upon and all around her, her roar heard throughout the house as she pounded the stones of Katie's flippant courage beneath her.

"All those things you said…" Hannah started. Jordan watched as Hannah's face moved from a visage of blank strength to dappled frustration to polished rage. "You're nothing but a player, bitch."

But so are you, Hannah. You never do it intentionally, but you get these guys and then you leave them, and you leave them in the crippling wake of your desire: torn, broken, and confused. We're all just brandishing our own guns of judgment, I suppose, pointing them at everyone but ourselves.

Katie sighed as she responded, Hannah's stern words seemingly taking root somewhere deep within. "I know, but at least I don't hide it, Hannah."

Damn, as much as I hate this girl…. But she's right.

"I'm a redhead, kissed by fire," Katie continued. "Get too close and you're likely to get burned."

I am fire, Katie. Not you. You are the thunder, and I am the lightning. You are all talk, the warning of the event already occurred. You may frighten and persuade, but I am the source of that fear and the physical existence of your empty words. I will strike without you. I come before you. But without lightning, thunder does not exist. Without me, you do not exist. I'm sure my denial of her earlier led to this moment, and that's the only reason you are here. I spoke. I struck. And here you are, the aftermath of my choices. Boast again, Thunder, and I will show you what fire really is.

In her hubris, Katie blew Hannah a kiss.

Huntress.

Katie then winked at Jordan.

Like aiming down the sights of a gun. One eye closed….

Katie turned from Jordan to Hannah's arm, avoiding the brunette's gorgeous, matte eyes—the eyes that stared like a snake, unblinking, ready to devour its prey. She seemed immune to the powerful gaze, though she respected it, never looking up.

Jordan watched Hannah as they both waited for Katie to retire beyond the bedroom door down the hallway. She was elated to see her finally gone, but before she passed through the door, Katie looked back at both of them, smiling directly at Jordan, ignoring Hannah still.

Still, you've got to admit, she's a confident one, the bitch. Either way, she's inspired in her own way. Once you've seen the villain, you know why you're the hero, even if you already had some vague idea before. Thank you, Katie. Thank you for all the venomous and terrible things you are. Without the cold, we don't know warmth. Without the darkness, can we really gauge what light is? Maybe that's what it is with Ari…. He's like nothing I've seen before—a soft-spoken lion that doesn't need to roar, merely shows his teeth…. Ari….

Jordan's thoughts of Ari mingled with her quiet thanks for Katie's crass, revealing demeanor. She appreciated this night in this concentrated moment, and she smiled back to Katie, seeing an invisible purpose in their meeting.

Jordan had been turned to coal by a heartbreaking phone call only hours before, wholly crushed by her ex's betrayal. Hannah had set Jordan on fire in their passionate moment in the car earlier, igniting her. The pressure that Katie had put on Jordan had compressed her into a diamond, shining like one never seen before—hardened through the struggle she had just survived. She shined like never before, made anew by the pressuring struggles that had turned her into this new and invaluable stone—a glimmering star in a universe all her own.

HANNAH

Hannah dreamed. Jordan was that dream.

She was awakened by a loud sound, and given the thunder that played on outside, Hannah knew what had shaken her into consciousness.

As she calmed herself, she noticed something was missing from her beautiful delusions, like gorgeous color in negative space. The subject was absent, but the picture was still mesmerizing.

That emptiness made itself obvious as Hannah rolled into the empty space beside her, which she had assumed was still occupied by her red-headed companion.

Katie was gone.

Hannah had no idea for how long.

Hannah sat up, keeping her gaze on the wrinkled sheets and tousled blanket that yielded no warmth for her. The tenant had vacated the premises and the house in which she felt such comfort had become cold and empty, all wires and chipped paint. Hannah shrugged, letting these taunting insecurities go, stretching her arms high into the air, letting out an indulgent sigh as her body relaxed. Leaning back, she scanned the twilit room with her waking, misty eyes. The raindrops gathering upon—and pitter-pattering against—the window were like an audience of tiny eyes, glistening in their awe, watching Hannah simply be. As they collected and descended down the foggy glass, she watched them and all the little glimmers that brought light into her world like the visible prayers of a thousand melancholy stars.

Becoming lost in this moment, she was stricken with the mild panic of loneliness.

Hmm.... I wonder where she went.

A noise of playful laughter greeted her ears from beyond the door left slightly ajar. One was Katie's. The other voice, however, sounded painfully familiar. The curiosity cut like a spiteful knife, her instinct inspiring the birth of a sharp jealousy within her.

Oh, you have GOT to be kidding me!

Rising from the bed with a preconceived notion of wrath building within her, she was ready to cast her judgments—toward whom, she had no clue.

Not gonna lose my shit. Not gonna let it matter. No matter what. Stay calm, Hannah. Stay calm.

Her feet landed softly upon the floor, the soft fibers of the rug gripping her around and between her toes. It felt pleasant to her, giving her a cushioned landing from what was otherwise an elevated, lofty position. She dressed herself with her scattered attire and tied her shoes. She stroked her hair back into place and with a quick shrug and a glance in the mirror across from the window, she made for the door. The giggling had ceased but had been traded for a dually voiced conversation, one that was unclear; but one voice, Hannah had observed, was definitely Katie.

Alright. So, that's how it's gonna be, then. Use me then lose me, huh? I don't get used. I get bored. But let's see what all the fuss is about.

She had no desire for stealth. She wanted to see it with her own eyes, obliterate the traitor, and resume her normal life.

It was fun while it lasted, I suppose.

She made her way down the hallway with a relaxed pace; not so quickly that she exuded nervousness, but also not so slowly that she seemed intimidated. The voices grew louder as Hannah got closer.

No. Hell, no! It can't be!

Hannah's heart sank, every crumb of her pseudo-confident pep-talk immediately swept beneath the rug of her insecurity, waiting in darkened patience for the roaches to come collect and devour.

She found herself paralyzed, numb, and very much the opposite of her genuine self. She was transformed suddenly. The light that radiated from her dulling—a light that had aged rapidly—became wizened and lethargic. She had lost her ability to move. She had lost her ability to speak. She had nowhere to be and nothing to say for the first time in a long time, and this paradigm shift had crippled her like an earthquake from which she had no escape. She stood trapped before the bathroom door.

Nowhere to run to, now. But what do I do? You really screwed up earlier, Hannah. You really messed up. Now you've unlocked Jordan's inner, hidden, sacred Pandora's Box…. You've given her away by trying to claim her….

That's why we're so close. But that's why it'll never work. It's like two magnets of the same polarity. They're the exact same magnet, with the exact same force, but they're so alike, they repel one another. And that's what you've done, Hannah. You've pushed her away, and here they are, two gorgeous guns—both of which you've loaded—and you've pointed them at your own head. You're always so careful.

She could barely breathe. The world around her fizzled and folded into nothing as she listened to the words of the spirited feminine din beyond the door. The shadows of their movement that danced within the light that crept from under the door made her jealous; but it was a jealousy that sat far away, staring deeply at her, unblinking—like eyes, lidless, studying her from within a private, subtle fog.

But this is absolutely your fault, Hannah. Think of how selfish you've been. Taking what you want with no consideration of anyone's feelings. You made Jordan uncomfortable. Now she's gone. You made fun of Michael, and all he wanted was you. Now he's gone. Maybe I should stop trying to gain and just be. I can't even move, right now. Seems like the obvious option.

Hannah shrugged, the only physical movement she could manifest, and she stood there dumbfounded by both her situation and her reaction. She had never questioned her confidence or her ability, yet here she had sampled that drab darkness, the taste of it resembling ash, where once existed the flavor of flames. This transition reminded her of the larger metaphor for herself, and it left a bad taste in her mouth. She became disgusted by both her descent into this unfamiliar state of self-hatred and the path and means by which she had arrived.

Katie, you little tour guide from Hell…. Fire hair and all…. I'm not Dracula. You are. You little blood sucker. You parasite! And I offered it to you. And what I didn't offer, you took….

In her mind, Hannah weighed indistinguishable thoughts that seemed more like feelings that had definition, as opposed to words.

Like a color that reminds you of a smell. Or defining numbers without reference to any other numbers—you know it if you know it. It's something you can't share but can only have. It's something you can't explain, but you know.

Hannah's thoughts dissipated into the ether, her mind coming to a dead end. The noise behind the door had died suddenly away, introducing a whole new wave of panic to Hannah's core. An abrupt silence like that typically meant only one thing: a silence much like the one Hannah had induced earlier when assaulting Jordan with her lips. The thought crushed her, reminding her once more of her inability to function. She felt betrayed. She felt almost nothing at all. It was an unfamiliar, distant darkness in which she found herself trapped, and her only means of escape was involved, likely trapped herself, just beyond the frustrating mystery of the door.

Suddenly, a voice—the familiar one that Hannah so dearly loved— came from the other side, countering the silence, bringing a morsel of comfort back to her arrhythmic heart.

A rustling sound came from beyond the threshold, and the doorknob shook with a failed attempt to turn it from the other side.

Someone is definitely not liking what is happening.

The clicking of the lock coming undone was like a tiny gunshot, killing her prepared ego dead.

Shit. What do I say? What do I say?! Hannah!

In her state, she was unready, unfocused, and almost unwilling to be here; but she had come here, putting herself in this potential path of self-destruction. She felt the fault had been her own.

But I didn't know it was going to be—

In the flash of an instant, Jordan stood before her, the light from the bathroom emanating from behind, illuminating her like an angel. Jordan glistened, reminding Hannah of the show of rain on the window, and the lightning that had awakened her.

It just ends the way it starts, I suppose. With a glimmer. With light….

Katie was also in the room, just as Hannah had suspected. Despite the passive rage that built within her during her trek to this spot, everything indulgent, impatient, invasive, or antagonistic faded with the darkness through the light that shone on the skin of her best friend—a friend that she had helped in redefining over the last few hours. Hannah felt like what she imagined the purest form of God would have been like in His creation of Lucifer.

My creation. My first. My child of light. And here you are, just like my little Lucifer, my creation, but not mine anymore. My favorite. My most beautiful. My love pushed you away from me. And now you consort with the wicked. How fucking poetic. And pointless.

Jordan stood there looking into Hannah's eyes, she as lost for words as Hannah felt.

Jordan looked as though she might cry from embarrassment.

Oh, my little devil. I forgive you.

"Hannah, it's—" Jordan said.

"Not what I think?" Hannah interrupted.

"Yeah, we were just having a girl's bathroom visit," Katie said. "No big deal." Katie shrugged and looked away and down to the floor.

No big deal? God is also judgment.

"Katie," Hannah started, slowly turning her head toward Katie, "don't say another damned word. Not yet. You'll get your chance to talk. You don't seem to understand—"

"This is the friend I've been looking for, Katie," Jordan interrupted.

"Oh, your *friend*, huh? Well, well, what a situation I've caught myself up—"

"Katie. Seriously. Shut. Up," Hannah interrupted.

"Yes, please," Jordan added. "She and I have a lot to discuss. Would you please excuse us?"

Jordan, I'm pissed off! Stop being so kind and humble!

"Well, I suppose I'll just be making my exit then," the red head responded.

Katie made for the door, but Hannah stopped her in the doorway, barring her exit with her arm.

Hannah looked Katie directly into her dead eyes. "All those things you said. You're nothing but a player, bitch."

But so are you, Hannah. You never give anyone a real chance, always investing only until the next better-looking, more elusive thing comes along. The farther the reach, the greater the desire. The vanity…. The easier it is, the harder you resist….

"I know," Katie said, "but at least I don't hide it, Hannah. I'm a redhead, kissed by fire. Get too close and you're likely to get burned." Katie blew a wicked kiss to Hannah, winked at Jordan, and calmly lifted Hannah's arm out of the way, Hannah's eyes never blinking nor leaving Katie's. The redhead let out a quiet, confident, sexy laugh as she left the two friends to be. Jordan and Hannah watched her as she entered the bedroom that Hannah so missed; but turning to Jordan, she smiled, and to Hannah's brimming surprise, Jordan smiled back. There was an air of forgiveness that had overtaken the atmosphere of dread and regret. The destruction had made way for new life. A new world—a brighter, more evolved world—was waiting to soon be born.

ARI

There was no point in attempting to dodge the heavy drops that fell like artillery all around me. I tore up the path as quickly as possible, knowing fully well the trees offered only temporary protection from the monsoon. I was becoming soaked, which I hoped would draw me from my agitated, argumentative state from my most recent conversation with Michael.

The sound of his feet striking the moistening ground behind me told me that he was right on my heels. It gave me a sense of urgency and pushed me to quicken my pace. As we breached the tree line, the rain worsened. The torrent that struck like hundreds of bullets shocked me, making my mind go blank, forgetting anything but the feeling of the relentless water on my skin. It was like an emotional vacation, and nothing but a great tranquility occupied my mind and body. I was unified in the release, and let my frustrations go. For just a moment, even Jordan did not exist for me. Nothing did. It was just me and the rain, myself and the source of all life; I, the resident—the water, my dwelling.

Just another flood, sent to destroy my world….

Modern Noah. Modern Job. The destruction. The struggle. All in one. Will I rise above and float on, or will I drown?

I'd rather be swimming in a river—the Jordan—that beautiful river of life…. What a beauty….

Michael was right behind me as we approached the house. We were both soaking wet, making our way through the maelstrom. I was the captain of the ship and he was my first mate, full of deceit and preconceptions of mutiny. The rain was the ocean that trapped us, threatening to swallow us whole. I was already drowning in limitless thought. Furthermore, the overwhelming events that had transpired were pressing me down like a cosmic finger into the mud of my drowning world.

We reached the door and I rushed to open it, passing quickly through.

"After you," I said, a cold, dead distance in his eyes as he stared out into the loud darkness, the rain no longer affecting him. He stood just outside the door, ignoring my invitation and how I held it open for him to come inside. He had the appearance of Michael, but he was no longer Michael. He was a hollow shell, and almost ghoulish in his suddenly wet, gaunt expression. The substances and party favors had disfavored him, shunning him like a wrathful god that imbued its punishment in the form of zombie-like dissonance. His grey shirt had become almost black in with its burden of wetness, and his hair was dripping.

In reticence, I kept my eyes on him as I drifted past. I was a hollow phantom, and Michael was simply hollow. I did not recognize him anymore. It terrified me, but what terrified me more was that he seemed lost in himself or far beyond. Either way, this statue that was once my friend was unfamiliar, and it left a lingering anxiety upon my skin; and as that commingled with the rain, I was doused in doubt, the thin layer of unknowing permeating me as it covered. The rain was an uncertain blanket, and it neither warmed me nor brought me comfort. I shed the 'lie blanket' as I moved indoors.

I attempted to shut the door to keep the rain out as Michael clearly did not wish to enter, but he kept it held open, his stone eyes fixated on the nothing that enraptured his undivided attention. His lips seemed to utter something, as though he was speaking to a ghost in its ghost language. It carried on into the air, lost to the sound of the droplets of rain that bombarded the back porch.

Again, I stood stock-still, the din of the kitchen party further blurring my overwhelmed ears. The party was beckoning my return with or without him.

"Michael Law, are you coming in?" I asked in an almost parental tone.

His only reaction was a shrug, one of distance and disillusionment. He no longer felt like a person but remained as the same shell I had been studying for the moments that strung along like an eternity pulled into a thin string.

Thin.

Weak.

I was mortified. It was as though we had fast-forwarded into a future, one that begged the reflection of a suffering life; like a cancer patient at the end of long road of recovery—exhausted, but living, technically, though wholly not his former self.

"Michael," I said. "Michael, are you coming in?"

The rain suddenly stopped as quickly as it had come, as though the sky had ceased its mourning. The sadness was over, and God was gone once again, the world freshly abandoned, with no purpose but the absorption of the broken ocean. The crowd went silent almost immediately.

We are made in His image….

"And we go silent with Him," I whispered. The silence was so thick, my lowered voice was clearly audible.

Michael turned slowly to me, forsaking what held his attention out there in the void, and as his eyes slowly rolled away from me to right at me, long hair dripping steadily before his face, a chill shot up my spine, stopping just behind my slowing heart. It all met together and caught in my throat. I could not speak, and I could barely form thoughts. All at once, the world froze, and the wet earth became an icy, unforgiving landscape before me.

"Ari, I have to go," Michael said. "It is time."

"What the hell are you talking about?" I said. "You've had way too much to drink tonight. You're staying here tonight." I grabbed his bicep as I spoke, its definition still so new and shocking to the touch, but like the stone man he was, he seemed to not feel it.

The mushrooms…. You should never have even touched those. Your willingness to please these women will be your downfall.

"That's not what I mean," he stammered, his words sounding difficult to enunciate, as though his tongue had gone numb. "Out there. It's all out there," he said, returning his gaze to the void beyond.

"Michael, I know I've been talking about God a bit tonight, but please don't mock me. Are you okay?"

The crowd began to stir, both in movement and in volume. The clouds were parting. I could tell because of the light of the moon gradually illuminating the ground outside, and as I got lost in the glimmer of the light, the crowd began to slowly grind around and pass me, like an amoeba passing itself through a prey too large to absorb.

"I—I've got to go!" Michael said, his voice's volume increasing as he spoke.

"But Michael! You've got to tell me what's going on! Please, tell me!" I said.

"No time but now. We'll talk later!" he said, shouting at this point. I looked around at the crowd engulfing me, the door still open. I looked back to Michael, but Michael was gone, lost in anonymity to the mass of the mob of darkness.

Have I done something wrong? What did he see? Where is he going? Michael, where in the hell are you going…?

MICHAEL

Michael followed Ari through what he thought was rain. It felt like rain. It smelled like rain. It was melting him.

Into what, he did not know.

It's all so strange, isn't it? The lightning. The rain. The voice. Who are you? You know me. You spoke like you know me, but you're like a stranger I've not met before yet known my whole life. Why tonight, among all this? What are you? What am I?

Running, running, running. Wet rain. Cold ground. You son of a bitch! How did you know my name? Must be the mushrooms, Michael. Don't lose yourself. Not here. Not at Ari's house. It's been a while, hasn't it?

So, remember who you are and handle it. Don't entertain such dark thoughts….

"But I am a dark thought, Michael Law. That isn't even your name as I know you. But if that is what you wish to be called, so be it…. I know who you are."

Who? Who said that? Hello? How are you inside my head? Show yourself cowar—

"Do not even say it, Michael. Don't you dare tempt me. I know you. You do not know me, but I know you, and that alone should quell your desire to affront me with any offense. Here we are, both of us, in your head, having a conversation."

Am I crazy? What the hell?

"Exactly, Michael."

What does that even mean?

Michael was at the back door of the house with Ari again. He was frozen with doubt and fear. Ari stood before Michael, holding the door.

Good host.

"Good host, indeed. You, first."

"After you," Ari said, waiting with patience on his face, the door in Michael's hand.

What the f—

"Watch your mouth, Michael Law. I have great plans for you."

What plans? What are these thoughts? You're losing your mind, Michael. That's all you've got tonight besides Ari.

"Yes, you lost your heart long ago, didn't you?"

I did. I definitely did.

"I have seen you suffer."

I have suffered. It's why I try to stay so strong. Wait…. Who are you?

Silence was Michael's answer.

Hello? Hello! I'm talking to myself, great. Maybe Ari is onto something. Maybe Beethoven will join us after all….

"Michael Law."

What?

Ari spoke to Michael, mirroring the voice that spoke to Michael in his mind. "Michael Law, are you coming in?"

Michael sat terrified at the coincidental prediction. Every word Ari was speaking, the voice in his head alluded to first.

Maybe time and space mean nothing… on mushrooms.

Michael laughed to himself. However, he could not speak at all. He could not move.

"Come, Michael. Come in. The door is open."

Perhaps I should. Ari is waiting.

"Not Ari, Michael. ME."

"Michael Law, are you coming in?" Ari said. Still, Michael was still. He was frozen, affronted by three voices: Ari's, his own, and the other.

But who is the other? Will you tell me?

Michael got no response. The only response he could offer Ari was a shrug, though that hardly communicated the struggle that he was enduring within himself.

"You are tired of the rain, aren't you—this 'God talk?' Listen to me, Child. I will help you forget if you let me, Michael Law. Remember your name—Law, Law, LAW!"

My name is…!

"Michael," Ari said.

Okay. This is weird now. As if it weren't already….

"Michael Law," Ari said.

"So, are you coming in?"

Ari spoke, interrupting the voice. "Are you coming in?"

Michael's mind had imploded. The third instance of repetition had eradicated his preconceptions of coincidence, the meaning of it all too much and heavy for his drug-encumbered mind to handle. He defragmented within himself, slowly turning to Ari, giving the best response he could. He could feel his words grinding in his head, like an ancient stone—a doorway to which the key had just been found, millennia later.

"I can stop this pain for you. Watch."

Just then, the rain ceased. The silence allowed Michael to reflect on the echoes that carried on within his head.

"I will leave you now. Come find me should you wish to entertain and entertain with."

But what is your name? Who are you?

"I am silence, as are you. Now, seek me, should quiet be your calling."

"And we go silent with Him," Ari uttered ruggedly beneath his breath. Michael could still hear him, despite the fragile breathy exhale that carried the heavy words.

"You must choose to save your friend, Michael Law. His path has been chosen, and you have laid it out for him. What will you do?"

Michael stood in disbelief.

"Save him. Farewell, until we speak again."

Michael gave no response. The moisture of the air seemed to evaporate around him, the heat of his heavy heart warming him as it weighed him down. His stomach sank like stone, steadily falling into the dark depths of his anxiety. The singularity that was his thought broke beneath the gravity of the weight, and in an instant, his physical self disappeared. He was light embodied. Michael decided his next move.

It chose me. It called my name. I must go. I have to know.

"Ari, I have to go. It is time," Michael said.

"What the hell are you talking about?" Ari said. "You've had way too much to drink tonight."

And still, I thirst.

"You're staying here tonight," Ari continued.

Like hell I am. I've got to go. I've got to find that voice.

"That's not what I mean," said Michael, fumbling with his words. "Out there. It's all out there." Michael peered back into the darkness, watching.

"Michael, I know I've been talking about God a bit tonight," Ari said, "but please don't mock me."

For the first time, Ari, I am not mocking you. I just need to know that I'm okay.

"Are you okay?" Ari asked.

The question forced an air of panic into the balloon of his heart. He could feel his heart rate increasing. His breath rattled as he responded.

"I—I've got to go!" Michael said.

I can't explain it. Time is wasting! He said I must 'save you.' But you don't seem in any danger.

"But Michael!"

No 'buts.' Only action.

"You've got to tell me what's going on! Please, tell me!" Ari pleaded.

I can't tell you. I don't even know, myself. It's all so mysterious….

Michael mustered up his final courage, decisiveness coursing through him like a purpose of which he had no knowledge. It stirred within him at first, and then it overtook his body, possessing him and dragging him back to the shadows.

No time but now, Ari.

"No time but now. We'll talk later!" Michael said, his voice increasing to a shout as he spoke.

As quickly as he had made his decision, Michael abandoned the doorframe, cutting through the shadows like a panicked light, hurtling through the unknown outside.

I will find you again.

And I will find 'you' first.

Michael was gripped in fear as he felt the separation from the party and Ari. Still, he pressed on, eager to meet what being had known him so well and knew him not at all.

Either I can hear the future, or you are real. Either way, I'm bound to find something, I hope.

PROVERBS

JORDAN

Jordan was stunned by her reaction to Katie's brash expression of emotion in the presence of Hannah, as Hannah had made it very clear that she despised the redhead and her crass actions.

"Well, that was weird," said Jordan, attempting to nullify the harshness of the air around them. She could feel the static coming from Hannah's body, watching her chest heave to and fro from what seemed like a comedown from the adrenaline that had undoubtedly overtaken her. Like a lioness wheezing after battle, Jordan's aloof comment seemed to go completely unheard by Hannah. Hannah was intent on her anger.

I've almost never seen you this way. Thank you for protecting me. I'm always so nice. I'm always so kind, even though it's ruined me at times. You…. You don't give a shit, Hannah. Always protecting what you love. I know you love me. Thank you.

"Hannah, are you okay?" Jordan asked.

Silence.

Jordan hated that she could not bring Hannah back to reality.

You're my best friend. It's over now. We don't have to worry about her anymore….

"We don't have to worry about her anymore," Jordan said, placing her arms over Hannah's soft shoulders. Hannah winced a little, then relaxed underneath the weight of Jordan's arms.

There you are.

"So…. Are we okay, now, Hannah?"

Hannah kept her eyes on the floor. Jordan moved in closer.

"Hey, listen to me. It's all okay. I promise," Jordan said. "Whatever happened in the car, it's gone. It happened in the past, and now we have now. Hey…."

Jordan watched as a tear fell from Hannah's eye, landing on Hannah's shoe.

"Hannah, honey, I've never seen you cry before. It's going to be okay. I promise."

Hannah slowly lifted her head, bringing her sad eyes to the level of Jordan's. Jordan did her best to mimic the sad expression on Hannah's face, her attempt to console without words—to empathize with the breaking woman in front of her.

"Jordan, I…." said Hannah, her voice cracking.

"Tell me," said Jordan. "Tell me anything. Whatever you need to say, say it. I promise I won't get upset or anything."

Hannah's eyes were glossy and red with the emotion gathering behind her face. Her quivering lip was a testament to her unbridled, unfiltered feelings, and Jordan stood before her, examining the changes in Hannah's face. Hannah's shifty, unfocused eyes told a million stories, all the frustrations and unknown goings-on of the passing night coming to a head in her mind, exploding inside of her with no path of escape. Beneath the pressure, Hannah was crumbling, and Jordan felt a slight twinge of guilt for her instigations.

"I…."

"Yes?" Jordan cupped Hannah's cheek in her hand. "Go on, sweetie. It's all right."

"I just can't right now," Hannah responded. "So much. It's all so much. I've been hoping to talk to you since the car, and still…. Still, I don't know what to say. I don't know how to say I'm sorry because…."

"Go on, Hannah. I'm listening now."

Jordan had exposed herself as well as she knew how. The diamond armor that she had put on throughout the night was coming off in these moments.

We all need something worth fighting for. Find the ones that you can take off your armor for.

"Because…" Hannah continued. "Because I…."

A millennium passed within Jordan's mind as she hung on the slow words falling clumsily from Hannah's mouth.

Anything you say is okay with me.

Hannah looked down, around at the floor, and then back up to Jordan's face. Another collection of tears, fresh and fierce, began to culminate in Hannah's eyes.

"…Because I love you, Jordan."

Jordan smiled at the words. She knew what Hannah meant, and hearing those words comforted her.

I haven't heard those words in so long, I've almost forgotten they exist.

"I love you, and I'm not sorry for it!" Hannah said, wiping her eyes, abandoning her eye contact with Jordan once more. "Seeing you become this new woman tonight…. Oh, hell! It's just absurd!"

The rain outside had ceased.

"I know it's my own vanity, but seeing you after *seeing* you for so long…. It's all just so overwhelming…."

"No need to apologize or feel guilty or shitty," Jordan said. "And Hannah, I—"

I love you, too.

Jordan poured every ounce of her caring heart into what she was about to say to Hannah, but Hannah cut her off with a gasp.

"I'm so sorry! I need some space. It's not you, I swear! I just need a moment, Jordan. Let's talk a little later. Tonight is for fun. We can save the serious stuff for another time," said Hannah.

"But Hannah—"

"No, I've made up my mind," Hannah said, wiping her teary face once more. "We'll talk later. I have much to think about."

Hannah turned and was down the stairs before Jordan could respond. The noise of the party downstairs filled Jordan's ears, and once again, she was in the dark, alone, and confused. Hannah had left her for the second time tonight, and she had no one.

Shit. It's all just shit. Muddy water….

"*Mud….*"

Jordan thought back to Ari and his obvious interest. She contemplated his goofy demeanor and his well-intended eyes.

Ari…. Ari….

Jordan gathered herself, shrugged with an exhale, and fought back the tears of uncertainty and frustration.

Go find Ari, Jordan, but don't go. No. And don't go falling in love.

Jordan made her way down the stairs, each step bringing a new revelation and understanding to her bustling mind.

HANNAH

Hannah stood and stood alone.

"Well, that was weird," said Jordan.

Hannah was completely numb to her friend's vain attempts to console—completely unreachable. The frustrations building in her heart were making her fit to burst, but instead, she imploded.

"Hannah, are you okay?" Jordan asked.

No. Hell, no.

"We don't have to worry about her anymore," Jordan said. The soft touch of Jordan's caring hand caused Hannah to jerk, surprised as she flashed back to reality.

There you are.

"So…. Are we okay, now, Hannah?"

What is 'okay' anymore, even? This is all so stupid. Always wanting what I can't have. Throwing away all that I can. Vanity.

Hannah could not even look at Jordan or anything but the floor, for that matter. She had once held her head high, but now it hung low, much like her self-worth as she had felt betrayed by not one, but two people she had come to trust.

I don't even trust myself anymore. Who I am…. What I've become tonight….

"Hey, listen to me," Jordan said.

Yeah, because that's worked so well tonight.

"It's all okay. I promise," Jordan continued.

Like hell, it is! You don't know! The shower. The car. This damned moment right now! Nothing is okay. Certainly not me!

"Whatever happened in the car, it's gone," Jordan said.

No, it isn't. It's all I've been able to think about all night. I really screwed up with that….

"It happened in the past and now we have now," said Jordan.

I don't have anything. Nothing at all. It's all just a bunch of bullshit. All of it.

Hannah began to weep inside. Slowly, but fiercely, emotion began to creep from her eyes. The blurry pain crawled to the surface of her vision. She was holding back as hard as she could, but she was overwhelmed.

"Hey…."

Jordan's voice was a distant echo rattling the caverns of her entire being. Down the soundwaves went, bouncing from surface to surface, on into the nothing below.

"Hannah, honey, I've never seen you cry before," said Jordan. "It's going to be okay. I promise."

Hannah lifted her head, the weight of it seeming unbearable to her. She could see Jordan's attempt to make the same concerned face as her, but it was in vain.

I'm already gone. But still here. Why?

"Jordan, I…" said Hannah. Her words were being drowned by the river roaring in her mind. She nearly choked on the syllables.

Jordan interrupted Hannah's thoughts. "Tell me. Tell me anything. Whatever you need to say, say it. I promise I won't get upset or anything."

That doesn't matter to me. Not at all. I need to focus on me. I don't give two shits how you feel about it, Jordan. But I do love you.

"I…."

If I tell you….

"Yes?" said Jordan. "Go on, sweetie. It's all right."

The inner conflict made Hannah sick with words, and suddenly, she vomited those words. "I just can't right now. So much. It's all so much. I've been hoping to talk to you since the car, and still…. Still, I don't know what to say. I don't know how to say I'm sorry because…."

Because I love you and I'm sorry.

"Go on, Hannah. I'm listening now."

"Because. Because I…."

I know we're just friends, but earlier…. But earlier you'd forgive me. If anyone would, it would be you. I'm so sorry, Jordan, but, I have to say it…!

"…Because I love you, Jordan."

Jordan's smile brought solace to the moment. Hannah felt she had been heard and not misconstrued.

I haven't said those words in so long, I've almost forgotten they exist.

Hannah had decided to let it all out. She felt as though she were shaking off the tremors of the earthquake that had silently rumbled on within her. She looked away from Jordan and, using her wrist, wiped away the subtle moisture that collected in her eyes.

"I love you and I'm not sorry for it!" she said.

I'm acting like I'm drunk. Simmer down a notch!

"Seeing you become this new woman tonight…. Oh, hell! It's just absurd!"

For a moment, you were totally new.

The sound of the rain outside dissipated.

"I know it's my own vanity, but seeing you after *seeing* you for so long…. It's all just so overwhelming…."

"No need to apologize or feel guilty or shitty," Jordan said.

Shitty is the word. I need to think for a while….

"And Hannah, I—"

No! Don't say. Go to your Adam, or Ari, or whatever. I need to think for a while.

"I'm so sorry! I need some space. It's not you, I swear! I just need a moment, Jordan. Let's talk a little later. Tonight is for fun. We can save the serious stuff for another time."

"But Hannah—"

"No, I've made up my mind," Hannah said as genuinely as she could. "We'll talk later. I have much to think about."

Hannah dismissed herself before Jordan could intercept her.

This party was a terrible idea….

ARI

Am I my brother's keeper?

I stood in disbelief at the speed in which Michael was gone. In a doorway, almost like a portal to chaos, I watched as a man I knew became a husk before my eyes, floating off into the unknown. It frightened me.

So strange. I've never seen him run from anything, much less me....

The moisture lingered in the air, a discomfort to my skin. The world suddenly felt out of balance—shifted and off-center. My empathy for Michael's obvious change in persona caused a change in me, and I could feel his unnerved demeanor throughout my soul.

What's gotten into you?

The rain had come and was gone, much like Michael, and I could control neither, it seemed.

God was fire.

Jordan was fire.

Michael was water.

My mind was drifting in the post-rain air.

And we—all of us—were being brought back down to earth.

Instantaneous gravity upon us all and we cannot escape it.... We are all such frail slaves to the Monarch's harmonious design.

"Still, Michael," I whispered. "What's gotten into you?" The darkness beyond the door that had swallowed Michael was swallowing me as well.

"Excuse me," came a strong feminine voice from behind me. I turned in time to glimpse the most indescribably flawless brunette I had ever seen flash by me, almost as if I had not even seen her at all, but more so imagined. In a flash she was there. In the same flash, she was gone. A living dream had passed me by, and I was breathless in my swoon; and much like the flash of an atomic bomb, the shadow of her countenance and stride were burned into my mind. I could barely make out the trace scents of smoke and wine in her wake—her memory and odor were all that was left behind of her blitzkrieg introduction to my life.

Drifting in like that, producing such a spark in me. You smell like smoke, but you've started a fire. Fire…. Eyes in the fire…. I may never see you again, but Jordan…. I wonder if she's even still here…. Drifting, both of them, in and out: their look—that scent—like a siren screaming, a warning for the beautiful chaos to come. And before shelter can even be sought…. The bomb of their presence goes off, destroying all—destroying me—leaving nothing but ashes and smoke.

Like smoke, they leave us. Like smoke, they start with heat, they drift, then they're gone…. Farewell….

Akin to my metaphor, I was becoming ashes.

Smoke. Ashes. Fire.

God. Jordan.

Will I ever see you again?

Thunder rolled outside, some distance away.

"Jordan," I whispered, barely audible amid the noise of the guests that surrounded me. I continued to stare blankly out the open back door, my eyes focusing on the void that had claimed Michael and me.

Jordan, if you're still out there….

"Jordan," I exhaled, lowering my head, closing my eyes.

"Yes?"

A familiar voice acknowledged it had heard me. My skin tingled as my mind erased itself, and disbelief gripped me like a child clutching its favorite toy. I slowly raised my head and turned.

The party mob was gone from me in a moment as my eyes attempted to take in the impossible sight in front of me. It began at the floor with red high heels, my eyes continuing their journey up two perfect legs, which hid at the thighs beneath a form-fitting black dress. The curves of the perfect hips led to a tiny waist, then two small but beautiful breasts that further guided me to the neck, then the chin, then lips and cheeks, finally meeting and diving headlong into the perfect eyes belonging to—

"Jordan…." I sighed, nearly brought to tears.

MICHAEL

Michael was a ghost chasing a ghost, and lost as he was, he was merely a shadow in a game of shadow-tag, hidden from light, blindly hunting, uncertain of the identity of his prey.

Am I even the hunter? Or simply a fly, running quickly to the spider…?

The pounding of each step smashing the wet earth was a small earthquake, muffled only by the wetness of the grass beneath. Moving as quickly as the descending terrain would allow, Michael trotted impatiently—to where exactly, he did not know.

Every step crushed the earth beneath.

The earth pressed back.

With his psilocybin influence lingering, each sinking step felt like a rabbit hole, and while his feet sank to rise to sink again into the wet soil, so mirrored the tempest of thought, metaphor, and reality—three pieces comprising Michael of all he was—a trinity of existence and non-existence; a duality both eternal and existential.

The hypocrisy of existence! Born against our non-existent will to live and to die….

Michael was halfway to the grove when he stopped. He was surrounded by the silhouettes of trees in the night beneath a clearing post-rain sky, the outdoor house lights vaguely illuminating Ari's home beyond the tree line.

"So glad to be away from it all—nice and alone. Peaceful," he said, turning his gaze to the mansion behind him. The faint smell of the dead fire lingered softly upon the air, and that very smell urged his hand into his pocket for his cigarettes. He procured one, lighted it, and, enthralled momentarily by the dancing flame of his lighter—

Little god….

—he stared into its colorful dance in the dark, suddenly terrified by his lack of vision beyond the flame. He let it go out, returning the lighter to his pocket, taking a drag of smoke in stride. Looking up, he exhaled his smoky breath into the air, the smoke passing through the dim rays of artificial light that shone through the trees, until it was gone.

Michael took another drag, folded his arms and exhaled again in the same fashion, watching and waiting.

For nothing.

I can't believe the rain didn't soak my cigarettes….

Michael laughed.

"What the hell am I doing out here?" he asked himself.

A low rumble of thunder sounded from far away.

"Well, at least the storm has passed."

Taking another drag from his cigarette, he leaned against a nearby tree, breathing out and taking in a long, clean breath. His mind began to come to terms with his hallucinating state, and a sense of calm and acceptance came over him.

I needed this. First Ari goes crazy, then I do. But I'm not the crazy one. All this 'God' garbage…. Ari's always got some weird notion about him. Too smart for his own good. I mean, I know he gets lonely, but Jordan? You just met the girl, man! Soft-hearted. And religion? In the same night? What is going on with you, man? You're insane!

Michael laughed to himself.

"I guess I can't blame you. We're all a little crazy tonight…"

Michael took another drag of his cigarette.

"At least I'm starting to get it back together…."

A rustling near Michael caused him to jump away from the tree upon which he was leaning.

"He-hello?" he quietly asked the darkness. "Someone there?"

No response.

The dark forest scene was eerily silent. He stared intently, peering in the direction from where the noise came, his heightened senses failing him as he discovered nothing. His ears could hear far-off animals, the rustling of leaves dancing to the music of the gentle post-rain wind. He could feel the air's embrace as it crept through the still shadows of trees around him, and its gentle caresses comforted him. He could still smell the perfume of the forgotten fire commingled with the dewy clean scent of autumn precipitation. The gentle light that could reach the earth was intensified by his dilated pupils, allowing him to see better in the dark. On his tongue, he could make out a myriad of flavors. Beneath the blanket of tobacco smoke and wine, he could still faintly make out the filthy flavor of the mushrooms, which, to Michael, suddenly reinforced their power with another subtle wave. Still, beyond all these flavors were two more—

Katie. Hannah. I can still taste them. The shame….

He hung his head to his chest, bringing the cigarette to his lips for another drag. Exhaling this time, he licked his mouth hungrily, savoring the remaining morsels of those two gorgeous creatures that clung faintly to his lips.

I wonder which one left this gloss on me?

Michael laughed once more, satisfied with himself in his reflection of moments of the past. Another drag of smoke climbed out through his smiling teeth as he pondered.

Another sound of movement stirred him, making him uneasy, as it was slightly louder and closer than before.

He brushed it off, dismissing it as nothing. He was focused on his thoughts and his senses. He was focused too intently on his inner visions of lust unconsummated, his failure to sexually perform becoming a hilarious joke unto himself.

I'll get my second chance. We'll just say I got to sample the meal—

Thunder rumbled again—again, far away.

—before I gorge myself on the 'spread', ha, ha!

Once more, he laughed aloud.

"And precisely what do you suppose is so humorous, Michael?"

Michael nearly jumped from his skin as that familiar voice boomed once more inside his mind. He tried to ignore it, shrugging his broad shoulders and taking another drag as he leaned back against the tree.

"Yeah… right," he said aloud, laughing to himself yet again.

I work with the sick. Sickness cannot heal sickness. I am not sick. I am not crazy. The mushrooms sure are doing a number…. No more drugs from now on. Never again.

Michael hit the cigarette again. He exhaled, eyeing two adjacent far-off lights through the trees in front of him. He looked away from them, then into darkness in the direction of where the fire once burned.

Let's see if we can't get that thing lit again. After all, the rain's gone.

Michael began his short trek toward the doused woodpile at the heart of the grove. The trees began to clear as he approached, the shadow of the bonfire's remains made more legible with his increased sight and the subtle light from the moon above. He, however, could see no gas can or dry tinder with which to reignite the pyre.

He took a drag from his cigarette, eyeing the smolder close to his face as it intensified.

That won't be enough….

He laughed again. "Hell, if Ari were here I'm sure he could pray me up some fire," said Michael, sarcastically chuckling to himself. "God's here tonight, isn't he, Ari?" Michael asked, mockingly. He gestured as if Ari were present with him. "Come on, why don't you pray me up some fucking fire, Ari? Come on, do it. Just for shits and giggles. Why don't you ask Beethoven and God to come over? We'll have some wine and coke with them, we'll all get wasted, and you can ask both of those deaf bastards to help us all see better!" Michael jested. "Since they can't hear and none of us can 'see', might as well help someone, *right?*"

Right, Ari?

He threw his finished cigarette aggressively into the woodpile, only to draw another out immediately, light it, inhale, and blow his smoke to the sky above.

"Only gonna listen to Ari tonight, huh?" Michael mocked. "If I were Ari, would you give *me* fire? Come on, Mister God—why don't you *show* me something!"

Michael dragged his cigarette, blowing it mockingly to the sky once more.

Silence. As expected. Par for the damn course….

Another drag entered and left Michael's chest, the smoke casted tauntingly toward the clouds for the third time. Michael raised his arms in expecting fashion, looking around him as if before an audience, seeking applause for his performance.

"What's wrong, Mister God? Did I get smoke in your eye?" Michael questioned defiantly.

Michael turned back toward the two lights he had seen earlier. As he dragged his cigarette, the lights intensified in brightness, as if reflecting the light from the cherry of his cigarette.

Keeping his unblinking gaze locked upon the lights, he hit his cigarette again, and once again, the lights grew slightly, both in size and in the intensity of their 'reflection'.

"You can't get smoke in your eyes," Michael spoke into the darkness, his tone becoming more serious and calmer. "Because you can't see anything at all. Because you're not real. You can't see a thing."

As he hit his cigarette, the two lights once more swelled, doubling in size. A chill ran up Michael's spine, though he did not waver.

"You can't see a thing, you blind, sky-bound bastard!" Michael shouted.

Michael took another drag, nearly swallowing his cigarette as he choked, the two lights having suddenly moved closer, undeniably nearer—and very near—to him. Their sudden shift caused him to lose his balance, falling, becoming seated and frozen solid in fear in the mud beneath him.

A voice came from the two floating orbs, which were now very clearly not lights at all but eyes.

"It seems you do not 'see' very well, yourself…" said the voice.
What in the fu—!
"MICHAEL LAW!"

HANNAH

Hannah was a blazing dynamo of fury, regret, and loneliness as she descended the stairs, and she, for the second time tonight, felt completely lost and alone.

That didn't go at all as I'd hoped. If only I'd not been so quick to give up and give in.... From one to the other—boy to boy, girl to girl—do you have any control, you idiot?! This façade of such a strong bitch, the mask for everyone to see.... But you know—you KNOW—deep inside, it's all just vanity! Narcissist! It doesn't matter what you need. It's what you want, and what you want is everything!

Hannah's thoughts were racing in and out, between and beneath herself, above and within. From all angles she was struggling with herself—with her view of herself—and her epiphanies were almost too heavy—too real—to bear. The constant heartbreaks and letdowns she had been enduring all night were cracks in her self-understanding, and those little fissures had finally begun to creep their way to her marble surface, where the wear and tear of all her trials were becoming visible for the world to see. Realizing that her weaknesses were becoming more outwardly obvious only broke her further, which worsened her frustrations.

Fuck! It's just spiraling! I'm spiraling.... How do I stop it? I don't know what to do! I run from one nightmare into another! Up the stairs to hell, down the stairs to a worse one.... Will I ever escape?

Hannah had reached the bottom of the stairs and stood in the foyer by the front door, tears of frustration forming in her eyes.

Too much tonight. Too much everything. Jordan was too much, so I overreacted. The wine was too much, and I didn't even have that much! Katie, Michael, me—all too damned much. And now too much thinking! I swear, I'm about to explode!

Hannah could hear footsteps descending the stairs.

Shit! Gotta get somewhere.... I can't talk to her right now. I've gotta—

Before she could form a plan, Hannah went into a panic, running to the living room nearby.

Empty? Strange….

There was no door to shut behind her, so Hannah quickly looked around for a hiding place. She looked at the recliner, which looked quite cozy to her; she looked at the plush couch and matching loveseat; she looked at the fireplace and the low coals which were smoldering calmly, light whispers of smoke climbing up and into the flue.

If only I could jump into the flames and die! Haha!

Her humor crept through her panic, a coping mechanism to try keeping her wits about herself as her mind fell to pieces. She tore her eyes from the fire, those phantom footsteps meeting the bottom of the stairs. She threw herself silently into the floor between the loveseat and the coffee table, out of view from the adjacent foyer.

This'll have to do, I suppose….

She positioned herself so that she could see who had come downstairs but could only make out the feet of the 'intruder' through the gap between the tabletop and the shelf beneath.

Red heels…. Good thing I took cover!

The shoes paused their walk, remaining still for some time.

Please go! Please just go! This is torture!

The right foot began tapping on the floor, as if in impatience, then stopped. Both heels turned back to the stairs, then toward the living room, where they froze for a few moments. Hannah's heart stopped.

Please, please don't come in here!

To Hannah's horror, one foot stepped forward as if to enter the room.

This is so much worse! This is going to be so embarrassing! What would I even say? What would it look like? What would she think? I clearly didn't think this one through….

Those familiar red high heels took a few more careful steps into the carpeted living room, where they turned toward the fireplace. Hannah closed her eyes to blind herself to the suffocating world around her. She slowed and quieted her breathing.

Why am I afraid of you now? I suppose it's my love for you, Jordan. I'm sorry for my impulses, for what I did, and I'm sorry for how this night has turned out. I should have just stayed home! But I saw an opportunity to help—No! You were suddenly single, heartbroken, and vulnerable, and I sought to take advantage of your frailty. That's what it was….

Am I such a narcissist that I didn't see it before? How could I be so blind?

Blind to my role as your friend, blind to my own needs… blind to my own selfish motives that I disguised as 'help'—as friendship. This is all my fault! I've built the bomb and whether I push the button or not, the blood is on my hands. I'm so sorry….

With her eyes still closed, Hannah felt lighter in her honesty with herself. She had been lying to herself in so many ways for such a long time, and now her sins were catching up to her, as she was starting to see.

Eyes closed, and now I see…. Beautiful.

Just, beautiful…. But what is 'sinful' anyway? Does my own happiness not matter? Of course, it does, but you love Jordan, do you not? And wouldn't you be so good to her? FOR her?

Tears began to form behind her closed eyelids.

I would be, but that's my choice, not hers. She's never liked girls like that, and I was such a damned fool to be so proud that I thought I could sway her. She just looks so good tonight, too, and out of nowhere. Hannah, you suggested her clothing because you thought it appealing. You invited her to this party because you thought it appealing. You got high with her and drank with her because you found her appealing in the way that you crafted her tonight. And now it's all falling apart.

A tear, followed quickly by another, rolled gently down her nose. It began to tickle, so she rubbed it away.

It's all about you, Hannah. You hide your self-serving motives behind a paper-thin veil of selflessness, and while others may not see it, now you do, and maybe that's why you've always been alone. No one's ever been good enough for you, have they? You need someone perfect, yet not more perfect than you, and yet look at how broken and flawed you are. The hubris…. The absolute lie of it all! You polished Jordan, broken, into a diamond, but now another wants her—hell, several maybe—and now you're jealous in the failure of your own scheming heart! Look at how long it took for you to run to another—not even an hour. Jordan said no, and suddenly, you're getting fucked up with strangers, ready to take and be taken by the first person to lure you in! And not only one, but two! Will it ever be enough? And WHAT is enough for you??

Hannah broke completely. In fearful silence, she openly wept, a hidden, frightened, broken child, ashamed of the pieces she had become. She once had been a mirror, flawless, clear, and reflective; yet her internal realizations were thoughts becoming stones that she was now hurling at herself, the mirror becoming broken—and by these thrown truths, her mirror-self was shattering, becoming many mirrors in one, finally able to see all the individual, broken parts of herself.

Nothing's ever been enough. You've thrown away some good ones, and now you've thrown away yourself. Maybe now, you know how it feels, Hannah. No one is perfect, and certainly not you! It will never be enough until YOU are enough. Until then, nothing will be, and you will be nothing!

"And I am not nothing!" Hannah breathed quietly, forgetting momentarily where she was, quickly putting her hand over her mouth. She opened her eyes to see that the shoes were gone from the room.

Thank God!

Hannah wiped her face and looked around to make certain that she was alone.

No one. Perfect.

She remained stationary for a moment, taking in her loneliness—the peace of it—and stared deep into the warm, low glow of the fireplace, the soundtrack to her solitude the ironic dull noise of conversations in the kitchen.

A strange new notion gripped her. She was broken, but now that she knew, she could fix herself. She was lonely, but now that she knew why, she could be more honest with her own heart. She was ready to not be so stubborn. She had learned much of herself this night, certain more lessons were yet to come.

And Jordan didn't find me….

She looked at the fireplace with a curious look. She furrowed her perfect eyebrows, closing her eyes.

God, I don't know if you're there or not, but if you are, thank you….

She opened her eyes to the fireplace's glow.

Thank you.

A log shifted in the hearth, sending sparks upward into the flue, a little ember reigniting as the wood bustled. Hannah gasped. It was a beautiful coincidence, but Hannah felt she had been heard, and a new hope came to life within her.

I've got to get out of this house! I need some air!

Hannah scanned the room once more, made her way for her exit, peered around the corner making sure of Jordan's absence, and fled to and through the kitchen. She kept her head high, making long, strong strides as to both cover ground quickly and not draw attention to herself.

She saw a man in a red shirt standing by the open door of the kitchen leading outside.

And the rain has stopped. Perfect.

In an inwardly frantic but outwardly calm stroll, Hannah made for her escape. As she passed the man in the doorway, she said "Excuse me," never giving him a second look. She was out the door. She was gone.

She was—

Free....

JORDAN

Jordan returned her heels to her naked feet before she descended the stairs slowly to be certain that Hannah had plenty of time to get ahead in her escape.

I don't need her thinking I'm following her. She needs space. She needs time. Not to mention, these heels don't exactly make stairs easy, especially on the way down. Oh, I hope I don't see her for a little while. We've all had enough 'awkward' for one night, I think.

Eventually, Jordan arrived at the bottom.

If I were Hannah, which direction would I go?

The living room before her was empty, save for the remnants of a fireplace, the glow within clinging to life. To her right was the front door—

—I would have heard it shut, had she gone that way, I think—

—and to her left was a raucous gathering of people in the kitchen, which had become the main hub of the party.

Most likely that way if I know her. Party animal, though she is quite different tonight….

Jordan began tapping her foot in contemplation, uncertain of what to do or where to go.

These floors are amazing. My shoes are so loud here!

Jordan chuckled to herself, loving this puzzle of chance.

Finally, a choice I can make, just for myself. But at what cost?

She turned to the bottom of the staircase.

I could go back…. No? Going back isn't moving forward, is it?

She turned back to face the living room.

Looks cozy in there. But it's empty, and I've had enough 'alone time' and 'emptiness' for one day. But still, that fire needs help. Ari needs to—Ari… where might you be?

Jordan took a bold step closer to the fireplace, breaching the broad doorway into the living room. The soft sinking of her feet into the carpet surprised her in a comforting way.

It's like a hug for my feet! How cute!

This carpet, the fireplace—I would never leave! I could live in here, I really could!

Jordan swooned.

If tonight goes well, maybe I will.

Jordan took a few steps closer to the fireplace.

Ari and Jordan, sitting right here, warmed by each other, and this cute little fireplace….

She looked down contemplatively, closed her eyes for a moment, and smiled to herself.

I've always been treated like I'm invisible, yet Ari…. Ari seems to appreciate everything about me. But he knows nothing about me. I suppose we don't have to 'know' to fall in love. I barely know a thing about him, but still, the thought is there…. What can you offer a man who has everything? He seems to need nothing but looks at me so… so… so longingly, like he would die without me.

Damn it. I must find him. I must know more about this man; dig into the mystery, at least.

Jordan opened her eyes, looking into the fireplace's low glow.

He has no needs. It's about what he wants—*that 'wanting' look he gives me. He sees right through and into me…. He needs nothing!*

Jordan smiled.

And I am not nothing!

Jordan jumped inside herself, as she could have sworn that she had heard her own thought with her ears. She looked around, finding no one.

Hmm… perhaps it's true, then, true enough for my thoughts to be spoken.

She smiled to herself once more, turned, and walked out of the room. She began to make her way up the stairs when she thought of Katie.

No. Can't go back to that, *that's for sure.*

Jordan sat on the stairs, indecisive, taking a moment to just be by herself—Jordan with Jordan—caught somewhere between the past and the future. A shadow passed over the light of the fireplace on the outskirts of her vision. She looked up and peered through the balustrade to see none other than Hannah darting for the kitchen.

Well, shit. Imagine that….

As Hannah made an effortless, quick stride to and through the kitchen, Jordan followed at a distance. Jordan made her way through the kitchen crowd just in time to see Hannah exit through the back door, which was open.

That red shirt…. Could it be…?

Jordan slowed as time did the same, Hannah disappearing into the darkness outside while the room and all its inhabitants became a muffled, distant blur. All that was and all that mattered for a fraction of time was Jordan and—

Ari!!

Jordan stood behind this man, still as stone, unaware that she was holding her breath.

What do I do? What do I say?!

"Jordan," the man said.

Does he simply feel I'm here? Ari….

"Jordan…." he said again.

Jordan could hold back no longer. The room snapped back into focus and time resumed its natural course.

"Yes?" said Jordan.

The man turned around, his head hanging. His eyes brightened as they began at Jordan's feet, slowly working their way up her body—

—You. You make me feel so incredibly beautiful—

—Seemingly taking in every detail, examining and remembering again, as if they had not seen each other in a lifetime. As his eyes moved up her legs to her breasts and to her face, they gradually brightened, as if the closer he got to seeing her face, the more of both light and life emanated from him. Eventually her eyes were locked with his, and all things mysterious and familiar became reunited.

"Jordan…." Ari exhaled, his breath nearly taken from him as he pushed it from his heart. Jordan saw a glimmer in his deep, brown eyes.

Ari…. Ari, you do love me… don't you….

Jordan's voice caught in her throat. For the first time in a long time, her silence was a comfortable one, and the silence spoke for her.

MICHAEL

His hands were bound in the mud like earthen shackles.

Michael's heart was a fury of beats, rhythmic and fast, and he could feel his blood pulsing through his frozen body at a terrifying pace. Whether the being before him was real, it mattered not to him. Be it his mind bending to the will of the drugs and drink, or he was merely imagining, Michael did not care. He was wholly terrified, and terrified completely.

The eyes studied Michael intently. Michael did not blink. Neither did the glowing orbs in the darkness. They glistened like two ominous stars in stark contrast against the silent dark abyss that surrounded them—the same abyss that was claiming Michael more completely with every passing moment.

"Who... Who are you?" Michael stammered, looking up into the flaring spheres that unblinkingly stared him down. Distant thunder gave voice to Michael's fear.

"Who?" its voice called. "Who I am is not nearly so important as *what* I am."

The being before Michael began to laugh a threatening laugh, with a sound that felt to Michael like many voices combined into one. Its voice was an omen to Michael, its dark prophecy telling of wicked things to come. The laughter echoed off the surrounding trees, a soundtrack of shadow accompanying an otherwise silent film of nothing.

"So... so what are you?" Michael asked.

Great. Just great. I've finally lost it.

The voice spoke again. "You've lost nothing but yourself, Michael Law, using your career in helping others to picture yourself a hero. You, son of arrogance, who justifies your insecurities—your cruelty— the way you treat those who love you.... You betray Ari over a girl only because you want what he has. You are weak—a vulture, feasting on the scraps of better men," said the being.

The words washed over Michael, passing him over, drowning him.

Can you hear my thoughts? This has got to be—

"All in your head?" the being questioned.

Michael's eyes widened, his pupils dilating in total fear.

"Yes," said the being. "I am in your head and your heart, empty and cold as it is."

I am not!

"I am not empty!" Michael barked, choking on his words.

"You can barely even persuade the lies to leave your mouth, can you, Michael Law?"

Michael ceased trying to speak. He was completely beside himself.

"You are empty, and you fill your void with more emptiness, sacrificing the security and happiness of those you call friends to elevate yourself," the being continued.

You bastard….

"Sight is the bastard, is it not?" the being immediately replied to Michael's internal insult.

Michael flashed back to his earlier conversation with Ari, his mind becoming a cinema of past regrets. He flushed with pale embarrassment. The truth of these words was destroying him.

"I only argued with him to challenge him," Michael responded.

"No," its voice said. "You challenged him because even if he is right unto his own terms, you simply must be more correct. He cannot just have his own happiness without you being a part of it or stealing it entirely. You are pathetic, Michael Law. But you may yet be redeemed."

"I don't need your damned 'redemption', do you hear me?!" Michael lashed out. "I'm a good person! I help the elderly. I make lives better! You can't tell me—"

"But I *am* telling you," the being interjected, "that you, Michael, are lying to yourself. You and your false masculinity. I'll ask this—was Jordan even beautiful to you before Ari made it known he had thought so?"

Michael moved to speak, but he choked upon his insight. He was digging so deep within himself that he was becoming buried beneath the dirt—buried alive in a grave of his own revelation.

The being continued speaking. "You see…. Do you see now? You could not bear him having independent happiness, of being happy in a state completely devoid of you! So, you decided to lie with two women to prove to yourself that you, in fact, can achieve more than he—that you would 'show him' you are 'better' simply because you saw the truth in their bond—immediate, perfect and undisturbed. You could not interject, so you attempted to win a game of quantity, your shallow mind believing you having two women could somehow bring you peace for your self-perceived failure. And how you would have been such a braggart if not for your complete failure. Fool."

No! It's not true!

"To hell with you!" Michael shouted. "To hell with you and to hell with—!"

A flash of teeth beneath the icy eyes gleamed in the darkness. The ground beneath Michael shook, moisture from the leaves above falling to the quaking earth from the shockwave.

"HOLD YOUR TONGUE, CHILD!" shouted the being, the one voice made of many physically rattling even the shadows that surrounded them. "You know I am correct! You know it is true, even if you desire to so adamantly blind yourself to it! And do not speak to me so! You lash out as a frightened, cornered animal, small and quite aware of its own doom to come. And what will you intend to do? Do you sincerely believe you can harm me, either with hand or word? I laugh at you, Michael Law." The being fell into a raucous laughter, nearly hysterical, yet fully angered. "What am I? What am I?! I am your guide, tonight and forever. But should you raise your temper or voice to me again, Child, I WILL PUNISH YOU!"

Michael retreated back inside himself, shrunken and frightened.

"Do not dare to ever address me in such a way again. I am here to help you. Soon, you will understand."

A thunderclap boomed overhead. A streak of light, bright and white-hot, screamed across the sky. The light of it illuminated the dark creature before Michael, and for a moment, Michael was able to wholly see his adversary.

The eyes that once spoke of intimidating fear were quite beautiful, holding within them a myriad of colors, some of which Michael could not identify.

A terrifying rainbow….

The cheekbones were soft, but sharply made, the forehead broad and commanding, with eyebrows that appeared to be made of light rather than hair, as did the mane of silken locks that bustled softly in the building, billowing breeze. The ears, mostly hidden by flowing hair, were well-rounded, perfectly placed, balancing the masterpiece they adorned. Lips, full, pursed, and prepared to deliver, rested beneath a nose, large and pronounced, which guided Michael's eyes to a powerful chin.

Such a powerful man, but beautiful like a woman....

The light from the thunderbolt dissipated.

"I am flattered, Michael," the being spoke, "but flattery is not a currency I accept. And I can NOT be bought."

"Bought?" Michael asked. "What do you mean?"

Michael stood up, wiping his hands on his wet pants, rising to his feet and feeling comforted suddenly within the intimidating presence of this majestic and frightful creature. He was petrified and calm in his stillness—understanding in his terror. With wobbling legs, he planted his feet.

Michael continued. "What are you? I'm sure you won't tell me *who* you are… but what… what are you? Beautiful and scary… human, maybe, but not quite…. Are you…?"

Michael ceased his thought. He could not bring himself to say the word that gnawed at his mind.

"Say it, Michael," dared the being.

I don't know if I can....

"You can, Michael," said the being, "and you WILL! SAY IT!"

But this is insane. I can't—

"SAY IT!"

Michael fell to his knees, his newfound strength gone from him, as if he had never had it. Tears began to mount in his eyes. His voice choking with fear once more, Michael knew he must do as he was being commanded. There was no winning this fight.

Because how could I ever win.... I back down from nothing.... But now, how? How could I...?

"How could you, *what*, Michael?" the being asked, reading Michael's thoughts still.

How could I ever....

"Yes, Michael?" the being continued.

"I could never beat a—" Michael stammered.

"Yes?!" the being asked curiously, stepping closer to Michael, which caused Michael's heart to quiver.

"A… a vampire!" Michael gasped.

Silence held sway over the grove with only a soft breeze giving sound to the silent scene.

Michael crushed his eyelids together, certain that the deathblow was sure to come. That paralyzing face, the beauty and the terror, commingled in one fearsome, awesome immortal—an immortal who wanted Michael as a slave, or worse, a meal.

However, no such attack occurred. Michael instead was met with, and surprised by, a hearty laugh, then a barrage of hysterical, booming laughter. Each laugh echoed through and off the trees. Michael began to feel confused and mocked.

"What is so funny?" Michael shouted. "Are you going to toy with me before you kill me? Is that your game? Well, do it, then. Go ahead and do it. I will not be made a fool! I will not scream!"

The being continued to laugh, regaining self-control, which then began its decrescendo into a low lull of internal chuckles.

"Goodness, Michael, I had no idea you had such imagination!" the being laughed.

Another laugh ensued.

"No, Child," the being said, its fit of laughter fading. "I am not one of those undead things with which your modern culture has become so enthralled. Am I so terrifying? And would you believe… no, I don't believe you are actually decided in your conclusion. Michael…. I never knew you had it in you…. Maybe, just maybe, there is some hope for you, yet. Sure, those blood-drinking night-walkers do exist…."

The being laughed again.

"But," it continued, "I am surely not one of them."

Michael exhaled a breath of comfort.

"No, I am something else, and far superior to them," the being said.

Michael looked up and into that gorgeous face.

"Something far more capable and older than those earthbound vermin," the being finished.

Its eyes flashed, and another light streaked the sky, ushering in a violent wind, forcing Michael to lower his head, still keeping his eyes on the one before him, where his eyes were frozen. Light rain began to fall, the moist air cut in half by yet another powerful lightning bolt that rushed across the canopy of the grove.

"Michael," boomed the voice as if harmonizing with the thunder from above. "Thou shall be visited of the Lord of hosts with thunder—"

The sky rumbled overhead.

"—and with earthquake—"

The ground shook.

"— and great noise—"

Michael grabbed at his hears, cupping them as he screamed.

"With storm—"

The rainfall intensified. "—

and tempest—"

A powerful wind tore through the grove.

"And the flame—"

Michael withdrew back into himself.

"The flame of devouring FIRE!"

The voice resounded through the grove, shaking Michael to his core. A lightning bolt tore from above, the hair rising upon Michael's neck as the arc of electricity flew past him, striking the bonfire pyre near him, igniting once more the fire in the heart of a downpour. He could feel its heat upon his skin, though he was not burned by it.

"Peace," said the being, and the rain stopped, yet the fire burned on, brighter and hotter than before.

Michael began whimpering, wet and unsure of anything. He rose up like a wounded animal, his head down in defeat and confusion. A hand lifted his chin until Michael's eyes met with those of the being towering over him.

"Do you understand now, Michael?" asked the being in a matter-of-fact tone, moisture forming in his brilliant eyes.

"No," said Michael. "Not entirely…."

"Why can you not admit to me, and more importantly, yourself…. Strange as it is, I have known you your entire empty life, and now you have finally surprised me."

"What do you—what—who—WHAT DO YOU MEAN?!" Michael cried, unable to comprehend the ridiculous thoughts that were occurring to his disintegrating mind.

"'Surprise,' Michael. Defined as a moment lacking expectation or predictability…." the being answered sarcastically. "Please do not play stupid with me. You might be losing, but you are better at this game. The guise of a 'king' for so long, and here you are, playing the role of the pawn."

Michael sneered at the insult. He thought for a moment, briefly trapped in the chaos of his swirling thoughts.

"Chaos," said Michael weakly.

"Yes, it is all chaos, is it not?" the being asked.

A great nothing.

"In the beginning, there was nothing," the being whispered.

It's all nothing.

"So…." Michael whispered back. He seized in his form. His flesh became frozen. His shell became ice. He was stiffened in fear.

"So," mirrored the being.

"So? So what?" Michael asked.

"If it is all still truly nothing—just nothing—surely, Child, you could start again. Unlearn everything you think you know. Unlearn yourself. Rebuild the man within," said the being.

Michael shuddered inside, seeing the truth in what was being said to him.

"In the beginning, there was chaos—nothing—and then *I was*. I became. Before this awful place," said the being, gesturing all around him.

"Then I really am imagining all this, because it sounds like you're saying…." Michael began to reason aloud. "God is nothing but a chemical need—a human desire—to embrace our mortality. It's all an excuse to justify violence, to be ignorant of the truth…. To vainly give our tiny selves purpose and the like of a false hope that something is there for us beyond all this." Michael mimicked the being, gesturing around them, as well. "It's all just accidental chemical weakness. Our strength comes from knowledge. Knowledge is truly powerful, not some non-existent bearded man in the sky! The sooner we accept that—"

The being smirked, a glimmer shimmering across its eyes, then it spoke.

"Do you not see me now, Michael? Am I not the evidence you need?"

"You are evidence of nothing but my own insanity!" Michael stammered. "I'm on drugs, and you are my hallucination. Nothing more than shadows of Ari's words playing back through drug-induced hallucination!"

"And what of the wind?" the being asked. "The heat of fire? The lightning, the brief storm? Did you imagine those, too, and the very real sensations you experienced from them? What of your soaking clothes? If I do not exist, then why this grip of fear you have found yourself caught within?"

Michael interrupted. "Chemicals, I tell you! Panic from cocaine, emotions from alcohol, and the hallucinations, the mushrooms. Shadows of my mind, dancing on the walls of my eyes. Shadows, and nothing more!"

The slight breeze ceased, and a strange calm filled the grove in perfect silence. Michael felt as if he had suddenly gone deaf.

The silence was broken by the being's subtle laughter, as though disturbed by a glass-shattering whisper.

"Shadows, eh?" asked the being in a curious tone. "Perhaps you know me better than you think. I leave you for now, ignorant child, but tell me, do you believe that evil exists?"

Michael was confused by such a simple question, obvious as the answer was to him.

"Of course, I do," Michael answered plainly. "It's everywhere! So, how can God exist? What kind of god would allow war and children starving… the list goes on and on and on!"

"Ah," said the being. "So, evil does exist. And if evil exists, good must also, correct?"

"Well, yeah," said Michael. "Obviously."

"Then realize, without the existence of good, we cannot understand evil, can we? Without a moral compass—a source of morality—we cannot gauge or discern evil," explained the being.

"That makes no sense," Michael laughed, the insanity of these statements causing him to briefly forget his prior fear. "Of course, we can!"

"No, Michael, we cannot," the being calmly responded. "Cold cannot be measured. It is simply an observation of the absence of heat. Darkness can only be measured by the absence of light, correct?"

"Well, yeah, that kind of adds up, but are you about to tell me how to measure something as outrageous as the idea of 'God'?" Michael sneered.

"Never mind that," the being continued. "Something eternal cannot be measured. Which is greater? Eternity or the vessel by which one can measure it? Would not then the container be then more 'eternal' than its eternal contents? Can you tell me how long forever is, Michael? What is the sum of eternity? I know you cannot fathom this, so allow me to explain plainly. You believe evil and good exist, but not a Creator, yes? Then hear this, and may it sink into your doubting mind. Do those that do evil believe they are wrong, even though you as a species somehow know that they are? From where does that knowing come? Morality is based on a commonly known instinctual in-born knowledge. You know that murder is wrong, for example, yes?"

Where is this even going…?

"Most understand that it is common knowledge. Shadows prove the sunshine, as evil proves good, and true good cannot exist without a subjective moral source to govern it," the being continued. "Shadows cannot exist without light, but light can exist independently. I will conclude this debate, for I must go now, but remember this, if nothing else—darkness exists because light exists first, as cold to heat and evil to good. Yes, Michael, the shadows indeed prove the sunshine, and evil proves that a law-giver, a Creator, does indeed exist as well."

That is absolutely ridiculous....

"If you will not see His light," the being pressed, "know that tonight, here and now, you have seen His shadow. Think upon what I have said here tonight. I am Bezaliel. It has been your honor to meet me. I will be watching you."

Another lightning bolt made its fast, brief course overhead, and Michael shielded his eyes. When he reopened them, the bonfire was still burning.

His clothes were suddenly dry again.

Bezaliel was nowhere to be seen.

HANNAH

She was an anxious medley of thoughts and feelings.

Hannah walked calmly across the back porch and down the steps to the driveway. Coming to the edge of the house where the massive structure met the driveway, she peered through the damp darkness down its length, trying to make out where her car might be and contemplating her long walk earlier down the same path.

So much change in so little time. It feels like a lifetime ago.

She smiled to herself.

"Hell, maybe it was," Hannah spoke aloud, her grin widening, her first moment of true happiness—unbridled by circumstance or other tangible means—a happiness that was happiness of its own accord: a satisfaction untainted and selfless, yet all her own. She folded her arms as if to embrace herself, a physical expression of her newfound self-love.

But that *'me' is behind me, now. I feel like I'm finally 'me', my true self.*

"No longer that fake bitch I always ran from, I guess," she laughed to herself.

Yeah, I can laugh at myself! And I can be strong. And I… I can be ME!

She gripped herself tightly around her midsection.

So, how do I let go now? I love this!

Her arms loosened a bit.

But I have to. I must let go. Of everything I used to be. But how do I kill my demons unless I face them?

Hannah took a few strong steps toward her parked car. Then, she stopped.

"No, no that…."

That moment—Jordan—such a total disaster.

She kicked a rock by her feet, watching it bounce along the driveway until it tumbled into the grass, watching as its journey unfolded.

But really….

A revelation crept its way into her mind.

But was it really that bad? Maybe embarrassing, and not the right time. Hannah, you really did kind of try to take advantage of a broken heart, but still…. You were at least genuine. It wasn't just sexual. Sure, you wanted her, and physically so, but at the core of it all, you do really care for her.

Tears began to form in her brightening eyes.

In the end, didn't you….

She sniffled, fighting back the coming outburst.

Didn't you just love her a bit more in that moment? Shallow, sure. And awful, awful timing, but what it comes down to….

Hannah blinked her tears away and looked to the cloudy night sky. She wiped her eyes with her fingers, smiling at the clouds, rubbing her tears into her pants.

What it comes down to, at the very end….

She smiled once more, staring above her.

…is love.

A low roll of thunder rumbled, filling the scene around her. She could feel every vibration flow through her, as if the sound had come from within.

So symbolic, Hannah. Silly bitch.

She laughed to herself. "I guess you can either be defeated by the storm or become it."

She stood a moment, took one last lingering look down the driveway, turned on her heel and headed back to the house. Halfway up the back porch steps, she stopped.

Memories of the night flashed through her mind in reverse—her ponderings over her trek back and forth through the house as her heart broke and blossomed; her hiding from Jordan's red shoes; her verbal quarrel with Katie in Jordan's defense; and the bathroom—the bedroom….

The bedroom…. What a miserable paradise of lies…. Girls can be so cruel….

She thought about meeting Michael by the fire, his strong stance and his then soon-to-be-broken confidence.

Michael, you pitiful bastard.

"I shouldn't pity him."

Hannah moved to the bottom of the steps, away from the back door.

But I do. What I wouldn't give to say 'Sorry.'

She placed her hands on her cheeks, staring at the ground before her.

I mean, look at me. Aren't we all allowed to make mistakes, after all?

Moisture, barely discernable, saturated the air around her.

"After all, we're only human."

Thunder filled the air once more.

"But we can be *more* human, I guess."

Hannah felt the ground beneath her feet rumble.

She laughed, then she heard what she thought to be a distant scream from behind her in the woods.

Okay, that was real! Had to be!

The wet air dropped in temperature around her, followed by a singular strong breeze that cut through her like an invisible blade.

As the breeze subsided, she could make out a voice that sounded close by, yet far from her.

"Fire!" was the only word she could make out. The voice was clear, yet echoed with subtlety, almost as if the sound had been thrown at her. She dismissed it as a passing thought.

"My god, the fire!" she gasped.

Hannah looked to the woods behind the house.

"Is someone on fire down there?"

No, they couldn't be. It's too wet. Stop freaking out, Hannah! It's nothing. This is all—

"It's all in my—"

A bolt of lightning silenced her as it rapidly descended, seemingly from nowhere, flowing like electric water right into the dense darkness where the bonfire remained.

"—head." Hannah heard the lightning strike something in the forest. Her jaw dropped, hanging open. A faint glow could then be seen far away and downhill, deep in the heart of the trees.

So far away and down the hill, too. And I can still see its glow. The fire. Fire….

She took several steps toward the distant light, stopping again as the moisture in the air faded as quickly as it had come. She stood still for several moments, not knowing what her next action should be.

A voice then came from the faint light.

"What do you mean?!" the voice boomed.

Anger. Someone is frustrated over there, or hurt, or something. What do I do?

Hannah's curiosity grabbed her by the heart, dragging her toward the focus of her inescapable interest. She made her way, quickly yet cautiously. Uncertainties and predictions ravaged her swirling mind. Before she knew it, she was down the familiar path through the trees, halfway between the tree line and the glow ahead. She began to make out a voice, which became clearer with every clumsy step.

She could hear a one-sided conversation as she got closer but could only discern murmurs—blurs of sound as she approached—until she could identify a silhouette by the roaring flames of the reignited bonfire.

It hit the bonfire?? That lightning bolt re-lit the damned fire!!

Hannah kept her thoughts within but stood in silent shock at the impossible chance of it all. The silhouette continued to speak, the words jumbled yet clear.

"Shadows of my mind, dancing on the walls of my eyes. Shadows, and nothing more!" said the lone silhouette.

So angry and frustrated. And alone. You're not much more than a shadow yourself, man.

What followed was a self-satisfied laughter, which sent a chill up Hannah's spine.

"Of course, I do. It's everywhere," continued the mysterious stranger before her.

No one on this earth is all over the place as badly as you, dude. Wow, get a grip.

"So how can God exist?" asked the voice. "What kind of god would allow war; children to starve—"

I think you're starved for more than attention, you nut-job!

"The list goes on and on and on!" the stranger continued.

Especially when you're crazy—wait…. WAIT. So familiar…. Michael?! Is that you??

"Well, yeah. Obviously," the silhouette said.

No. Way! It can't be….

"Can we—" Hannah said aloud, clapping her hand over her mouth, fighting to be silent.

I'm a new 'me', and you obviously aren't you anymore… Can we just start over?

Hannah thought about his strong body and those piercing, unshifting, cold, handsome blue eyes.

"That makes no sense," continued the singular voice. "Of course, we can."

The hell…? Can you hear me?

Hannah doubted her own sanity.

Michael, can you hear me??

"Well, yeah, I guess so," came the familiar voice.

Hannah let out a loud gasp but was muted by yet another bolt of lightning that made her jump, and she could feel the heat as her hair rose up all over her body, surprised that its proximity did not singe her.

Definitely real!

Silence became the soundtrack for the grove. Hannah stood, awestruck, studying and contemplating. The crackle of the fire and Hannah's quickened breath was all she could hear in the mystifying, smoky darkness.

SONG OF SONGS

JORDAN

Disbelief was the sole theme of her mind as Jordan swirled and swooned over this surreal moment.

I suppose I shouldn't be so shocked. After all, he does live here.

Jordan thought back to her first impression before even meeting this man—her host—seeing all the detailed planning of the food spread, the drink selection, and all those unnecessary but appreciated additions to the bathroom shelf.

Tampons, for God's sake. Even tampons. What a guy….

As Jordan stared, lost in Ari's eyes, she was crumbling and reforming, a feeling of completion overtaking her soul.

Annihilation never felt so good…. Isn't it too soon to feel this way? Play it cool, Jordan. You're meant to be here. Here. And now.

She moved to speak, but Ari spoke first.

"Seems like you're meant to be here, doesn't it?" he asked.

It's like you can read my mind. You see right through me. You see me.

Jordan stood still for a moment as she shook frantically inside.

This isn't the same Ari. This isn't the same man I met hours ago. The same, but different. Like, calmer. More confident. Maybe distant or lost somewhere inside himself? What happened to you?

"I wanted to be here," she responded. "I've felt like running, leaving, so many times, but something kept me here."

"I'm glad you stayed," said Ari, his voice weakening with each word.

I hear the strength behind your voice, outwardly fragile as it is. You were so shy and shifty earlier. It was cute, but now… now it's like you've grown from a timid boy to a stone-skinned man in mere hours.

Ari's eyes glistened and Jordan felt her own eyes following suit, their souls mirroring each other through the hallway of their shared unbroken stare. The spark between them exploded in an invisible supernova in the transparent space between them.

"I am, too, now, Ari," she said. Jordan swallowed hard, blinked in a slow, longing manner, and reopened her eyes to the man she had just instinctively claimed. "But I have to ask, if it isn't weird…."

"Yes," said Ari, his eyes becoming more focused. "Ask me anything."

"Has something…?" Jordan began to ask but stopped midway through. Thunder echoed from outside as well as within her heart. A flash of light enveloped her as Ari's lips collided with hers, and in her forced silence, her heart screamed with joy.

Finally….

Her eyes wide with surprise slowly began to close as her lips embraced his, and in a brief moment of that short eternity, she was moved within, her inner fire bursting into a passionate, engulfing inferno. All her thoughts were kindling and underbrush, and in the blast of heat within her, her thoughts were eradicated. Her mind had become a calm world of nothing—a peaceful nothing—and ash-like snow fell all around. It was a scene of post-violence solace. Then, everything and nothing combined into one, all things became nothing at all, and her emptiness was filled as she was.

Weightless, thoughtless, and happy, she melted into herself, then melted into Ari and the warmth of his embrace. The inferno of passion intensified, destroying completely the self-doubt, the pain and the nagging weight she bore in her heart from the stresses of the evening. The heat fused back together the pieces of her previously broken heart, her soul solidifying like iron in the furnace of his blazing touch.

You truly are the fire to my phoenix, Ari. Don't stop kissing me.

Jordan had lost track of time, as if it had stopped, and despite her desire to continue this moment forever, she pulled herself away to look upon him—to confirm the moment was reality.

I almost just can't believe….

Ari opened his eyes, cleared his throat, and as he banished the obvious swoon from his face, he smiled a subtle smile and spoke.

"I can't… I just… Wow…. That felt as though we've done that before," he said.

"Almost like meeting the first time, right?" asked Jordan. "But after meeting lifetimes ago."

Ari smiled again. "Yes, Jordan," he said. "Exactly."

As he spoke, his eyes showed that his mind had become distracted once more. Jordan had to investigate. She kissed him with a quick peck on the lips, then asked, "What is it? What's troubling you? You can tell me."

His eyes glanced to the door next to them, then out into the darkness beyond. They then moved their focus back to Jordan's feet, repeating their slow crawl up her figure where his sight rested and loosened as they returned to Jordan's eyes.

"It's nothing. Let's not worry about it. Not right now," he said.

"Are you sure—" she said.

"Some just cannot be saved, I guess," Ari interrupted, shrugging his shoulders.

That's true, but still not absolute.

"You know, some of the hardest ones to reach are the ones who need saving the most," Jordan said.

Look at me. An hour ago, I was lost in this place, and in these moments, I feel like 'me' again. Whatever it is….

"Don't give up," she continued. "Whatever it is, I'll help. Tell me."

Ari looked back outside. Jordan grabbed his face with her hands, pulling his focus back to her.

"Hey, dumbass," she said. "Stop being difficult. It's *him*, isn't it?" Jordan laughed. Ari smiled.

That smile. Imperfect, but perfectly imperfect. Beautiful….

"It is," Ari admitted. "I just… I don't know what to do. You here. Him out there. I mean… shit."

You can go anywhere as long as you take me with you…. With you, I'll go anywhere. Be cool, Jordan.

"If you need to go find him, you can. I don't mind," she said.

"I can't ask you to go with me. It was pretty…I don't know, *weird*, when he left, just running off like that. I've never seen him behave that way before. I'm concerned," Ari said.

I'm concerned for you. I don't care so much about him, but if it makes you feel better….

"Don't ask, then," Jordan said, "but we're going."

Ari looked at Jordan, his pupils dilating and his gaze deepened. He shifted his focus to the window and the outside world beyond, then coming back down to the floor, he ultimately rested his eyes back on Jordan's eyes. A slight moisture had settled upon the surface of hers. Ari smiled a slow smile, at which Jordan shuddered with delight as a smile of her own began to take shape.

Jordan took Ari's hands into her own. "Come on, let's go," she said, keeping her eyes on his, nodding toward the door.

Ari closed his eyes, reopening them as he inhaled deeply, saying,

"Okay."

Jordan felt a rumble within her, even beneath her feet, as she trembled inside his confirmation.

Almost before the words had left his mouth, Jordan was dragging him in tow, tearing for the door; everything and nothing coursing through her racing mind. Halfway across the porch, Ari's grip tightened, stopping her in her tracks.

These stupid shoes….

Ari turned her around on a dime, pulled her close, and kissed her. As their lips met, a rogue lightning bolt shot from above, striking somewhere nearby. Jordan felt the hair rise on the back of her neck. Moisture and coolness filled the air around them.

Jordan was startled but kept kissing Ari. Finally, he grabbed her face with his hands and pushed her back, apparently unfazed by the electrifying crash.

Almost as though he didn't even hear it…. But look at you, so worried-looking.

"Why do you look so scared, Ari?" Jordan asked. "Do storms bother you?"

"Not at all," Ari replied, a quiver in his voice. "But Michael is out here somewhere. I need to make sure he's okay…"

"I understand. Let's go make sure," she said. They took off for the woods, together this time, Ari leading the way.

ARI

I looked on into those perfect eyes before me, stone-still. I was calm outside, but a crazed fury moved within me.

This is not the same Jordan, yet here she is. Something, though…. Something is different. More on-edge with more obviously on her mind. This night has been a small eternity for us all, I guess. Long night…. She seems… uncomfortable, but not because of me…. You belong here, dear.

"Seems like you're meant to be here," I said calmly. "Doesn't it?"

Jordan's eyes quivered, her emotions meeting together behind the thin curtain of those gorgeous orbs. She hesitated to answer, clearly thinking over her response.

"I wanted to be here," she said, reserved.

And I'm so glad you are, sweetheart.

"I've felt like running… leaving… so many times…" she said.

I'm so glad you didn't. I'd run with you if you need to run.

Her eyes were far away, but her focus snapped back to meet my gaze as we spoke.

"But something kept me here," Jordan said.

The sentiment in the complex simplicity of her words broke me as it built me anew. A light was born in me, and suddenly the world and all its problems disappeared for a moment. My voice barely held together as it escaped my lips.

"I'm glad you stayed," I said, smiling. I could feel my eyes wash over with suppressed emotion, the glimmer in my eyes matching, I imagined, what Jordan was feeling in this moment made simultaneous. I could feel Jordan as she was feeling me, and in our intimate, private little cosmos, her stars aligned with mine, and mine with hers. Our shared unbroken stare was the mirror through which we mimicked one another's reflection, the two becoming one.

The two are as one, and the one, two….

"I am, too, now, Ari," Jordan said, the words triggering another wave of feeling inside herself. She made it so obvious by her slow blink, swallowing whatever words had attempted to escape. "But I have to ask… if it isn't weird."

"Yes," I responded. "Ask me anything."

Please, God, please don't let me mess this up!

"Has something—"

Jordan…

Before I realized my body was moving, my lips were upon hers; my entire body was tingling, my toes and fingers were red-hot, and my face was flushed. It was as though my heart had died in its journey to discover new life.

This perfect face. These perfect lips…. This perfect night. I could stay here forever.

I squeezed her more tightly as our kiss lingered on. Jordan then pulled away, and I opened my eyes to hers as everything I could ever remember wanting appeared before me.

Jordan….

I cleared my throat, stunned and amazed. "I can't…   I just… Wow. That felt as though we've done that before."

I wonder how many times over how many lives, and now we've found each other for the first time again.

"Almost like meeting the first time, right?" Jordan said. "But again, after meeting lifetimes ago."

Or every single lifetime we've ever known. Ari, you're being a fool right now.

"Yes, Jordan. Exactly," I said, smiling so wide it almost hurt.

You might just be my new best fr— Shit! Michael!

The oasis of peace that Jordan had brought me had become once again dried and shriveled with the thought of the man that disappeared into the rainy night. I looked to the window, and into the night beyond. My thoughts were scattered like drops of rain, crashing all around me. A quick kiss from Jordan brought me back to my body.

"What is it?" she asked. "What's troubling you?"

I can't say.

"You can tell me," she continued, comforting me.

I looked to the door, thinking of Michael, then I looked to the night outside, wondering how lost he had become. My gaze then went to Jordan's bright red, sexy shoes and up her perfect body to her perfect face, and then to her perfect eyes. I gasped inside my chest with calm delight.

I can't worry her. I don't want to make her worry for me.

"It's nothing," I lied. "Let's not worry about it. Not right now."

She sees right through my bullshit. I can tell.

"Are you sure?" she asked plainly, as though telling me she knew the answer already.

You've saved me tonight, Jordan, but I must save him now. It must be me. Still, I feel lost, even here with you. Damn it.

"Some just cannot be saved, I guess," I said, shrugging. The empty words expressed my blanking mind, and my ability to think had begun to shut down.

"You know," Jordan said, calming me, "some of the hardest ones to reach are the ones who need saving the most."

The words stung me like a syringe injecting me with hard, simple truths.

"Don't give up, whatever it is," she said reassuringly. "I'll help. Tell me."

I investigated the distance beyond the window.

Jordan. Michael.

"Hey, dumbass," Jordan said, once again bringing me back to her. I giggled inside. "Stop being difficult."

I am being difficult, aren't I? Even when this feels so easy. So simple.

"It's *him*, isn't it?" she asked, laughing. Her laughter caused me to smile against my stubborn will.

"It is," I responded.

I can't lie to you anymore, even if the lie is disguised as silence.

"I just…. I don't know what to do," I said. "You, here. Him out there… I mean…."

Jordan.

"Shit." I sighed.

I don't want to leave you….

"If you need to go find him, you can," she said. "I don't mind."

Really? You don't? It's too soon for me to go dragging you into my problems, honey.

"I can't ask you to go with me," I said. "It was pretty… I don't know… weird, when he left, just running off like that. I've never seen him behave that way before. I'm concerned."

"Don't ask, then," Jordan said, "but we're going."

That understanding heart…. You're saving me all over again. You are my favorite drug, my heroine.

I looked to the window, then to the floor beneath me, smiling as I looked back up to those perfect eyes that again glistened like a thousand stars. Jordan shook slightly, smiling herself. She took my hands into hers saying, "Come on, let's go."

I closed my eyes, inhaled a deep, slow breath, and said, "Okay." She was already dragging me toward the doorway.

What a damn woman.

As we conquered the distance of the porch, I gripped her hand tightly, pulled her back to me and kissed her. The moment our lips met, the sky celebrated the magic we manifested. A lightning bolt exploded, passing us by before it struck the ground a close distance away. The universe acknowledged this fateful meeting that could not be denied. The surprise of the event made Jordan shake, but she kept her lips on mine, unfaltering in her affection. I ignored it for the sake of this unbreakable moment. I took her flawless face in my hands, gently pushing her away. I could feel my eyes widen, wholly overwhelmed.

"Why do you look so scared, Ari?" she asked in endearing fashion.

I'm not scared at all. Not anymore.

"Do storms bother you?" she continued.

Maybe the storm in my heart. I never want to lose you.

"Not at all, but Michael is out here somewhere," I said, my voice shaking. "I need to make sure he's okay."

Even if he can be a bit of a bastard at times.

"I understand," Jordan said. "Let's go make sure." She smiled, and I took that as the final nod of understanding. I led her down the steps. We were two stars blazing like comets into and through the great abyss of the unknown beyond.

HANNAH

Hannah could still feel the warm static in the air around her from the lightning strike that narrowly spared the fire-illuminated silhouette before her.

Jeez, that was close!

As her heart beat heavily on, Michael seemed to be frozen in place. She slowly made her way to the edge of the open grove, unsure if she should approach Michael.

But I've got to know….

She was suddenly out in the open in the clearing of the grove, and as the open air embraced her, her mouth fell open, and words began to escape its hollow dryness.

"Michael, are you okay?" she asked, the hoarse words barely discernable. She cleared her throat to herself, swallowed what little she could, and repeated herself. "Michael? Are you okay?"

Michael remained unmoved. He stood still and glared at the embers deep inside the heart of the woodpile. Hannah was a foot away from Michael before she stopped in her curious tracks.

"Michael, can you… can you hear me?" she said.

Michael seemed completely deaf to her voice.

Maybe the lightning injured his ears? What the hell!

"Michael." Her voice rose, which still garnered no reaction. She was right behind him, and still, he had not moved.

"Michael!" she cried, further raising her voice. Her hands gripped his strong shoulders.

Built like a brick shithouse….

"Michael!" she repeated, to no avail. "Michael!" Her voice was shaking with worrisome fury. She began to physically shake him.

"MICHAEL!"

A short breath was audible despite the crackling coals becoming still once more. He had again become frozen, clearing his throat, speaking suddenly through a voice that crackled like the fire, haggard and broken.

"Um, yes?" he said dully with distant intention.

"Michael?" Tears formed in her eyes. "Can you hear me? I know you don't remember—"

"Hannah," Michael said flatly. "How could I forget a voice like that?"

Still, he did not move. He simply stared forward, the smoke commanding his wholly divided attention. Hannah's eyes widened as she banished the approaching tears. She walked around to his front, facing him, looking up into his dulled, yet brilliant blue eyes that she could see, even in the dark. She desperately clasped his face in her hands. Still, he did not budge.

She thought about their first meeting. She thought about their broken, humiliating interaction afterward. She contemplated Katie's coldness and how she pitied Michael in that moment.

This soft man trapped inside his own hard body…. What a damned shame.

His eyes closed then reopened. Hannah could see a bit of moisture clinging to the surface of his sapphire irises.

"What's wrong? Are you okay?" she asked, tears still in her eyes.

I don't get emotional for ANYONE. What the hell is this?

Michael inhaled deeply, closing his eyes. He exhaled strongly as he reopened them, looking up and away, blinking away his obvious sensitivity, a mix of vulnerability and shame commingling in the shallowing depths of his expression.

"I… I don't know," he said, toneless and barren-voiced, his gaze shifting to the sky, to the pyre, then to the ground. Slowly, his focus rose to Hannah's eyes, looking both into and through her.

"Are you even here right now?" he asked. Hannah felt that he was not speaking to her but *at* her, his inquisition empty and coreless. Her heart sank into her stomach, where it burned in a shallow pond of acidity and anxiety—burning and writhing as it sought to be rescued from its own drowning.

I've seen you be so cold, but it feels like a rebellion. You want to love, don't you? But you can't…. Why can't you?

She realized why she yearned for him so longingly. It was not his devilishly good looks or his stone-cold demeanor that had both pushed and pulled her like a bipolar gravity. It was her similarity and her desire for love—a love she wanted but had not yet learned to reciprocate.

Perhaps that is our common ground—my attraction to you. Michael, you don't know how to love but you need it. You're just cold and alone. Maybe that's why you're back here by the fire. You can't expose yourself, totally and completely defended…. Maybe you need someone to infiltrate and to take you over from the inside…. The same thing I need.

"You know that is why I'm here, I think." She was embarrassed by her honesty, yet not ashamed.

"What's that?" Michael asked dully.

"Stubborn bastard," Hannah said. She moved her hands to the back of his neck, massaging as she gripped, and pressing her lips to his, coming to life as she died, this object of her affection seemed to finally belong to her.

But do you, though? Do you belong to me?

Michael lifted his eyes to hers, despite his greater height, and cleared his throat. "We've only just begun," he said, which confused Hannah. He seemed to answer the question she had thought to herself.

"Have we begun? Begun what?" Hannah asked, her voice breaking. "What is it we're beginning?"

A wind blew through the grove, and the bonfire wafted its haze toward them, surrounding them before it dissipated. Michael shook his head and rubbed his eyes.

"Hannah," Michael said, a shaken look in his eyes that glowed like the rest of him in the dark. "When did you get here?"

Hannah was stunned, and suddenly all the hope she had begun to feel—the warmth of a light she had never felt—was gone as it seemed to her that Michael had only just arrived.

Of course…. I've never been ignored to my face…. It's about damn time.

MICHAEL

I'm here. I'm there. Everywhere and nowhere. All at once, and yet not at all….

Michael's dead eyes stared into the seeds of fire that smoldered and glowed in their quiet, ambitious hatred as a thin pillar of smoke rose into the shadowed heavens above. The flames born of those seeds burned on, warming his face in the chilly autumn air. His ears rang from the lightning bolt that birthed the flames, like an unholy blacksmith. The hair all over his body had only just begun to rest from the static-infused atmosphere. His vision began to regain its composure, the effects of the sudden flash diminishing—his eyes finally adjusting to the fire's light in the darkness and the opaque picture beginning to become clear. The rising smoke was collecting what little light it could, a thin obelisk in the abyss of the grove.

A voice suddenly cut through to his damaged eardrums—an echo—barely audible, as if coming from within his own subconscious.

"Michael… Are you okay?"

Exhausted… just…. Fucking exhausted….

Another echo reverberated through him.

"Michael?"

What is a name, even?

"Are you okay?"

What does that even mean? Yes. And, still, no. Absolutely not.

The familiar, disembodied voice of Bezaliel came creeping, recognizable this time. "Michael," the voice said. "Can you…."

"Can you hear me?" Bezaliel continued.

Michael's mind remained blank and his mouth hollow.

The voice became louder, obviously agitated, and more adamant to be heard. "Michael."

Michael blinked, still unmoved within.

"Michael! Michael!!"

Bezaliel was practically talking to stone, the hardened shell of nothing Michael had felt and become.

Michael felt his body shaking against his own volition, as if gripped and rocked by invisible hands.

Is this even my body anymore?

The voice had clearly reached the point of rage as it repeated his name.

"MICHAEL!"

Michael's body was an abandoned house. His heart was a silent basement, his mind a television portraying nothing but the static of chaotic white noise in a living room occupied only by the ghost of himself. The voice had become an aggressive call from far down the hallway of his mind, yet he could practically feel the lips pressed to his ear. He could smell the breath by his face. He could feel its heat upon his neck. It smelled like smoke. It felt like hot iron pressed to his flesh.

He rapidly inhaled in modest shock and exhaled with timid relief. The relief and modesty shocked him with a weak current, much akin to a massage of the heart. The tiring current lifted him up along with his shoulders as he inhaled, the invisible ghastly hands upon him squeezing the breath out of him once more. He cleared his throat in anxious relief, his voice narrowly escaping his dried lips.

"Um…."

To feel or not to feel? Is feeling nothing feeling something?

"Yes?"

The voice ignored his question as it demanded Michael's attention, a saddened tone replacing the angry one, as if both defeated and concerned.

"Michael?"

That is what they call me….

"Can you…?"

The voice had begun to gradually shift from the concerned masculine to the caring feminine; from one familiar tone to a familiar other.

Yes, I am, I think…?

"…hear me?" it asked, the drone of this thunder-induced deafness subsiding, his ears seemingly mostly recovered. The voice's tone had become clearer.

This voice…. I hear you…. But Bezaliel, this is not you…. Someone familiar and more real, more feeling…. More…. More real…. That caring voice. The compassion…. The veiled face I can hear but don't fully recog—WAIT!

Yet another shock, more full and powerful, pulsed through

Michael.

I KNOW YOU.

"Michael," it said once more.

This voice…. This tone…. This…. This love…. This love that I ignore but feel…. That I forget, but still remember….

"I know you don't remember…" the voice answered.

BUT I DO. I remember you, and how could I ever forget? The ever-beautiful, the ever-compassionate—

"…Hannah," Michael said with relief, blankly.

How could I forget?

"How could I forget a voice—" he said, hollow.

A face. A body—

"Like that," he continued. Still, he only stared blankly forward. Michael thought of her, an angel with black wings, saving him with her darkened luster. Subtle tears welled in his once empty eyes.

"What's wrong?" her gorgeous voice asked.

I mean, what's right? What's wrong? Everything and nothing. The same things that I am….

"Are you okay?" her voice persisted.

No. Hell, no.

Michael breathed in deeply from nostrils to lungs and from body to soul. He closed his eyes and exhaled, reopening his eyes as clarity came to both his spirit and his vision. He became aware of the tears that had met in his eyes, blinking them away.

Am I okay? Am I all right? Is anything right? And if not, how have I been so wrong all along? I just don't know.

"I…."

What is that, even, the 'I'? What am I?

"I don't know," he said, resolutely.

Michael looked up, hoping to cast the tears back inside his confused head. He looked at the fire before him.

The aftermath….

He looked beneath him to the ground below.

The beginning.

He realized that the voice he had been hearing had been coming from Hannah herself, and not at all his imagination, as Bezaliel had.

She is real. And she is here and now. How long?

Michael recognized her as the fog of his mind lifted, the real world manifesting itself as he became in touch with his physical self once again.

"Are you even here right now?" Michael asked, as though

confused by his own presence. He was being torn between two worlds.

I am here. Damn the past, but how I love it. Without the stones of the past, we can't hope to cross the river of the future. And that is how we have the 'now'. We may stand. We may drown. But we continue to cross. May we appreciate the awful steps behind us that guide us to the shores we seek.

His vison had totally cleared, his ears fully healed from the lightning's shock.

Hannah's face, perfect and welcoming, beckoned him to cross over his internal river of doubt, to join her—to be with her.

"You know," she said, audibly and real.

Yes, Hannah. Now I think I really do.

"That is why I'm here, I think," she said.

I know it is. He was my shadow, and you are my light. And how the darkness has made me appreciate you. Now, Hannah.... Because of you, now I truly see. But... is that what you think?

"What's that?" Michael asked, attempting clarification.

"Stubborn bastard," she replied. He felt her feeling hands grasp the back of his neck, further reassuring her actual presence. Michael's eyes rose to meet Hannah's, clearing his throat as she overtook his entire focus. He was taken aback by her honest, unrivaled beauty, as though seeing her for the first time.

Sure, we have our brief history....

"But," he said, "we've only just begun."

Haven't we, sweetheart?

"Have we begun?" she asked, her tone hopeful yet broken.

Once again, yes, we have.

"Begun what?" she pressed.

Well, Hannah, our beginning, of course. Our real beginning. The failures before were our prelude, and these broken stones are now our foundation.

"What is it we're beginning?" she asked.

A breeze cut through Michael, and he was unsure if it was real air or simply a tingle he had summoned from within. The smoke seemed to have felt his concern, as it enveloped him, stinging his eyes—which he rubbed and opened—only to watch the smoke abandon him.

Smoke always flees the flames. And these flames of passion.... Let the smoke go. Let it run. I will embrace the flame. GIVE ME THE FUCKING FIRE!

"Hannah?" Michael asked.

You're really here, now. But when? Here you are, both before me but suddenly inside me, my spirit. How did you get in?

"When did you get here?" he asked.

The past....

The fire within and around Michael had finally been born, and life had begun to become something he both felt and knew.

The present....

It's about damn time.

But even still, the future to come....

And come whatever may.

The drugs had finally begun to wear off.

It's about damn time.

ARI

A heightened sense of things had gripped me by the backs of my kidneys, my adrenaline rapidly coursing through me, exploding like little volcanoes through my pores.

The combination of fear of the abrupt lightning strike and the electricity I gathered from Jordan's lips fueled me like the positive and negative ends of an erratic battery, clashing upon me, the man in the middle. The anxiety of my worry for Michael only increased the rush, the droplets of water cooling me, flecking the backs of my legs as I rushed headlong toward the woods. Jordan's strong, perfect grip held my hand as I guided her behind me.

I looked back to make sure I was not dreaming. Surely enough, there she was. My senses were finally being honest with me.

For once tonight....

I slowed our pace as we drew nearer to the tree line, eventually coming to a halt. Jordan skidded behind me, seemingly unable to judge the pace of my deceleration, bumping into me. I was amazed at how she kept her footing, even in those clumsy, gorgeous shoes.

When stars collide....

"What is it?" she asked, her voice almost a whisper, coherent and clear.

"Listen," I said, putting a finger to my lips as I turned to face her perfect face in the dark. Somehow, in this weak light, she appeared more beautiful than she had before, which I thought to be—

Impossible, and yet it is so. Stunning.

She exuded a light of her own, like a powerful candle in a paper lantern. The moonlight lent its glow to her gorgeous features. She was a beautiful actress commanding all the attention of the stage of the forest unto herself. I, her lead support, forgot even myself as I stood in brief shocked silence at the awe and wonder of the idol that was Jordan. I had to snap myself back to reality, remembering I was a man on a mission. My heart was thumping in my chest for reasons too numerous to comprehend.

"Do you hear that?" I asked. I could have been alluding to my racing heartbeat; I could have been hinting at the breeze that seemed to whisper foreign, calming words to my heart as it swayed through the treetops; but my question was more accurately referencing the voice I heard coming from within the core of the grove beyond the trees before us.

"I… I don't hear anything, Ari," Jordan said.

"Listen. Listen closely," I said to her. "From there," I continued, pointing toward the trees. She took the hand I had raised to point, bringing it down to the level of her hips, grabbing and pulling the other close. Her hands were within mine, resting on top of them, and she lightly squeezed my hands as though to comfort me. She closed her eyes, and leaned into me, her ear turned toward the forest.

A voice was speaking—I could tell—though from that distance, clarity was impossible to discern. Nevertheless, I could tell the syllables kept their rhythm; but in its echoed repetition, the voice grew louder and more panicked with each rendition, getting clearer with each delivery.

"Ari, what—?" she began.

There is definitely someone down there.

"You don't hear that?" I asked. I knew she had to be able to hear the distant murmurs.

But perhaps she just doesn't want to. Maybe, just maybe….

"I know, Jordan, I know," I said, squeezing her hands tightly in assurance. "But listen. Someone is down there."

The voice beyond had gotten louder, its echo losing its power, its clarity coming closer to being intelligible.

"Maybe it's—" we both said simultaneously.

"MICHAEL!" shouted the voice, the voice of a woman, and Jordan and I looked at each other. Her eyes opened frighteningly wide—as wide as I imagined mine to be—and our collective shock both enamored and froze us still.

"Michael!" I cried.

"Hannah!" said Jordan, anxiety coursing through her tone. "That's Hannah!"

Jordan more strongly grasped one hand, relinquishing the other, sprinting immediately with me in tow toward what we thought to be Michael and Hannah.

I swear to God, Michael, if you are hurting this girl…. I'll…. I'LL….

No, he wouldn't hurt anyone. Maybe a bit of a brute, but not cruel. Michael, please be okay. Please, please just be you, still.

I could feel the lingering euphoria of the drugs from earlier, an abrupt farewell as they weakened on their way out of my body.

No, he's got to be in trouble!

Jordan was simply not fast enough.

Those damned shoes…. Sexy as they are and so damned impractical.

"Wait, stop," I said. She seemed to not hear me at all. "Jordan. Wait…."

She turned abruptly, clearly panicked and frustrated. Her wide eyes said all they needed to—that she was in no mood to stop, but stopped, she had.

I let go of her hand, latching on more strongly with my gaze, reassuring her non-verbally that she and all her thoughts and feelings were safe in my presence. She nodded and kissed me with a quick peck on my cheek. I nodded downwardly toward her feet, and she smiled a brief smile before nodding back to me. As if understanding my silent offer, she placed her hands on my shoulders, slightly pushing me down.

This girl can read my mind. Maybe even my heart.

I knelt slowly to not throw off her balance as I descended. I touched her shoes first to communicate my intentions. She gently lifted her leg, surrendering it to me. Sliding my hand from her ankle along the back of her smooth, supple calf, I held it in place as I gently removed her first shoe.

Setting it aside on the ground next to me, I repeated my sultry action with the other leg, giving a loving squeeze to the latter. Before I took off her remaining shoe, I looked up and into her eyes, and they communicated back with so many deep, unspoken things that did not need saying.

Understanding.

As I knelt in awe and stillness, my heart plummeted like a comet into my stomach and filled my core with light. The drugs and their effects had faded.

Weak psychedelics, thank goodness….

She was my drug now.

I wanted more of her.

Before I could swoon further, she snapped out of the swoon of her own. A smile crept across her face as she acknowledged the same unheard words—in thought—that I thought we were sharing. She laughed abruptly as she slapped my shoulders with her hands in apparent dismissal.

"Okay, Ari. Hurry up. I'm worried. I'm…." she started.

"You're mine," I said, "if only for a little while. I know you're scared. Don't be."

She breathed in and I breathed out. "I know, but hurry up. I just… I just… need to know…."

"I know," I said, laughing a tiny laugh. She began to laugh as well, she and I stupidly giggling in unison.

"Okay, seriously hurry!" she urged.

I gave no verbal response. I simply set to my gentlemanly task. Removing the other shoe, I set it on the ground alongside the first, kissing her lifted knee. Gathering her shoes in the opposite hand, I rose to grant her the empty hand.

Let her lead. Give her the power. She is the queen, after all.

"Lead the way," I uttered.

"Yes, sir," she said, giving the power right back to me.

So equal. Such balance…. Where have you been all this time?

She kissed the hand she held within her own. Barefoot and courageously, she dragged our collective binary body toward the epicenter of her concern. The strength of her pull on me shocked me, forcing me to drop her shoes on the edge of the path as we accelerated toward our friends. I tried to speak up to let Jordan know what happened, but I knew she would rather leave them behind for the sake of getting to her friend faster.

We can always get them on the way back.

Those heels—those perfect metaphors for her passion, appeal, and her anchor to the earth—they were gone, behind us, once clutched possessively in my hand.

Like particles of light, we rushed through the cleared path I had kept meticulously manicured, with only the noise of the moistened ground to break the silence of our flight. The voices from beyond grew steadily louder as we neared them, broken as their vocal pattern was.

As the trees began to thin, the moonlight intensified, as though it had been replaced by a silver sun. Jordan's body had become wrapped in angelic light as she kept my hand in her grip.

God had answered my invitation.

He had done so through this hidden gem—this messenger—and she and all she had said and done and been had perfected her accidental, consequential purpose in the moment.

I, the crucifix and she the girl-Messiah nailed to me, saving us all in our marriage of sacrifice. My God-sent savioress…. God…. I see You now….

We were then at the edge of the clearing, a miraculously surviving fire and two silhouettes before us. A broken conversation was occurring between the two solid shadows before us.

It's them! Both of them!

We crouched down, Jordan and I, both knowing as we approached that both Michael and Hannah were safe, and safe with one another.

See, Jordan?

I looked at her, as she looked at me, both of us relieved.

He is who he is. He has always been a good man.

I thought back to all the betrayals and double-crosses and snide, back-handed ways he sometimes would dismiss my care for him.

But still, I always remember you, Michael—a bit of an asshole at times, but always, always a good man. I remember. That is my forgiveness as your best friend. I always remember. And that is what I will always remember, my brother!

"I know you don't remember," Hannah's voice said, seemingly answering my meditations.

Oh, Hannah, if you only knew….

"Hannah," Michael said, almost coldly.

You will soon be forgotten. Maybe you already are. A pawn in his game, sacrificed for the queen ever-yet to come. Isn't that right, Michael?

"How could I forget a voice like that?" Michael asked her.

Well, damn. Maybe I'm wrong, once again.

I looked to Jordan, that dream-clad silhouette of hope in the moonlit night.

You're all that is right, when everything else is wrong. It's all so wrong.

"What's wrong?" Hannah asked.

The hell? Am I still tripping? Michael, you must be. You never chase. You love being chased. And like a wasteful spider, you draw in your prey, only to discard them after the kill, after the thrill of the hunt is gone. You get what you need, and you throw the rest away.

"Are you okay?" Hannah asked him, concerned.

No, a nice guy, sure, but a monster to women. Which is why he always gets the ones he wants. And I—I'm almost always left with nothing. Okay, sure, Hannah, but I don't think you will be.

I investigated Jordan as she looked on at the scene unfolding before us. Her eyes were fixed upon the couple conversing as we watched.

Like Your Watchers, God, on the outside looking in, waiting to influence; waiting to pounce, like a starving wildcat with a buffet of sin on its table.

So, what will you do, Michael? Have you changed? Will you throw this one away like all the others? You must still be tripping. Are you still tripping? Is this a new you?

"I...."

You. You're my best friend, you bastard.

"I don't know," he concluded, his voice cracking under some invisible emotional weight I had only just begun to recognize.

Fake tears? No. But why this sudden genuine feeling? I've never seen you cry, never lose sight of your strength, fake as it can be at times. Is this you? Am I dreaming? And Jordan.... Here, with me, in this perfect moment. We hid our whole lives from each other, now here we are, hiding together. Is this real? Am I even awake? Am I even here right now?

"Are you even here right now?" Michael asked, his voice still building in its breaking.

Well, damn. I guess we're both unsure of that one. Maybe we'll never know.

"You know," Hannah said.

Every thought I had seemed to be audible to them in this trading of questions answered—questions I was certain that I had not asked out loud. Yet here they were, with Jordan on my mind; the three of them possessing my thoughts, invading the empty space inside—a place that was my own. Even still, I seemed to be the only one absent.

"That is why I'm here, I think," Hannah said.

Maybe it is. Maybe you're supposed to show me a different side of this man. Could it be you, Hannah? Are you the one to finally wake him from his neanderthal slumber? Or maybe just to drive me insane.... Either way—please, Hannah, teach him. Teach Michael to truly love.

Love, Michael. Learn to love. The law is love, and as Law is your name, so should Love be your nature....

"What's that?" Michael asked.

I was no longer shocked at this ridiculous situation—the craziness and the chaos of this string of maddening events that had become my newly adopted reality.

"Stubborn bastard," Hannah laughed.

I laughed to myself in the silence of my empty mental chamber.

You couldn't have said it better, girl. Maybe he sees you because you truly do see him. Maybe he just needed what I've needed—to be seen for the monster he is, yet sought, regardless. Maybe love found you, after all. Maybe love comes for us all—all of us tonight.

I thought back to my lonely living room and the thoughts I had had within it hours before, when loneliness was my sole companion.

Love is blind and God is Love.

Perhaps He is blind, being Love, after all. And He just happened to blindly stumble upon the world's finest group of lost children He's ever met. We're all just separated from You, aren't we? Like the father come home to see his kids after years of absence, here we are, just being the lost ones that we are, even as you find us again.

Well, welcome home, Dad. I'm glad to have You back. I've been blind, too. We are made in Your image, after all. You've hidden from me, in the shadows for years, yet here You are, now. Or maybe I've been hiding from You. Either way, thank You.

"But…." Michael said before giving another pause.

I closed my eyes, drifting into the darkness they provided—a black dream. Coming into that darkness, I had awakened into a void from the dream that Jordan was—a dream from which I longed immediately to slip into and revisit.

Now that I'm awake, God, can we start over again?

"We've only just begun," Michael said, like Michael the archangel, speaking for the God he now served, if only in voice and not action.

"Begun what?" Hannah asked. "What is it we're beginning?"

I'm certain we are all about to find out.

A breeze moved through the treetops, rustling like the voice of God, as though acknowledging my acknowledgement of Him.

Or maybe just the voice of a lost angel. Lost and now found. Like Jordan. Like me. Like—

"Hannah?" Michael asked.

Yes. All of us, really. But since we've all been lost and locked away, how did we find each other? How did we escape, if we have escaped, at all? Lost, all of us, but all searching, in our own ways, for a way out. Of all the nights…. How did we escape? How did we get here? Found within the lost, like sight in an abyss, or 'feeling' emotion. Michael, we've been friends forever, and I've always felt you were the lost one. Maybe you were the first to get out. Maybe your example of being awful to women is what showed me what not to be; and if so, I appreciate the lesson, brother. You've unlocked the door from the outside. I'm here now. And I'm here for you.

"When did you get here?" Michael asked.

Maybe my whole life, Michael. But then again, maybe, just now.

I looked up into the blank canopy moving with the movement of God.

It's about damned time.

JORDAN

The moistened ground narrowly claimed Jordan's heels with each step as she briskly followed behind Ari in their frantic pace toward the tree line.

Damned uncomfortable things!

Ari was moving quickly, keeping a respectful speed.

He must know I'm struggling.

Their mouths silent and their footsteps loud, Jordan gripped Ari's hand more tightly—part desperation, part affection. As they approached the trees, Ari slowed his pace, then stopped. Jordan slid through a muddy patch, bumping into Ari.

When stars collide…. Clumsy, reckless stars….

"What is it?" she asked, her anxiety unhidden in her clear whisper.

Why are we stopping? We've got to get down there!

"Listen," Ari said, placing a finger to his closing lips, Jordan then feeling a tingle of passion crawl through her body, a modest shockwave bursting forth from her center, exploding outwardly to her extremities. She loved the way he was taking control. She lusted after his manner of controlling her.

You can try, mister. I swear I'll take you down with me.

Jordan laughed to herself in her soul.

My heartbeat…. Is it the running or this nervousness? This nervousness you put in me…. Can you feel it? Can you hear my heart, Ari?

"Do you hear that?" Ari asked.

Damn, really? I guess you can, after all, lie. Lie…. Lie to him, Jordan.

The treetops rustled and swayed with the wind that moved through them.

"I…." she began.

I hear everything.

"I don't hear anything, Ari," Jordan continued.

We don't have time for this!

"Listen," Ari said.

Don't tell me what to do!

"Listen closely," he urged.

But, God, how I love it, from my very core.

"From there," Ari said, pointing to the infinite shadows before them.

Take control, Jordan. Hannah will be fine. Why are you even panicking about her? She abandoned you. It's not up to you to fix it all. You can... you can let it go.

Jordan looked at the hand Ari had raised as he pointed onward.

Let it go. But in the meantime—

Jordan took that hand, and then the other, into her own.

—you can hold on.

With her hands on top of Ari's, she pulled them down, allowing the weight of his arms to guide her motive, bringing his hands within hers to her hips where she secured them. She squeezed his hands with hers, pressing her dominance, leaning into him to solidify her power position. A distant echo of a voice caught her attention from far away, to which she lent an ear.

This moment, interrupted, like everything else....

"Ari, what—" Jordan began to ask before she was silenced.

"You don't hear that?" Ari interjected.

I hear nothing but the sound of our hearts, Ari. Now, I just kind of want to be here with you. The rest.... It's just not as important.

"I know, Jordan," he said, reassuring her concerned thoughts.

I know you do. I know you know.

"I know," he repeated.

I know. More than ever, I know.

"But listen. Someone is down there," he said calmly.

Jordan could hear muddled voices from beyond the darkness. She thought of her panic that had bought them both here, then relaxed once more into the calm of the present.

A rollercoaster from hell....

The dulled voices had suddenly become clear and audible in their fervor as one voice, familiar but forgotten, rose above the rising wind, cutting the stirring air. Jordan's voice escaped her lips as her eyes widened, her realization shocking her out of her thoughts, bringing her back to reality.

"Maybe it's—" Jordan said, thinking of Hannah once more, her forgotten mission returning to its place of priority.

"MICHAEL!" Ari said, his voice shaking. Whether it was from

excitement or fear, Jordan could not discern.

"Hannah!" said Jordan.

I'd know that smoky, sultry voice anywhere!

"That's Hannah!"

Without thinking a further thought, Jordan let go of Ari's one hand, squeezing more tightly the other before rushing off toward the voice down in the grove.

Guiding Ari haphazardly behind her, she darted as quickly as her high heels would allow.

Can't stop. Won't stop.

"Wait," Ari said.

But what if she's in trouble? That sounded so serious! No. I won't wait.

"Stop," Ari pressed.

Just shut the hell up, Ari! I adore you but stop telling me what to do! I need you right now. I need you to listen. I need my king to follow me right now.

"Jordan, wait!" Ari continued.

He had triggered her frustration. She kept her thoughts calm, but her body, she could not hold back. Stopping and turning on a dime, she looked into Ari's concerned, comforting eyes, her own eyes wide with power and conviction.

Ari let her hands go, as if trusting her to return. Jordan nodded in acknowledgement, all her inner fight leaving her, and she leaned into Ari, kissing him on the cheek. She pulled back, her eyes slowly opening to Ari's, and she lowered her head as she smiled. Her heart was full, and her mind was blank.

Take them off. We can move so much faster that way. And I'm not afraid with you.

Jordan placed her hands on Ari's shoulders, lowering him, as if with a slight, forced permission, silent and strong. She lifted one leg, offering Ari to do what she already knew his gentlemanly heart to do. Ari knelt to her feet.

Bow to the queen, king.

Ari lightly tapped one of her shoes. Jordan understood, and Ari understood her. She was lost in a fog of battling emotions as he took her leg into his modest, strong hands and claimed her, she offering herself one piece at a time. She lifted her leg, allowing him to hold it—own it. Her hands on his shoulders, she leaned on him, trusting him with all her weight, her balance, and her heart.

The way he's taking such care, yet taking control…. My God! Where have you been? The soft touch, and the firm grip. The passion and delicacy in the strength. The sensitivity in the quiet, manly nature.

Jordan's shoe slipped off into Ari's hand. He set it aside, then moved on to the other leg. Jordan simply watched this slave-king do her bidding, but of his own volition.

She could not bring herself to take her eyes off the show unfolding on the ground before her. She was impressed. She was stunned. She felt safe for the first time during this entire night—maybe longer. She smiled an uncontrollable smile at him, unending and immortal. She could not seem to remove it from her face.

It was only she and Ari, darkness surrounding their combined light; two binary stars alone together in a vast vacuum of whatever. Then, Ari looked up into her eyes.

She did not budge.

She did not blink.

She was right at home in the presence of a comfortable stranger.

In the beginning was nothing. And then something happened. The darkness brought light, and light brought much more. From darkness, all came to be, and in this particular darkness, two lights burn as one. We are slaves to each other's gravity, spiraling and spinning in chaos until we crash into each other, the ultimate end bringing on the ultimate beginning—new life.

Jordan smiled again, her revelations pouring like a summer sweat out of her flesh.

That's enough for now, mister.

Jordan slapped Ari's shoulders, relinquishing him of his task, confessing her own newfound, playful affection.

"Okay, Ari," she said.

You've got me. You soft stone….

"Hurry up," she continued.

But take your time.

"I'm worried," she whispered.

About 'her'.

"I'm—"

"You're mine," he said, cutting her short.

Well, no shit, you idiot!

Jordan laughed inside herself.

"If only for a little while," Ari continued.

Until the light burns out. Until forever can't keep up anymore.

"I know you're scared," he said.

But I'm not. Not any-fucking-more!

"Don't be," he concluded.

Ari's reassurance had lain her final doubts to rest.

Jordan breathed in deeply, her soul relieved and satisfied.

I know….

"I know," Jordan said, her thought and voice escaping simultaneously from her silent heart and open mouth. "But hurry up."

Or take your time. Whatever.

"I just," she said. "I just—"

Just what? Just everything. And nothing at all.

Perfection. But what's it all for?

"—need to know," she said.

"I know," Ari said.

The seriousness of her thoughts had both inspired and broken her. She laughed as Ari laughed, and in that symphony of mirrored humor and connection, Jordan, like so many pieces of herself, had formed back together—a beautiful mosaic of imperfection.

She broke herself from her mind. Reality awakened, and so did Jordan.

"Okay, seriously. Hurry!" she urged.

Ari had no hurry in him. He calmly released the other shoe from her burdened foot and unburdened her. He kissed the knee he held, and Jordan lit up. Her light was quiet—her spirit relieved.

"Lead the way," Ari said.

I will. I so will.

"Yes, sir," she said with hopeful calm.

Jordan kissed Ari's hand and let it go. She wanted to say more, but she had said everything with her silence.

Taking Ari's hand in tow, with the rest of him following, she and Ari took off once more toward the wooded path, onward toward their friends. Her heels were left behind, muddy and cloaked in shadows and forgotten.

As they traversed the trees, the moonlight gained luminosity, and everything became clearer the deeper Jordan and Ari ventured into the woods. The trees became increasingly thin with each of their steps as the light of the moon took over the scene.

Dodging a branch every so often, her eyes focused on what lay ahead of her. Jordan briskly guided the pair of them to the edge of the grove. She slowed her pace, minding the volume of her steps, becoming stealthier the closer she brought them toward Hannah and Michael.

No need to rush in. Looks like they're just talking. Good.

Coming to the very edge of the tree line, she crouched down. A burden of great weight had lifted from her heart. Still, she did not wish to be caught spying.

This feels so wrong, but I can't just rush in there. That'd be awkward.

The moonlight had reached the apex of its intensity and Michael and Hannah were clearly visible.

Jordan looked at Ari, who returned her gaze, both of them apparently relieved at the spectacle at which they had arrived. Hannah and Michael were clearly amid a meaningful conversation.

Good thing I held back. Good job, Jordan! I can remember to be good to myself sometimes....

"I know you don't remember," Hannah said, surprising Jordan with the timing of her words.

"Hannah," Michael said. "How could I forget a voice like that?"

The conversation began to confuse Jordan.

Haven't they been speaking this whole time? Like, who the hell is he talking to? Are you weird after all, Michael?

"What's wrong?" Hannah asked, a bit of concern now audible in her voice.

That's what I'm saying. Are you okay, Michael? Is Hannah?

"I... I don't know...." Michael said.

I don't think any of us know anything anymore. This night.... It's been so... odd... At least they can't see us. At least they don't know we're here.

"Are you even here right now?" Michael asked, once again psychically responding to Jordan's inflective inquisition. However, what concerned Jordan more was the shift in Michael's voice, as if a sudden fear had taken hold of him.

Are you okay, dude? Maybe you need someone strong like Hannah to keep you level.

"You know, that is why I am here, I think," Hannah said.

I think so, too. This guy is obviously off his rocker.

"What's that?" Michael asked.

Oh, for God's sake, idiot! Just listen to her. Men are so damned dumb sometimes.

"Stubborn bastard," Hannah replied.

Tell him, girl.

Jordan laughed in her spirit, proud of Hannah, still surprised at the investment she was making in a man—any man—at all; especially this one that seemed so stupid to Jordan.

"But," Michael said, his tone flat, before halting his speech. "We've only just begun," he continued, catching up with his thoughts.

"Begun what?" Hannah asked. "What is it we're beginning?"

Who knows.... Tonight has been one for the books. Maybe we're both growing up. Maybe…. Maybe we're learning, and you know what? It isn't half bad.

Jordan shuddered at her own thought, a brief excitement rushing over and through her just as a breeze above swayed over the treetops, as though she had moved them by sheer will, like a discharge emanating from her soul.

"Hannah?" Michael asked. "When did you get here?"

OKAY. WHAT?! Is this guy serious? What game is this?

Jordan was twisted with confusion.

Oh, shit. No, he must have seen us! Please, no! But honestly, we've been here for some time. He was bound to find us!

Jordan stood up, owning her discovery.

It's about damned time.

KATIE

Katie awoke from her stupor as a bolt of angry lightning screeched across the sky outside, rudely waking her from her half-sleep.

"Fuck!" she shouted, waking in immediate terror by the abrupt raucous beyond the window. The covers of the cozy bed flew from her and she instantly desired more drugs.

"Shit, what time is it?!"

She looked out the window, the moonlight falling softly on her crimson hair. She was tingly with the chemicals coursing through her and shaken back to earth from her distance from reality. Katie was half in and half out, both beside herself and deeply within, yet separated and bonded.

She was lonely, she was alone, and she was torn between war and peace—satisfaction and rage. Her roots and branches were both grounded and reaching, and she was stretched between both truths.

"Where the hell did they go?"

Definitely didn't stick around. Michael never did bring me that water. I don't expect Hannah to return, at all. Oh, well. They never do. They always just leave.

She was gone, herself. A passive rage crept over her, and it inflamed her, lighting the wick of her anger, the sparkle of her inner demons shining as it burned, encroaching upon the core of the bomb that was her impatient heart.

"Fuck them," she said aloud, both angry and sad. She was still reaching out but hating her willingness to feel anything for those that felt nothing for her.

Michael. Hannah. Shouldn't someone had been here by now?

She rolled over in her fiery confusion.

She then heard a voice.

"Awaken, Child."

…Um, what the hell?

Her beautiful red hair a mess, she stared into the darkness of the room.

Child, who? What dreams was I having?

Katie could then hear quiet, low laughter from somewhere nearby. A gust of wind rocked the window.

Jeez, I need to wake up.

Katie rubbed her tired, waking eyes, rolling over in bed toward the bedside table. Picking up the book and drugs, she set them in her lap, beginning to grind its contents to finer particles. She grabbed the dollar bill from earlier, tightening its roll. The powder on the book a haphazard mess, Katie knelt by the bedside and inserted the bill into her nostril, inhaling a large amount of cocaine. She knew she had done more than she had intended. She had no care, regardless.

"Damn," she said, leaning back as she sniffed inwardly, pulling away from the book as she rubbed at her nose, sniffling. "That's what I'm talking about."

Katie stood up, moving the book from the bed to the table, turning to get back into bed. However, she stopped and turned as her body began to chemically change, her mind altering its state, and her energy level was rapidly skyrocketing.

"Well, one more couldn't hurt." She returned to the cover of *Dracula*, repeating the ritual, using the opposite side of her nose this time. Again, she sniffed upwardly, rubbing her nose once more, blinking her watery eyes. She blinked heavily several times, looking around to investigate her changing perception of her surroundings.

There. No more dreams for now.

She sat on the bed, her back to the window.

But didn't thunder just wake me up?

She looked back to the window.

"No rain…?" she whispered to herself.

Am I still dreaming?

She inhaled strongly through her nose to ingest any bits left clinging to the inside of her nasal wall. A wad of powder and mucus shot back to the back of her throat which she swallowed, gagging. She could feel her pupils dilating. Her skin began to vibrate.

"You think this is a dream?" came the same voice from earlier.

Katie jumped from the bed to the floor, terrified, looking around the dim light of the bedroom.

Okay, I know I heard someone…. I'm tripping….

She slapped her face and ran her fingers through her hair, shaking her head. She looked to the door, then once more to the window.

Still, no rain…. So weird….

Katie picked up her cigarettes from beside the book on the table and a nearby lighter. Putting a cigarette into her mouth, she walked to the mirror on the wall opposite the window. She studied her visage via the moonlight descending through the glass. She pulled the lighter to her face, lighting her cigarette, blowing the smoke at her reflection and watched as it billowed and rolled off the clean surface, spreading out and rising into the air.

"I've got to get out of this room," Katie said. She set her cigarette in an ashtray on the table, put her pants back on that had lain askew in the floor, then her shoes that lay next to where her pants had been. She gathered up what cocaine she could remove from the book's cover, putting it back in the tiny bag she had left in her pants pocket. She left the dollar rolled up, slid it into her pocket along with her cigarettes, the bag, and checked her person for her phone, keys and wallet.

She began to leave the room but stopped to examine herself in the mirror once more before leaving. She liked what she saw. She nodded to herself, and put the cigarette back to her lips, taking a puff. As the ember glowed hot, then diminished, she looked at the reflection of the room behind her, seeing what appeared to be two eyes glowing from outside the window.

Katie gasped the smoke from her lungs, turning abruptly in fear toward the window, seeing nothing. The eyes were gone.

"What the fuck," Katie whispered, disbelief overtaking her. The hair on her body stood on end and her heart began to beat faster. She hit her cigarette again then exhaled, moving cautiously toward the window. She peered outside, looking in all directions, seeing nothing out of the ordinary, which somehow made her much more nervous. Her breath quickened and she dramatically dragged her cigarette two more times in rapid succession. She had smoked it halfway gone already.

Looks like nothing. I'm being paranoid, but still….

"Yes, still," she heard, the voice coming from behind her. Katie turned slowly to face the source of this voice, terrified and nervous. Her eyes were as wide as her mouth as she rotated slowly and silently, her electrified skin the only energy she could harness to keep her from becoming entirely frozen.

As she completed her turn, there she saw it—a large looming silhouette, barely illuminated by the moonlight—a shadow embodied before her.

Katie shrieked in dreadful terror, dropping her cigarette from her mouth to the floor, backing up to the window, nearly breaking through the glass. She was made into stone by the paralyzing gaze that crept over her.

The same two glowing orbs she had seen in the mirror manifested themselves into reality as two eyelids closed and then opened to reveal them. The shadow grew as it stood on the other side of the bed, spreading what resembled wings as it stared at, through and into her.

"Hello, Katarina," the being said in a deep voice. "Did you sleep well?"

"HOLY SHIT!" Katie gasped, caught somewhere between a whisper and a scream.

"Well, I have been called much worse, but please, watch your language, young lady," said the shadow. "You may fool these humans with your strong demeanor, but you and I both know you still possess a child's heart."

Katie attempted once more to distance herself from what was in front of her, putting more pressure on the glass behind her as if either to escape through it or climb backward up the wall—up and away from this creature—this speaking shadow—before her. She was hearing the words, yet her fear had paralyzed her mind. She could neither comprehend nor respond. Then, words began to weakly form and fall, trembling from her lips.

"Wha—Who the hell are you? *What* the hell are you?" she inquired.

"You seemed lonely," said the shadow. "I thought I might grant you some company."

"WHAT ARE YOU?" she hoarsely yelled.

"Do not be rude, young one," said the shadow. "You know what I am. Fallen, like you, but hope remains for both of us. How did you sleep?"

"Li—like shit, but what do you want?" Katie asked, her eyes still wide open.

"Want?" asked the shadow. "I have not been asked what I want in a long, *long* time, Katarina."

The shadow took a step aside, moving toward the door, its head downward in thought. Katie could see the being for what it was.

Wings. Glowing eyes. Beautiful, really....

"What do I want?" it said.

"Yes! What do you—? Why are you here?" she asked.

The being paused for a moment, then spoke. "You are so inquisitive. That is good. It means that you are likely willing to listen."

It turned to her, its awesome size becoming apparent, glowing with a light from within that was not light at all.

"What do I want? I want to be here, and that is why I am. And I always achieve my ambitions."

The being moved two large paces toward Katie, rounding the bed in process. It knelt next to her frozen frame, she once again pressing herself against the window behind her as the being's face came within mere inches of her own. Powerless to escape, she could only stand still, drawn into the glowing eyes before her.

In those eyes she saw galaxies and a battle between all things light and dark. She saw hope and loss, the past and the present, and she saw herself—her life flashing before her in seconds—including the reflection of her terrified face.

The being breathed in deeply, exhaled, and spoke in a voice both coarse and beautiful, like multi-colored sand falling through a polished hourglass, both spent and eternal.

"I am Bezaliel. I doubt you have heard of me."

Katie calmed down, becoming more relaxed, this being's voice and demeanor becoming less intimidating with each passing moment. Still, she kept her hand to the window, bracing herself against its frail support.

Seems nice enough but could turn on me at any moment....

"I promise you, you are safe with me, Katarina Avery," Bezaliel said.

You can—

"Read my mind?" Katie finished the thought. "And you know my name? Even my last name?"

"I know much about you," responded Bezaliel, reassuringly closing and opening his eyes. "Everything, truly."

"But... but, how?" Katie gasped.

"I am one of the Old Ones, something in which you choose to not believe," he said, his voice brightening. "Would you care to guess before I tell you?"

No. No! Just... no! There's no way! There's just—I'm losing it....

Katie looked around the room— at everything and in every direction where Bezaliel did not stand.

"You're going crazy, Katie," Katie said to herself. "You're on drugs, you're drunk, and you just woke up. This is a dream, a damned dream, and you just—just wake up, damn it!"

She slapped herself across the face again, then touched her pocket where her paraphernalia was kept. As the sting from her hand crept across her cheek, she returned to some form of reality—or so she thought.

Katie smelled burning, recalling immediately the cigarette she had dropped moments earlier. It had begun to char the carpet, the odor in the air foreshadowing a flame that threatened to go ablaze. Quickly, she bent to pick it up, stopping halfway down, looking up to check her senses. There still, Bezaliel was unblinkingly staring at her.

Fuck. Why are you still there?

The grin beneath Bezaliel's eyes only widened as his eyes narrowed.

"I have already told you. Now, if you please, mind your language. You are above such foul words," he said.

Katie looked down as if to ignore him or forget him entirely. She wished so desperately that he would be gone.

She let go of the window, picked up the cigarette that still smoldered, rubbing the burnt patch with her foot where it once laid.

"So, you think you are good at extinguishing fires, do you?" Bezaliel asked, reminding her of his presence.

Katie stood still, wordless.

"Wonderful, how as even a child kissed by fire," Bezaliel said, stroking her red hair, "can still suffer from it. You have only 'dipped your toes' into it, but still, you cringe at its power, small as it is."

"What is it you're telling me?" Katie asked.

You only speak in riddles....

"There are no riddles, if one knows how to interpret them," Bezaliel responded to her thought.

"So," Katie said, stepping around Bezaliel to the foot of the bed. "Let's just say you are real. You know my name. You're both scary and pretty. You can read my mind, and you know... you know my name.... Are you a gho—" Katie said turning, her sentence dying in her mouth as she turned to see he was gone. She looked around the room, seeing nothing but the mirror, the disheveled bed, and the table along with all its contents.

"A... ghost...?" she finished.

Phew.

Just a weird lingering dream.... Thank god!

She pressed her hand to her chest, breathing herself back to peace, her heartbeat slowing with each beat. Standing upright, she patted her pockets, double-checking that she had everything.

Seems okay....

She looked to the window and the mirror, then to the table, and finally the bed.

Time to go!

Katie turned around to head for the door, immediately halting her stride. She was face-to-face with the gorgeous terror that was Bezaliel's chilling beauty, once again.

"Not just yet!" Bezaliel bellowed, his voice filling both the room and Katie's mind. Wholly shocked, she stumbled backward, falling to a seat on the foot of the bed. Her anxiety had returned, as if it had never left her.

"A ghost, you say?" Bezaliel's voice roared, maintaining its violently compassionate tone. He then laughed an equally powerful laugh, as if in mockery. "What is a ghost, Katarina?"

"A—a ghost—a spirit—someone dead, but not—not *gone.* Someone—" she said.

"Yes...?" Bezaliel insisted, pressing Katie to finish her thought.

"Someone—someone passed on. Someone who's died, but refuses to... I don't know... move on?" She was suddenly unsure of herself.

"Oh, yes," he responded, laughing to himself in a self-satisfied tone. "Someone who has died, tethered still, to the realm of the flesh. No, trust me, Child, if I could escape this prelude to Hell, I would. I assure you, nothing clinging to true life lingers here."

Bezaliel looked down, then up, an expression of sadness coming over his face.

"We all want to go home. Well.... Most of us," he said, the intensity of his voice shifting to a melancholier tone. "We want to go home, even if we—even if you—do not know where that is. These substances with which you poison your body," Bezaliel said, gesturing his hand toward Katie's pocket. "Is that not how you escape the pains of this world? How you forget—temporary as it is—that you are anchored here? My child, my dear Katarina, you are a fire, and you are not meant to extinguish yourself in such ways."

Katie understood him, finally, remembering the broken life that had brought her down the path of her broken, reckless lifestyle. A tear gathered in the corner of her eye, then rolled down her cold cheek.

"I know," she said, shrugging.

"I know you know," Bezaliel said, stepping forward and wiping the tear away from her face, kneeling before her seated frame. "And that is your frustration. Such fire inside, yet you cannot burst. How the world holds you back—traps you within yourself. So much like a matchstick unable to spark, but already burnt out—used up and useless, underutilized, then discarded. Everyone always abandons you, do they not?"

Katie looked Bezaliel in his eyes—eyes too close but not close enough. She wanted his warmth but feared the heat of his presence.

"Yeah," she said, looking into the mirror. "They always leave."

"And yet the drugs cannot make them stay? Child, they simply cannot handle your fiery spirit," Bezaliel said.

So kind. So insightful.

She had only just realized that she had felt him touch her, diminishing her prior conclusions.

"No, you aren't a ghost, are you? You're not a ghost at all," she whispered.

Bezaliel closed his eyes and reopened them as he smiled and stood, then took two steps back, tucking his wings behind him.

"No. No, I am not. One day, soon enough, I will be, but mercy can be afforded all," Bezaliel said. "Even the damned."

Bezaliel looked to his hands as he outstretched his arms, his wings spreading to their full span, conquering the width of the room. "Burns may wound and heal, but fire can kill," he said. "Perhaps that is what holds you within yourself."

Well, hell, maybe....

"Hell, exactly," he said. "Empty as this room, consuming like an insatiable darkness, devouring like a furnace with no walls." Bezaliel looked behind him to the bedroom door. "And certainly no way out," he continued, his voice shaking.

"What does this have to do with me?" Katie asked. "I want nothing to do with this—this night, this emptiness, or this damned room!"

"You feel trapped, do you not?" Bezaliel asked, looking back to Katie. "You and the room are one, as I and this world. You are far from all you love, and you cannot even love yourself, can you? Indifference from those who abandon you, and only punishment from anything—or anyone—you truly come to love. And yet the only one to ever love you needs you more than you are able to provide, which only wounds you further. Your grandmother loves you, but you feel completely guilty not being able to give her the time you want to give her from your shame of your habits, which you imbibe to escape the pressure of the responsibility of being all she has. It is a vicious spiral of constant self-destruction, is it not? Why am I here? You are so much like me."

Bezaliel pointed to a candle upon the bedside table, urging Katie to look at it, which she did. As she looked upon it, Bezaliel spoke. "As a flame upon a candle, we are watched as we glow, sometimes brightening, oftentimes dimming. Yet even though we waiver or blaze, change color or shrink, spread or remain stationary, one truth is clear: whatever we make of ourselves or choose to do with our brief lives is of our own will. But all things aside, we are merely watched, weighed, and ultimately judged by our Father Flame, the Source that gives us brief existence in how we compare to Him in our effects upon the darkness. The very same Source that would watch us—whatever our journey—burn in whatever mode we select, the wax of life dwindling and melting at our own selected pace...."

He paused, keeping his hand up, gesturing toward the candle, yet he looked up, to and through the ceiling. "Until there is no more wick of life left to consume. Until we are snuffed out, the purpose always eluding us, but within...." He looked back at Katie. "But within, we know the purpose to be the burning, itself—the light expelled, or the shadows made."

Bezaliel closed his eyes, then opened them. He moved through the air in fluid effortlessness, landing next to the candle, continuing to speak as Katie watched, enthralled.

"God is a fire," he said, lowly, "and we are each, in our own little flickering embers, a part of Him; and through us, He burns on until one of us is but ash and smoldering wax."

As he finished speaking, Bezaliel waved his hand over the candle, the wick suddenly coming to life with a flame of many colors—a tiny flame that filled the entire room with a light that was not light, and a warmth that was not heat. Katie could now see this being for what he truly was.

Oh. My. God.

"He is still my God, too, Child," he said, abandoning the candle as he rounded the bed where he again came face-to-face with Katie.

"You are, aren't you?" Katie asked.

Bezaliel smiled.

"You, Bezaliel. You're an angel," she said, nearly choking on her words.

"I was, once, and so innocent, yet here I now wait, waiting," he said, smiling more broadly. "We are both, children of fire, in our own way, awaiting the inevitable, unable to escape."

Katie nodded, lowering her head in understanding.

I—I can't argue. Even if I leave…. Even if I find 'them'.

She thought of Michael and Ari—of Jordan and Hannah—and all the invisible faces in between.

Even if I find them…. I still won't find….

"Yes?" Bezaliel urged.

"I STILL WON'T FUCKING FIND *ME!!*"

Bezaliel stood, flapping his wings, quickly returning them to their resting position behind his back. He brought his forefinger and thumb to his chin, as if to ponder.

"And neither shall I, as I once was. My fate is certain," Bezaliel said. "I have ruined myself, but you, Child…. For you, there is still time." Bezaliel laughed. "The irony of time. As I am above and beyond it, still I am a slave to it, my freedom my release—my doom… my judgment. Ironic as it is, further still, that though your kind ages and dies—'forever' has still not evaded you. Will you do something for me, Katarina?" he asked.

"I don't know…."

"I need you to be the fire you always have been. I need you to explode. I want you to be…" Bezaliel rushed to Katie's face, coming in close. "I want you to be the candle—to burn in passion and life and not in suffering as I am damned to be."

Katie looked once more to the candle, this newfound metaphor for herself. "I could piss that fire out," she said.

Bezaliel laughed. "Good. Then now is your time."

Katie looked back into those cosmic, understanding, wickedly beautiful eyes. "I can burn so much brighter. Bigger, even."

"Good girl," said Bezaliel. "Then be snuffed, rest from your labors, and be born again. Be renewed."

The flame upon the candle erupted into a tiny blaze, Katie feeling its heat upon her neck and back. Her eyes widened as Bezaliel's hand passed over her face. Her wide eyes closed and she fell back onto the bed, sinking quickly into a deep unnatural slumber.

All she saw was darkness and Bezaliel's eyes off in the distance of her immediate dream before they vanished.

All she felt was cold, the candle a long-forgotten thought in her transfer between realms.

All she tasted was chalk, the gritty flavor of the drugs that still lay within the prison of her own body.

All she smelled was sulfur and the cigarette burn on the carpet from before.

All she could hear was Bezaliel's echoing laughter, comforting her and urging her to fall more deeply into nothing.

Nothing was her final thought before drifting back into dormant peace.

Nothing. What I was and what I will be. Nothing. Simply, nothing….

It's about damned time….

HANNAH

Hannah was silent and her mind was blank, her heart hardened like stone. She wanted to cry but could not. She wanted to scream but could not form a voice behind her quivering lips. The tears in her eyes welled up but would not flow, as if gravity had abandoned her, leaving her floating in an empty sea of confusion, all alone.

She hovered, surrounded by silent, kinetic chaos, the galaxy of her heart tightening in on itself, a black hole of frustration and rage consuming it from the inside out. As the spiral tightened, her thoughts quickened—thoughts that did not seem to exist at all. Her inner silent screams reverberated off the walls of her interior echo chamber of torment, and she loved the pain.

She exploded despite her secret love for her suffering.

"What the fuck, Michael?!" she said, her tone amorphous yet focused.

"Wh—what?" Michael asked, shaken. "What did I do?"

"Do?! Almost nothing, and yet everything! What do you mean 'When did I get here?!' I've been here forever, you idiot! I mean, what game are you trying to play?" Hannah had become lost in hysterics. She could hardly form the scathing words she was summoning to injure him.

I want you to feel my pain, asshole!

"But, babe," Michael said, his shaking voice giving Hannah hope that perhaps he was being genuine.

No! Don't you dare! Don't you DARE!

"Don't you dare gaslight me like this, you son of a bitch! I've heard it before from better men than you, Michael! You think because you're all tall and handsome… that I'll just GET OVER IT, HUH?" Hannah had caught herself yelling at him, her voice reaching a heightened tone, her sense of control quickly fading and dying.

"Hannah, please," Michael said, stepping toward her. "Please, listen to me."

Listen? LISTEN?!

"I've been here, talking to you this whole time, and you've treated me like a fucking ghost! I'm not here for your convenience!" she continued, laying into him, taking advantage of his vulnerability as he had so mindlessly taken advantage of hers. She was a victim who had now gained the upper hand, and she intended to take full advantage of her newly empowered position.

Take your punishment like a man, you…. You…. YOU!—

"You little boy!" she shouted, swinging her arms down angrily to her side. She closed her eyes, and the tears finally began to flow. As they cascaded like two tiny raging rivers down her face, they eroded away her weaker bits, and all her insecurities and self-doubts with them, carving her into a purer, stronger, more self-aware version of herself.

I haven't found you yet, still, have I? Whoever you are…. Wherever….

The tears began to flow more heavily, her disappointment taking her over, possessing her—consuming her.

"You pitiful excuse for a man," she said, wiping at her teary face, embarrassed and angry at herself for showing such weakness.

Honesty is what it is. To hell with honesty. It only ever gets me hurt in the end.

She looked down at her shaking hands, then between them at the ground beneath her feet, frozen in rage. Though she wanted to run, she was simply too infuriated to do so.

She could not bring herself to scream anymore. She had become disappointed in herself for not being more aggressive, despite her hurtful words. She had become disappointed in herself for losing control, also, all while hating herself for all the past heartache she had tolerated and just now confronted. She despised herself for not killing him with her hatred, disgusting herself further for allowing him to make her hate him like this in the first place.

Fuck. Just…. Fuck!

Hannah imploded, a flustered contradiction, her fire suddenly burning out. Her tears had ceased, dried up from within, and her spirit along with it. Her arm fell back to her side, wet with her undead tears, and she was suddenly a withered husk before Michael.

She looked to the pile of wood that had reduced itself to a smoking ruin.

Just like me, no life left in it…. Damn it. Damn him. Damn you, Michael.

"Hannah," Michael said, assuring her. She ignored him.

And damn me, too. Me, especially.

"Hannah, honey," Michael continued.

Whatever. What. Ever. Don't 'honey' me! I'm so done….

Just then, Hannah felt warm despite her newfound coldness. She felt comfortable despite her shaken state. She fell silent amid the raucous of her internal, chaotic din. She felt trapped, yet free.

Michael, you son of a bitch….

She felt safe, and as she calmed down, the inner storm finally tapering, she realized that Michael had embraced her with his honesty, loving her with the promise of his lie.

You…. Michael, you man! You stubborn, stupid, caring, handsome, beautiful man!

She loved this moment—how he was here when she needed him, never mind that he was the source of her current stress.

Now was what mattered.

'Now' is all there is….

All her inner fire had condensed. Its matter had concentrated. It exploded and burned out. It gathered, bound, burst, and from it, a new universe had been born.

Hannah was Hannah again—renewed, catatonic, and comfortable.

"Hannah," she heard, Michael breathing her name onto her neck. "Hannah, you wouldn't believe me if I told you…."

Hannah felt the cold sting of Michael's tears on her neck.

Damn you. Damn you, Michael.

Hannah pitied him, and her heart softened.

So vulnerable. So stupid.

Hannah laughed within herself, then laughed out loud—a modest one—a snicker fading as she buried her wet face into his strong chest.

"Michael, I'll believe you if you tell me. Please—" she said, fighting more tears of honesty. "Just tell me…."

"You promise you'll listen?" he asked.

I'm here, aren't I? Are you? Are you still here?

"I'm still here, aren't I?" she asked, half-crying, half-laughing. She snuggled deeper into him.

"I'll listen. I'm listening," she whispered, wrapping her arms around him.

Michael took several long, deep breaths. He became hard against her but did not withdraw. Then he cleared his throat, exhaling once more upon her neck. "I would rather show you than tell you," he whispered back. "Better for you to see than hear…."

All I feel… it's all nothing and everything and you, Michael. And aren't you all of this… and none of this…. Everything and nothing….

"I love you and I hate you," she whispered.

And you, Michael—you fall somewhere in between, I think.

"Then show me how you feel," Michael said. "Put me in the middle, until I can show you better."

Michael squeezed her more tightly, and Hannah lost herself, tangled in the safety blanket he had become. She breathed in, then relaxed, exhaling a powerful, slow breath into Michael's chest, glancing off the heart she could hear and feel beating within his ribcage.

"Show me," she whispered, muffled, as she was still caught up in him.

"How would you like me to do that?" he asked.

Hannah snorted in disappointed laughter.

Stupid boy….

"You just don't take a hint very well, do you? You perfect idiot," she said, her voice still slightly muted. She pulled her face away from him, looking up into his listening eyes, beckoning him with hers.

Then, all went to beautiful black as she felt his clumsy lips press into hers.

As quickly as her thinking had slowed, now it had stopped completely. Her mind was as equally empty as her heart was full, and she kissed him back. Her spirit lifted inside, and she could feel her body lifting from the ground, Michael hoisting her up. She wrapped her legs around his waist.

Fingers danced rhythmically and uncontrollably through hair. Tongue danced with and over tongue. The lock that had kept Hannah's inhibitions bound melted in the presence of the heat of the moment, no key now necessary to access the limitless treasure beyond—the treasure that was the true Hannah within.

There was only one thing she had kept to herself, and she wanted to share it with this man-boy that had come to understand her.

Despite his rampant stupidity….

He kept her held in his elevating grasp, not overly forceful but enough to make her feel safe. He pressed a sealing kiss of pause to her wanting lips, holding its clasp for moments that passed like rapid epochs. He pulled his face away, slowly opening his eyes to her slowly opening eyes, both he and she simultaneously flustered—both mutually aware of their shared desires.

"I don't take hints," he whispered strongly, admitting it to her itching ears. "I take what I want."

The fucking confidence. More confidence than sense. Perfect.

Somewhere inside her, a drop of honey had fallen from the comb, struck the bedrock of her soul, and watered, with richness, a rapidly growing garden. Flower after flower bloomed in spite of its barren inclinations; and deep inside of her, a new Eden bloomed in fast-forward, all manner of potent flora and fauna becoming instantly manifest, spreading like a virus of creation at the heart of her core—the nucleus of her center—setting itself on fire in the process. Birth and death and beginning and ending all culminated into one in the ecstatic agony of her own selfish pleasure.

Her euphoria had conquered her, her new favorite drug, and she wanted more. She had gained herself yet given herself up to him.

"Then take what you want, babe," she said.

Take me now....

"And take me where you want," Hannah continued, in quiet confidence.

Hannah, stubborn as she was, had surrendered herself. She had not, however, admitted defeat. In her own powerfully-feminine way, she was prepared to conquer this mountain of a man as he conquered her—sweating, grueling, and rewarded—wounded by the struggle as she scaled his summit, punished by the journey; the punishment making her conquest all the sweeter and more savory.

Michael, pulling from her ear, maintained the honesty in his eyes, and the power of those clear blue irises destroyed the last brick of the stone castle wall that defended her from herself. Any remnant of any wall that remained had crumbled, and she was happy to let her sanctity go, her defenses shed, ready to be conquered as she conquered.

Michael laughed to himself in the full, open, unabated presence of Hannah.

"Would you like a tour of the house, Hannah?" Michael asked in calm confidence.

His laughter implied an assumed answer, she felt. His tone implied an assumed outcome. Still, he left the decision to her, and as the power was now in her hands, he had given her the choice, even though he assumed a tone that he had already decided for her—something she quietly loved.

"Take me anywhere. Just take me," she said.

She knew what she had given up. She knew what she had attained. She had become a queen of sacrifice, yet a queen nonetheless, and still a queen yet to be crowned. She was about to conquer his kingdom. His desires both mattered to her and held no consequence.

She was about to be the master—the mistress—of both domains, and she had no apology to offer, in either case.

Make a move, you fucking coward.

Michael repeated himself. "So, the house?" he asked.

Hannah laughed to herself.

"The house, the fire, the now. Now is the time," she said.

Michael smiled and laughed. He set her on the ground, taking her hand. "Then let's go."

The unending confidence…. Perfect.

Hannah gave herself over to him.

You're mine.

Michael said not another word. He took her hand, kissed it, and she followed in tow as he guided her to wherever—the altar of her surrender and the temple of her desire.

I am the queen.

The shadows of trees passed her by like her fluid thoughts as she was guided up the path to the comfort of the mansion—a comfort she had long-discarded for the sake of her own passion.

She was reckless. She was in control.

Hannah was finally Hannah.

I won't apologize anymore.

The grove had become a forgotten memory.

Never. Never again.

The night disappeared behind her. A new dawn approached her in the middle of the nighttime autumn morning. A sun rose in her heart, the shadows fading from her sight, the horizon a blazing dynamo of promising potential; a hot wire cutting the sky from the ground, severing the past from the present and her hopes from her reality.

MICHAEL

Michael's mind was a stirred pot of numbing nonsense and frivolous focus. He was both taken aback and giving in to the gorgeous sight before him, his tattered focus sharpening, like waking into a heavenly dream from a demon's nightmare.

Man, that was weird….

All he knew was that he had lost his mind—yet there she was, the contents of his empty heart personified before him. Hannah was tangible but far from his reach.

Her angry, hysterical demeanor confused him.

To reach and to touch, but never hold…. It's like the future. You reach to grab it, but by the time you have it, it's become the present. The ever-eluding…. What the fuck….

"What the fuck, Michael!"

Michael shook awake from his foggy daydream. Hannah had truly and wholly arrived.

"Wh—what?" he asked, unsure he had even spoken. "What did I do?"

This is bullshit. WHY CAN'T I WAKE UP?!

"DO?!" Hannah said, her voice escalating to a fervor. "Absolutely nothing—"

Nothing, nothing, nothing….

"—and yet everything!" she continued.

Everything, everything, everything….

She continued to dig into him.

"What do you mean, 'When did I get here?!'" she asked. She was obviously troubled.

I have totally screwed this up—

"I've been here forever, you idiot!" she shouted.

Right into the ground, I go. Yes, I am an idiot.

"I mean, what game are you trying to play?" she asked,

hammering further into him.

This is not a game. But if it is, I am losing, for sure.

I refuse to lose you. Not again.

"But, babe," he said, a reckless attempt to salvage the pieces of the heart he had so clearly broken.

Even in the moonlit dark, he could see her pupils shaking with rage.

Brace yourself, brother. The storm is about to rock this ship right to the goddamned shore.

"Mind your language, Michael Law. God damns no one. He merely separates those who choose Him from those who prefer to obey themselves. Take it from my 'shadow'. We all choose. And He gives us the freedom to choose either path. At the very least, you are not a slave. And His love is so pure that even in His strength, He will not force you to love Him back."

Michael heard that mystical, familiar voice but ignored it. Still, he had heard. Hannah's crippling cries deafened his ears and she became his focus.

Maybe she could love me back. Maybe…. Maybe she already does. Hell, I don't even know what love is.

"Don't you *dare* gaslight me like this—!" she shouted, her voice crisp and diminishing.

Gaslight…? Here we go again.

"You son of a bitch!" she continued.

And again and again and again…. It's all bullshit. It's always the same bullshit.

"I've heard it before—" she started.

Yup. Different, Hannah, but all more of the numbing same.

"—from better men than you—" Hannah continued.

Better? No, not a chance.

"—Michael!"

My name. Such a common name. So uninspiring. But better? No. Just shut up, Hannah. You're losing it, honey.

"You think because you're all tall—" she said.

Sure, tall. Whatever that means…. "—

and handsome—" she added. *Yeah,*

I'm not ugly. So-the-fuck-what? "—that

I'll just—" she persisted. *Just what,*

Hannah? That you'll just—

"—GET OVER IT, HUH?" she screamed at his face. Her voice became hoarse in its delivery, fading, yet clear.

You're going crazy. Maybe my 'crazy' made this happen. I've had 'Hannahs' before. But 'this' Hannah…. I don't want to lose this one—'this' Hannah. Those perfect eyes, crying, now. Because of me. How I feel and hate this pain.

Michael saw her chest rise and rapidly fall, and he began to both hurt for and with her.

For the first time in my entire lonely, selfish, sad, pathetic life. Hannah, don't leave…. This is when they always leave…. This revolving door of 'now'.

"Hannah," Michael said, struggling to speak the name. "Please…."

I AM A MAN AND I DO NOT BEG! BUT! I…. I…. I am begging now….

Michael's heart had overtaken his rationality. He stepped forward a bit, breaching Hannah's comfort zone.

"Please," he said. "Please, listen to me."

You've only just arrived.

"I've been here—" she said, erratically.

And just in time. "—

talking to you—"

Yes. Yes, me.

"—this whole time—" she continued.

What perfect timing.

"—and you've treated me like—"

A princess? A queen, even?

"—a fucking ghost!" she concluded.

Oh. Well, damn.

"I'm not here for your convenience!" she said.

And yet so impossibly 'right on time'. So convenient. So convenient…. I've got to be a man about this.

"You little boy!" she yelled.

Michael stiffened, his heart turning to stone, knowing he had betrayed Hannah's heart, and for once and the first time, he cared that he had.

As Hannah's eyes cried themselves closed, Michael died a bit inside.

All he could see now was her pain. He felt it within himself, and suddenly—

So. So, this is what love feels like.

Finally.

His heart leapt out of his body in joy.

"You pitiful excuse for a man…." she said.

His heart retreated back into him, sank and drowned.

Even the fire itself quieted its flames as Michael and the bonfire both seemed to lose their fervor in solidarity. Only little flames, smolders and smoke remained.

I'm burnt out, too, it seems.

Hannah stood silently before Michael's silence, they, the two of them, two mute gossamer reflections. They both hated. They both loved.

Hannah wiped her now-flowing tears from her perfect face. Michael self-destructed at the sight. He watched as she looked away, her eyes drifting like smoke to the drifting smoke that rose up from and abandoned the dying, clinging pyre of firewood. Then, it ceased—the smoke gone and the fire now completely dead.

Hannah. Hannah....

"Hannah," Michael said as she blatantly ignored him.

"Hannah," he repeated, unheard.

"Honey," he attempted, hoping she would not ignore him again.

Sweet, like honey sticking to my tongue....

She did not recognize his plea.

Only one move left to make....

He stepped forward, taking her into his arms, wrapping her tightly in undoubtable security.

Infiltrate. Infiltrate when the walls go up and diplomacy fails. Make her hear you!

Michael, heeding his own advice, brought his lips to her neck, both cold and warm with death and life.

"Hannah," he said, weakly letting himself go.

Michael thought of the angel from earlier—an angel in which he did not believe.

And yet....

Here an angel stood, dark hair aglow, her eyes radiating—a vision of glory and a possible proof of perfection.

Those perfect, perfect—

"You wouldn't believe me if I told you," Michael said, exhaling onto her neck.

Just... all of you.... Perfection.

Michael began to weep. Hannah laughed a quiet laugh, which at first felt like her revenge upon his prior ignorant thoughtlessness; but as she nuzzled into his chest, he knew it to be a laugh of comforting joy.

"Michael," she said, muffled. "I'll believe you if you tell me."

But you'll just think I'm crazy.

"Please, just tell me," she continued.

I don't want to lie to this girl. The truth only ruins things. And lies make me feel like shit....

"You promise you'll listen?" Michael asked, reluctantly.

They make me feel like shit, but at least lies don't leave, like everything else.

"I'm still here, aren't I?" Hannah asked, cuddling into him further, her tone caught somewhere between elation and misery.

You are, but people are so afraid of the pains of truth. Like shying from a medicine for fear of the pain of the needle, no matter how trivial or temporary the sensation. The cure hurts, so we hide from it, while the sickness of loneliness kills us a little at a time. So stupid. Is this even me?

"I'll listen," Hannah said.

No, maybe 'hear' me, but not listen....

"I'm listening," she continued, lowering her voice to a tone of more concrete sincerity, her arms slipping around his torso, cradling him.

I don't want to concern you with my daydream—that hallucination. I can't get it off my mind. Not with you here, teasing me with your honest touch, pressed firmly on my body with your body.

Michael was thankful for the darkness as he began to glow red-hot in his face, his pants tightening as he became aroused, hardening against her softness.

Own it, Michael. Just own it. Honesty and truth, after all.... Let her feel that needle. She'll come to love the 'sting' of your truth in the end.

Calmly clearing his throat, alleviating his lingering discomfort, Michael exhaled a hot, loving breath onto Hannah's inviting neck.

Give her the damned medicine. Heal her. Give her what she wants. Give her what she needs.

"I would rather show you than tell you. Better for you to see—" he whispered.

And feel....

"—than hear," he finished.

"I love you," Hannah responded, a jolt of satisfying discomfort coming over Michael. He was becoming immediately confused in both the brashness of the statement and its abruptness.

"And I hate you," she followed, whispering to herself now, another shock slowly washing over him. Both statements, entirely opposite in nature, provided the same response in his spirit.

I guess I'm just not sure which I believe more, or which one I prefer. Both could come of some use, I suppose. Maybe words are not the way.

"Then show me how you feel," Michael said.

Between love and hate…. I'd rather be between those perfect legs…. Between, yes, and within.

"Put me in the middle, until I can show you better," Michael flirted, his subconscious emanating from within him.

His passion teetered on the edge of recklessness, and he squeezed her more tightly, pressing his hardness against her, taunting her sexuality with his, both demanding and begging for her to respond.

She understood.

Hannah pulled in a breath as it was taken from her, then exhaled, taking it back for herself. She reclaimed her authority as she quietly conquered him with his own thoughts.

Michael's excitement rose with his heightening senses, his heartbeat increasing in rapidity, as if to flutter from within his chest. He knew she could feel him in all the ways that he knew how to bare himself to her.

"Show me," she whispered, and Michael contained his frenzy at her dare, remaining calm amid the battle of lust he had been fighting within himself—a minuscule battle in the grand scheme of the sexual war that she, Hannah, had instigated.

Show you? Hannah, my sexy little perfect angel, I would love to.

"How would you like me to do that?" Michael asked.

Let her believe she's leading, even though you are the beast in control.

Hannah let out what Michael thought to be an ugly but charming laugh.

"You just don't take a hint very well, do you?" she asked.

No. I never have.

"You perfect idiot," she said in what sounded like a mix of sarcasm and playfulness. He looked down to, into and through her. It appeared to him that she had seen the mischief in his eyes, and she pulled away. Her watery, honest eyes met his, crippling him in their complex, exposed, inviting gaze.

There you are.

Michael's vision sharpened like a seeing sword, ready to pierce and prepared to penetrate. Lost in thought, Michael lost his balance, tipping forward, falling into her. He disguised his drunken fallacy by anchoring his lips to hers as he stumbled, hoping to make his kiss seem intentional.

She immediately began kissing him back, Michael fading into euphoria. He had to further tempt her, so he lifted her from the ground— their lips unparted—taking her up and away from herself by taking her up and into his arms. As he lifted her from the ground, she wrapped her legs around him, each of them claiming the other.

He kissed her with a desperation he had never known. She had sketched a new man upon the wayward page that Michael had always been, yet the paper man he was began to fold and unfold, the lines of his past emptiness beginning to become filled in by the hands—the soft touch—of this angel-artist.

I can't handle this. This is too real. Maybe I'm the one that fears your needle, your medicine….

He kissed her with a slow last pass of finality, putting the period on the sentence of the moment. Michael withdrew his tongue then pressed his lips against hers once more, as if to say goodbye. He then separated from her. As his eyes opened, hers were opening.

I prefer the honesty. The straightforward….

"I don't take hints," Michael whispered to her eyes, the portal and doorway to her heart.

I want you.

"I take what I want," he whispered further.

He felt her flower gather dew between the legs that had bound him like a rope—a rope that was the lifeline to the death he had become willing to die for her.

He felt the newborn heat.

He felt the fresh moisture.

I want you.

And now. Right fucking now.

"Then take what you want, babe, and take me where you want," she breathed.

Michael, awestricken by her confidence, backed his head away from her ear, laughing as he withdrew.

His goal had become clear to him, like a race he had won before it had even begun, or like a chess match he was playing against himself.

He could not lose, victory being his only option.

Knowing her answer before he had posed the question, he said, "Would you like a tour of the house, Hannah?" He then gave a muted laugh, ashamed of making his confidence obvious. In the same turn, he ignored the shame, burying it in the black hole of his intention.

"Take me anywhere," she said, her voice coy but assertive. "Just take me."

Soon, Hannah. Soon.

"So," Michael reiterated. "The house?"

Hannah laughed a brief laugh.

My god, how I love the sound of that laughter…. That song….

"The house," she said.

The only heaven I have to look forward to….

"The fire," she said.

The fire—the hell I've endured without you.

"The 'now'," she said.

All I ever have…. And it's about that time.

"Now is the time," she concluded.

Just a little longer….

Michael laughed through his smile as it crept across his stone face gone soft. Michael used his strong arms to set her back on the ground, hating letting go but loving how she was about to bounce back to him and belong to him. He took her hand, claiming it as his own.

These stupid things that Ari believes in…. God, Heaven, hope…. You are my goddess, Hannah, and I crave your heaven. You are the only heaven I want. You're the only devil I need. And if you are my paradise, take me inside yourself. Let me inside of you. So, if I'm forgiven…. Angel, open up to me more than just your wings.

"Then, let's go," he said.

"Then, I'm all yours," she responded. "If you can handle me."

Michael was so taken aback by her powerful words that he could only blindly react, giving into his nature and instinct, a neanderthal with a human heart, torn somewhere between mankind and humankind, brutish action melding with refined calculation.

They were ascending the path toward the house before he had realized he was moving. Hannah's hand in his hand, he gripped tightly as she gripped more tightly back, both of them refusing to let go or let up.

The lights of the house came closer in a blur of desperation and focus—control and powerlessness.

And yet the light behind me eclipses all. Blind me. Blind me and forsake my sight….

My goddess of the midnight sun….

JORDAN

As Jordan stood, Ari took her hand, holding her fast. The prickling electricity in her chest dissolved with his comforting grip. Jordan turned to look back to Ari, away from the pair of quarreling lovers-to-be by the fire pit.

"We're fine," Ari whispered only to be interrupted by Hannah's anger as she shouted.

"What the fuck, Michael!"

Ari stepped back from Jordan in surprise, letting her go as he turned. Jordan barely noticed as she swiveled on her feet in curiosity.

"Wh—What?" Michael asked her, his voice apparently broken—for what reason, Jordan could not discern. "What did I do?"

Yeah, what did you do? Or fail to do? I'm watching you, Michael.

Hannah's response cut Jordan's ears like a rusty razor, dragging, cutting, and uncleanly so.

The honest way I know you to be. First time you've been 'you' all night, to be honest.

"Do?!" Hannah shrieked. "Almost nothing, and yet everything."

I see why you and Ari are friends, Michael.

Jordan laughed to herself silently in the cage of her body.

"What do you mean 'When did I get here?' I've been here forever, you idiot! I mean, what game are you trying to play?" Hannah said. She was obviously furious, and rightfully so.

"But babe," Michael said.

Babe? What have I missed?

Hannah's continued hysterics cut off Jordan's thoughts, loud as they were.

"Don't you dare gaslight me like this, you son of a bitch!" she shouted.

But maybe he isn't. I just can't figure Michael out....

"I've heard it before from better men than you, Michael!" Hannah continued. "You think because you're all tall and handsome… that I'll just GET OVER IT, HUH?"

But Hannah, tall and handsome—wealthy, even—they've never stopped you before.

There's something different with this one. I can see it. I'm sure you see it, too, don't you, Hannah.

"Hannah, please," Michael pleaded as he took a large step closer to her. "Please listen to me."

Maybe you should just let her speak and sweat out the fever.

Hannah lost it.

"I've been here, talking to you this whole time, and you've treated me like a fucking ghost!" she said.

I feel like a ghost, myself, right now, hidden in shadows, hiding from the light.

"I'm not here for your convenience!" Hannah continued. "You little boy!"

Hannah slung her arms down to her sides. As Jordan saw it, her rage had become physical. "You pitiful excuse for a man," she said, her voice donning a new armor of frailty. Jordan watched as her arm rose to her face, wiping away the tears she could hear falling from Hannah's face. Then her arm fell limply to her side. The fire reflected Hannah's melancholy, hiding its own face from the tears that burned too hot for even the fire to endure. The flames fell low, and smoke began to billow from the tall pile of wood.

Oh, Hannah.

"Hannah," Michael said in a subtle way as if to calmly interrupt her, to reassure her of his presence. "Hannah, honey," he continued. And then, to Jordan's pleasant surprise, Michael embraced Hannah, something Jordan loved witnessing. Michael spoke but was whispering in an intimate tone that Jordan could not make out.

I'm no longer part of that moment. It belongs to them now.

Jordan heard Michael's mumbling then Hannah's laughter as she drew herself closer into Michael's silhouette. Then Hannah wrapped her arms around Michael.

You did it, you son of a bitch.

A tear of empathy was born in Jordan's eye, happy for Hannah, and perhaps Michael, as well. More low speech followed, and in her witnessing, Jordan turned back to look at Ari, whose eyes pierced her, a mirror of the moments passing before them as though Hannah and Michael's shared passion had reflected off Ari's eyes, pouring out of him like the moon reflecting the light of the sun from the other side of the world. Jordan took Ari's hands into her own, and could hear

Hannah clearly as she said, "I love you and I hate you."

Hannah's words became Jordan's thoughts as she studied the man in the twilit dark before her.

Yes, love and hate. Ari, I love this moment. I hate that it hadn't happened sooner.

The conversation between Michael and Hannah faded to nothingness behind her as Ari was once again all that there was. There they were, Ari and Jordan, thieves of a moment not their own, stealing it, leaving empty the coffers of the victim-pair they had left behind.

Maybe they'll be watching us soon.

"Would you like a tour of the house, Hannah?" Michael said, barely audible. Jordan giggled to herself, her thoughts taking a more intimate turn, thinking to herself of all the beautiful, reckless, lustful, loving things she might do with Ari if not for fear of their discovery in the dark.

The mystery. The secret.

"We can just stay right here," Jordan whispered to Ari's ear, leaning in, answering Michael's question as if Ari had asked it. Jordan could hear Michael laugh a clear, distant laugh far behind her, reinstating her brewing inner mischief that she had begun to plot.

"I don't care where we are as long as you're there," Ari whispered back into Jordan's ear.

Anywhere.

"Take me anywhere," Hannah said, echoing Jordan's mischievous thoughts.

Yeah. Anywhere.

"Just take me," Hannah could be heard saying.

Even my best friend knows what I want and what I need.

"You heard the woman," Jordan whispered, still only an inch from Ari's ear. She could practically hear the hair raising on his neck, the temperature of his body gaining heat as she pressed the buttons of his heart and soul, receiving the reaction that she wanted. She knew that Ari understood her, a feeling she had had about him since their first meeting—a trend he had maintained throughout the night, even in his times of absence.

"I didn't hear a woman," Ari said, "but I do hear *my* woman."

Jordan was beside herself. Ari had built a literal fire to which all could gather, yet amid the crowd, she stood out, had been so perfectly, passively claimed, and felt as though she was the sole reason for the entire party. At the whim of his perfect, well-timed words, the fire he had built within her had ignited, destroying her and then bringing her back to life. He had killed her from within yet shown her a sense of passion she would not otherwise have known.

So, so this…. This is Heaven…

The house….

"The house," Hannah said.

The fire….

"The fire," Hannah continued.

"Ari," Jordan said, speaking to him. "All I need, honey—"

"The 'now'," Hannah said.

Exactly. Now. Right now.

Hannah's voice was a metronome in time as she and Jordan's voice combined in an identical declaration.

"Now is the time," Jordan whispered further to Ari as Hannah spoke to Michael. Then, Ari laughed as Michael laughed, their tone of satisfaction a beautiful song of shared purpose—a purpose they had simultaneously achieved and celebrated.

Hannah, I love you, but I wish you would LEAVE!

"Then let's go," Michael said.

Jordan exhaled in relief, now fully exempt from any prior doubt she withheld for him.

Michael, you angel. Thank you.

Jordan heard Hannah say something, but she could no longer be bothered or concerned with the outside world. Ari had grasped her hands with his strong hands, pulled her in, and kissed her with a kiss to end all kisses. She was overwhelmed like an over-fueled star, burning its way to a fast oblivion, incinerating all within a galaxy's reach of her sexual might.

The echoes of the real and present world faded in the form of Hannah's and Michael's footsteps as they bolted hurriedly up the path toward the house, away from Jordan and Ari like a rogue comet.

They're gone….

"They're gone," Ari said just above the level of a whisper.

Jordan laughed in his face, only inches away, embarrassed by her recklessness.

"But we're not," Jordan said. "We can stay here."

Jordan gasped inside as Ari spoke.

"This is the only place I know—here—with you," he said.

Jordan grabbed Ari by the hips, guiding him toward the crackling grave of the fire.

"Then," she said, guiding his body closer to the smoking rubble, "you aren't going anywhere, mister."

She stumbled and fell, Ari's body tumbling on top of her, the woodpile only feet away.

Why are we wearing clothes?

"Hey," she said, her hands all over him.

She stared into those mirror-eyes of his with her own. Reflection bore reflection and in the infinite exchange, forever promised itself, unending—a black hole swallowing itself. All manner of physical law, mathematics, and time dissolved in a clash of incalculable emotion.

Their lips met like two continents colliding as if to destroy the very world they inhabited. Neither cared, ignoring the destruction. Both were willing to die for their passion, like a flame consuming a candle, depleting the wax to burn as brightly as it could. The diminishing wax served as a timer—a period at the end of the sentence of life—to decide just how long that wick should last.

And damn it all—how we also burn each other down. Too many wicks in the wax, consuming the finite, begging to be infinite.

Ari's lips were pressing Jordan into paradise. Her world was breaking apart, much unlike the portions of her mouth.

Nothing does, but I wish this could last forever.

His fingers were in her hair and on her body. His hands were caressing her sweetly in their powerful ownership of her, taking and borrowing, yet giving back, only to take over and over again. Jordan lost herself in Ari as he disappeared before her, the pair of them becoming two invisible ghosts within the fog of their togetherness.

Those two lost souls haunted the same house—a house they had so separated themselves from, yet begged to return to again.

We always find our way home.

A cold wind cut through Jordan and Ari, the dead fire, and the grove. The trees swayed. Ari and Jordan did not.

Wherever home is….

That wind, slow-rolling and modest, stirred the coals of the pyre just enough to cause it to roar back to life and light.

Jordan was the fire and Ari the wind.

The pile of smoking wood engulfed itself and the shadows of Ari's face—a face gone into the violence of the waged war that was once a sleeping heap of resting rubble.

Dead bodies everywhere, and here we are, as alive as we've ever been.

They kissed perpetually and without discretion.

The fire had come back to life, and so had Jordan.

Nature forsook her inhibitions, reflecting them back. Jordan was lost in the swoon of Ari's charms and honesty. She was lost in the molding of his will, broken as it was.

I could stay here forever.

Jordan became lost in the moment as she blacked out in her swoon, her spirit satisfied as Ari began to satisfy her body—her body the door to the pleasure of her soul.

ARI

Jordan stood where the tree line broke and I could feel her curiosity blanket itself with the impulse to both fight and run. She wanted to protect her friend, but her reticence spoke of her uncertainty to whether she needed to.

I understood her thoughts and concerned heart because we now shared a heart, conjoined by our mutual dilemma. Her anxiety had triggered mine, making me uneasy and ready to pounce to protect her. It was good that I felt this discomfort because it allowed my adrenaline to ready me to catch her by the hand, stopping her from rushing toward our friends that stood out in the open. I hated making that choice for her, but despite the obvious argument in which the two of them were so loudly engaging, I trusted Michael.

He can be an asshole, but at his core, he really is a good guy. Michael, don't screw this up. Don't sit in the lap of my trust to slap its face.

I regained my composure, her touch calming me, reminding me of my strength. Simultaneously, I was reminded that I was her protector and I had to be strong for both of us in this moment that I knew would have destroyed her without my presence. Our hands still clasped and I was a good king, standing both alongside and behind my queen.

I gave her my most honest look, stepping aside to let her inside my eyes—eyes that fell more delicately upon and into her. She turned to catch my eyes with hers as I whispered to comfort her.

"We're fine," I whispered to her in my attempt at a sultry voice. The moment and atmosphere I had tried to create was destroyed by Hannah's abrupt voice of rage.

"What the fuck, Michael!" she screamed.

I was so startled that I stepped back and away from Jordan. Hannah's unnerving, shrill voice astonished me, and I released Jordan's hand in the brevity of my shock. Jordan turned away from me, facing the drama in the grove once more. "Wh—

What?" Michael responded. "What did I do?"

Michael, don't be an idiot right now. Please. Be bad at being stupid, just this once.

"Do?! Almost nothing and yet everything," Hannah proceeded, verbally digging into this man that was Michael Law—the friend that had become my enemy, and yet one that I loved. He was once again my friend, yet now so far from me.

How did we ever come to this? How—When did we get here?

Hannah's continued diatribe seemed to juxtapose my thoughts.

"What do you mean, 'When did I get here?'" she shouted.

Hannah, I guess Michael has been 'Michael' to us both tonight. But damn, there's just something about him. You just can't help loving the guy.

"I've been here forever, you idiot!" she continued.

I feel like I've been here longer. This is so damned awkward!

"I mean, what game are you trying to play?" she yelled.

Game? This feels like hide-and-seek if you're asking me.

"But, babe," Michael said.

Babe? Right. The endearing game, the words the pawns, moving along a colorless black and white board. You sacrifice everything you have to just to topple another king while you try to claim the queen, only to toss her, along with every other piece, back into the box until the next game of more of the same.

"Don't you dare gaslight me like this, you son-of-a-bitch!" Hannah said, becoming ruthless.

Michael, perhaps this is no queen you can so easily take. Michael, I do believe you are in trouble. She's keeping you in check—constant check—and you're stumbling, stuttering, and failing to make a move. The queen might just claim the king tonight.

"I've heard it before from better men than you, Michael!" she said, further chipping at Michael's ego. "You think because you're all tall and handsome that I'll just GET OVER IT, HUH?!"

She's about to out-Michael you. Will you run? You always run from what doesn't come easily to you.

"Hannah, please. Please listen to me," Michael said.

You're about to be put back into the box, man. I see why you love this girl so much, Jordan.

Hannah could not be restrained. Her rage seemed limitless—reckless and without apology.

"I've been here talking to you this whole time, and you've treated me like a fucking ghost!" she responded.

Same here. Tell him the truth he needs to hear. I've always held back.

Correct him. Fix him, please, Hannah. Now, at least, someone else knows how I've felt.

"I'm not here for your convenience, you little boy!" Hannah shouted, her arms falling aggressively by her sides. "You pitiful excuse for a man." Hannah's voice had become weaker in strength and tone as she brushed her face with her arm, shunning the tears that could be heard in her calming words. The two fires—the bonfire and Hannah's flaming spirit—were both quelled to the state of smoke and ashes.

Tell him. Say what I never could.

Her shift of tone touched me in some way, convincing my heart to empathize with her pain—a pain he had made me feel for years. She was speaking my past sufferings, bringing them into the light of the truth. She was personifying and embodying rages I had clung to throughout the past, letting them out, unleashing justice and vengeful hell upon Michael. She was accurate and effective in her attack, something I had always lacked. That harsh past had caught up to him in the form of Hannah, and I was stunned as my future—Jordan— was right here before me, the melding of all forms of time—past, present and future—coalescing into some form of existence that was neither.

I was stunned by it, wholly impressed by this girl.

While I did have these thoughts, I felt I had betrayed Jordan by my enthrallment with this woman, me realizing how distracted I had become by Hannah, who was my true voice speaking to my only true friend. While I did now understand Jordan's and Michael's love for this immaculate creature, I could not afford nor bring myself to be so emotionally conflicted. Michael was right there before her. Jordan was right here with me, though her back was now to me; yet I could not justify betraying both her heart and my love for that heart. Just because she could not see my internal argument did not mean it was not betrayal. I was cheating her and on her in a game she was not even aware that she was playing.

I felt like a complete coward hiding in the shadows, shadows looming like the guilt that surrounded and consumed me, like the fascination with this distant girl—Michael's girl—and I became somewhat lost in the weight of my unjustifiable thoughts. Jordan was still there with me, right in front of me.

Do I want what I want? Or cultivate what I have? Will I choose the mystery of the appealing unknown or choose what or who has already chosen me? What do I do?

My thoughts were killed dead, murdered by the cold hands of

confirming disappointment as I received my answer.

"Hannah," Michael said. "Hannah, honey."

I watched, both crushed and relieved, as Michael melded with Hannah, a marriage of smoke-wrapped silhouettes. Michael took Hannah into himself, embracing her, and she embraced him back.

Their conversation continued in whispers and intimate talks that I would never know, and the illusion of my nighttime daydream faded away with that embrace I was not meant to see. I was a witness to the crime of my own insecurity, and Michael Law had lain the law upon me, condemning me in the courtroom of my own hypocrisy. Unbeknownst to her, Jordan was the jury, sentencing me to internal death, entirely unaware that she had killed a man many times herself tonight. She had also brought me back to life several times throughout the evening. I decided to rise again, reborn and resurrected by her light.

And this time, I swear, I will not be lost in the dark again. Ever. Never again.

Michael uttered something quiet to Hannah, undiscernible. Hannah laughed and I felt cosmically mocked by her laughter, knowing then that my thoughts may have been the sin that casted me from the heaven that was Jordan. Still, Jordan did not abandon me.

A second chance at a second chance.... I don't deserve you, but I'll never abandon you again, Jordan. And I'm sorry.

I'm so, so sorry....

My eyes began to moisten with silent apologies, each micro-droplet a dialogue of words I could not say—a multiverse of regrets, each one more sorrowful and honest than the last. I looked at the back of Jordan's head, imagining those perfect eyes that resided on the other side, like a love I desperately missed who was an entire world away. The tears that formed were the unsent letters that my love would never read. As I spiraled into a breakdown, Jordan turned to look at me. She had released Hannah from her concern. Michael had been forgiven and understood by her.

My unwritten letters had somehow been delivered. Jordan read each of them as she turned the pages of my eyes, reading the story of my thoughts.

"I love you and I hate you," I heard Hannah say, my heart telling me that Hannah was speaking to me, reflecting Jordan's unheard disappointment in my failing of her.

I love you, Jordan. And right now, I hate me.

Jordan's eyes became my own as I looked at her, and Jordan was peering through me.

The surrounding world disappeared. No Michael. No Hannah. No trees nor darkness, nor God. Jordan was all there was—Jordan and me—and I was at peace.

All thoughts became dead and silent to me in the whirlwind of emptiness that consumed my perspective like a black hole, all of reality devoured in an instant. Just as I was about to cross the threshold of that event horizon, Michael's voice summoned me back to the safety of the shadows of the grove.

"Would you like a tour of the house, Hannah?" Michael mumbled.

THE house? You mean MY house! My home, you bastard!

Jordan let out a stifled laugh as if reading my mind, cracking up at the hubris.

You two go on to the world I've built for you. Use it at your prideful will. I'm just the god you now forsake as you defile the place I've made for you TO EVEN FUCKING EXIST!

I focused my gaze more sharply on Jordan.

"We can just stay right here," came Jordan's voice, whispering to my pleading, failing heart. Michael was laughing, mocking me.

Fuck you, Michael. But I can't be angry with you, even though I am. Without you making me jealous, would I have chased her the way I did, even if I chased her only in my living dreams?

I spoke, keeping my voice low to remain silent in the role of my half of the quiet secret Jordan and I shared, and were.

"I don't care where we are—" I said.

Can we just go somewhere far away? Another country? Another planet? Even Heaven itself?

"—As long as you're there," I finished. I realized I had been whispering into Jordan's ear, right next to her incredible face.

Once again, Hannah spoke what I had thought—what I imagined Jordan's thoughts to be.

"Take me anywhere," Hannah said. "Just take me."

"You heard the woman," Jordan said. I blushed as my instinct was confirmed. My excitement must have become obvious because my skin tingled and my mind emptied itself. I became hot all over and I knew Jordan could feel the building temperature. I became increasingly nervous in my comfort with her, and words—nervous words—poured from my basic thoughts. I had become a lifeless machine, my emotions blindly driving the empty vehicle.

"I didn't hear a woman, but I did hear *my* woman," I said.

I was stunned by what I had so naturally said. My instinct had escaped my lips with no thoughts to stop them or filter them at all.

You clumsy man. Clumsy, drunk and staggering…. Tumbling, falling. Falling deeper into her, sinking, drowning in the river Jordan…. And what a gorgeous death to die….

"The house," Hannah's voice came.

MY house!

"The fire," she said.

MY fire!

"Ari," Jordan said. "All I need, honey—"

"The 'now'," Hannah interrupted.

OUR 'NOW'!

"Now is the time," Jordan said, her whisper sharp and seductive.

I laughed, and as I did, so did Michael.

I then had an epiphany.

One is one. And one is the other. While we both have our 'other', we share the same 'other', and each 'other' speaks for each other. Thus, the others speak and become the other 'us'. Our voices are spoken by mouths not our own, but isn't that conversation? Is that not how we come closer? By seeing something of ourselves within someone else? And vice versa? We have a common source. God is here. The branches, they all go different directions, reaching out from the same trunk, and the roots do the same as they go down. Different directions, up or down, choice and consequence, heaven and hell…. It all comes from one seed. And that seed is the purpose of all life. The purpose—that seed— is love…. What other reason do we have to exist? Love is all that is eternal. Nothing but love lasts. Even the stars remember the heat of the passion of the burning of mutual hearts. Love can be etched upon the very sky, and even if the world dies, the echoes of love go on, even to the very door of Heaven. Whether God is real or not, a love like this would either give Him hope in our pathetic species, or cause Him to awaken from His slumber, His very nature finally realized in how true this feeling truly is. He rises from His slumbering grave, awakened by a love that rivals His own—Jordan, I am yours.

Even after we are gone, our story will still be told among the stars, and I love you. Jordan and Ari, and how we make the very stars quake with jealousy….

Take me back to my house, Jordan. Take me home. Take US home.

"Then let's go," Michael said, Jordan exhaling as he spoke the words I had hoped she would say. Her lofty strong breath was a breath of fresh air, and I inhaled it deeply into myself.

Then let's go. You said it, Michael.

I could no longer hold back. I was a light in my own darkness, I my own question as my answer stood before me.

I'm all yours. I'm all yours, Jordan.

I grabbed her hands with mine, pulled her close, and with a kiss that I planted upon her, I became lost. I was rising high into the sky, then to the wherever beyond, and all within the 'self' I lost within her.

I could vaguely hear the stomping of feet as Michael and Hannah clumsily stumbled away like the echoes of my beating heart that faded into the ether as Jordan kissed me back. One echo drowned out the other.

Michael and Hannah….

"They're gone," I said, the words crawling from my paralyzed lips.

It was only she and I, and Jordan laughed a happy laugh. She exuded satisfaction and unbridled elation, the same feelings that she had instilled in me.

They're gone, sure….

"But we're not," Jordan said.

Not at all, dear.

"We can stay here," she continued.

'Here' is perfect. You're perfect, Jordan, in all your imagined ways.

"This is the only place I know," Jordan said.

YOU are the only thing I've ever truly known.

"Here," she said, "with you."

I had no time to feel the full force of her words as she grabbed me by the waist, dragging me—not against my will—toward the pyre.

The fire I built for you…. Before I knew you, you ARE my fire. There is nowhere else I would rather be….

"Then, you aren't going anywhere—" she said.

Wherever you take me, I'll go.

"—Mister," she finished.

She stumbled backward as she dragged me into her, and I was so invigorated by that '*mister*' that I fell apart inside. My soul and body crumbled, and I collapsed on top of her.

I looked deeply into her, discovering her in a new way, caught somewhere between '*Hello*' and '*Where have you been?*'

Hi.

"Hey," she said playfully.

She was driving me insane with lust.

"Hey," I concurred. I was hesitant to move too quickly. Instead of digging into her, I dug my hands into the dirt on either side of her body.

The house and I are one. And as a house, I am someone's home—Jordan's home.

The walls I had built to hide from the world over the passing years had become a safe haven for her. She had unlocked my door, moved in, and made me her domicile—her shelter from the world.

I stared into her, amazed. Amazed, she stared back. Then I kissed her. And kissed her. And kissed her more. I could not separate myself from her as I kept kissing her, unable to let go, too paralyzed in my passion to separate.

I lost control of myself. I forgot my body, and in my trust, I lost myself longingly to her. I was a body all over her body—a spirit becoming more lost in her spirit. As physical connected with physical, something beyond that—something we more deeply shared—fused together.

I'm home. The house is my house, but Jordan, you are my home. MY home.

A cold wind shredded the treetops, chilling my skin as I was warmed inside. The breeze stoked the dead coals near us, bringing them back to life as I sprang back to life myself.

I was once so dead. Now I live again.

I kept kissing her. Kissing her was all I could do and all I wanted to do. She became the purpose of my existence and my purpose in general. She both took my breath from me and returned it. In her circular dichotomy, she became the inspiration for my circle of life— my birth, my life, my death, and my resurrection.

We are all made in His image, as we're told….

God, you have sent me an angel.

The newborn fire crackled in unison with the fire I felt within.

And Your angel is mine, now. Maybe we—You and I—are not so different, after all.

God had spoken to me, and I had heard His voice in the form of this angel beneath me on the ground.

So, who did I really invite here tonight? You or her?

If He had responded, I had ignored it and His fiery form to better focus upon His angel who had become my own; one I could see and feel and touch with my hands. I kept my eyes closed to Him despite His bright, mighty, burning presence.

He whispered to me in crackles and shifts, much like He had when I had spoken with Him in the living room earlier, His flaming tongue the fire within the fireplace. Now that He had sent me something I could not deny, I could not look at the fire that I could feel growing stronger with each passing second.

While the growing inferno only feet from us increased in heat and light, so did I inside, becoming increasingly more fervent and lost behind the veil of Jordan's body. My belt came undone, and I pushed my pants to my feet, kicking them off my legs. Each kiss and caress pulled me deeper into Jordan's spirit, and as our souls melded together, I realized we had joined physically as well. Her panties were on the ground beside us, and she had drawn me deep inside the warm, wet center of her body.

Jordan gasped in pleasure, the sweat of nervous satisfaction gathering all over me, a hot bolt of desire rushing up, down, and along my spine. Her eyes rolled into the back of her head, further with each thrust, the fire near us growing as the fire within me increased in size and heat, almost as if complementing my burning soul as mine connected with Jordan's.

My fingers interlaced with hers, her eyes coming back into focus on me as I looked into the eternity of Jordan's eyes. Her thighs began to tighten around me, and her moans had become more closely knitted and rhythmic.

So, this is Heaven. And God is right there, chaperoning.

She bit her lip and nodded, telling me she was close to the climax I wanted so badly to give to her. I was getting closer to achieving that goal, myself, for us both.

My passion is hers. Her passion is mine.

Tears of pleasure welled up in her eyes, and she stopped biting her lip as her mouth opened wide. Her eyes closed as she focused on the sensation that built within herself, mounting like the love I made her feel.

"Ari," she gasped. "Ari. ARI!"

Her fingers crawled quickly to the base of my skull, grabbing what hair she could on the back of my head. In reciprocal fashion, I reached my hands to her waist, grasping with all my strength, squeezing and taking total control of her body.

She screamed out into the darkness as her eyes locked more securely onto mine; and as her pupils dilated, her thighs quaked, her hips swirling about like a petite hurricane. She had reached the apex of our mountain of love, and so had I.

"Jordan!"

I had neither time nor impulse to pull away from her, but as my body did what bodies do in such a moment, I began to tear up myself, my eyes watering with unspoken emotion, releasing without any remorse all I had within me.

As I reached my peak, Jordan had frozen in focus on the physical sensation we simultaneously experienced. The fire next to us became literally white with white-hot heat, climaxing with us as it reached with its flickering fingers toward the sky that looked down upon us—two earthbound stars that refused to relinquish each other. God, Himself, had acknowledged this once-in-an-eternity union that He had both organized and witnessed.

Jordan's head fell back as the bright, day-like light of the fire perfectly illuminated everything that she was. She laughed a laugh of complete satisfaction, raising herself up to me in awe and appreciation. She kissed my lips, then I kissed her forehead, pulling myself slowly from her body. As we separated from each other, I began to cry and so did she. I sat back, and with my naked bottom in the dirt, I pulled her up and seated her in my naked lap, resting my head to her bosom, letting go, allowing my tears to freely flow. She rested her head on top of mine, stroking my hair, comforting me in my masculine weakness. She placed kisses here and there. She cried along with me.

"Ari," she said. The fire hissed as though echoing my name.

"Ari, I love you," she said, comforting me.

My tears dried up immediately, as I loved that phrase too much to shed any further tears.

I've got to be strong for you.

"Jordan," I said, lifting my head from her, looking up at her watery eyes. "I love you, too, and I feel like I've loved you forever."

Thunder rumbled in my heart as actual thunder filled the sky and the grove around us. The fire that had blazed so incredibly before extinguished itself in fast fashion as if exhausted, just like Jordan and I were exhausted. The thunder was the fire's final breath before its exodus into the unknown.

"I feel the same way," Jordan exhaled, breathless.

I picked up her underwear, sliding them back onto her body, up past her ankles, then her calves, taking advantage of the opportunity to touch again those incredible thighs as I slid them up and into place. As I let go, they made a snapping noise, right where they were meant to be, and I could feel the warm moisture of her satisfied flower as I took my hands to her hips, kissing her knees again. I sat back, pulling my pants up my legs, fastening my belt and adjusting my zipper as Jordan watched in satisfaction—a flirtatious smile moving across her face. I watched her closely as she watched me put my shirt back on.

I realized that my clothes had become dry.

I'm not surprised, really....

"That was rather unexpected, wouldn't you say?" she asked, laughing.

I finished putting on my shoes and stood, offering her my hand, which she took, and I lifted her off the ground to her feet.

I studied those feet for a moment then said "Sorry, honey, but I lost your heels back there somewhere…."

Jordan only shrugged, embracing me, her head relaxing against my chest.

She was all I could see and feel in the nearly empty, newborn darkness; and she was all I needed—all I had ever needed.

Even in this darkness, your light illuminates all. You are like a black diamond of a perpetual sun, your black luster the only light the moon cannot deny.

"Shall we start another fire?" she asked playfully.

We will, my love. Soon enough. You're the only fire I need.

I looked to the woodpile flickering and flashing next to us, then back to Jordan. I grabbed her delicately by the face, lifting it from my chest to my face. Honest eyes met honest eyes, the moonlight combining with the bonfire's now steady orange flame, both of them providing for us the blessing of true sight.

"Whenever you want, sweetheart," I said, as if coerced by a hidden instinct of which I had not previously known.

Jordan looked to the fire next to us, then back to me, smiling.

"So, the house?" she asked, picking up the green handbag that laid askew on the ground near us.

"I couldn't have said it better," I said, returning her smile.

"Then let's go," she responded.

"You know the way," I said.

Maybe we'll find your shoes….

"I mean, you can carry me if you like," she teased.

I turned around, answering her request, offering my back to her.

The last time I'll ever turn my back on you….

She hopped on immediately, those incredible legs wrapping strongly around me, her arms enveloping my neck. Piggyback, I carried her shoeless body up the path toward the house.

A house we will share….

Forever, I hope.

She kissed my neck from behind as we traversed the path back to the house, away from the grove. I smiled and laughed to myself.

I hope we never leave it. I could die happy there. We can just be there, together, forever.

I had never felt so strong in my life. I had shed the weight of the world to carry *my* entire world—a world I wanted to live in and love, and one that wanted and loved me back.

So, this is Heaven. I guess I don't have to die to get there after all….

HANNAH

People in great numbers were leaving the house as Hannah guided Michael up the steps of the back porch toward the kitchen. She could see through the window that only a handful of guests remained.

Not many. Perfect.

Hannah stopped, grabbing Michael by the face before walking through the door, kissing him lightly on the lips, stepping through the doorframe with Michael right behind her.

We're going upstairs, right now. I can't wait anymore.

Hannah had a head full of steam and her heart full of intention as she recklessly and purposefully dragged Michael behind her. Halfway through the kitchen, Michael exhibited resistance, pulling against her passion, stopping her in her tracks. Hannah stopped and turned to face him.

"What is it?" she asked. Michael was studying the spread of alcohol on the kitchen bar, and Hannah immediately understood.

Okay, fine. One more for the road, as Jordan would say….

She smiled.

"You go on ahead. Remember the room from earlier?" he asked.

Hell, yeah, I remember. How could I forget? Where we met…. Where we so awkwardly met….

"Yes, sir," she said.

"Go on ahead. I'll make us a drink. What would you like?" he asked.

Hannah thought for a moment.

Don't want to get too fucked up. Something mild but familiar.

Hannah thought back to the glass of white wine she had abandoned at home.

Pure. Slow. Simple.

"White wine, if its available," she answered.

"Perfect. I've got you," Michael said, keeping his eyes on her.

"Perfect," she said. "I've got *you*, when you get there."

And I'll have you and you'll have me, over and over and over again.

Hannah winked at him, turning to head upstairs, his hand striking her backside, both turning her on and making her feel safe.

The perfect amount of force…. Michael….

Hannah moistened at the sensation of the impact.

She turned to make one last pass at Michael before making her exit. The last of the crowd was leaving through the door through which they had just passed.

"I'll be waiting for you in the bedroom," she said, blowing a kiss to him as he winked back at her.

I can't wait…. I cannot fucking wait!

As Michael turned toward the bar to set himself to his promised task, Hannah turned toward the hall leading to the stairs.

She ran her fingers through her own hair, flipping it at the man left behind—a final flirtation, not caring if he had seen or not. As she passed the living room, she thought of her flight from Jordan earlier.

I'm not hiding anymore!

Classical music resounded from the sound system, a fire still burning in the fireplace.

She approached the stairs, stopping at the bottom, looking up at them.

This stupid barrier. The climb from Hell into Heaven…. Get up there, Hannah.

Hannah thought of rewinding in fast-forward up the stairs that were her escape only an hour or so earlier.

Well, back down, um, 'up' the rabbit hole….

She rushed up the stairs as quickly as she could, looking backward and down, her heart filled as she had faced the fear of her past, conquering who she once was.

I've come a long way. In just one night. This night…. Yeah, screw this night. I'm gone, and so are you, Jordan. I swear to fucking god, if Katie…. Goddammit, Katie…. I had better fucking not…!

She turned away from the stairs to the hallway before her.

Where have you gone?

Hannah shook her head.

No matter. I'll find you, but not until 'he' does. Be good to her, Ari.

Hannah continued her steps toward the bedroom, feeling a twinge of discomfort in her loins that begged to be addressed.

Damn. Gotta piss.

She looked to her left, saw the light coming from the crack of the half-open door of the brightly lit bathroom, and she entered quickly.

This place…. Jordan, Jordan…. And Katie, Katie, you bitch! What a total bitch! To hell with you and your red hair, you selfish slut! I fucking hate you!

She shut the door quickly behind her, as though that might silence the voices in her head—voices that she treated as though they were chasing her—but they were screaming at her like prisoners tortured inside the steel and stone cage of her mind.

Hannah locked the door, deaf to the cries of her suffering, sighing with relief.

Then, she turned to examine herself in the mirror.

Damn it, you're beautiful!

She stepped toward the mirror, facing the 'self' that was merely her reflection, seeing who her past self was, reveling in her evolution from the Hannah then versus this new version of herself.

Much, much better.

The twinge in her body assaulted her once again.

God, I've got to…!

Hannah dropped the toilet seat with force, the sound of it striking the porcelain bowl with a loud bang.

Her pants were down, and she was seated, the sound of liquid immediately striking liquid.

Oh, yeah…. That's what's up.

She leaned upon her knees giving into the ecstatic release of pain. She sat in the bliss of that release and paused, seated and relieved.

Hell yeah.

Hannah finished, stood, and washed her hands in the sink, looking at herself once more in the mirror before her. She thought of Michael.

Clean hands for an unclean motive….

Hannah exhaled, looking down.

Whatever. We are where we are….

Hannah dried her hands, took one last pass at her reflection, then turned the doorknob, exiting the room.

Michael, I can't wait to let you fuck me.

And I can't wait to fuck you back, you confident, handsome…. Damn it!

As she left the bathroom, she turned left for the bedroom down the hall, her clean hands and filthy mind a gorgeous duality of destruction.

She looked to her right to the stairs, pondering their meaning through all the night, then back to her left. She made her way toward the bedroom door, pausing as she stood before it, forsaking the past the stairs meant for the purpose of the future she and Michael promised one another. As she grasped the doorknob, she stopped to think.

Jordan, you'd better be safe. You'd better be happy. Michael… you, sir, had better be ready for me.

Hannah breathed in preparing her body and soul for the pleasure to come.

Michael, are you ready? Because I am. Thank God, I'm finally experiencing something real. Thank God….

She pushed the door open ready to conquer as her heart opened.

"Hannah…" came Michael's voice.

Her heart lifted up and out of her chest as the door slowly opened.

Hannah's eyes opened wide, her jaw gaping, her body frozen like a winter stone.

"MICHAEL!!"

ACTS

KATIE

In the chaotic nothing of her nightmare trance, Katie heard a faint knocking at the door of her mind. She awakened and stirred, confused and flustered.

"Hey, honey," came a familiar voice. "Are you ready?"

To be awake? To be alive?

Katie stretched as she sat up in bed, crossing her legs.

Give me whatever you want me to have. I'm tired of being alone in this room.

"Come on, big boy," she said. "It's been too long."

Katie recognized that it was Michael. She was fully prepared to exact her sexual revenge upon him.

Her sleeping thighs had awakened to the sound of his powerful, blond-haired, sapphire-eyed voice. She was a snake eating her own tail. She was eagerly prepared to devour.

Katie was willing to die by her own hand, so long as revenge was her pleasure, and pleasure was her revenge.

MICHAEL

Damn, what an amazing body….

The lights from the house better illuminated Hannah's figure as Michael followed her, narrowly tripping over every other step as he stared unblinkingly at her gorgeous frame. He was mentally blank, awestricken as her legs climbed the steps, her bottom bouncing left to right and right to left as she ascended toward the back door of the house.

What. A. Woman.

Before he knew it, they had arrived at the back door.

Holy. Fucking. Shit. What a fucking goddess!

Hannah caught Michael by surprise as she abruptly turned, grabbing his head and kissing him, forcing his mind away from his perverse mentality and reminding him she was much more than a physical object.

But how I would love to get physical…. …Put my hands all over that. Everywhere….

She pulled away as strongly as she had pressed herself to him, walking through the door in a calm hurry as she took Michael's hand, guiding him.

I can't wait…. But perhaps another round before we get down to it….

Despite Hannah's surprising strength dragging Michael along, the kitchen bar and the limitless alcohol upon it caught his eye. He gave resistance to her pull, pulling back on her hand, asking for silent permission to slow her progress.

She obliged immediately, stopping and turning swiftly to face him, allowing him to explain his thoughts.

"What is it?" she asked, turning her head in the direction Michael was facing. His intention was obvious to her. Hannah's grin told Michael that she understood and had accepted.

"You go on ahead," he said.

But to where? How about where we first met?

"Remember the room from earlier?" he asked.

I try to not remember. You didn't matter so much then, and neither did I, honestly…. Not nearly as much to me as my own embarrassment, but things have changed. Things are different now. There is more, now, to life than me…. Never thought I'd ever say that.

"Yes, sir," she acknowledged, and her words and tone sent a powerful sensation up Michael's spine.

But I am still in control, apparently. Guide her. Show her. Tell her….

"Go on ahead. I'll make us a drink," Michael said.

If you trust me….

"What would you like?" he asked.

Hannah paused in thought for a moment, then answered, "White wine, if it's available."

So commanding before, yet now you're being more reticent; mannerly, even. I think we're good for each other.

"Perfect," he said.

You've got me…. And….

"I've got you," he continued, staring into her fiery eyes.

"Perfect," she said, mimicking him.

Yes, you are…. Are you my flawed heaven or my immaculate damnation?

"I've got *you* when you get there," she flirted, winking at Michael, stunning him.

As she turned to leave for the bedroom, Michael could not restrain himself from eyeing her behind again, slapping it with his hand, unable to control himself, with a force half strength, half affection.

Make her feel safe, but remind her who daddy is…

Michael watched as the shockwave rolled through her frame. As she stepped away, she turned to look at him, his eyes meeting hers, both silently communicating. A great portion of the anonymous guests were departing to go wherever they may. Michael hardly noticed, as they were a passing blur, Hannah the only thing clearly in focus in his sight. She blew him a kiss then spoke a temporary farewell.

"I'll be waiting for you in the bedroom," she said, Michael winking at her, unable to do much else. She flipped her hair at Michael as he looked longingly on, traversing the doorway to the hallway. Then she was gone, a sensual apparition that had disappeared, but still haunted the house of his mind. Though he was studying the bar in careful thought, he still could see her silent, flirtatious, final goodbye from the corner of his eye.

Even when I'm not looking, I'm watching. Eyes don't always need to see to notice things.

Michael snapped himself from his daydream, setting to his task.

Don't want to make her wait too long…. Hell, I can't wait much longer, myself.

Michael looked frantically around the available contents of the bar.

I don't know shit about white wine! Chardonnay? Grigio? What the hell should I choose? FUCK!

Michael saw an unopened bottle of expensive bourbon next to two half-empty bottles of white wine, their variety something that he could not comprehend.

He tucked one bottle under his arm and grabbed both wine bottles before he began his rush toward the stairs.

The scent of fire—that familiar odor—caught his nose as he passed the living room, Beethoven's "Moonlight Sonata" catching his ear. Michael thought back to his mockery of Ari earlier.

Well, maybe Beethoven 'is' with us tonight. And maybe not as dead as I thought. Shit. I'm sorry, Ari. I wish I could tell you, but Hannah is waiting…. Soon, friend. Soon.

Michael stopped at the foot of the stairs.

Damn. Torn between two second chances. I guess one will have to wait. Sorry, Ari. I hope that that 'Jessica'—um, 'Jordan'—girl can keep you company for now…. She's going to have to. Hannah is waiting.

Michael ceased his thought, tearing up the stairs. Once at the top, he saw that the bathroom door was shut, the sound of water striking water coming from beyond the door where he stopped.

Someone's peeing rather loudly, and damn, now I've got to piss, but I can't make her wait any longer. I can't wait, either. So close. She's so close. Just one door away.

Michael set down one wine bottle, opening the bourbon under his arm and took a long drink from it.

There. That should do the trick.

Replacing the cap, he returned it underneath his arm and picked up the wine bottle from the floor, hurrying to the next door down the hall.

Here we go…. Are you ready, baby?

The liquor began its sneaky work, and Michael tingled with both excitement and a fresh wave of drunkenness.

Tomorrow is going to be one hell of a hangover.

Michael put the bottle from his right hand under his arm adjacent to the bottle under his arm. Gripping them to his side, he used his free hand to gently knock on the door, alerting Hannah of his presence, hoping she was naked and ready.

Hannah, our lives are about to change.

Michael turned the knob and entered. There she was on the bed, ready.

Oh, I can't wait to open those legs and get in between them. To own them and all the things in between….

"Hey, honey," Michael said, fighting to remain calm. "Are you ready?"

Hannah sat up in the dim light and stretched, crossing her legs. The moonlight added a pale hue to her skin. A candle flickered on the bedside table. Michael quickly forgot its allure as the bourbon began to take its effect upon him.

"Come on, big boy," Hannah said.

I'm coming soon enough…. And so are you….

"It's been too long," she continued.

Michael wasted no time. He dropped two bottles to his feet and approached the bed, taking a longer walk to the side of the bed opposite the window. He carried the one bottle—the bourbon—and set it on the table after taking another large drink, leaving the top off.

"Michael," said Hannah. "Is that you?"

"Yes, it's me, babe," he said.

You sound different in the dark. You must be ready….

Hannah scooted herself up and nearer to him.

"Do what you want," he said.

"Yes, sir," she said.

'Yes, sir,' she says. I could get used to this. I'd better be a good boy.

Michael became hard behind his zipper.

Good. Not like last time.

The bourbon had accomplished its task.

Both blind and seeing more clearly than ever, he dropped his pants to the floor in focused frenzy. Grabbing Hannah by the hips, he pulled her to him and spread her legs apart. Pushing her panties aside, he thrust himself into her wet, inviting center.

Every stroke was an apology for his past misdeeds and failures.

"I love you and I hate you," she said, gasping in between each syllable.

I hate me, too…. But….

Michael was approaching climax, and all too soon.

But I love you, Hannah. I think I do.

"Come for me, Daddy," Hannah said.

Michael had reached his peak, unleashing all his newfound passions inside of Hannah—no regrets and no apologies. He could hear the thud of the liquor bottle falling from the table, striking the floor. Hannah moaned, pleased by his pleasure, no matter how brief the encounter might have been.

Wow…!

Michael pulled himself slowly from her, inhaling and exhaling even slower as he withdrew, his heart and feelings resolved and satisfied, finally able to satisfy himself and the girl who had so stealthily stolen his once-unattainable heart. The dancing candlelight flickered upon her sweat-covered skin.

"Oh…" he said, a broad smile spreading the entire breadth of his face as he looked up, licking the sweat from his lip.

Hannah, say my name. Just once, say my name.

"Michael, say my name!" she gasped.

Michael's climax had finally resolved as Hannah moaned in heightening pleasure, laughing in satisfaction.

Oh….

"Hannah…" he exhaled heavily as his heart became heavy as well.

Wait. Wait!

Michael's happiness suddenly faded. Something was not right in this moment.

You sound…. Hannah?

A voice from the door screamed his name in broken terror.

"MICHAEL!"

The effects of the alcohol had temporarily lifted, and he was caught up in a wave of all-confusing panic.

Michael turned from the naked body before him to face the voice—that beautiful, familiar voice—that resonated so angrily from the doorway.

Even in the dim light, he recognized the figure as the voice confirmed his sudden and surreal nightmare.

There Hannah stood, far from him and not at all beneath him, and all the emotions he had felt both before and during his recent experience evacuated his body. He had become an experimental husk of nothing and exasperated regret which supplanted his once full, inspired self.

He turned from the figure in the doorway to the figure on the bed, briefly considering his surroundings, gathering himself.

Oh, shit.

Katie lay beneath him.

Hannah—the real Hannah—stood in the doorway.

Oh! OH, SHIT!!

He bent to pick up his pants from his ankles, clumsily and rapidly pulling them up, fastening them into place as he scoured his mind and heart for the words that refused to materialize. He stumbled in his hurry, bumping into the table next to him. The candle fell over on its side, rolling along the table, off and onto the floor.

Katie laughed a laugh that filled the room like a chorus of multiple voices—a layered laugh Michael could hear but chose to ignore in his scattered state. He looked at Hannah, staring with dead eyes. She was frozen in place, much like his mortified heart.

"Hannah," he said. "Hannah, please! I can explain!"

Michael abandoned Katie's presence, almost falling as he approached Hannah.

What the actual FUCK!

Hannah looked down and away, folding her arms.

Michael stopped a foot shy from her, knowing well enough to not attempt to touch her.

But how I want to touch her. To comfort her…. What the fuck is going on?!

"Hannah," Michael said, his voice breaking.

Hannah remained as silent as the grave.

"Hannah," Michael repeated, reaching to touch her, despite his prior thoughts. She resisted, pulling away from him.

"Don't touch me!" she shouted. "You… you…. You motherfucker!!"

Michael could see her shaking in rage.

Fuck! What do I do? How could this happen?

"Hannah, honey, please. Please listen to me…" he said weakly.

Katie's laugh once more filled the room.

Michael turned to scream at her, his frustration linked to both his anxiety and his heartache.

"Shut up, bitch!" he stammered, turning to Katie.

"Shut up, bitch!" Hannah harmonized.

Their voices joined in a unified chorus, a song of hysterics.

One last song…. One last song before…. You leave me…. And probably forever….

Michael turned back to Hannah.

"Hannah, honey, please. I thought…" he pleaded. "I thought she was you!"

He reached to stroke her cheek, a helpless plea for understanding—the knocking on the door of an empty, unforgiving house. She quickly withdrew.

His heart fell empty into his empty stomach. His racing mind dissolved into a blur.

Hannah rubbed tears from her eyes, looking at him once more before she began to fully weep in her rage.

"No," she said, her voice broken into many pieces, each piece cutting Michael as they fell to the floor between them.

"Hannah," he said, looking to the floor as if to examine the invisible shards on the ground. He knew he had lost her.

Hannah shook her head as Michael witnessed a tear fall from her shaking head. It struck the floor, making an echo Michael could hear. It was an echo heard throughout the universe, yet an echo—a symphony of sadness—only for him and his crying queen. In the reverberations of that echo, Hannah made one last pass at Michael, her combined emotions too confusing and heavy for him to handle. As it broke him into sand, she left, like a wave from the incredible ocean that she was. She had come ashore—to *his* shore—washing away the footsteps he had left on her heart, eradicating any evidence of his presence. Michael had been erased, and Hannah had erased herself from his life as she quietly wept, sprinting wildly for the stairs.

Katie lay behind Michael, but Michael was alone. He was a wisp of smoke in a room of ghosts. He stood there, hating himself, when a familiar laugh filled both his ears and his body.

I've got to get the hell out of here.

That ominous disembodied laughter resounded within Michael once more.

Get out! Get out of my head!!

Michael turned to look at Katie in hatred and disdain. Between the bed and the window, a shadow with glowing, powerful eyes stood, staring at him before they turned to Katie. Then, the shadow was gone.

You bastard!

Bezaliel, you fucking coward!

"You bitch," Michael said. "You've taken EVERYTHING from me!"

Katie laughed once more, sitting up, then falling to her back upon the bed.

"I take what I want from now on," she said.

Michael stood there, seeing his old self in her honesty, believing her—he, the proof of her promise.

With a resounding, layered voice, she spoke. "I AM FIRE!"

Michael scowled at her then looked to the window. He looked to the candle burning on the floor. He laughed a scathing laugh of hatred.

"Then burn, bitch," he said, slamming the door shut.

Michael thought of Hannah, forgot his anger, and was out the door.

I've got to find you! I've got to explain!

Michael fled through the doorway, leaving Katie behind, pursuing a future he was certain no longer existed.

He stumbled down the stairs, the liquor's will reclaiming his body, taking him.

"I take what I want, too," he said, falling in a mad rush down the stairs.

And I know what I want….

The faint echo of laughter met his ears, chasing him as he chased Hannah. He was, by his own hand, destroyed as he sought to create a new world for himself.

KATIE

Katie loved how Michael dropped the contents he was carrying, stunned as he was by her. She loved even more how quickly he floated across the room to the side of the bed between her and the mirror.

In a flirtatious tone, she asked a question to which she already knew the answer.

"Michael, is that you?" she asked as he conjured another bottle, taking a quick, deep drink from it and setting the open bottle on the table next to the candle.

"Yes," he said. "It's me, babe."

Her eyes rolled as she ignored him, despite her desire to linger upon him.

What do you want from me? Is there anything I want from you, really?

Katie moved herself to the bedside, hanging her legs off the side, ready to open them for him—he, a guest unexpected, yet welcome.

"Do what you want," he said.

"Yes, sir," Katie said, knowing how it would destroy him.

Her 'yes, sir' had stirred him. He had shown up for her, despite his earlier contradiction. He had become ready to give her what she wanted all along.

What I want…. No, to hell with that…. Give me what I need!

Michael unfastened his pants and Katie moistened as Michael's strong hands grabbed her by the hips, she giving him no resistance as he pulled her body closer to him, spreading apart her weakening thighs.

She descended further into chemical frenzy, that familiar sensual odor filling her nostrils as he pushed aside her underwear.

Good. No time for foreplay.

Michael was fully inside her immediately, and she was impressed by both his size and the strength and rhythm at which he administered his power, even more vigorous than their first encounter. Every stroke brought her closer to her climax, and every stroke was more powerful and calculated than the last.

God, I've never had it this good! So decisive and passionate! It's like you hate me but you're so damned loving. So perfect.

"I love you," Katie said before her lips could stop the words from escaping.

Michael continued his work.

"And I hate you," she followed, attempting to right the wrong of her loose tongue.

Both are true….

She could feel the familiar swell of Michael approaching his finish. Realizing this, it brought her closer to her own, their pleasure mutually increased by the pleasure of the other.

So fast, Michael. But damn! Me too!

"Come for me, Daddy," she sighed, wanting him to finish along with her in simultaneous release.

Michael began bucking his hips, thrashing her sensitive interior as he reached his goal, and as she felt the contents of his body fill hers, she released herself. Katie heard the dull thud of the liquor bottle striking the ground, her face flushing as her body vibrated, unable to hold back any longer.

Yes, sir!!

She had only just realized she was covered head to toe in sweat, and she was impressed by the speed at which Michael delivered her.

He pulled himself from her body, every inch felt as she begged in her mind for more. Michael moaned as he withdrew.

But maybe later. Lay down with me, won't you?

Michael's obvious satisfaction resolved her own, and as her bodily tremors settled, she examined this man as he looked up to the ceiling.

"Oh…" he moaned.

Just say my name.

Michael licked his lips.

Say my name, Michael. Say my name!

"Michael," Katie said. "Say my name!" she moaned, laughing.

Michael kept his eyes up as he spoke.   "Hannah…" Michael sighed.

Wait… Hannah?

HANNAH?!

Katie became infuriated and confused but held her tongue, completely stunned.

Hannah!? HANNAH! Still thinking about her! Well, at least I got what I wanted. No one wants me…. No! TO HELL WITH THAT!

You stupid bastard. You haven't changed at all!

Katie was shocked and hurt but kept her composure as a voice filled the room with a scream.

"MICHAEL!"

Well, there she is, douche bag. Go get her. Get out of here.

Katie's mind broke as her heart did the same. She laughed a wicked laugh inside herself. She took an evil joy in watching her once-strong lover fall to pieces in grief as he looked Katie over then to the angered shadow in the doorway. She happily watched as the color and confidence flushed from his face, a change so drastic she could see it in the twilit darkness.

Katie donned a crooked smile as Michael hastily put his pants back on, falling into the table in his drunken, panicked stupor. She heard something fall on the bedside table, then to the floor, but she ignored it for the showing of Michael's embarrassment, which she fully relished. She could not hold back her laughter at this cartoon of a man falling apart before her. However, her laughter felt as though it were not her own, as though multiple voices were laughing in unison.

"Hannah!" he said, his voice shaken.

Oh, that name that I loathe but love to hear. And how crazy you sound saying it. Serves you right!

"Hannah, please!" he stammered.

Yes, Hannah, please. Please stay and watch this womanizer crumble to pieces.

"I can explain!" Michael said.

I'm sure you can, buddy. Go on. This should be fun to watch.

Michael stumbled as he left Katie's side, hurrying to be nearer to Hannah.

Idiot.

Michael stopped short of Hannah.

"Hannah," Michael pleaded. "Hannah…."

"Don't touch me!" she shouted.

Even though you want to so badly. I love what you did to me, but I hate it was meant for her. I hate you both. But….

Katie felt sympathy for Hannah as she stammered in her rage.

"You… you," Hannah said, struggling to get the words out of her trembling mouth. "You motherfucker!"

"Hannah, honey, please," Michael begged. "Please listen to me!"

I love how broken this bastard is. You couldn't recognize your own woman, you drunk moron. Hannah, I feel sorry for you…. But what a funny situation!

Katie laughed again, her laugh once again powerful, layered, and almost not entirely her own. She could hear the echo of the voice of the shadow-angel from earlier harmonize with her laughter, knowing then that he was nearby. She looked around but could not find him, though she could feel him watching her as Michael and Hannah yelled at her in unison.

"Shut up, bitch!" they shouted, Katie unaffected by their emotional explosion.

Bitch? Hannah, I'm on your side, sweetie. I understand his rage toward me, but Hannah? If you only knew the way he fucked me… the way he fucked me when he thought I was you….

"Hannah," Michael repeated, desperately. "Honey, please. I thought—"

You only think about yourself, asshole.

"—I thought she was you!" he continued, pleading and on the edge of audible tears.

Katie thought she saw Hannah resist Michael's attempt to touch her followed by a saddened gasp of misery coming from Hannah's lips.

Girl, I feel sorry for you. Why don't you come over here and let me show you how appreciated you are.

"No," Hannah said. Katie knew she was addressing Michael but felt she was answering Katie's thoughts, responding accordingly.

You're a goddess, Hannah. You're the hottest girl I've ever seen. A shame it was this lame ass—and not you—all over me.

"Hannah," Michael said once more.

Say her name all you want. She can't hear you.

Hannah turned and was gone.

Great. Ruin it for us both, Michael. Thanks, jackass.

Katie watched as Hannah passed from her sight, Michael so obviously withered and defeated and lingering. That familiar ominous laugh bellowed alone this time, apart from Katie's harmony, another laugh of the same nature following.

Okay, seriously. Bezaliel, are you actually real?

She felt her hair raise up, feeling something next to her. She looked up to her left next to the bed just in time to see the familiar glowing orbs of Bezaliel's eyes disappear. Katie then turned back to Michael, his eyes glowing in the same ethereal fashion. She could see them clearly, even from across the distance of the dark room. They appeared as though they were glowing red, his rage preternatural and visible in their glare.

"You bitch!" Michael shrieked.

You are the bitch, you bitch boy. Don't go making any more mistakes. You can't afford another.

"You've taken EVERYTHING FROM ME!" he cried at her.

You are exactly right, dickhead. Everything!

Katie chuckled at Michael, intentionally mocking him. She sat up to speak but fell silent, dismissively, as she fell onto her back.

She stared blankly at the ceiling.

I've lost all I've ever had, even when it wasn't even mine. So….

"I take what I want from now on," Katie said, dully.

Yeah! Yeah, whatever I want! I'm so tired of being shit on! I've been burned so many times…. You can't hurt me! I will be what has hurt me so many times before! I will become the suffering! I will be pain as long as it keeps me from feeling it, myself! I've been burned and burned and fucking burned! I will do the burning from now on! From now on…!

Katie giggled with a maniacal tone as her hatred washed over her like lava, her own mouth becoming a volcano.

From now on—

"I AM FIRE!" she cackled.

"Then burn, bitch," Michael said, his tone cutting her but with an intention of pain to which she had become numb.

Michael slammed the door and was gone. Katie paid his sudden absence no mind.

Once again, she heard the disembodied laughter, both within and outside herself. An uncomfortable happiness embraced her weeping heart. It was a happiness that was not happiness at all, but—

—Justice.

Whatever.

Katie fell back into her prior trance, her inner darkness balancing the outer darkness of the room.

I am fire.

She drifted into a familiar daydream.

Fire. Damn it all.

Katie recognized the smell of smoke as she faded into herself.

Fire…. Burn it all down.

The candle flickered on the charring carpet next to the bottle of bourbon that had fallen from the bedside table.

HANNAH

Hannah was at a loss for words. Her present was broken. The future she had imagined was shattered. Her heart was in pieces. All that was full was Michael and Katie as they filled one another, and Hannah's pulverized heart was the fading, falling, hollow shards left in the wake of their meeting.

Tears flowed like tiny mighty rivers down her pretty, folded face. She was rapidly down the stairs, passing the living room in no time. She heard classical music still playing from within as she passed.

Sad music for sad 'me'. How fitting!

A pair of violins danced around one another in song as she passed by. She thought of Michael, deepening her misery.

Maybe we are the violins, dancing in and around each other. Delicate. Intimate. Fragile as strings. Ready to break one another.

Another wave of anxiety gripped her by the heart as she speedily made her way through the kitchen.

And now that song—our song—is over.

The last few people were leaving through the kitchen door, Hannah pushing them aside as she barreled through them, casting them away as she attempted to delete the memory of the treachery she had just witnessed.

Damn… DAMN!

As she broke through the tiny remainder of the crowd, she broke through the clouds of her miserable, crumbling world—a sky through which she was falling—one through which she had once flown. She stopped on the porch, feeling the eyes of the offended mob still in the kitchen behind her.

I have never cared for the judgmental eyes of others. Probably why I've never given a shit. And I'm not about to start now. Fuck you, Michael. You fucking asshole!

Hannah peered at the sky in lonely silence.

Truly…. I am truly alone.

One final tear fought through her closing eyelids, coursing down her cheek.

But I have always been. I've always been alone, to be honest.

A low rumble of thunder met her ears.

I'm not about to break down now. No, I've gotta keep it together! This always happens, though. It's the broken world, breaking itself all over in some sort of suicide-revenge. These poor souls, robbing each other—thieves, stealing from each other's empty houses! But I have also been the thief. I've been so shitty. Maybe I deserve this, just a little bit.

Hannah opened her eyes to the clear sky above, a solitary raindrop striking her forehead right between her eyes, taking her breath from her chest.

Not a cloud in sight. Odd….

Suddenly Hannah felt less lonely, and as she heard the creaking of the opening door behind her, she fled, rushing down the back porch stairs.

These stairs…. Michael's eyes on me…. Someone is always watching, huh….

Hannah was in the driveway rounding the corner of the house, following its path to the only place she knew solitude; the place of her last happy memory—her car.

I'm always running…. Running away from a world that I don't belong in.

Hannah thought of Michael and the magic that was now lost. She thought of Jordan and how she had brought her to this party to help her escape her own dismal reality.

To help you escape to only be trapped, myself. I've got to get the hell out of here! I swear to God, it's like looking for a key that I have hidden so well, I can't even find it! …To a door to a room that I've locked knowing that I am that very room! And now I can't even get inside myself! FUCK!

Hannah arrived at her car.

This driveway was so packed a few hours ago….

She quickly procured her keys, fumbling with them as she unlocked the door.

Guess the party's over.

She opened the car door, quickly sitting down in the driver's seat.

Ah… Finally….

She inserted the key into the ignition, feeling the engine come to life at the strong turn of her key.

Finally, I'm in control again! For the first time, in so, so long….

She sighed, closing her eyes, sitting back in her seat. She peered out through the window, gazing at the house; and as she reminisced on the memories of the night that overwhelmed her mind in their rapidity, one thought—the origin—overwhelmed her more than the others.

Jordan….

She looked in the direction of the passenger seat through the window where Jordan was seated earlier. She thought about her best friend, regretting herself and her lack of self-control, hating herself for being the catalyst of all the wrong she had created and endured throughout the evening.

Damn…. If only I had held back, we could've just had our girl's night. We could have just, damn, I don't know…. We could have just had fun! But, no, Hannah, you've always got to be so ridiculously selfish!

Her lips trembled as regret after regret filled her mind, each memory more painful than the last.

I tried to save you, Jordan. I tried to help you escape your pain—yourself. I tried to dig you out of your sadness, and I lost myself along the way, buried under the dirt of my own digging… in so many ways….

Maybe I should keep digging, bury myself, and get even more lost. I'm suffocating already, so why not?

Hannah checked her rearview mirrors through the blurring vision of her saturated eyes. She breathed in, put the car into reverse, and backed it up, putting it into drive, looking at the reflection of the house in her rearview mirror. She put her foot to the accelerator, beginning the journey of her escape from this place.

A shadow, fast and nearly unnoticed, was catching up to her, which she ignored.

She can call if she needs me. You'll be safe with Ari. He's no 'Michael'. Stay happy, Jordan. I love you.

Hannah pressed her foot more heavily to the accelerator pedal, speeding down the driveway. In moments, she was on the road, escaping the night that had destroyed her. Feeling the power of the machine through the steering wheel in her trembling hands, she felt she had finally regained some sort of control of her life.

Finally….

Freedom….

ARI

I kept my eyes focused on the ground, mindful of the path, careful to not trip or stumble over any objects that may have interrupted my purpose of getting my angel, Jordan, back to safety. I thought over and over about the romantic activities that she and I had just shared. I tried to shake them from my mind, maintaining focus on being her protector and deliverer, getting her to the house safely. Still, my mind was constantly invaded by the passing memories of our recently shared passion, this goddess that once lay beneath me now clinging to my back.

Every angel needs a god. Let me be yours.

Every now and then, a little kiss would meet the flesh of the back of my neck. Her breath on my skin was a refreshing breeze, rejuvenating me, helping me to forget my physical exhaustion, despite her, my lightweight burden, who was no burden at all.

I did not even mind the annoying nature of her handbag as it bounced up and down on her arm, and me, with every step of my eager feet.

Each shoeprint was a conquered kingdom. As we got closer and closer to the house, I appreciated every conquered step.

Occasionally, I readjusted her body, never letting loose the firm yet intimate grip I kept on her thighs. My breathing became more rapid, the true exhaustion setting in.

"Hey, are you okay?" Jordan whispered into my ear.

I've never been better. Happiest I've ever been.

"Yeah, honey, I'm fine," I said, each syllable a heavy breath as it left my mouth.

"You can let me down, king. I'll be okay," she said.

As we arrived at the top of the back porch steps, I set her down, turning to her.

"I'll never ever let you down, Jordan," I said.

She kissed me, thunder rumbling in the distance.

"I know," she said. She smiled a smile so powerful that it took me aback; and stunned, I simply stared at her. She shifted her body in a beautiful way, folding her arms, looking down and off to the side. She looked down to her bare feet then back up to me. The glistening of the moon in her sunrise eyes nearly killed me.

I was awestricken and eager to get her inside. The house was close. It appeared to me that the last of the guests were leaving.

"Come on. Let's go," she said.

I smiled, both at her and inside myself.

"Let's," I said, lifting her by her waist, kissing her as I held her in the air. I set her back down on her naked feet.

As we turned for the door, Michael approached us, and he was completely frantic.

"Have you seen Hannah?" he said. "Jordan, I've lost her! I fucked up!"

"Michael," I said.

"I haven't seen her in a long time," Jordan lied, keeping either of us from having to explain what we had just seen, those two lovers, Michael and Hannah, loving in secret shadows—a secret Jordan and I were not meant to know.

"Shit, I *have* to find her," he said. "Ari, I love you, brother, and I'm so sorry. I'm sorry for everything!"

"Michael," I responded. "It's okay. Are you okay?"

"No," he said. "Hell, no. If you see her, tell her I'm looking for her!"

"Okay, man," I responded weakly, casting an awkward glance at Jordan, who apparently dismissed my notion that her friend was missing. She winked at me.

Michael, are you that much more drunk right now?

"We'll catch up soon, but now I've gotta find her!" he said.

"Michael, are—?" I began to ask, but my question was cut short as Michael jumped down the full length of the stairs, fleeing like a thief around the corner of the house toward the driveway.

Jordan and I looked at each other, shrugging.

"Well, that was awkward," Jordan said. "Hannah is fine, I'm sure. She always runs from real things."

So does Michael.

"So does he," I said. "Maybe we could let them have their first fight? Just for now?"

Tonight is you and me. Michael can wait. He's probably just wasted.

"You sure we shouldn't check on your friend?" I asked.

Jordan pondered for a moment, looked to the sky, then back at me. She then looked down, laughing.

"I'm so sure," she said. I paused to take in her coy confidence, but she snapped me from my thinking before it could begin, slapping me on the chest with both hands. "Come on, mister," she said playfully. "Take me inside."

I could only nod in understanding.

Yes, ma'am.

A few more guests departed, gliding past us in a blur. She was my sole focus.

The house should be almost empty. Perfect.

I scooped her up in my arms, carrying her like my bride toward the bed of our consummation. She lit up like the only star in my sky, and I was happy to have that one light to hearken to and follow.

"God, you're cute," she said. I blushed but kept to my purpose.

"You're not so bad, yourself," I said, unable to come up with anything clever. Still, she laughed.

As long as she's laughing....

"You're such a nerd," she responded.

You have no idea....

We arrived at the back door.

"Allow me," she said, reaching out to open the door before us. I used my hip to keep the door ajar, carrying her through the doorway feet first.

Before I knew it, we were past the kitchen and then the living room. Johann Bach played in the air, and I could smell the smoke from the fireplace.

God....

I thought about the body I had claimed as mine just minutes before. I wanted to see it from a better-lit perspective.

"Set me down," she said as we approached the foot of the stairs.

"You've got it," I said, and she was off, defying gravity as she floated up the stairs ahead of me, above and beyond.

I could not pry my eyes from the curvature and sway of her gorgeous frame. I lost myself in the movement of her body. She gained the top then turned to look down at me. Despite her incredible speed, the whole moment passed in slow motion, her perfect thighs extending from that little black dress, pulling me further into stupor.

"Well, you coming or not?" she asked.

I stuttered. "Uh, yeah, sorry!"

I made my way up the stairs—my stairway to the sky above—where my angel waited for me. As I reunited with her, I kissed her forehead, taking the lead and guiding her to my bedroom. The smell of the fireplace revisited my nostrils as we passed the guest bedroom.

Strange… I don't think I've ever smelled the fireplace from up here….

"Ari, do you smell… something burning?" she asked.

"I'm sure it's just the fireplace. Might even be the smoke from the bonfire sticking to our clothes," I said.

I should have swept the chimney. It'll take forever to get this smell out of here.

"Well, let's go to bed and take these smoky clothes off," she flirted.

"Good idea," I said, and as we made our way to the bedroom door, I slowly turned the knob, keeping my eyes on Jordan, letting her lead the way inside.

"Always such a gentleman, aren't you?" she said.

"Maybe just this once more," I said, thinking of all the things we were about to do to one another.

"Mmm… Good!" she said, taking my meaning quite well. "You're quite the devil, aren't you? Follow me. I want to see where the devil sleeps." She entered the dark room.

I stepped in behind her, turning on the light switch by the door. She turned away from me, standing in awe at the incredibly clean master bedroom.

The chandelier that hung from the ceiling was impressive, yet understated, its many lights lending a soft illumination to the space. A plush crimson comforter was neatly placed atop my clean, white sheets. Several pillows lay at the head of the bed, matching the color scheme of the sheets and blanket. The dark hardwood floor contrasted with the brightness of the colors of the bed in a majestic way. My bookshelf on the opposite wall rose nearly to the ceiling, all manner of hardback classic literature filling its shelves. My record player, which had had no use for some time, begged for my attention from its place by the side of the bed nearest us; and next to that, a shelf full of vinyl records stood proudly, which contained a library of varying taste. A short hallway exuded light through which one could access my bedroom walk-in closet, and then the private bathroom beyond.

"Ari… this is incredible. I love this room! Is there a bathroom this way? I have to pee," she said.

"Sure," I said. "It's right that way." I pointed to the small hallway. "I'll put on some music."

"Okay, thank you," Jordan said, wasting no time in heading to the restroom. Once again, I watched her body move in that voluptuous way that I had come to love as she passed through the hall, disappearing behind the bathroom door.

I walked over to the door, taking my shoes off, then moved to the record collection, perusing it for the perfect choice. I must have taken a long time deciding because I could hear the toilet flushing and then the sink running. I gave up my search and sat on the bed. After a few moments, she emerged through the door, sparkling in the light of the chandelier, her green handbag no longer on her arm; and as I saw her in clear light for the first time in what seemed like forever, my jaw practically struck the floor.

"Why is it so quiet in here?" she asked.

I looked her up and down, dumbstruck.

"I suppose you've just shut me up," I said, "in all my favorite ways."

Jordan smiled, making her way to the shelf of records. "Then I'll pick," she said, her back to me as I kept my seat on the bed, allowing me to continue appreciating her flawless beauty, her passive way of exciting me, being so close but just beyond my reach. I stood up to make my way to her, but she had chosen a record at random, laying the disc on the record player, expertly placing the needle into its proper position. She turned to me as the record began to spin, and Mozart once again filled my ears.

Amazing. Perfect. So, the night will start and end with you, huh, Amadeus?

A hauntingly beautiful beginning reached my ears, mirroring my rising and falling heartbeat with the rising and falling of the music.

"'Agnus Dei.' Good choice, honey," I said.

"I don't know who she is," Jordan said.

I snorted in laughter. "No, dear," I said. "It's Mozart. 'Agnus Dei' is the song."

Jordan donned a look of embarrassment. "Really? I'm sorry I don't listen to th—" she said, but I had interrupted her unnecessary apology with a kiss. "It's very beautiful," she sighed.

You couldn't have chosen better. I couldn't have chosen better…. Jordan….

"You're very beautiful," I said, knowing fully well how cheesy my words must had sounded. She breathed in and out, my words clearly hitting their intended mark. "Dance with me, won't you?" I asked.

Is this too much? The music? Me?

Without a word, she pulled me close, our hands interlocking as my other hand found her waist, hers finding my shoulder, and we began to sway. The song ended. More Mozart—'Kyrie'—began to play. As the music guided us, I pressed her pretty head to my chest as we learned more of each other in a new way. I kissed the top of her head.

"I'm so glad I found you," she said.

"I'm pretty sure we found each other. I've been lost for so long," I said.

The more lost I get in you, the better I know myself.

"Me, too," she said, "but we've got plenty of time to explore that. For now, we've got tonight."

"And tonight—and you—is all I need."

"Well," she responded, pushing me onto the bed, "tonight is all we've got. And it's all I've ever really had."

I sat up, saying, "Well, you're stuck with me now."

If that is what you want.

"I'll be stuck with you forever, Ari," she said.

I scooted my body closer to her, taking her hands and pulling her close to me, positioning her between my dangling legs.

"Then get stuck to me now," I said, and I pulled her in on top of me. We began to passionately kiss each other.

"Yes, sir," she said, whispering between kisses.

My eyes closed and we kissed deeply, our hands everywhere at once. As she unbuttoned my shirt and pants, I removed her dress.

There we were, two people as one, glistening in glowing bliss beneath the light of the chandelier. As she lay on top of me, she placed me inside of her body, a sensation both familiar and new. 'Kyrie' lulled to silence. As I breached her center, Mozart's 'Dies Irae' began to play, the perfect soundtrack for the perfect moment.

As Jordan looked down upon me with her gorgeous blonde hair about her gorgeous face, tears entered her eyes, a mixture of pleasure and vulnerability I had never witnessed before.

"Can we just stay like this forever?" I asked.

Jordan smiled through her happy tears.

"Yes, forever, my love," she breathed. "And if I go, you go with me."

Tears then began to fill my own eyes.   I had never felt nor portrayed such honesty in my entire life.

"I go where you go, sweetheart," I said.

To and through whatever heaven or hell awaits us.

I heard a low rumble of thunder from outside, nearly eclipsed by the increasing rapidity of Jordan's breath.

JORDAN

So strong and accommodating…. I feel like a little girl again…. How wonderful.

Jordan squeezed Ari's torso with her thighs as she bounced on his back, every step he took being a step closer to the house and her heart. Her handbag was slung carelessly over her elbow, repeatedly bumping both she and Ari's arms as he carried Jordan to his castle of light.

Closer to the house, the bedroom.

Jordan found herself planting little kisses on Ari's neck here and there, unable to resist reminding him that she was there—there with him and there *for* him. Jordan could not help loving his periodical lifting of her body, returning her intermittently to a comfortable place on his back.

Whatever you've got to do, babe. Toss me around…. I love the way you squeeze my legs. Just enough danger in the security.

Jordan could feel Ari becoming tired.

"Hey," she said. "Are you okay?"

You smoke too many cigarettes, babe. We've got to get you off those…. Though, after the sex, I could totally go for one myself.

"Yeah, honey," Ari said. "I'm fine."

She could hear the struggle in his voice.

No need to be strong for me right now, though I do appreciate it! Hell, you've reminded me that I can stand on my own, for the first time in so long.

"You can let me down, king," she said.

Don't take his strength from him.

"I'll be okay," she continued.

Ari kept her closely bound to his back as they mounted the steps of the back porch.

Had to do just a little extra, didn't you? A king, indeed.

Ari returned her bare feet to the floor.

"I'll never ever let you down again, Jordan," Ari said.

I believe you.

Jordan kissed him, silently admitting her trust in him. Thunder rumbled.

"I know," she said, warming from within. Jordan could not fight the smile that covered her face, and it only grew larger as Ari's deep, caring eyes penetrated her to her soul. Jordan folded her arms, looking away from Ari in innocent joy. Jordan looked down to her feet then back to Ari.

I'm so glad those awful shoes are gone. Much too 'Hannah' for my taste, even though they are mine…. They just don't match my spirit. But I do wonder where she is. Probably off somewhere with Michael.

The final wave of lingering party guests seemed to be departing past Ari and Jordan as they stood in loving, lustful stalemate.

Ari, please just don't be a good host for once. Just let them go. We'll have the whole house to ourselves soon, even though I just want the bedroom.

"Come on," she said. "Let's go."

"Let's," Ari said, smiling at her. He picked her up by her waist, making her quiver inside as he kissed her lifted body. As he set her back to her feet, a figure aggressively approached Ari from behind.

Ari! Look out!

"Have you seen Hannah?" came a familiar voice. "Jordan, I've lost her! I fucked up!"

So tall…. So concerned. It's got to be….

"Michael," Ari said, his calm voice balancing the dynamic of Michael's hysterics.

Michael, don't ruin this moment! I'm sure Hannah is fine! Maybe you need this wakeup call, just like her.

Jordan thought back to her watching Michael and Hannah from the shadows earlier.

"I haven't seen her in a long time," Jordan lied.

And maybe I've never truly 'seen' her a day in my life.

"Shit!" Michael persisted. "I have to find her!"

So, you screwed her over like she screws people over. When selfishness meets selfishness, at least one of you dumbasses has got to learn something.

"Ari, I love you brother," Michael said, "and I'm so sorry! I'm sorry for everything!"

Well, maybe she was the asshole this time. Hannah, will you ever change? It's okay. It'll be okay.

"Michael," Ari said, "it's okay."

It sure is. And if not, it will be.

"Are you okay?" Ari pressed.

Always the champion. Always the quiet king.

"No. Hell, no," Michael said flatly.

Maybe Ari and I are the only good to come from this shit-show of a party. So be it.

"If you see her, tell her I'm looking for her!" Michael said.

I won't say a damn word. She's got to find herself first, if that's even possible.

"Okay, man," Ari said, Jordan impressed by his cool reply.

How I love your erratic, overthinking mind. But you never cease to surprise me.

Ari looked to Jordan, as if acknowledging her thought. Jordan winked at Ari, returning his misunderstanding to him.

"We'll catch up soon," Michael said, "but now, I've gotta find her!"

But again, you'll never really find her. She's got to find herself first.

"Michael, are—?" Ari moved to ask, but Michael had already fled.

Fake alpha….

Michael jumped down the full length of the porch stairs, landing in a clumsy manner, and was off around the corner of the house—gone. Jordan shrugged her shoulders in indifference, Ari shrugging back.

Perfect. So, all either of us care about is 'now.' I love this. Still, what weird timing. Damn you, Michael.

"Well, that was awkward," Jordan said. She could see the blatant concern on Ari's face, thinking he had become worried about Hannah missing, if only for Jordan's concern herself. "Hannah is fine, I'm sure. She always runs from real things."

And no one is more real than she is. Mostly, she runs from herself.

"So does he," Ari said.

Maybe he's running from her, too. Running right into the fire too hot to actually hold onto for too long.

"Maybe we could let them have their first fight?" Ari asked.

I don't think we really have a choice. Hannah will have to learn her lesson one day. She hurts people, then she runs, like a cowardly parasite. Maybe tonight, she's running into herself. I hope Hannah has gone off to find Hannah.

"Just for now? You sure we shouldn't check on your friend?" Ari asked.

Jordan looked to the sky and then to Ari.

The weather has been so odd tonight. The sky, the world beneath it. So much crazy stuff has gone on tonight.

Jordan looked to her bare feet, thinking about her first meeting with Ari, this reserved, handsome man—the man who had offended her at first—who hadembarrassed her—by commenting on the mud on her shoes. Jordan laughed at the memory in contrast with the present.

You struck me as such an asshole. I'm glad fate gave us a second chance. I'm happy with you. Let those two work out their issues. I can't be her stepped-on support system forever. Someday, maybe today, she'll learn to stand on her own.

"I'm so sure," Jordan said.

So, let's move forward with 'us', instead of moving backward with them.

Jordan used both hands to pat Ari on his chest.

"Come on, mister," she said. "Take me inside."

I want the grand tour!

Several guests passed them, and Jordan felt safe with Ari in the anonymity of being both a part of—yet separate from—the small crowd as it passed by and through them.

Jordan was then off her feet, snatched up and being carried in Ari's arms. She was both surprised and elated, this gift of a moment making her incredibly happy.

"God, you're cute," Jordan said, studying the face of this romantic, awkward hero of hers.

"You're not so bad, yourself," he said.

You're just so lame sometimes. I absolutely adore you.

Jordan laughed.

"You're such a nerd!" she said.

As he carried her to the cusp of the door, Jordan spoke. "Allow me," she said, reaching out while Ari still held her, not wanting to let him go, trying to meet him halfway in the chore of opening the door.

She floated in his arms through the empty kitchen, save for the lingering alcohol buffet on the kitchen bar. They passed by the living room, a classical composition that she did not recognize coming from the speakers within.

It's pretty. Strange, but beautiful.

The mixture of Ari's scent blended with the warm notes of burning wood in a fantastic combination. Her senses heightened amid the euphoric atmosphere.

They had reached the stairway. Jordan looked up at the numerous stairs and decided Ari had carried her far enough.

"Set me down," she said.

Doesn't mean you're letting me go.

"You've got it," Ari said, honoring his word. The second her feet touched the floor, her excitement for the future boosted her like a rocket to the top of the stairs. She could feel his eyes all over her as she turned back to him.

"Well, you coming or not?" she asked.

Ari struggled to get the words out as he said, "Uh, yeah, sorry!"

Oh, checking me out, were ya? I like that.

Ari took to the stairs like a blur, he, the opposite side of Jordan's rubber band finally springing back to her; and there, he kissed her forehead.

She appreciated the gesture, but her other senses prevailed, despite how much she loved his lips on her. She became concerned, the smell of something putrid burning in the air as they navigated the hall toward the bedroom.

"Ari," she said, "do you smell something burning?"

Seriously, what the hell is that smell?

"I'm sure it's just the fireplace," he assured her.

Well, that would make sense, but….

"Might even be the smoke from the bonfire sticking to our clothes," he continued.

Okay, that makes more sense. But I didn't smell this while we were downstairs. Of course, there was a LOT going on…. Maybe it's nothing…. But I…. Nevermind.

"Well, let's go to bed and take these smoky clothes off," Jordan said, returning to the magic of the present, shrugging off her worries.

"Good idea," Ari said.

They had reached the door of the bedroom, Ari opening the way for Jordan to enter, stepping aside.

"Always such a gentleman, aren't you?" Jordan asked, loving his consistency.

"Maybe just this once more," Ari said, Jordan loving his flirtatious wit.

"Mmm…" she uttered, expressing her love for his dynamic playfulness. "Good!"

And here's to all the 'once more's' to come. Time and time again.

"You're quite the devil, aren't you?" she asked.

And by you, my fire has begun to truly burn. A devil, indeed. And you've drawn me into the calm warmth of the fire you started….

Jordan led the way into the darkened tomb of Ari's bedroom with no light to illuminate her path, trusting the darkness, and wholly in him.

"Follow me," she said. "I want to see where the devil sleeps."

Or doesn't sleep, in this case.

Ari followed suit, tailing Jordan in the dark, turning on the light switch by the door.

Holy shit! What a palace!

Jordan was stunned.

The first thing she saw was a dazzling wonder of a tastefully ornate chandelier that hovered over the room—a room cloaked in neatness and attention to detail. The bed was immaculately made, the color combination of the blanket and sheets perfect in their display of powerful comfort. The quantity of pillows were many but not superfluous, and yet were tasteful. The carpet of the hallway gave way to a dark wood floor of rich depth that reflected the chandelier's light with just the right amount of luminosity, absorbing and reflecting simultaneously in a balanced symphony of melodic and harmonizing hues. The bookshelf that climbed to the ceiling bore literature bound by impressive leather and gilded, embossed script. The final object that had caught her eye was an ornate record player, flayed open, ready to be used, yet bare; and next to it, an impressive wooden shelf with an equally impressive selection of records. Jordan cared not what they were, though she hoped to find something new and approachable.

Across the room, she saw a doorway leading down a short hall into what appeared to be a tiny, tucked-away bathroom, solely for Ari's use. It became obvious that the whole diorama of the layout was an ascended cave—a heightened escape—to which Ari could retreat, from both the world and himself. This was the unknown corner of the spectrum of the multi-hedron of his reality. This was his escape from his escape, and one more piece of Ari added itself to the puzzle that Jordan sought to understand. She noticed no windows at all.

A perfect cave. I'm going to sleep like a baby tonight.

"Ari, this is incredible!" she said.

So incredible! So intriguing, but so comfortable. I feel like I'm home in a place I've never been before. This room…. This room is a perfect reflection of you! This room hides from the house like you hide from the world! And I found you both. How amazing….

"I love this room!" she said.

And I love you, too.

Her thoughts interrupted themselves as nature called from within, and a dreadful need took control of her mind. Jordan looked to the miniature hallway, suddenly a slave to the urgency inside.

"Is there a bathroom this way?" she asked, stepping toward the door already. "I have to pee."

"Sure," Ari responded. "It's right that way." He pointed to the hallway to which Jordan had referenced.

Thank God!

"I'll put on some music," Ari said.

Wonderful. Leaving me to my needs, being there only when I need you. You're something, aren't you?

"Okay, thank you," Jordan said, sprinting for the door, closing it quickly behind her. She laid her handbag beside the sink upon the countertop as she passed it which bore shining gold fixtures and white marble inlay, the hand towel red like the bed comforter, neatly folded, hanging on a golden rod that reflected the warm glow from the bright bulbs whose light became diminished as they delicately poured through their opaque marble glass covers.

The curtain that hid what Jordan guessed was an equally impressive shower was grey, accentuating the off-tones of the marble theme of the entire room. All these details, however, barely registered in her mind as she deftly passed them by, desperate for the toilet she so adamantly sought. Quickly, she was seated, lifting her short dress, planting herself haphazardly upon the cool seat, immediately relieving her bladder in a small waterfall of pleasure and pain.

She leaned upon her knees as the relieving sensation took over, embracing the powerful release. The silence beyond the closed door told Jordan that Ari was waiting for her to return, entertaining himself in her absence. She finished her task with a final push, stood, turned, wiped herself, and flushed. She adjusted her dress then moved to the sink to wash her hands. As she looked into the mirror, she saw the dirt and soot on her face and chest, evidence of her prior antics all over her.

Filthy.

I brought the fire in with me....

She picked up several of the disposable hand towels on the sink, laughing at her flippant self-mockery. She looked into the mirror's reflection of her own eyes, and as dilated pupil gazed into dilated pupil, an unending, cyclical self-examination took place. As mind bled into mind and heart melted into heart, soul met with soul—the original and the imitation—staring into one another. While they both exemplified some truer version of Jordan, whether disconnected or tangled, neither could touch the other via the immeasurable yet close distance between the two sides. Both she and her reflection lacked the ability to truly meet one another, perpetually without the other. Both saw into the other but were eternally separated, unable to coalesce.

In this moment, Jordan was meeting Jordan for the first time, a meeting that truly bore no physical meeting at all.

Jordan dabbed at the dirt upon her skin, removing the muck and soot from her chest and face.

But even if I could meet myself, I only know that I can be this woman because, while it was inside me this whole time, I was a hidden room—like Ari's room— and he opened the door for me, in either case. I've got to get back to him!

Jordan tossed the paper cloths into the nearby trash can, washed her hands, shimmying her dress more securely into place, taking one last look at herself. Satisfied, she moved for the door, opening it, escaping this realm of escapism to retreat, ironically, back to a place of comfortable vulnerability, leaving her green handbag behind.

Such a cumbersome thing, anyway….

As she emerged from her quiet place, she asked, "Why is it so quiet in here?"

Ari was seated on the bed as his eyes ascended and descended, his gaze lain heavily on Jordan's gorgeous body.

Good boy, Ari. That's a good boy. Let your eyes do the talking.

"I suppose you've just shut me up, in all my favorite ways," he said.

Then don't speak. We don't have to talk anymore.

Jordan walked over to the selection of vinyl records.

Damn. My face is getting sore from all this smiling. I'd better get my shit together. Since you can't seem to make up your mind….

"Then I'll pick," she said, keeping her back to Ari who was seated on the bed as she set to her self-appointed assignment. She was stunned at the broad measure of the selection before her.

What to choose? I want to set a mood, but I don't know what half of this shit is! Oh, well….

Jordan selected one at random paying no mind to what was printed on the record's spine.

Screw it. It doesn't matter. The music is just background noise anyway.

Jordan drew the vinyl from its sleeve setting it on the turntable, smartly setting the needle into place on the outer rim of the disc.

I know what I'm doing, Ari. Does that surprise you?

Before the music even began, Jordan spun around in blind confidence to face Ari, who remained seated.

Hell, he doesn't care about which one I choose, either. I could play nothing and still he'd wait for me right there, in his infinite patience, exactly where he wants me to join him.

As the music began to play, Jordan knew she had chosen correctly.

Yeah, it's not my thing, but it's beautiful, and…. Wow!

The introduction had settled and a heavenly chorus of angelic voices took over, followed by a rising melody—one as beautiful as it was ominous—then back to a movement of quelled melancholy.

Yeah, this is perfect. Good choice, Jordan. Good job.

"'Agnus Dei.' Good choice, honey," Ari said.

Damn, I'm good. But 'Agnes Day'?

"I don't know who she is," Jordan said in coy fashion.

Ari exploded in nasal laughter. Jordan knew then that she had gotten something wrong.

"No, dear. It's Mozart. 'Agnes Dei' is the song," Ari explained.

Jordan felt the heat rise into her face, knowing she was turning red.

Damn it!

"Really?" Jordan asked. "I'm sorry. I don't listen to th—"

The music had reached an overwhelming peak. Her embarrassment was silenced as her quiet lips were sealed with the press of Ari's mouth against hers. "It's very beautiful," Jordan continued. The music descended into pretty voices once more.

Beautiful….

The song ended. Ari spoke to Jordan and the newfound silence.

"You're very beautiful," Ari said. "Dance with me, won't you?"

Yes, of course, but which song is next?

Jordan moved to Ari, summoning him from the bed, her actions portraying her silent acceptance of his offer. A new song was about to take over. The needle moved, bringing in the next track that almost terrified Jordan. She trusted Ari's taste, however, as she trusted in her record choice. They began to dance.

As they moved together, so did the music, and as she gained comfort in the moment, the music became prettier, and it made sense to her as it complemented the romantic mood.

This really is beautiful. The music. The 'us.' And it's like this song; it starts off ugly but gets more beautiful as it goes on. Giving the music a second chance paid off, like the second chance I gave you. You are the music. I see it now, the connection. The metaphor…. Maybe I could figure you out if I could understand what you like—what you're about. I'll get there. And I know you'll do the same for me. I'll try. I know you will.

"I'm so glad I found you," she said.

"I'm pretty sure we found each other," he replied.

We sure did. And I'm finding myself as I lose myself further into you.

"Me, too," Jordan said, "but we've got plenty of time to explore that."

And explore each other.

"For now, we've got tonight," she continued.

"And tonight—and you—is all I need," Ari said, swaying Jordan in his arms, Jordan swaying within his embrace.

Jordan stopped her dance.

We came to do what we came to do. We can stop this literal song and dance.

Jordan separated herself from him.

"Well," Jordan said, pushing Ari back onto the bed. "Tonight is all we've got. And it's all I've ever really had."

Jordan felt heard and understood as she studied Ari on the bed.

"Well, you're stuck with me now," he said.

I'm okay with that.

"I'll be stuck with you forever, Ari," she said.

As long as you keep showing me all of you while I show you all of me. Deal?

Ari pulled Jordan closer to him between his seated legs, bringing her closer to him and closer to her comfort.

That'll do. Gotcha.

"Then get stuck to me now," Ari said. He pulled her on top of him, both surrendering to the other, kissing each other deeply, reaching beyond the soul—the core—of one another. Jordan could hold back no more.

"Yes, sir," she said, her voice quiet as her heart pounded in her chest.

It took no time for Jordan to begin undressing Ari, her instinct guiding her actions.

Yes. Absolutely, yes.

Jordan took Ari, sliding him inside of herself as she lay on top, owning him. The song that played died out as they both died and were reborn. A new song had begun as had a new beginning for both of them.

I wish we had a set beat to do this to, but how intense this is…. The touch, the sound. It's like being the dirtiest angel in Heaven, making love while the better angels look on and sing. How sinfully romantic!

Joyous tears cloaked Jordan's gorgeous eyes, and as the pleasure set in, Ari spoke.

"Can we just stay like this forever?" he asked.

If God won't kick us out of paradise for our love—our beautiful love—then, sure, forever will do just fine.

Jordan smiled, looking down at Ari as she continued rocking back and forth on top of him. Each press of her body was a milestone in the living romantic history of her new life.

"Yes," she moaned. "Forever, my love."

But God would send us to hell for our sin, right? But what a pretty sin. I would go to hell with you if it meant being with you. Heaven is not heaven without you in it. So let us go wherever tonight.

"And if I go," she continued, "you go with me."

Jordan knew her words had hit her intended mark. As her tears multiplied, she looked through blurry vision into Ari's eyes that had begun to weep in elation, like hers.

"I go where you go, sweetheart," he said, the sound of his voice crumbling beneath the weight of his heavy words.

Ari's mouth closed, his eyes rolled back, and a whisper of thunder met her ears from outside. All she could hear was beautiful music—the music, itself, and the dissipating thunder—and the shared chaos of rhythmic breathing. She and Ari were composing a song—a passionate symphony of their own.

Maybe a storm is coming. Perhaps we are the storm, ourselves, the lightning and the thunder being poetic destruction. And from such an awful beginning…. We've come a long way in such a short time….

MICHAEL

Michael descended the stairs like a lightning bolt, striking the floor at the bottom with a loud thud as he leapt down and over the last half of the staircase.

I've got to fucking find her!

He stormed past the living room that was still emanating music that was audible even in the empty kitchen. Soon, Michael met with the departing remainder of the crowd lingering on the back porch. Michael looked them up and down, each guest individually, head to foot, and did not find Hannah there.

You couldn't have gotten that far, right?!

Michael looked to the sky for answers and saw nothing but stars and a taunting moon, as it was full and bright—everything Michael was not.

A wisp of a cloud passed quickly over the moon, casting a temporary shadow on the dying party along with Michael's world. The stars seemed to dim for a moment as Michael paused to think about the night and his experiences with Hannah, the only thing he could think about.

"I can't just stand here!" he said aloud.

The crowd had finally abandoned the porch. He saw a couple standing alone, together, cloaked in the moonlight beyond his personal shadow. The man had picked up the girl and set her down. Michael heard the voice of the man, and it sounded so much like—

"Ari! Have you seen Hannah?" he asked in rushed panic. "Jordan, I've lost her! I fucked up!"

Ari's voice came back to him, calm and brief. "Michael—"

"—I haven't seen her in a long time," Jordan interrupted.

Well, aren't you just two peas in a fucking pod, finishing each other's sentences! I want my pea. I want my pod! WHERE THE HELL IS HANNAH?

"Shit!" Michael said. "I have to find her!"

Look at you, looking for a girl you barely know, hunting her down, while you've treated Ari like shit for it forever. He's always had your back, and while you rely on his goodness and faithfulness to pick you up when you fall, you cling to him and drag him down when you've overwhelmed him. And you become angry with him and call him weak, even when you are the life-sucking disease that broke him down in the first place! You fucking, goddamned PIECE OF SHIT, MICHAEL!

"Ari," Michael said. "I love you, brother!"

Still, you're looking for Hannah, and that's why you need him now, just like always. Empty words, Michael. Empty fucking words. Apologize.

"And I'm so sorry! I'm sorry for everything!" he said.

I truly do love you, man. Can you ever forgive me?

The tone of Ari's voice surprised and comforted Michael.

"Michael," Ari said, "it's okay."

No, it isn't. How could I ever make it up to you, the love you have for people? While I just take and take and take from them!

"Are you okay?" Ari continued.

Same damned Ari. Same damned Michael. Nothing changes. No, I'm far from okay. You're here but gone. And so am I.

"No," Michael said. "Hell, no."

I'll have to make everything up to you, but I don't know how. I suppose it'll have to wait. Damn it. Damn it all! To hell with all this!

"If you see her—" Michael said.

Hannah, I'd just love to see you again. I'd love to explain.

"Tell her I'm looking for her," he continued.

"Okay, man," Ari said, sounding indifferent to Michael, Ari obviously distracted by Jordan. Michael both loved and hated what he was seeing.

Fine! You two be happy! I'll just get lost! And hopefully I'll find my girl along the way. You always make it look so easy, don't you, Ari! Fuck this! I'm going for what makes me happy. But keep your cool, Michael. Keep your cool.

Michael smiled a false smile neither Ari nor Jordan saw.

"We'll catch up soon," Michael said, "but now, I've gotta find her!"

And maybe find myself, too.

Ari's sympathetic voice met his ears, but Michael dismissed the sound for the sake of his pursuit—a pursuit he may have been journeying in vain. Michael leaped down the porch steps like the stairs earlier, evacuating a world he hoped to forget as that same world so apparently hoped to forget him.

Fuck them all. All of them. And fuck you too, Hannah, if you've abandoned me!

Mid-stride, Michael debated where Hannah was most likely to have fled.

Not in the house and definitely not back at the fire. That meant too much to her, and me, too. No, she's….

Michael rounded the corner of the house with his incredibly athletic stride.

Her car! Damn it, Hannah, if you're leaving—you'd better not be running like this! You're stronger than this! We deserve better than this!

He stood at the front corner of the house where the driveway met the structure of the mansion, peering through the moonlit darkness in which any car lights may have belonged to her. Only two red, angry taillights glowed in the absent light, and Michael broke into a run.

It's gotta be! It's gotta be! Please!

His heart quickened as his breath followed suit, both mimicking the other while they fatigued. Michael could vaguely make out the shadows of bodies in various seats of various cars, but his desperate instinct pushed him toward the one that had just started.

Please!!

As Michael gained the length of the driveway, getting ever-closer to his target, the headlights turned on.

Please, no! No!

The car he targeted reversed wildly into the driveway, then quickly made its way to the road beyond.

Got to be her! Hannah, please don't leave!

Michael was faster than the sedan that moved into gear, but as man's passion met with machine's indifference, he was defeated, his heart crushed by sheer inhumanity.

The sedan's back tires spun, sending rocks and dirt and dust at Michael. As he shielded his eyes from the blast, he kept his pace, and momentarily, he caught up to the driver's side window, looking in as he ran. His breath was depleted, his heart was full, and his purpose was somewhere in between.

There she was in the driver's seat, teary-eyed and strong, flinging herself away from the party, the world, and Michael in particular.

That second of time became a slow eternity, like he was on the cusp of the event horizon of the beauty of the black hole of anguish she had suddenly become. She tore through his universe, absorbing all the light he had left to contain before absconding with it. She was blurring and devouring all around her—all light, all life, all everything, including time, itself.

Michael—and space, time and hope itself—became lost in the vortex of his loss embodied in Hannah. As she sped up, she left him, leaving him abandoned, confused and angry. He was desperate to reach out, though he knew he could not touch her, given both the spatial and emotional distances between them.

He kept his pace, she accelerated, and he fell behind her in a cloud of dismissal and future memories lost. She was forever away in moments; yet he still chased, hoping for a pause in her escape, a pause that never occurred. Foot over stumbling foot, he pushed himself to his physical limit in his chase. The sedan did not stop, and as the tires met the road, the screech of their meeting defeated Michael as he slowed to a halt, his heart skipping a beat despite its desperate struggle.

Michael looked to the cloud of dust in the moonlight as light passed through the darkness of his unwanted and unintended goodbye.

Well, farewell…. Should have gotten her number. Damn.

Michael's present faded and was crushed beneath the weight of his past and future, the walls of each destroying him between the immense pressure of his memories and revelations, chipping away what he once was.

Using the sand to which he had been reduced, he became a formidable basis for the building of a potential personal empire; yet his empire was broken into pieces before it could form, his shards scattered to the wind—he, the sand in her windstorm, lost to her wilderness. His future was being taken from him, even as he looked upon its departure like a dreamy-eyed child, weeping as he awakened—awakening to a life without the dream he had craved to become lost within forever.

He disintegrated.

Bezaliel. You fucking bastard!

Hannah was gone. Michael was equally gone. His whole world crumbled in his wanting, empty hands.

As he watched the dust cloud dissipate behind Hannah's car, so did his hope for something he had never known—a true connection with someone besides himself.

She was gone like the gravel behind her. Like dust in the nonexistent wind, she evaporated by her own will, and Michael disappeared within the trauma and reality of her choice.

Goodbye. Goodbye, Hannah. Goodbye, me.

Michael stood still as his past, present and future fled from him in a plethora of appreciations and regrets.

I've been such a piece of shit. Hannah…. Ari…. I'm sorry. I'm so fucking sorry. Well, what to do, now?

'Nothing' was all Michael knew. Michael also became that same 'nothing'—shadows of dust, and dust in the shadows.

In a cloud of his own, he vented his frustration in rebellion, leaving the pieces of himself in the accumulations of all his past mistakes. Michael stepped back, looking to the road, disappearing into the dark, retreating headlong toward the house.

At least I was alive there. At least I didn't hate myself.

The driveway was an unforgiving walk of shame and unforgiveness.

Tonight, and all of it. Let it burn to the ground! And to hell with the fire, itself! To hell with this party. To hell with this night! I've got to escape, but I'm too wasted to drive. Where to go?!

Michal despised the idea of returning to the house, where Katie might be waiting for him.

That bitch! That selfish, selfish bitch! No, can't risk that. I might just do something, something I might regret. I guess there's only one place to go, really.

Michael picked up the pace of his stride, eventually breaking into a full run. As he bolted toward the bonfire, every step increased his rage.

Bezaliel…. You were even there watching me with Katie. I saw you there! And you did nothing! NOTHING! YOU KNEW AND YOU DID NOTHING!

"How dare you…."

I'm not even sure I believe you're real, but how I hate you so much right now! Almost as much as I hate myself! You have explaining to do!

Something inside of him snapped and he could hear it—a sound much like shattering glass.

"And I want an apology," Michael wheezed, each syllable an exhausted breath that his falling feet pressed from him. "You'd better be there," he continued, boiling with fury. Michael had arrived at the tree line, where he stopped and stood.

He stepped past the first trees and began his trek into the dark heart of the forest. Mid-step, he drew out a cigarette and lit it as thunder echoed around him with the click of his lighter.

The glow of the cherry at the end of his cigarette was the only light Michael could see.

REVELATION

KATIE

As Katie journeyed through her nighttime daydream, she was floating like a ghost down a narrow, infinite hallway; and at the end of the phantom tunnel was a small doorway. The walls were made of innumerable terrifying faces that stared at, into, and through her. Sconces lined the walls, the candles upon them perpetually melting down and then back into themselves, their haunting flames eternal in their self-sustainment. Wax melted down along the sides, creeping up back to the top in a perpetual cycle.

The only escape—the only way out—was onward. Every step closer to the end of the hallway granted her no progress. The door in the distance kept shifting farther and farther away from her, as though Katie was pursuing it in vain on an eternal, horrific treadmill. The air, as thin as it was, sounded like a dull soundtrack of droning static, harmonizing with the echoing, agonized screams around her. With every step, the flames of the candles on the walls became larger and brighter.

Let me out! LET ME OUT!

"NO!" a voice boomed, resonating off the walls of faces, the candles' flames rising in height and heat. The flames themselves produced a symphony of sound, each one Katie passed emanating a burning voice that melded chaotically—and beautifully—with all others. The melody was haunting and angelic and vibrant. It made Katie feel connected yet separated, almost as if her soul begged to escape her body as it more aggressively pursued her center.

As much as it is within as it is outside of me…. Like my soul performing a song that only my body can hear….

The symphony rose in fervor and eloquence, a wrathful undertone supporting the entire movement. The music was angry and beautiful, unlike anything Katie had ever heard before.

Such gorgeous, aggressive music…. It's like the lightning of my soul and the screaming, the thunder of my suffering.

"Now, you understand," said the voice.

I think I do. I can even smell the rage—that impeccable rage—that I've hated and nurtured inside myself for so long.

Katie smelled smoke though the candles produced none.

"My child," said the voice.

"Bezaliel? Is that you?" Katie asked.

Smug, satisfied laughter coursed down the hallway and off the walls.

The scent of smoke took hold of her.

"Why can't I wake up?" Katie asked.

"You are not meant to," said the voice. "Not yet."

The candlelight intensified, their glow reaching a point of blinding brightness. Katie kept to her pursuit of the light at the end of the haunting hall. The surrounding candlelight had become so intense that the unattainable radiance of the door forever away became eclipsed by it. The corridor itself gradually became nothing but white-hot light; the light itself becoming a second darkness in which she became lost, losing any bearing she had for a route of escape.

Soon, Katie could not see her hands before her face in lieu of the brightness that now surrounded her. It had overtaken her, filling her inside, drowning her from within. As she more deeply felt the intense heat and glow invading her body, it also infiltrated her mind and soul. All she could see and feel was a light unlike any she had ever witnessed. All she could taste was hopelessness, her escape now seemingly impossible. All she could smell was the ever-increasing scent of smoke, putrid and charred, though she could see no smoke around her in this ethereal hallway of fear. All she could hear was that familiar ominous voice, reverberating all around her, even inside her private thoughts which had become as blank as the empty whiteness that enveloped her.

"You are so much like me, Katarina," said the voice. "So surrounded by light that you are now lost in it, and you have lost your way. But you can find yourself once more. All you must do is give in. Trust me. Do you trust me?"

The smell of smoke became stronger and stronger as Katie's will weakened. It began to choke her lungs.

"But if I can't wake up, how am I supposed to do anything? I can't even see!" she said.

"But do you trust me?" it asked again. "Did I not grant you your desires with Michael? Did he not leave by my hand so that you may know that he is not to be for you? You may yet wake up, Katarina, but first…. First you must *awaken!*"

"What does that even mean? Why are you trying to confuse me? Bezaliel!" she said in desperation.

"All I will say is that you must heed my example; a light so bright that it terrifies, but should you give into it—its perfection—" the voice said, "you will come to see that it is the apex of all creation, and even some things beyond it."

"But… but I can't choose for myself?" she asked. "Don't I have a choice? You've taken my 'choice' from me! So, I either make this my home and call it heaven, or I resist it and it becomes my hell? A place of helplessness and torture, either way? Please let me out! Please, please, just wake me up! Let me choose!"

Bezaliel laughed. "Katarina," he began, "you understand, do you not? I was born a slave to the idea of perfection, and as perfect as my existence was, I chose to follow another path, if only to simply choose for myself, no matter the consequence. And like you, I trapped myself in my own autonomy. Sometimes it is better to be happy than to become stubborn with thoughts of freedom. Sometimes, that very idea of freedom may lead us to nurture the thought that what we want is better than what we have. This is the path that led me here, as well as you. You pursued a selfish idea of happiness—something better, you thought—giving in to your base desires and fabricated wickedness as you discarded the beautiful soul you were meant to be, abandoning your true purpose—all for the sake of your reckless idea of self-sabotaging revenge. You began to hate your Creator for what the *world* has done to you; and while you tell yourself repeatedly that He does not exist, still, you continued your path of indulgent, narcissistic martyrdom, all to spite Him. And still, you blamed Him, hating Him more and more for the consequences you brought upon yourself. You chose your loneliness, and with the freedom of choice that He gave you, you used it as a weapon against Him, though that weapon you forged was your own selfish sword that you pointed at your own heart. 'Slowly kill yourself to wound Him', correct? And how has that gone for you, Katarina? So now, here we are. I do not judge you, but this is the reason why I am both here, and you are now here with me. I may be a discarded child, but that does not mean that I escape His will. He calls to all of us, and though we may ignore that call, eventually, we all—every created thing—answer in the end, responding in one way or another. The grass is not always greener on the other side—it is greener where you water it, a lesson I wish I had learned long, long ago."

The candles dimmed to a more palatable light, the hallway becoming a corridor of shallow illumination, and the eyes of Bezaliel, along with his massive frame, became all Katie could see.

"Give in to me and let me save you," he continued. "Sometimes heaven is darkness and hell shines brightly. You must embrace them both to truly exist, as they both are very, very real. Will you wake up? Will you awaken?"

The smell of smoke had overtaken all of Katie's senses, burning her eyes, choking her voice, and depleting her nose's capacity to sense any other odor. She could even feel its particles clinging to her skin.

"So, what will you choose?" Bezaliel asked. "Freedom? Or happiness?" he asked.

Katie closed her stinging eyes.

"Well, if happiness is this prison, away from the world, and freedom is the real world that I despise so much..." she said. "I choose...."

Tears rolled out from her closed, smoke-stung, weepy eyes, carving a soft path like two tiny rivers down her cheeks. The smell of smoke had become so potent that she began coughing, her ability to breathe becoming an increasing struggle.

"I choose..." she repeated.

Katie became lightheaded and dizzy. The grip of smoke in her lungs strangled her words.

What the hell is going on?

Her spoken thoughts were broken by the intermittent breaths that were interrupted by the imagined smoke that paralyzed her voice. She struggled to speak the punctuated words that she could hardly form from the caustic air around her, though no smoke or fog could be seen.

"You've taken... my choice... from me..." she said, struggling to get the words to leave her mouth as she gasped and choked. "Heaven is a prison.... And hell is the punishment... for wanting to be free...."

"YES. Yes, Child! Now, you understand!" Bezaliel said. "Now you understand it!"

The hallway of light and darkness dissolved into nothing. Katie jumped awake in the bed, fleeing her nightmare. She immediately began coughing. The bedroom was no longer filled with moonlight, but with thick smoke and the glow and heat of fire. As the candles of her dream haunted her in her waking subconscious, their fire had become real, chasing her into the real world, burning in rage beside her. The smoke she smelled in her vision now made sense, and she fought to catch her breath.

Her eyes were watering, as they had in her dream. She could barely see through her struggling eyes as the rampant cloud invaded her lungs, making her even more dizzy and nauseous.

Michael's final words echoed in her head.

"Then burn, bitch."

I am fire, after all…. Guess I'm finally home….

She looked to the window, contemplating jumping through it to her safety. The fire licked at the bed and had reached all the way to the doorway. She quickly got up to make her daring move, but fell down just as quickly to the floor, her spinning head getting the better of her.

You've taken my choice from me, Bezaliel. How unfair….

"How… un… fair…" she wheezed, coughing in between syllables. She could hear the faint sound of music, both pretty and wicked. The growing fire was louder, still.

Such pretty music. And life is so ugly. And this is where mine ends….

"I *am* fire…. How… appropriately… poetic. How… stupidly… symbolic…" she said, as she began to black out.

"Child, if you will not choose…." Bezaliel said, his voice coming back into play.

I… don't… have… the… strength…. You've… taken… that… too….

"Then I will have to choose for you," Bezaliel said. "So ironic I should play the role of the god that takes your choice from you, as mine did from me. You are like me in so many ways, Katarina. Come with me. Come with me or perish."

"Fine…" Katie said, passing out completely with her final breath.

"That is no answer," Bezaliel said, "but you are coming with me. Now!"

Katie felt a physical rush from beyond the darkness of her wilting consciousness. The smell and burden of smoke was lifted as the sound of breaking glass filled her ears. She could breathe once more. Her eyes no longer burned, and the heat of the bedroom inferno had faded away in place of the cool autumn air. She came to and, opening her eyes, she saw the sky and all the clear stars in the sky above, past the face and eyes of Bezaliel as he looked down upon her. His smile was both terrifying and comforting, but she loved how amazing it felt to be safe in this moment, away from the consuming flames.

She coughed for a few moments, then spoke.

"Is this..?" she asked. "Is this a dream? Am I…. Am I dead?"

"No, Child," Bezaliel said, comforting her. "You, in fact, have never been more alive. Once we face the fires—the light and the shadow of death—the darkness of existence is not such a terrible alternative. After all, the stars owe their stark beauty to the darkness that surrounds them."

He let out a brief laugh and Katie felt the rumble in his chest as she realized he was holding her in his arms. She became comfortable as she embraced the safety of the moment, the safest she had felt in as long as she could remember.

"You… you saved me. But why?" she asked.

"Because," he said, looking back down to her. "Because you are worth saving."

Katie motioned a silent request to be set down, and when her feet met the ground, she leapt into the arms of darkness that had saved her life. Bezaliel returned her tiny embrace.

"You could have just let me die," she said, weeping into his chest.

"You are like me, Katarina," he said. "You, like me, have been dying for a very, very long time. It is time to live again and be alive—truly alive. Come be alive with me."

Katie squeezed him tighter before releasing him, leaning back, looking into his loving, fear-inspiring eyes. In those eyes, she saw her past, present, and future; a future which was now possible because of this shadow-savior.

"I owe you my life," she said.

"Your life is what I offer you, Child. Will you come with me?" he asked again. "I offer you the choice I never had—to live beyond the consequences of life."

Katie smiled at his eyes then looked to the canopy of the sky as a shooting star cut across the clear expanse above. Looking back to Bezaliel, she grew warm within, a comfort she had not felt for most of her broken life.

"Let's go," she said. "Show me how to live."

Bezaliel smiled back down at her, offering his hand.

"Come," he said, beckoning her, and Katie placed her hand into his. They began walking together, Bezaliel leading the way toward the tree line and the grove beyond. Katie looked to her side as a silhouette ran up to the cleared path that led to the heart of the forest. It paused, then proceeded into the thick of the trees.

"There is something I want you to see," Bezaliel said, and Katie followed him through the uncut wilderness. Katie looked back to the house and to the window of the room through which she had escaped by the hand of her dark guardian angel. The window glowed bright orange, filled completely with the fire that had nearly devoured her.

She looked back to her host, following him deeper into the trees, away from the house and the inferno, until it was nothing more than a memory—unforgettable—behind her.

Thunder dully called from somewhere far, far away.

HANNAH

Hannah recklessly took turn after daring turn as she raced along in anger and sadness down and through the country roads toward her apartment, half-fighting and half-loving the tears that threatened to overtake her rage-shaken sight. Caught between fury and melancholy, she had no regard for the safety of her body as she pursued her home. Hannah kept her windows down and her radio off to fully concentrate on the road. Her seatbelt dangled next to her, unused.

Her eyes were unblinking, dedicated as she was to getting home and to putting this entire night behind her.

It sticks with me. But why? Something doesn't feel right.

Hannah continued peeling through the streets, streaking by the houses, neighborhoods and buildings on either side passing her by in the blur of her speed and confusion.

He seemed so sincere! The way he looked at me…. The way he touched me…. He not only told me so, but he showed me that he wanted me. So, why? Why Katie?

Her foot eased itself off the accelerator as her thinking began to bring her calm, her erratic mentality dispersing in its chaos, receding in momentum. Her logical mind had finally begun to communicate with her broken, deaf heart once again.

She looked out of her window at the glowing moon, distracted from the road ahead.

All I did was stop to pee, and he was already on her—inside her…. The things he said. The things he did. It doesn't make any—!

She returned to reality just in time, slamming on her brakes, bringing the car to a screeching halt. She stopped just shy of running a red light at a four-way intersection.

As the car rocked, Hannah slid violently forward, almost striking the steering wheel with her chest. She heard a thud come from the floorboard of the passenger side, and as she roughly settled back into her own seat, she put her hand to her chest, feeling her now-racing heartbeat and nervous breathing.

She looked down, inspecting herself, putting the car into park.

Damn, that was close! Should have just run it!

She looked around the intersection, the light still a violent neon red.

I'm in the middle of nowhere! What is this intersection even doing—?

Hannah thought of the thud. She looked to the passenger seat, then the floor. Hannah sighed as her eyes found Jordan's phone lying there, a souvenir of better days. She looked up and through the windshield at the empty street before her, her headlights illuminating a short distance before the streetlights swallowed their light, along with the surrounding night that occupied the space around them. She could then smell the odor of burning rubber coming from her tires.

Darkness and nothing everywhere, and just this one oasis of life's evidence here, in the middle of nothing. And all there is… this light—this one light….

Hannah laughed in lieu of, and in spite of, her panic. Her mind was racing as she was rudely stirred from her heartbroken daydream.

One stoplight hovering over four roads in the middle of nothing—of nowhere—in the dark….

Wait!

Michal went upstairs to meet me, right? Wait! I stopped to pee…. He thought…. I bet he thought she was me!

That 'must' be it! Katie, just always so conveniently…. What a bitch! What an opportunist bitch! Damn! It's just like the party, but here… here I am truly alone. No 'Katie' to scold here….

Hannah looked back to Jordan's phone in the floor.

She can't even call me….

Hannah sat upright.

"She can't even call me!" Hannah shouted. "Should I go back?"

The red light turned green. Hannah stayed put.

Damn that phone! I should be going home, but here you are, Jordan, calling me back to you, with a phone you don't even have!

Hannah reminisced on her meeting with Jordan by the bathroom earlier.

We promised we would talk again. And I've run away!

Hannah pondered on the night's events.

And Michael, I didn't give you a chance to explain, either, and I've run from you, too.

She thought about her life prior to this night.

And the only reason I—we—even went to that party was to get you away from yourself, Jordan, but….

Hannah shrugged, sighed, and collapsed inside and out.

But, hey, we both know I went there in hopes of being seen—finding that man that doesn't exist, yet there he was! I felt so understood by him.

Her eyes began to water as her inflective deliberations overwhelmed her heart and soul.

I went there tonight to get away from myself. So much to love about 'me' and still, I ran. I just run. I always freaking run! I'm always just running away!

Hannah shook the tears from her eyes as she shook her frustrated head.

"Damn it!" Hannah shouted, pounding the steering wheel with her fists as she screamed, venting her mounting frustration.

"Damn it, damn it, damn it, and damn *me!*" she said through gritted teeth.

She shifted the car into drive, firmly gripping the steering wheel. She slammed on the accelerator with her foot, making a screeching U-turn in the middle of the intersection. Her tires smoked and screamed. The green light turned yellow.

"Screw caution!" she said aloud, yelling at the light in her rearview mirror as it became red once more. "I'm going to be *me* from now on! And I'm going to let others be who they are, whether they keep up or I leave them behind!"

My standards have always been so impossibly high, yet I blame everyone else for my loneliness…. It's time to stop being so damn selfish! It's time….

Hannah pressed even harder on the accelerator, zooming down the country road.

It's time to fix me, time to fix what I've allowed to be broken. I've got to fix this mess between us, Jordan! Michael, we have so much to talk about, ourselves.

Hannah's past became her future as she pursued both at once, aiming to mend them in her chasing of their conjoined revelation.

She fastened her seatbelt as she sped down the road away from that fateful crossroads, directly into the center of another; one she had, until now, left behind. As the seatbelt clicked, a loud roar of thunder filled the scene as the world outside passed her by in a speeding blur.

"Michael," she said, "I'm sorry, and I hope you are, too!"

She focused her eyes on the road—a path both behind and ahead of her—her passion purposeful and her newfound purpose melding into her passion.

"I'm going to fix this," she said. "All of it."

Hannah pressed her eyes to the road, squinting ahead in anger at her past self, sharpening her sight upon the woman she had suddenly become, focusing upon the approaching unknown.

It's time to put out the fires I've started—the fires I've fed.

"Jordan," Hannah said to herself, "I'm coming."

She sped back toward the house, the wind howling past the car windows as she shed her chrysalis, finally proud of herself, becoming more hopeful, compassionate, forgiving and—

—Ready to love. It's time to let the walls come down a little. Maybe not all at once, but maybe a brick at a time.

"And give some love back to the world," she said. "Jordan…. Michael…."

Hell, maybe even you, Ari. And especially you, Hannah. Don't forget to leave some love for yourself.

"I'm coming for you…. All of you."

Hannah smiled to herself, then at herself, as she locked eyes with her own reflection in the rearview mirror.

"All of you, especially *you*, Hannah," she spoke aloud, reinforcing her self-reassurance. She looked to the moon as though silently speaking to it. Suddenly, the moon was replaced by darkness, its glowing face now hidden behind a pitch black veil.

Hannah sighed deeply, released her breath, and looking back to the road ahead, she sped off into the night. The lights, the shadows and all things in between disappeared behind her. All that was behind Hannah was Hannah. All that was before her was a Hannah she was eager to meet, and she was wholly her current self, at long last.

MICHAEL

Michael was an empty husk as he tumbled in rage through the thicket of shadows. He could feel the heat of his anger on his skin as goosebumps raised up on his arms, increasing in severity with each step. The smoke he exhaled as he feverishly smoked his cigarette rose up and out of him, the fire within him burning, his mouth a fuming chimney.

Making his way to the bonfire, he thought of Hannah and the memories they had made when they shared each other's company on the same dark path that he now walked alone. For the first time in a very long time, Michael felt true sadness, his confidence wavering as he fell to pieces inside.

I am not this weak!

Michael stopped as he came to the opening where the bonfire resided, his cigarette nearly finished. He threw it to the ground, stepping on it, snuffing its glow.

But I can't help missing her!

He stepped closer toward the woodpile, his fists shaking by his sides. His fit of anger was cut short by a sudden sense of fear. He looked around and saw nothing there.

Bezaliel…. Is that you? I can feel you watching.

"Are you there, you coward?" Michael asked, his voice resonating through and back from the surrounding trees.

No answer came.

"You just hide in your damn shadows, don't you?!" he shouted.

Michael took another cigarette out of his pack and lit it, the flame of his lighter reflecting off two eye-like orbs that floated just beyond the trees before him. Then they vanished.

"You son of a bitch!" shouted Michael. "I knew you were here!"

Michael ran for the spot where the eyes had been, but found no one and nothing.

"Coward…" Michael sneered through gritted teeth. "Coward!"

He took a drag from his cigarette, blowing his smoke into the space where Bezaliel's face once was, mocking and daring him.

"All you do is run from the fires you've started," Michael said to the empty air. He looked down, hitting his cigarette again.

"And yet," Michael continued, his rage subsiding, "don't I do the same?" Michael spoke, his voice quivering to a whisper. He turned to look at the woodpile, falling to his hands and knees as he replayed in his mind his moments with Hannah earlier. His cigarette weakly rolled from between his fingers to the ground as his strength left him.

"I always lead them on, don't I? I make these women fall for me, and when it gets so real that I become uncomfortable, I leave them, without a word," he said. "I start a fire in their heart, give them hope, and then I run, leaving them to burn out to nothingness, choking to death on the fumes of their own emotions."

Michael began to weep, realizing the errors of his past with no way now to correct them.

Hannah, why? Why did it have to be you? Why couldn't I just learn it all before you? Why? Why did you have to be the lesson? I should have learned by now.

"And now that I have found what I want," Michael said, sobbing, "she's gone. She's just, she's just gone! She's gone and I'm just out here, alone and crying in the damned dark, yelling at shadows!"

Michael used his arm to wipe the tears from his eyes and punched the ground with his fist.

You said I was to save Ari, Bezaliel…. And look at me now….

"Look at me, now!" Michael yelled at the ground beneath him. "I can't even save myself! I couldn't even go back to the house!"

Katie, that must've hurt like hell when I called you 'Hannah'. It wasn't supposed to be you! And Hannah, Hannah…. I am so, so very….

"I'm so sorry, honey," Michael wept. "I'm just… I'm just so sorry, and this is all my fault! If I had just been the man you deserved already…. You should never have been the lesson. You're the one I want to apply this lesson to…. And now I'll never be able to…."

Michael stood up, wiping his tears away, accepting his failure and the difficult wisdom he had learned by its misery.

"Bezaliel!" Michael called to the void around him. "You told me I had to save Ari! Seems like he's done a pretty good job of saving himself, finding something real like Jordan. Ari," Michael continued, Bezaliel leaving his mind in place of images of Jordan with Ari. "Ari, you deserve what you've found. I've dismissed you this whole time, and I've been so selfish…. You deserve a girl like that, and I deserve what I've gotten, too. I deserve this loneliness. I see that now. I see it all so clearly, now, ironically, in a place so dark and lonely as this…."

Ari, I don't know about saving you, but you've been saving me all along…. I've always known it.

"And maybe that's why I've treated you the way that I have," Michael said, continuing to speak to Ari as he stood alone in the woods. "To hell with me. I've been jealous, putting on this macho front, and all to diminish you, because I've just been jealous. You're a good man. I am not. Hannah was right to call me a boy. I'm so sorry, my brother."

"Michael," came that ominous, layered, familiar voice. "You understand, now."

I knew you were here. But I can't be angry with you anymore. Not when the mistakes have been mine.

"I'm tired of blaming others for the consequences of my choices," Michael said.

"Good," continued the voice. "Good. Now, I can leave you, Michael. Ari will need you. I do not lie."

"Then I'll let him have his night with his dream girl. I'll just go. I don't want to interrupt him now," Michael said.

"No, Michael," said Bezaliel, coming into view. "You must find him now. Now is the only time you have."

"What do you mean?!" Michael said, looking around himself.

Michael bent down to pick up the cigarette he had dropped, placing it in his mouth before he dusted off his knees. No answer came, and no one was anywhere to be found.

"Well, I guess that's that," Michael said. "Tomorrow is a new day, I suppose." He reignited the cigarette.

"NO! NOT TOMORROW! NOW, MICHAEL LAW!" Bezaliel bellowed.

Michael spun around, exhaling the smoke he had just taken in.

"What the hell do you mean by *now?*" Michael asked, gesturing to the woodpile. "The fire is dead. Everyone is gone!"

Michael looked up.

The stars, the moon…. They sure are awfully bright tonight….

The full moon faded abruptly to pure black, erased completely from the sky. Stars, alone and bright, were suddenly the only lights in the autumn sky.

An   eclipse?

What the fu—

In the sudden, frozen, pitch-black darkness, Michael heard a dull roar from behind him, accompanied by crackling and creaking.

But the fire….

"It's not even burning, anymore!" Michael said, his voice shaking. "What the hell is that soun—?"

Michael's lips trembled as the cigarette fell from his mouth. Before it even hit the ground, Michael was in a full sprint toward the house. He became a shadow dissolved at full speed into the shadows of the wooded path.

Fuck! Ari! ARI!!

Michael panted and stumbled over his own feet as he ran, petrified inside, toward the house—a house that was nearly fully ablaze with angry fire. It had caught fire itself, somehow, and that fire—the light of it—could be seen, even through the thick trees of the shadowy grove.

Holy shit! ARI!! Please, please—! Please, let me get there in time!!

Bezaliel's laughter was all Michael could hear, his ears almost deaf to the shock of the sight of the house; the house that was Ari's home, nearly fully engulfed in bountiful flames.

With each step, Michael shed another layer of his past self, donning the armor of the man he was becoming, trading cowardice for the heart of the hero he thought he was about to be forced to be now.

Ari…. Ari…! I hope I get to you in time…!

ARI

I was dreaming of Jordan as we lay next to each other, as if dreaming within a dream.

As I dreamed of her—my naked body entwined within and around her naked body—we slept off the fatigue of our desire. Despite our shared, deep rest, I stirred and rolled over to her, pulling her closer to me. The scent of smoke was the only thing that eclipsed her perfume, the ladder overwhelming the former. I ignored all my other senses as I looked over the body of the flawless sleeping angel in my bed.

"Hey," I said, brushing the hair from her face. A slow, tired smile crept across her countenance.

"Hey," she said, stirring as she opened her eyes. "Ari, tonight…."

"Good morning," I said, kissing her forehead.

"Is it morning already?" she asked, rising up in bed, coughing. Ari froze inside as Jordan's eyes looked to the closed door, widening in immediate fear. "Ari! ARI!!" she gasped.

"What?" I asked. I turned to face the direction of her attention, then consumed by fear, myself.

Smoke was billowing through the door cracks, and Mozart's "Requiem" provided the soundtrack for the most terrifying moment of my life, my anxiety multiplying by the moment. I only then smelled that of which Jordan had warned me as we traversed the hallway earlier.

"Oh… Oh, shit!!" I said. I leapt from the bed, naked and dizzy. The flickering glow of the fire beyond the door danced upon and through the smoke as it crawled through the gaps in the frame, thickening as it crept. I could feel the heat in the air as my senses returned to me. I had snapped awake from the dream that was Jordan's presence into the nightmare of my burning house.

I made for the doorknob, pulling away immediately as it scorched my hand.

"Shit!" I said, abruptly.

I shook the pain from my hand, looking at it, then looking to Jordan, who had turned to stone in panic.

I cannot—I CAN NOT PANIC!   I HAVE TO BE STRONG! FOR HER!

Even if I cannot be strong for myself….

"Ari, I'm scared," Jordan said, emboldening my protective instincts.

I have got to save you!   An angel should never die!   Especially mine! Especially you!!

I reached for the blanket that she and I had wrestled to the foot of the bed in our lovemaking. I wrapped it haphazardly around the hot doorknob and twisted it, the doorknob giving no purchase to my grip.

No! No, I will not fail you, honey. My God, I love you, woman. I. Will. Not. Fail. You.

I began to cry.

How could this have even happened? Is this a dream? Please be a dream!

I choked back the tears of terror, grasped the blanketed knob with all the strength I could muster, and turned it, the door finally giving way. The rush of heat that met my face was unlike any pain I had ever known; comparable only to the pain I felt within when I first saw the unbridled fear in Jordan's eyes.

Smoke rushed the door, nearly filling the room. The hallway was consumed by flames. I could feel my pupils dilate as they took the scene in, widening as the rest of my eyes had, unable to comprehend what my eyes were seeing.

We can't get out that way….

I realized that I had received what I had asked for throughout the entire evening.

God…. God is a fire….

I turned as my house was being turned to ash before my very eyes, and with me inside. The house was being destroyed against its nonexistent will, and despite my fear, I looked back to Jordan, which placed a smile on my otherwise blank face.

"God is here now," I said.

God.   You heard me.   Thank You!   And You even sent an angel, a messenger, and there she is…. She's here with me….

I kept my gaze intent on her as I kicked behind me, slamming the door shut with my foot.

But not in Your face, Father. Thank You for hearing Your son. Thank

You. Thank You. Thank You.

"Ari, what the fu—!" Jordan said, but my lips collided with hers as I dove across the room to the bed. The fire and all the awful possibilities it threatened were forgotten. God was all around us and through us. Here before me, kissing me, was His messenger. As I closed my eyes, I watched hers close as well. I was comforted by her comfort.

The fire that promised to kill us held no comparison to the fire that we felt inside for each other. We were more alive than ever. Our passion was illimitable, and God, Himself, despite His power, could not supersede the flame inside.

He is a Flame, eternal. And so are you, Jordan. If God is Love and Love is blind… and yet you see me, Jordan, even with your eyes closed. You are God. The fire is God. But how much more brightly you burn…

I looked to the door.

"And now, we all die together," I said under my breath.

And don't we always…. We are made in His image…. If we go down, becoming ashes, doesn't He, also? Will you, Father? Will you become the ashes You made in this 'image' You created?

Ashes to ashes to ashes.

I pressed my nakedness to her nakedness, and we were an image of God mirroring Himself, one creation loving the other; and as the heat rose against my back, I embraced this woman's warmth—this woman that had become as much a part of me as my very soul. God, in all His forms, was before, behind and within me.

We become ash. After all, You made hell, didn't You? And in Your image, we're damned all the same.

I had my angel. I had what I needed. I could feel the flames growing as they pressed the door, their heat licking at my back. I did not care. All the evidence I needed of God was right here, and I loved her.

Jordan…. So perfectly named….

I closed my eyes as I continued kissing her in my incomparable adoration. As the smoke overwhelmed me, I began to drift into a dizzy swoon, consumed by love, and I felt a warmth within; a warmth with which the fire could not compete.

"God is a fire!" I said.

In His image….

"AND SO ARE WE!" I said loudly, coughing.

"I'm getting sleepy," Jordan said.

I was becoming increasingly lightheaded, and our combined

coughing became a sad symphony.

"Then, let's go to sleep, my love," I said, the room now unbearably hot. The smoke had become too thick to overcome. The exhaustion had taken over. I kissed her forehead and hugged her tighter in a vain attempt to both comfort her and shield her from the heat. "And when we wake up, this will only be the start of our story."

"Agreed," she said, snuggling into me, her voice weakening, another violent cough erupting from her perfect mouth. She kissed me as her strength rapidly waned.

I drifted into a darkness I had never known before, the icy hand of death reaching to shake my hand in the center of the inferno that was my home. I heard Jordan's voice, which sounded distant.

"Ari, my love," she said, weakly.

"Yes, sweetheart," I replied, barely able to speak.

The needle on the record player stopped and Mozart went silent. The distant scream of the now-waking smoke alarm met my ears.

"Can we just stay like this forever?" she asked.

"Of course, we can," I replied. "And when we wake up, we can start our forever together."

"That… sounds… nice…." she said. "Forever is all I want with you… I'm glad we met."

"And we… we have… such a long… way to… go, honey," I said, our voices growing thin as the oxygen thinned around us. "I'm sorry…. I'm sorry I couldn't… save… you…."

"Oh, Ari… You already… saved me… tonight…. Thank you," she whispered.

I was nearly passed out when Jordan's voice called to me once more.

"Ari?" she asked.

I love how you say my name….

"I love you," she said, her sentence unbroken. "I love you… so… much…."

"I love you… too… Jordan," I said. "You are… my absolute… favorite…. Sweet dreams, sweetheart…."

"Sweet dreams," she said. "I'll see you… really soon…."

That was the last thing I heard as darkness swallowed me.

Silence. Peace.

God…. Life…. Death….

And of course, Jordan, the center of it all….

I love you….

JORDAN

Jordan was in and out of sleep as she half-dreamed of Ari, still conscious of her reality—Ari's protective cuddles—that was her entire world.

So cozy…. I'm finally where I need to be…. I swear, I could die tonight, and die happy.

"Hey," Ari said, and Jordan heard, abandoning her dreamlike state. She felt a loving finger drag across her forehead, brushing her fallen hair from her closed eyes.

"Hey," Jordan responded, mimicking the softness of Ari's voice.

The events of the night raced through her mind. Ari was still there with her, and that was all she needed.

Tonight has been… it's been a miracle. You saved me tonight, you know.

"Ari," she said. "Tonight…."

"Good morning," Ari said, playfully interrupting her.

God, I love that, when you hear what I haven't even said….

Jordan blushed within herself, the warmth of her vulnerable safety fueling the warmth in her face as Ari kissed her forehead.

That subtlety…. The power in it….

"Is it morning, already?" she asked. She sat up in the bed, her dreams of Ari and the assault of memories they had made together consuming her mind. She felt a sting of discomfort in her nose and chest and began coughing to relieve the tingle.

Something is wrong. Very wrong.

As she rose, she looked into and through Ari; and as she peered beyond him, she saw the cloud of smoke that cloaked the doorframe.

Oh. My. God! I have got to be dreaming!

"Ari!" she gasped. "Ari!!"

I'm seeing things! No way this is happening!

"What?" Ari questioned.

Come ON! You don't SMELL THAT?

Ari turned away from Jordan, then froze stiff.

This music! The smoke! They seem to feed one another. Damn it! I knew I smelled something burning earlier! Ari, why didn't you listen to me? Why?!

"Oh," Ari said. "Oh, shit!!"

We don't have time to be strong right now! We've got to get out of here! Open the window!

No, there… there are no windows….

No escape….

She felt the tickle in her throat crawl down into her lungs where it began to choke her, her eyes desperately scanning the room for an exit that did not exist. Soon, that tingle crept its way down between her legs, and she somehow felt aroused as she watched Ari, her hero, leap from the bed like a knight in flesh armor, prepared to meet their fiery foe. Smoke lined the ceiling now, and while her terror intensified, so did her respect and admiration for the man who was staring at the smoking door—death's door—willing to battle the hopeless inevitable for her.

Jordan looked on as he grabbed at the doorknob with his hand.

Why can't I bring myself to move! I should be helping him!

Jordan sat on the bed, petrified.

"Shit!" Ari yelled, yanking his hand away from the doorknob that wounded him.

The pain you endure for me….

Ari looked at his hand, then to Jordan. She could see the fear in his eyes as he peered directly into her soul.

And yet I know that fear is not for himself, but for me. I see it. I see it for what it truly is. Death is tapping on your shoulder. You're facing literal fire, and all you care about is me…. I fear, too. I fear for your fear. But I still feel safe, somehow, because you make me feel safe. But for you…. For you, I'm….

"Ari," Jordan said. "Ari, I'm scared," and Jordan's voice fell back on itself, her voice crumbling as she tried to match his strength, hoping to keep his worries at bay for the sake of them both.

In a flash, Ari lunged for the crumpled, plush blanket that lay in a heap at the foot of the bed. As quickly as he had grabbed it, Ari used it to grip the doorknob, tugging violently at it to no avail. Jordan felt a sharp sting of pity as Ari began to weep at his failed attempt.

It's okay, honey. But keep trying! I believe in you!

Jordan began to weep in reciprocation, but stopped herself.

No. No! I will not give up like that! Keep trying, handsome! Keep trying! Don't give up because I won't give up on you!

He adopted a determined look in his resolute stance as he turned with the blanket in hand. He wrapped the doorknob with it once more, and with strength that was more than strength, Ari pulled the door open, wildly swinging as he forced it to bend to his will.

Jordan's fear met with arousal as the door flung open. Ari became a silhouette, becoming the painted subject upon a canvas of fire, the heat of the blaze reaching Jordan's face. She raised her eyebrows in both fear and wonder as her man, naked and brave, stood before an undefeatable enemy; yet there he stood, regardless the odds, fighting for their survival.

Ari looked to Jordan as a knight of old, facing the flames of the fabled dragon, and that dragon was spewing smoke and fire into the room, thinning the air with each exhale, bent on suffocating murder. Jordan could not take her eyes off Ari's strong backside, the effects of the flash of initial fiery light dissipating, allowing her eyes to focus upon him.

Oh my God…. We'll never get out of here!

"I…" she said, too quietly for Ari to hear over the roaring flames.

Ari turned on his heel, facing Jordan. The terror that had consumed her left her. As Ari faced her, even within his crimson outline, she could tell he was—

—Smiling?

"God is here, now," Ari said, and Jordan did not fully understand his meaning, but she was taken aback by his voice as he spoke in a voice that was not his own—as if singing in spoken word with an accompanying chorus—an effect by which Jordan was both alarmed and calmed. Jordan jumped as Ari used his foot to kick the door shut behind him, looking deeply into her.

You are the first person to ever truly 'see' me. Will you be the last? Why here? Why now? Why this night of all nights?!

"Ari," she said in confusion. "What the fu—!"

Ari was suddenly across the floor, falling on and into her, meeting her with a kiss; a kiss of heat and light had helped her forget the angry blaze that threatened to engulf them. Jordan forgot her questions. She forgot her answers. She forgot the fires that brought light to her dark night. She forgot the fires that brought warmth to her cold world. She forgot Hannah. She forgot herself. The only thing she seemed to be able to think about was—

I'm so glad I lost those god-awful shoes….

Jordan closed her eyes as Ari's closed, two doors shutting at both ends of a private hallway that was the connection between them. Ari pulled away from their passionate exchange. Jordan's eyes watered in desperate longing as she imagined the future of which she was about to be robbed.

I have never lived before tonight… truly lived. You've given me so much, Ari. You, you miracle of a man. You have taught me so many things about myself, and have given me a way to be myself with someone, finally. You make me feel like I'm enough—more than enough—and I see that I've done the same for you. I love you for that. Thank you!

She smiled in acceptance of all things.

I am finally alive.

"And now," Ari said, "we all die together."

Together. I like that.

Ari melded his body to hers, and by the heat of the forge of the blaze of the room, they had fused into one being.

She was the sword and Ari was the blacksmith. As his sweat fell upon her, she became both his weapon and his defense. They deeply kissed. She felt she had become the source of his strength and his bravery—Ari neither willing to let her die, nor she willing to go on in life without him.

The fire is you, Ari. It always has been.

"God," Ari said, "is a fire!"

Ari pulled away from Jordan to cough as the smoke continued its suffocating work on him.

And so are we, Ari. So are we!!

"AND SO ARE WE!" he bellowed.

Jordan wished to respond, but the thinning air had begun to fail her.

I'm about to pass out…. Is this the end? Don't let him know…. Keep him feeling strong. He's been so strong.

"I'm getting sleepy," Jordan said.

She and Ari coughed simultaneously.

That sound of married, gorgeous, terrible chaos….

"Then let's go to sleep, my love," Ari said, kissing Jordan's forehead, squeezing her more tightly. "And when we wake up," he continued, "this will only be the start of our story."

A story? I like that. I love a good story. And I love 'us'.

"Agreed," Jordan said, nestling into the protection of Ari's body. Jordan coughed again. She kissed Ari with a kiss that spoke of new beginnings, as well as—

Goodbye….

Jordan began to fade away. She summoned what little strength she had left to speak one final time.

"Ari, my love," she said.

"Yes, sweetheart," Ari responded, his voice losing strength as did his body, loosening its grasp on her.

The flames roared ever louder, but Jordan could still hear the record player cease motion as the needle stopped. The hallway smoke alarm began wailing, as though mourning its failure in warning them of the danger that was now upon them. She thought of when life was much more beautiful—when life was still a possibility.

"Can we just stay like this forever?" she asked.

Forever…. It sounds so nice….

"Of course, we can," Ari said.

Promise?

"And when we wake up," he continued, "we can start forever—"

I like the sound of that—forever. Take me there. Keep me there. "—Together," he finished.

Perfect.

Jordan struggled to summon the strength to speak.

"That… sounds… nice," she said, fading. "Forever is all I want with you…."

Strong, large tears flowed reticently from her puffy eyes.

If only these tears could put this fire out…. But I died a long time ago. You've resurrected me. Thank you, Ari. Thank you so much. You're the best second chance I ever had….

"I'm glad we met," she said, drifting.

If only we had more time…. There is still so much to share….

"And we," Ari said, his voice becoming more distant and broken, "we have… such a long… way to… go, honey."

I like that. I can live with that.

"I'm sorry…. I'm sorry I couldn't… save… you," he said.

But you have! And amazingly so!

"Oh, Ari," Jordan said, "you already… saved me… tonight…. Thank you."

We saved each other from ourselves. And if 'God is a fire', then this is heaven, and we're finally home. We're going home together, as we were meant to. Born to…. Dying to….

"Ari?" Jordan said, her head spinning as her vision became spotty. "I love you. I love you… so… much…."

Ari snapped awake for a moment, his last strength fighting off the inevitable permanent sleep to come.

"I love you… too… Jordan," he said, the honesty of his voice the only strength Jordan could discern in the broken breaths of the only person who had never failed her in her entire life. "You are…" he continued, "my absolute… favorite.…"

You're my favorite, too! Get some sleep. We have such a long journey ahead of us.…

"Sweet dreams, sweetheart," Ari said, his voice lower than a whisper.

"Sweet dreams," Jordan said, a tear coursing down her cheek before it evaporated into the hot air.

Ari did not respond.

Ari was gone.

Jordan spoke to the silent shell of the man she loved that lay next to her, still between her and the approaching flames.

"I'll see you… really soon.…" she said.

I.…

Ari, I.…

.…

.…

I love you.

Jordan faded into the strange wilderness of a familiar darkness, a darkness she had never known but recognized.

Blacker than smoke and warmer than fire.…

So, this is love.

Ari.…

I love you.…

MICHAEL

Michael heaved and wheezed, his hopes of finding Ari the loud echoes in the chamber of his heart as it pounded vehemently in his chest.

With every step, the heat of the burning house grew stronger as the breeze eroded his skin—a duality, like himself—and he was caught between the cooling of his bravery and the fever of his fear.

He took two steps at a time as he mounted the stairs of the back porch. The heat was unbearable, stunning him where he stood. Michael could only stand like a stone as he sized up the awesome power of the flames.

You must save Ari!

Live or die, I've got to try!

Michael took a step forward toward the door, but a clap of lightning subdued his progress. He stopped as an electric bolt danced all over the moonless sky. As the flash of light faded, Michael watched in disbelief as two golden lights, like two shooting stars, rose through the roof, lingering for a moment in the air above the decaying mansion. The sound of thunder dissipated, those two lights circling in geometrical dance around one another, like two binary stars caught in a gravitational waltz. Then, they rose like bullets into the sky. Soon, they were gone into the abyss above as if never even there, seemingly lifted by the flames that continued to devour the house.

The lights faded into the great beyond. The moon which had been absent once again revealed its full, shining face. Its light illuminated the shadows that the house had cast upon the scene in its murderous anger.

Okay.

Michael took a deep breath. He could taste soot on his tongue.

Let's fucking do this!!

Michael made for the door, opening it in fear and desperation.

The fire was confined to the upstairs portion of the house. While no flames were anywhere to be seen upon entering the kitchen, smoke filled the air around him. He began violently coughing, throwing his forearm around his nose and mouth. His eyes began watering and his skin became immediately hot with the heat trapped by the surrounding walls.

Ari, where are you?!

Michael thought back to his last encounter with his best friend.

You…. You were with Jordan!

The bedroom!

Michael made for the hallway and the staircase at its end. Music met his ears as he passed the living room.

Winter…. Vivaldi…. I remember this one. Ari loves this one.

No time! I've got to find you!

"Ari! Ari, where are you?!" Michael began shouting. "ARI!"

Michael continued his pursuit of the stairs. Turning by the handrail, he set foot on the first step, the heat from upstairs accosting his face. The heat only worsened with his next few steps, his eyes on his feet as they made their arduous journey to the landing above. Michael began coughing again, the stinging in his eyes now unbearable. They watered uncontrollably and Michael was paralyzed by a wall of hot air. Stunned, he stopped to look at the top of the stairs above him. His eyes widened as they begged to shut, tortured as they were by the elements.

Oh. My. God.

The landing above him was nothing but light and darkness embodied by the heat and light of the fire—the shadows, the chill of the presence of the smoke above. His heart skipped several beats as the air in his lungs fled in fear. He choked in his throat. Michael became lightheaded, collapsing on the stairs where he stood, grabbing the handrail beside him for purchase and balance, missing and falling.

No…. No! I can't save you if I don't save myself, first! Fuck! What do I do? I can't die, not now! Ari…. Ari, and Hannah…. And me…. So much to live for…!

"Ari," Michael said, coughing and becoming dizzier with each passing second. "I'm sorry. I'm so sorry, Ari…."

Michael fell, rolling down the stairs. He crashed into the wall at the bottom of the stairs. He began to give up.

No! I am not weak! I may be a total asshole, but not tonight!

Michael looked himself over, then up the stairs. The flames were crawling toward him.

I have got to get out of here!

Michael moved to stand and stumbled. Falling into the wall behind him once more, he coughed in lieu of the building wall of smoke that had caught up to him.

Live, Michael! Live!

Michael made for the back door in the kitchen. As he passed the living room, however, a glint of flame caught his eye amid the smoke, enrapturing him. He stopped in his tracks. The smoke thickened as it descended downstairs and still, Michael was distracted by a little flame that glowed through the shades of doom that surrounded him. Michael stumbled, enamored, into the living room, coughing with each step. In the fireplace, a fire still lived. In that fire, Michael saw eyes—like those of Bezaliel, but more powerful in a multitude of ways—eyes that felt like his own—but were something more than himself.

Vivaldi played on.

More loving, those eyes, whatever that means....

Those eyes grasped him and dragged him deeper into depths of himself with which he was not familiar.

Something new. Something.... Something good....

As Vivaldi's dissonant notes and flawless progression took him over, Michael felt a warmth in his core—deeper than his heart—and burned more aggressively within than without.

Vivaldi's 'Winter' thawed, and 'Spring' took over as Michael fell forward, his hand cooled by the brick of the mantlepiece. He leaned onto it desperately to support himself as he fell, folding beneath his increasing weight.

Those eyes.... Those eyes right in front of my very face, burning deeper than fire, like lava in my veins, pouring right into my heart....

Michael became sick at his newfound weakness—this 'sensitivity' that had claimed him in his morose revelations—his own personal failure.

Ari, I....

Michael stumbled, his knees buckling.

Ari....

Michael's knees struck the brick outlay of the fireplace, his hand slipping from the overhead brick right into the flames of the hearth. He withdrew his burned hand immediately, he nearly too lightheaded to even feel it—the pain, the clinging awareness of his nervous system still fighting to survive.

His body grew cold as his skin began to rapidly dry within the growing heat of the tomb of flames. The smoke took him over, and Vivaldi's 'Spring' was all Michael heard as he drifted into a coughing fit—an episode—the final one—that claimed him in the shadows of the inferno.

Michael admitted defeat and closed his eyes.   Unwanted sleep called to him. Michael heard its call and surrendered to it.

Ari…. Ari, I tried. God, if you're there….

Even as the noise of the chaos around him dimmed as he fainted, Michael could still hear the rustling of the logs in the fireplace.

Darkness.

Peace.

Here, I….

"Michael? Michael?! MICHAEL!"

Bez…? God…? Is that you?

"Michael, come on, we've got to get out of here!"

No, but yes….

Michael had given up.

But that voice….

Is that you, God? You sound familiar. You sound….

"Come on, babe! Get up!"

God, you sound like a woman….

You sound….

"Michael, come on, we're leaving!"

You sound like Hannah….

All Michael saw was black.

HANNAH

Hannah hunched her shoulders as she tightened her grip on the steering wheel, skidding off the road, back into Ari's driveway.

She pressed the accelerator to the floor, more speedily getting herself to the house, but—

—Oh… OH MY GOD!

She slammed on the brakes, gravel flying as she skidded to a halt. Before her was a moonless sky and a massive house crumbling to the earth, burdened by the crippling weight of a massive fire that crowned the head of the impressive structure.

The hell?!

"Jordan!" she said, dismissing her shock, slamming the accelerator to the floor, the gravel beneath her tires rattling the undercarriage of her car. Her windows were down, and as she got closer to the house, she felt the gradual increase of the heat of the Ari's burning residence. She unbuckled as she hurriedly parked her car, drawing out her phone from her pocket, quickly dialing 9-1-1. She rushed toward the house as she saw a silhouette, tall and still, standing by the back door. Hannah became stone, herself.

"9-1-1, what is your emergen—" came the dispatcher's voice.

"It's on fire! The house is on fire!" Hannah said, vomiting the words from her mouth.

"What is your location?" asked the dispatcher. Hannah could not answer as she watched on in horror. Two bright lights, golden in color, rose through the roof, rising up and into the sky in a circular dance until they were gone.

The moon came out from its hiding place.

"I'm not sure of the exact address. It's the only house on fire on Shadow Chapel Road! Please, send help, and hurry! The house is—" Hannah said, stopping as she watched the silhouette on the porch hurry inside. She recognized the face of the shadow as it passed through the door.

"Michael!"

You fool! You damned fool!

She thought about the moon; the binary lights of gold; the fires, both great and small; and she and Michael. Her mind spun in frustration as her thoughts twisted with anxiety. She was a scattered mosaic and her thoughts were a labyrinth of confusion.

Damn, they'll never get here in time!

"Someone just ran inside! The entire upstairs is completely on fire! Please send help now! Michael!!"

The moon....

"Ma'am," came the voice of the dispatcher.

What the hell is happening tonight?

"I've got to go! Someone just ran inside!" Hannah said.

"Ma'am, do not go inside. Wait for the fi—" said the dispatcher, but Hannah had hung up the phone already. The fire grew and grew more rapidly with each passing second. Thickening smoke crawled from the broken window on the far side of the house, the black clouds pouring out as the flames licked against the outside of the window frame.

I've got to.... I can't.... I've....

Hannah knew what she had to do. She thought about the light at the intersection and its metamorphosis from green from red. Michael had been inside longer than she could bear, so she rushed the steps, her mind now empty of all thought, her instinct taking over completely. As she topped the stairs, the heat stunned her, and she briefly reconsidered her choice.

Shit! Michael, are you crazy??

"Ugh! What the hell!" she said. "Can I do this?"

The red light....

If only I hadn't stopped at that light so long, I would've been here in time to stop you from going in, Michael!

"I—I wouldn't be in this fucking position! Damn it!"

She began thinking of her shortcomings, her constant second-guessing and her judgmental nature. She regretted those regrets, and something clicked within her mind—an epiphany she could apprehend without fully comprehending.

I can't be a coward anymore! I swore I wouldn't be! The green light! Still, how could I have predicted this?!

Hannah looked up at the house as the heat of its blaze became hot and close to her face.

Well, shit. No time like the present, I guess. Let's do this!

Hannah took a deep breath, flinging open the back door to the kitchen. The heat pressed itself against her face, taking the breath from her lungs, almost knocking her down. The amount of smoke that had begun to fill even the downstairs was astonishing.

Damn! Michael, you strong, brave…. Jordan…. Jordan, just please, be okay. I hope you're far away from here!

Hannah barely made it through the kitchen before she became lightheaded and dizzy. She could hear coughing and beautiful music coming from—

—The living room!

She wrapped her arm around her face to guard her mouth and nose from the smoke. Her eyes had begun to water heavily.

"Michael?!" she yelled, trying to speak over the volume of the flames.

She received no response.

"Michael?!" she shouted as she made for the living room, each step through the thickening smoke gradually taking her sight from her. She rounded the corner, through the doorway, and she could barely make out the shape of a body lying unmoving on the floor in front of the fireplace that still crackled with life.

Fire. Fire everywhere.

"MICHAEL!" she shouted, expelling her fear-flooded, clumsy thought.

She rushed to him, kneeling next to him, tears coming to her eyes as she reached to shake her fallen hero.

"Michael," she repeated. "Come on!"

She began weeping, helplessness overtaking her.

"We've got to get out of here!" she shouted, unsure if he could hear her at all. "Come on, babe," she continued, her voice shaking as her heart slowly broke. "Get up!"

Please get up! Please, please get up! GET! UP!

"Michael, come on!" she pressed.

We are getting out of here if I have to drag you out, myself!

"We're leaving!" she yelled. She attempted to lift Michael, but his incredible lifeless weight was too much for her.

No! No time for weakness! We're getting out of here! We're going to live!

The fire in the fireplace roared to life and Hannah heard a voice.

"Now is not your time, Hannah, and it is not Michael's time, either. Do what you came here to do. Let that be your strength," the voice said.

The fireplace then extinguished itself and that solitary light that shone through the thickening smoke was gone.

The smoke must be getting to me. Michael, we're getting out of here! Alright, you heavy bastard! Help me out!

Finding a strength within herself she had not known before, Hannah lifted Michael with all the power she could muster. Coughing repeatedly and her vision becoming increasingly spottier, Hannah hoisted his heavy, lifeless frame onto her back. She carried him through the kitchen toward the back door to salvation. Her head became as foggy as her sight in her smoky struggle, she becoming more faint with every step.

No, not here! Not yet, damn it!

She coughed again, more stars crowding her vision. The smoke, the heat and her unconscious burden were all battling against her willpower.

Almost... there....

Halfway across the kitchen, her strength had given out. Her steps were slower, heavier, and less rhythmic.

Al... most... there....

She began to pass out, overtaken by all the elements that vigorously fought to destroy her.

Heat... and pressure.... When they are applied to coal, they turn into diamonds. Coal burns unless it transforms. And I am not burning today! Not today! Not tonight! And not ever!

Despite the weight of her lover and her thoughts, she lunged for the door with Michael in tow. With their combined weight, they fell into the door, catching the latch handle, causing it to open violently. As the door burst from the frame, Hannah and Michael fell onto the porch outside. Lying on her back with Michael beside her, Hannah looked up at the house that had nearly taken her life, along with Michael's.

Still too close....

Her head was still buzzing and she was completely spent. She got up with her remaining stamina and dragged Michael to the steps, studying the distance to the ground below.

Michael, I'm sorry. You'll thank me later.

She heaved at his body, pushing him down the steps. He landed in a heap at the bottom with a crunch. Collapsing, herself, she knelt, rolling herself crudely down the steps toward him. As she met the bottom, her trajectory took her up and over Michael's body where she lay by his side, exhausted. Michael lay next to her, both he and she upon their backs, and Hannah summoned the strength to sit up to kiss Michael's forehead before lying back down, looking to the sky that had brightened slightly with the coming dawn.

What a beautiful sky, a sky I almost didn't see....

She lifted her weak head, looking to the tree line. There, she saw two figures—a girl with vibrant red hair and a massive humanoid shadow behind her.

Katie....

A touch of anger rose up in Hannah but she no longer had the strength to feed it.

Katie, the child of fire.... Well, I faced the fire....

Hannah fell back once more into a lying position, closing her eyes.

I faced you and I beat you. I won....

Hannah passed out to the faint sound of sirens approaching.

Jordan.... Jordan....

"She is gone, but she is safe," came that familiar, mystical voice.

Hannah smiled to herself acknowledging the voice.

The world faded to black.

MICHAEL

Michael flashed awake from his feverish dreams to a clean, white room. His chest and lungs felt sore, much like the rest of his body. He looked down at himself, his body in a robe, a needle in his arm, and the beeping of machinery all around him. A sudden headache was upon him as he sat up, wincing in pain. He looked around the room, finding a sleeping angel in the chair to his right.

Am I dead? Is this heaven?

He began to weep as he said her name, overcome with disbelief.

"Hannah?"

It can't be!

"Hannah?"

His tears began to flow heavily as he both appreciated his life—barely intact—and saw the only thing that he had ever truly loved. Hannah stirred at the sound of his voice and she opened her eyes to him.

"Michael," she said, sleepily. "Michael!" she repeated, but elated. She threw herself at him, squeezing him with affection, a pressure that increased the pain he had just begun to realize.

"Ow!" he said, laughing as he placed his arms around her.

"Michael! I'm so sorry! I thought you were going to die!" she said, choking on her words. They both started weeping in each other's desperate embrace.

"How… how did I get out?" Michael asked.

"Honey, that doesn't matter!" Hannah said through her tears. "What matters is that you're safe!"

So, you saved me. It wouldn't be the first time, sweetheart. Thank you, and I love you. You came back for me….

"Where is Ari?" Michael asked. "Is he okay?"

Hannah withdrew, then returned to squeezing Michael, her tears increasing.

"Michael, I…" she said.

"And Jordan?" Michael asked. "I tried…. I tried to find them. I couldn't find them!"

"I'm so sorry," they both said simultaneously. Hannah looked at Michael with a look of horror.

"Michael, I… I don't know how to say this," Hannah said. "I just, I just don't know. They, the emergency crews… they found us, then brought us here. From what I understand, the house didn't fully collapse. They've put the fire out, but… but…."

Hannah began sobbing uncontrollably.

"They never found them! They never found their bodies!" Hannah cried. "No bones and no evidence of them being in the house at all!"

"Well, it sounds like they made it out, somehow," Michael said as he tried to console both himself and Hannah. Maybe they left before the fire spread. Did they go to Jordan's place, you think?"

Hannah's horrified look worsened, and letting go of Michael, she stepped back, pulling a phone from her pocket, eyeing it as her tears completely overcame her.

"She…." Hannah began mournfully. "She can't say. I have her phone."

"I'm sure she's fine," Michael said, lying down, realizing his pain. "Wherever she is…."

"I hope so," Hannah said, "but we know that *we're* okay! And if they weren't found at the house, that's a great start!"

Michael reached out and took Hannah's hand, drawing her close to him.

"She's fine. As long as she's with Ari, then Ari is with her, and they're okay," Michael said, encouraging her.

"Thank you. That's comforting to hea—" Hannah said as a knock came at the door. A doctor walked in, his eyes widening in surprise.

"Oh! You're awake, Mister Law! How do you feel?" he said.

Michael laughed.

"Like hell," Michael said, "but better knowing *she's* here," he continued, gesturing to Hannah.

"You're very lucky to be alive," the doctor said. "I'm Doctor Gabriel," he continued. "Let's check your vitals."

Doctor Gabriel moved across the room, checked the machines, and then began to look Michael over.

"Mister Law, you are very fortunate. You almost left us for a minute there. How do you feel?” the doctor asked.

“Like hell, like I told you,” Michael said.

“Sorry,” Gabriel said. “I suppose this is a bit of a shock for me to see you awake so soon. You’ve had quite a night.”

I’ll fucking say I have. But an even better day….

Michael looked at Hannah, smiling.

“I had an angel go into hell to save me. What can I say?” Michael said. Hannah shuffled her feet, looking down in shyness and blushing.

“He’s a survivor,” Hannah chimed. “We all are today.”

“I’ll say you are,” Doctor Gabriel said. “Well, Mister Law, you are a very lucky man. While you’re awake and fairly coherent now, I’d still like to keep you at least through the night just to make sure you remain stable. Your injuries could have been much worse, but you inhaled less smoke than we originally thought. One night should suffice, at least until we have more information.”

All it takes is one night, these damned days….

Michael pondered, knowing well that his opinion did not matter.

“Yeah, that’s fine,” Michael said, looking at Hannah. “But what about Hannah?” Michael looked deeply into her eyes as he spoke her name.

“I’m sorry, Michael, but while she was medically cleared in the ambulance, we would like to ask her to go home and rest, which will allow you to be less distracted and focus on your own rest. We found no reason to make her stay here at the hospital, and I’m sure her own bed would suit her better—more comfortably—for the time being. We have more tests to run on you, Mister Law, and—”

“I love her,” Michael said, interrupting the doctor as he kept his eyes locked on Hannah. “She should go home for now.”

Hannah looked at the floor, then into the world beyond the window.

“Honey,” Michael said, Hannah averting her gaze back at and through him. “We have plenty of time to spend together. You saved me tonight. You go home and get some rest, babe.”

Hannah’s spirits lifted at his words and she looked with a vibrant smile at the doctor, despite her tears, then back to Michael.

“Okay, handsome,” she said, standing slowly. She stepped forward to kiss Michael, kissing him longingly. He kissed her back, matching her passion.

“Oh, well, if there is no objection—Hannah, is it? I would ask that you leave so we can keep a closer eye on your boyfriend.”

Boyfriend…. You know what? I like the sound of that.

Hannah blushed a bright red, looking Michael deeply in the eyes as he peered into hers.

"Yeah," she said, stepping back from the bed, looking Michael over as he gazed upon her. "Yeah, that's my boyfriend." Hannah smiled at Michael as he grinned back at her. The true pain in his body had now become apparent, despite his medicated state.

I might need more than just today, after all. I hope she'll come to visit.

"But we did find, well," Doctor Gabriel began, "well, I can't say with Miss Hannah here, Michael."

"That's okay," Michael said. "Anything you have to say to me, you can say to her."

They both turned to Hannah.

"We found a lot of narcotics in his system," the doctor said. "We're needing to look into the situation further, Miss Hannah."

Damn, I could have gone without them knowing all that....

Hey, she did those drugs, too, damn it! Wish I'd been 'cleared in the ambulance.'

Michael laughed to himself.

Hannah looked at the doctor, then nodded to Michael before she kissed him once more.

"Doctor Gabriel, may I have a pen?" Hannah asked, keeping her eyes on Michael.

"Uh, sure," he said as he pulled a pen from his pocket, handing it to her.

"And paper?" she asked.

"Sure," the doctor obliged, tearing a leaf from his tablet, handing it to her. Hannah scribbled her phone number down, folding the paper in half and kissing it before handing it to Michael, who took it with a gentle quickness.

"Call me the moment they let you go," Hannah said, "and call if you need me for anything at all."

"You got it, babe," Michael said, blushing now, himself.

"Love you," Hannah said.

I love you, too, gorgeous.

Michael winked at her, blowing her a kiss. Doctor Gabriel blushed at the genuine sweetness of what was happening before him. He then turned, opening the door for Hannah.

"We have your number at the front desk," Gabriel said. "We'll update you with any developments, and of course, you may call as you wish."

"And call me if I can help," she said, "in any way."

"Yes, ma'am," said the doctor.

Hannah took one last glance at Michael as she walked backwards through the doorframe, Michael her only focus as Gabriel slowly shut the door.

HANNAH

As the door clicked shut, Hannah stood for a moment, pondering all the events of the night before. Then she thought about Jordan.

I wish she would call already. I know you're out there… somewhere….

Before her tears could start again, she pulled out her phone and called for a cab. She slowly walked the lonely white halls to the elevator, took it to the bottom floor, and waited for the driver to arrive. In every car that passed her on the street, she saw Jordan's face in their passenger seats.

The driver showed up within minutes.

Thank God. I just want to go home.

She got into the back seat, exhaling heavily. The driver looked at her in the rearview mirror, examining her exhausted eyes. She knew he could smell the lingering burnt odor on her clothes.

"Long night, Miss?" he asked.

"You could say that," Hannah responded, her words like sand on her tongue. She swallowed her sadness, thankful to be alive and that Michael was alive as well. She snapped herself out of her forthcoming emotional relapse.

"I'm sorry," said the driver. "Where to, Miss?"

"Take me ho—" Hannah said, stopping herself mid-sentence. "Actually, take me to Shadow Chapel Road, please. My car is still there."

"Shadow Chapel? Not where that house caught fire last night, right?" he asked.

Hannah looked out of the window at the buildings that lined the street, imagining them all ablaze with Jordan trapped inside. She struggled behind her eyes, fighting the urge to cry.

"Yeah," she said. "The same. I had to ride in the ambulance here to be checked out."

And to be there with Michael. I didn't think he would ever wake up! Thank

God!

"Well, I'm very glad you're okay," the driver said. "At least they haven't found any bodies so far."

"Yeah," Hannah responded, knowing inside herself that she was the furthest from 'okay' than she had ever been in her life. "Thank you."

"Okay, Shadow Chapel Road, it is," the driver said, and they were off to their destination, Hannah fighting her nerves and painful memories the entire way.

MICHAEL

Michael kept his eyes on Hannah as the door closed.

"You really care for her, don't you?" Doctor Gabriel asked.

"You have no idea," Michael said.

"She saved you, you know. Without her, you surely would have died."

"She's been saving me since the moment we met," Michael said confidently. "It doesn't surprise me at all that she's done it again."

"Well, something to look forward to," Doctor Gabriel said, returning to the machinery to which Michael was connected.

Definitely. I wish I could have left with her.

"Doctor? Was anyone else… found in the house?"

"No," Gabriel responded dryly. "You and she were the only people found at the property, as it stands now. No fatalities were reported, thanks to Hannah."

Michael laid back on his pillow, closing his eyes.

Ari, where the hell are you?

"You know, Doctor," Michael said. "I believe I did die in that fire. The old me, at least."

"Well, I think that is a very positive way of looking at it," Gabriel said. "There's nothing like looking death in the face to make one feel most alive, I think."

"I couldn't agree more."

"But for now," Doctor Gabriel continued, "we want to keep you throughout the day and overnight to keep an eye on things and make sure there are no complications. Miraculously, your cigarette habit helped your lungs better withstand some of the impact of the smoke inhalation you've suffered. Be that as it may, I do strongly urge you to quit."

Nothing like little sips of death to help one ease into the 'big drink', I guess…. Dying practice….

"We do expect you to make a full recovery in time," the doctor continued, "but for now, rest, Michael, and we'll revisit your progress later this evening."

The doctor nodded and turned around, reaching for the doorknob.

"Uh, Doctor?" Michael said.

"Yes?" said Gabriel, turning to face him.

"One more thing…. If you hear of an Ari Cayne being admitted, will you let me know? I have a million apologies to make to him."

Michael's eyes began to water with regret as he mourned inwardly and outwardly.

"Certainly," said Gabriel, "but for now, please rest, Mister Law. I'll update you with any information that comes my way."

"Thank you," Michael said through his breaking voice.

"Rest now, Michael. I'll check back in with you in a little while."

Doctor Gabriel exited through the door, shutting it behind him.

Ari, please be okay. You've always been a survivor.

Hannah was his final thought as he closed his tired eyes and drifted. Michael began crying heavily in silence.

You're an angel, Hannah. Hell, you might even be God to me….

Michael's tears and breathing slowed, allowing him to slip into a darkness—a peaceful one—devoid of all things.

Perfect.

HANNAH

As the cab pulled up the driveway, Hannah continued reliving her memories with Jordan and the last true time they had spoken. She thought about how she had not yet known Michael then, and when she saw the decrepit, charred remains of the house coming into view, she thought of Ari and how, by his invitation, her entire mind, heart, and life had changed forever.

"Wow," said the driver. "Are you sure you want to be here so soon?"

"Yes. I need my car for when Michael needs me."

"Ah," he said. "I understand."

They pulled up the driveway until the car stopped and shifted into park where caution tape hung loosely across the gravel path.

"Here we are, Miss," the driver said. "Anything else I may do for you?"

"No, thank you. I've got it from here."

Hannah reached for the money she had in her back pocket to pay the driver.

"Oh, no, that won't be necessary," he said, waving the money away. "This one is on me. You've been through quite enough."

Hannah was too exhausted to express her appreciation with the tears of thankfulness that begged to surface.

"Thank you, sir!" she said with weak enthusiasm.

"Call if you need us again," the driver offered as Hannah exited the car. "Do you want me to wait here for a while?"

"No, I'm fine," she said. "You've done more than enough. Thank you for your kindness!"

"Let us know if you need anything else, Miss," he said, and Hannah shut the door.

She looked up at the mansion, whose upstairs had been completely ransacked with destruction. The lower level was seemingly untouched, aside from major smoke damage, yet the upstairs was a charred mess. The house appeared to Hannah as if it were two different structures crudely stacked on top of each other, the top half still slightly smoking from the residual heat.

What a shame.

She looked down at herself.

What a miracle.

Her car was the only one left in the driveway.

Not yet. I want to see that grove again—that magical bonfire—in the daylight. Just one last time....

Her mind was a rushing blur of recollection as she pondered the evening like a film in fast forward. As she reimagined her discovery of Michael in the darkness and smoke, she was already down the path, deep into the clearing in the woods, the pile of wood before her.

What the hell? It's not even burnt! It's like it never even burned at all!

"But I saw it! I know I saw it! Am I going crazy, after all?"

"No, you are not crazy," a voice said from behind her.

Hannah spun on her heels in surprise. Before her stood a massive shadow of a being with mighty wings and gorgeous, golden, infinite eyes. Hannah stumbled back and fell to the ground in total shock, crawling backward until her shoulders touched the unscorched bonfire behind her.

"Do not fear me, Hannah," said the being. "Michael—your Michael—reacted the same way."

Hannah's eyes were wide with disbelief.

"You... you were the reason he was acting so weird! You're real?! What are you? What do you want?!" she said, barely able to form the words. "And the fire! I saw it burning, myself! What the hell is going on here?!"

"Hell," he said, "is quite the opposite of what is happening here. Hell is my home away from home, and this place is much more... tolerable... than that place."

"And how do you know my name?" she asked.

"Child," he said, slowly walking to her. "Do not be afraid. I will not harm you. I doubt *He* would allow me to if I even so desired." He turned his head upward, looking at the sky. "So many questions, yet I know that you already, in your heart, know the answers." The being expelled a modest laugh. "Yes," he continued, looking back down and into Hannah's eyes. "I was the reason for his strange behavior. As you can discern, meeting one like me for the first time can be quite... disconcerting. I apologize. I did not make me this way. We all are made the way we are meant to be made, including yourself. I should not have to apologize any more than you should, Hannah."

She sat there, frozen, listening to this creature speak.

"Yes, I am real," he said, stepping even closer to her, folding back his wings. "As real as you. I am what you call an angel. I am, simply put, a messenger. I am a Watcher—Fallen—as some say. As far as what I want?"

The being knelt, now face to face with Hannah, and she became comforted by the unexpected, unexplainable beauty of his eyes.

"As far as my desires, Hannah," he continued, "well, as a messenger, I have a message for you."

"Wh— what would that be?" Hannah stammered in curious fear.

"The wood behind you is not burned, though it *did* burn, because not all that catches fire turns to ash," he said. "And that is what I mean to tell you."

Jordan's face filled Hannah's mind.

Jordan, I love you…. I miss you….

"Yes, Jordan, the one you love most of all…. She is why I am here before you."

"Do you know where she is?" Hannah asked, her interest overpowering her terror. "Is she… is she… dead?" she continued, swallowing hard. The being laughed, filling the grove with his beautiful, haunting song.

"Death is no end, I assure you," he said, "but no, she is not dead as you know death, and neither is Ari, for that matter."

Hannah teared up, the subtle glimmer of hope she had clung to bursting into a vibrant explosion of light inside her heart.

"What do you mean?! Please tell me!"

"I will tell you," he said, "though the entire answer may disappoint you. It will, however, I believe, offer you some much-needed consolation."

"Please, just—"

"She is not dead," he said, cutting off Hannah.

Hannah sighed with relief, the floodgates of her eyes breaking wide open.

"Let it out," he continued. "I understand, Child, but please, collect yourself and listen to me."

Hannah wiped her eyes with her dirty hands.

"You see, your love for her…." he said. "Love is a saving thing. It is in our nature, and you are made in His image. As His image is Love, Love is your nature. A miracle that it exists, still, in such a hate-filled world, and that is why she is not dead—the unabated, honest, perfect, unshackled love that she feels for Ari. It is the same pure love that Ari feels for her. Love has saved them, in a way."

I don't understand.

"I will help you understand," he said.

"You can read my mind?"

"And your heart, as well, like theirs, and that is the point at which I would like to arrive," he answered. "You see, they should have perished in those flames, but the One that made us all saw the purity of their affection—the very reflection of His nature—and He could not bear to let them suffer so. So, to be brief, Hannah, He *took* them."

"Took? Took them?" she asked.

"Yes, *took* them. Like Elijah and like Enoch, they are with Him now, but they did not die. While they are no longer in this place, they—both of them—did not die a physical death. Simply put, they are no longer with us in this physical realm."

So, those two golden lights…. Those…. THOSE LIGHTS WERE JORDAN AND ARI?!

"Yes, those two lights were your friends."

"But, but what does that..?"

"What does it mean?" he inquired. "For you, most importantly, it means that you may see her again, though perhaps not on this earth. I do not have all the answers. But, yes, you very well may see her again. There is hope. Even for one who is damned as I am, there is always hope, even in hopeless times."

Hannah leapt at him, wrapping her shaking arms around his massive body. She began crying as he cried with her, touched deeply by her pure emotion. She had transformed from the selfish Hannah she had once been into the newborn Hannah, who had become selfless, strong and decisive.

"That is all I mean to tell you," he said. "Now I have delivered my message. I must go."

"Wait!" she yelled. "I have more questions!"

"Do not we all?" he asked her. "But that is the beauty of life—to seek secrets and the truths they bear, never knowing if we ever shall truly know. Take that with you, and carry it like a beautiful burden, Hannah."

They let go of each other.

"Until we meet again," he said, and he turned to leave.

"But wait!" she cried in desperation.

"Yes?" he asked in a tone of annoyance.

"What… what is your name?" she questioned.

"That is not important," he said, "but I am known as Bezaliel, the 'Shadow of God'. Just know that I am always watching, a Watcher as I am. Hannah, you are never alone, even at your loneliest. When no one else is, He is there, I assure you. And perhaps myself, should He allow it to be."

"Bezaliel?" she said. "Thank you."

Bezaliel nodded to her in silence, turned, and disappeared.

Hannah sat a moment, weeping to herself, a confusing mixture of sadness and joy overwhelming her entirely.

Thank you! Thank you!

Moments of uncontrollably appreciative mourning passed. Hannah collected herself and stood up, looking to the sky above.

Hmmm….

Her mind blank and her heart much lighter than before, she made for the path leading out of the clearing, looking back to the woodpile one last time where it stood, unscorched.

Amazing.

She made her way up the path, stopping every now and then to take in her surroundings before returning to the real world beyond. Halfway up the trail, she saw a glint of something bright red in the foliage several feet from her. She walked slowly over to the object, bursting with happiness as she discovered she had found—

—Jordan's shoes…. Oh my God! I can't believe—! Thank you, Angel!

Hannah gripped the shoes tightly to her chest and sprinted for the car, tears of happiness coursing down her smiling face.

"Amazing! Simply amazing!"

Opening her car door, she set those dirty, red high heels in the passenger seat next to Jordan's phone and started the car.

Reborn…. How appropriate….

Hannah took one last look at the house before pulling down the driveway, then onto the street, watching the cigarette smoke billow through the cracked window, up and far away from her.

Hannah's mind was as empty as it was full during her drive home. She was as confused as she was understanding. She was hollow yet fulfilled.

As she pulled into the parking lot of her apartment, she pondered on everything and nothing. She collected her things—Jordan's shoes and phone among them—and exited the sedan. She smiled at her reflection in the black glass screen of the phone, still beside herself from the prior night's events—even more so from her encounter with

Bezaliel—and yet further still at the woman she saw in the reflection looking back at her.

She was now a woman, the girl she once was burned away and lost forever in the trials of the flames.

She locked the car door, then made her way into her apartment.

I'll take a shower later. I'm exhausted….

She locked her door behind her, headed upstairs, changed into her sleeping clothes, washed her face in the upstairs bathroom sink, and examined herself in the mirror.

A new woman. A totally new person, Hannah. Maybe tomorrow…. Maybe…. Maybe today….

She went into her bedroom and turned on the television, collapsing onto her bed.

"Two found injured, one still at the hospital being treated for injuries," came the voice of the news reporter onscreen. "None reported dead as of now, though two bodies are still missing, according to authorities…"

Hannah immediately turned the television off, teary-eyed, but feeling stronger than she ever had.

I know you're okay, Jordan. And now I know you are. I KNOW you are!

She laid down on her thick comforter, not even bothering to cover herself.

I am all that I need.

She plugged her phone into her charging cord and set it on the bedside nightstand.

Just in case Michael calls….

She set Jordan's phone down next to her own.

Dead, but not dead….

Laying her head on her pillow, her excitement, stress, comfort, and any feeling she had at all faded as her eyes grew heavier and heavier. Rolling onto her side, she looked on as a beam of light, singular and radiant, cut through the window, illuminating the glass of sauvignon blanc she had left behind, unfinished, from the night before.

Newly illuminated, transparent and pure. And unfinished.

Hannah smiled to herself as she closed her weakening eyelids.

Like me…. Just… like… me….

Perfect. Just… perfect….

Hannah's eyes were closed and locked shut as she drifted into blissful, peaceful rest. She was immediately asleep, and the beautiful nightmare of the night—the house and all things lost and gained—was finally behind her.

Perfect, everything….
Soon, Jordan….
Very soon….

ARI

I opened my eyes to Jordan, who was standing next to me, enshrouded in clean, white light that glowed powerfully from within, around, and through her. Music unlike anything I had ever heard filled my ears, warming my heart and putting me at incredible ease. For countless reasons, I wanted to cry, but the tears would not come.

"Good morning," I said to her, looking longingly into her eyes and touching her cheek.

"Hi," Jordan said. "Where are—? What happened to the fire?"

There will always be a fire in your eyes, Jordan, and it will burn forever in my heart as I will forever burn for you.

"The fire is behind and beneath you," came a voice—one that I had never heard but was strangely familiar. It was one voice, powerful yet comforting, reaching my ears from every direction. "Welcome home, you two."

Home?

So, this is home now....

As long as she is here with me...

This is home.